KERRY J DONOVAN

ON THE MONEY

ᵛINCI
BOOKS

The Ryan Kaine series by Kerry J Donovan

Vinci Books

vinci-books.com

Published by Vinci Books Ltd in 2025

1

Printed and bound in Great Britain by Clays Ltd, Elcograf S.p.A.

Chapter One

Tuesday 26th January - Byron Codell

Brooke Street, Walthamstow, London, England

Thou shalt not steal.

Bible said it loud and clear, and Bible was Goddamned fucking right. One of them Ten Commandment things.

Byron Arlon "Barcode" Codell didn't know which Commandment exactly, but that didn't matter a damn. What it meant mattered. Mattered big time.

Steal something, anything, food to survive even, and the thief would suffer the flames of hell for all eternity. Thieving fuckers would burn forever. That's what Bible said.

Yeah, that's right, stealing did a person's soul no good in the afterlife, no good at all. But who gave a shit for souls? If that same thief took from Barcode, bad things would happen in the here and now. Right away. No one stole from Barcode.

Ain't no one gonna mess with Barcode no more. The ink lines on the back of his neck were a permanent reminder of what happened to anyone who tried to fuck him over. Barcode wasn't never gonna take no disrespect. Not no more.

Which was why he was aiming to climb up on the garage roof in the middle of the night.

Some fucker were dipping his greasy fingers into Barcode's pie, and that certain someone was gonna lose more than the same sticky fingers. The thieving pig-fucker was going to die.

Wrapped up in his heaviest parka and dressed all in black, apart from the white lines on his trainers, Barcode pulled the fur-lined hood over his shaved head. He cinched the drawstring tight under his nose to cover his mouth. Side flaps and fur threw his face into deep shadow.

He stuck his head over the top of the shoulder-high, wooden fence, and checked out the sloping back garden.

Nothing much had changed since the last time he'd been there, or since the old man kicked the bucket. Such a shame, but old people died, didn't they? Nothing shocking in that. Nothing at all.

Unlike last time he'd climbed the fence, the crib stood dark as night.

No lights shone from the kitchen window over the shitty patch of land that had once been an okay back garden, with flowers and vegetables and shit. Back before the old man took ill and his wheelchair became his legs.

Stupid, old man thought he was still relevant, still worthy of respect. Not in Barcode's books. Cripples was a waste of space. A waste of oxygen. A blight on the world. Should be swiped from the area, moved into homes. Culled or something.

But the old geezer were pushing up the daisies now. Gone to his Maker. Nothing mattered to him no more.

The old man's grandson, Darwin Moore. He mattered, though. Still stayed in the house, but only on weekends. Never on a Tuesday. Darwin, the college boy geek, spent the week studying somewhere up north, which were the reason the house stood empty.

Perfect.

Even if the old boy had still been alive—sitting behind his net curtains, in front of his TV—he'd have been lost in his favourite soap. For the old, TV stood in for "product", the street drugs Barcode and his posse shifted by the baggie load. Gramps woulda been sitting with his back to the window and the sound turned up loud enough for a deaf dog to hear the dialogue from a couple houses away. Nah, the old sod wouldn't have noticed an armed assault force scrambling over his garden fence, let alone a stealthy black dude with a barcode tattoo on the back of his neck.

After pulling on his leather gloves, Barcode grabbed the top of the fence and vaulted over, landing in a patch of soft, sticky mud. He scuffed his tracks as he headed down the slight hill. Although the old bastard hadn't been in the back garden for years before he croaked, on account of his wheelchair, no telling when Darwin would venture out for a look-see. Didn't make no sense to leave a clear trail.

The crib—a two-bedroomed, end-of-terrace house— had to be worth a fucking mint, even in a shitty area like Brooke Street. Darwin shoulda sold up soon as Gramps kicked the bucket. Fuck knew why he didn't. Probably wanted to keep it in memory of his dear, departed grandpa and his poor, murdered mother. Stupid, sentimental fuckwit should be living for the moment, not dwelling on the past. No profit in it.

The mother weren't all that bright neither. Shouldn't have left the crippled, old man on his own to fly off on a hen's night. And why Amsterdam, for fuck's sake? What was wrong with London? Bitch coulda had a good time down the West End for the same scratch as flying to Dutch-land.

Paid the price though, didn't she? Mrs Moore and the others who died on that flight. Served her right. Served them all right. Blown outta the sky in a fireball.

Barcode smiled. Wished he coulda seen the boom for real and not just on some shaky phone footage.

Must've been a hell of a firework show.

Eighty-three dead. Either burned to charcoal, crushed on impact or—much worse—drowned in the freezing North Sea.

Yeah, Barcode woulda loved to have seen it in real life. Such a buzz.

Ah well. Can't do nothin' 'bout it now.

Keeping close to the fence, staying in the deep shadow, Barcode crept around the garden, the tall grass swishing up to his knees, soaking the legs of his jeans. He made it to the rear of the garage. The metal wheelbarrow was exactly where he'd left it, leaning against the garage wall. He used it to boost himself onto the flat roof.

Again, keeping close to the end wall of the house, Barcode scrambled on hands and knees to the front of the garage and squatted.

Simples.

Gave him the perfect view.

One of his own crew, fucking scumbag, had been dipping his fingers in the till, which meant the total take was coming up five percent short. Not much, but significant. In any other business, the shortfall mighta been explained away by bad weather keeping the punters off the streets and outta the shops. But in his industry, clients would crawl over shattered glass and sell their babies as sex slaves to raise the cash to cover the next fix.

Nah, a drop in revenue meant only one thing.

Thievery. Plain and simple.

He'd first noticed the shortage a couple days ago.

Up front, he thought about running to Top Man, but that would only have reflected badly on Barcode. It would probably have dropped him well and truly in the slime. No telling what TM woulda done. The invisible fucker might even put the evil eye on Barcode for dropping the ball. After all, the thievery was happening on one of Barcode's pitches. Made him responsible for clearing up his own mess. In the end, Barcode made up the shortfall from his personal cut, but that couldn't last forever. If the thieving fuck kept getting away with it, he'd only get greedier. Eventually, Barcode wouldn't be able to cover the losses and that wouldn't do. Not at all.

It had to stop, and stop right away.

If he didn't flush out the scumbag and deal with the prick before TM sussed out the losses, TM would probably decide Barcode wasn't up to the task of running his own crew. And that would put a cramp on his plans to move up in the Tribe and reach his ultimate goal.

Move TM aside and take over.

Complete and utter domination. The only thing that mattered to Barcode. But he was smarter than them mugs who tried to take over by playing hardball, all gung-ho but no smarts. Barcode played the long game. Over time, stealth were better than shock tactics.

He sucked air between his teeth, smiled, and settled down to study one third of his crew. That week's evening shift. If he'd worked it out right, it wouldn't take long to prove.

Barcode pulled a pair of stolen binoculars from the pocket of his parka and sat cross-legged on the tar-covered roof, hidden deep in the shadows. He raised them to his eyes and started in on the spying.

As he watched, his anger built.

He fed on it. Used it. Enjoyed it. Anger kept him warm.

If emotions made the man, Barcode was a man built of fire and rage. World saw him for what he was—big, powerful, angry. But there was more. Below the surface, hidden deep, lay ambition and a brain to take him to where he wanted to be. And a street-level, middle manager wasn't nearly the final destination.

He'd go further. Much further.

Barcode was going to the top. Wouldn't be easy. There were plenty of faces standing between him and TM's spot. Yeah, plenty of wannabes, but none with Barcode's patience or smarts.

To TM and his lieutenants, the Heavies, Barcode weren't nothing special, not yet. But he was worth more than they knew. Even his handle meant more than he let on. The tat on the back of his neck—the barcode that gave him his tag—actually meant something. It wasn't just a random load of fat and thin vertical lines. No way.

At aged twelve, he'd been turned on by a movie about a hired assassin who wore a barcode tattoo on the back of his neck. The young Byron wanted a tat just like it. Thought it would be cool. Saved up his hard-earned for months and spent hours each week in the school gym, building his muscles with weights, and his reflexes with the speed bags.

According to the rat-faced, broken-toothed tattoo artist who inked him, the vertical, black lines he'd etched into young Byron's dark skin displayed nothing but his name, his handle—Hitman #48—and his date of birth.

"Barcode" was reborn that day, and he was totally fucking psyched. But, weeks later and after the scabs had healed, when he ran a Tesco's barcode reader over the lines, the code gave a different result. It spewed out an insult to his mother and her love life. Even though he was fired up and spitting bullets, Barcode never told no one about how he'd been screwed over. Kept it to himself. Never allowed no one to run a scanner over the tat again, neither. Nobody could never accuse Barcode of being shit at keeping secrets.

Months later, someone out walking found the same rat-faced, heartless fucker who thought it funny to play games with his needle gun and mess with a teenage kid. Found him floating face down in the Thames, missing his eyes—and his heart.

Barcode didn't tell no one he'd done the deed, neither. Yeah, Barcode could keep a secret all right.

Later, the filth tried to finger him for the deed. They call him in to "help with they enquiries". Yeah, right. The fuck with that. Barcode were too smart for them. Ran rings around them during the interrogation, and they still didn't have no clue.

Since then, he coulda paid another inker to cover the lines, change them, but he left it untouched as a lesson to himself not to be so stupid again. And besides, Barcode was, as the tat actually said, a Big Black Bastard.

Too fuckin' right I is. And nobody's ever gonna say different.

In the dark and the cold, Barcode watched and waited. And he smiled.

BRUTUS.

Yep.

Had to be Brutus.

Couldn't've been no one else. No one else on his crew had the balls, or the stupidity.

The minute he discovered the pilferage, Barcode knew it had to be Brutus, the third mini-leader of his posse.

It had only taken a few seconds to rule out everyone else.

First, he cleared Petey. No way his blood, his brother, would do nothing to drop Barcode in the brown stuff. They'd known each other since nursery. Grown up together. Petey was as honest as any dealer had a right to be. Petey would die for Barcode and Barcode would let him.

Ha!

As for Rhino, the second stringer, Barcode cleared him almost as fast as he cleared Petey. Rhino didn't have the stones, or the need. The musclebound cretin didn't partake of the product, not even occasionally. Fine, upstanding member of the Tribe, he was. Didn't even smoke normal cigarettes. Treated his body as a fucking temple, and worshiped his pregnant squeeze, Ariel. Top of all that was the clincher—Rhino, the scar-faced bugger, didn't have the smarts to rip no one off without giving himself away in seconds.

That left Brutus. The third wheel. The third deputy. The bastard in charge of the pitch Barcode were watching through the binoculars.

Brutus.

You stupid, greedy, selfish fucker.

He had to go, but …

Barcode couldn't deal with the thief without proof. The Tribe had its rules, and any member who pointed an accusing finger without proof was liable to find himself in as much trouble as the tribesman he accused.

Nah, Barcode needed evidence, which was how come he ended up sitting, cross-legged, on the flat, garage roof freezing his nuts off, risking butt cramp and piles.

As it happened, it only took twenty-five minutes to eyeball the act.

Slimy bastard!

Barcode spotted it when the fifth customer of the evening handed across her small bundle of creased notes— probably earned from lying on her back and spreading her scrawny legs. As the bitch scurried away, her fix held tight in a grimy fist, Brutus handed the cash to his rider, Lil' Aran, who slid the notes into his backpack.

Lil' Aran, ten years old, no more, spent the shift pedalling up and down the lanes between all the pitches, ready to make a lightning split the moment the bacon shoved they noses into Tribe business.

The routine was slick and simple. Barcode designed it for the purpose and it worked real well.

Customer arrives.

Money passes from customer to dealer—in this case, Brutus.

Dealer tips the nod to rider.

Rider—Lil' Aran—rolls up on his BMX, takes cash, hands product to Brutus, and buggers off up the lane in a flat-out, wheel-spinning sprint.

Dealer passes product to customer.

Junkie buggers off, happy as shit, transaction complete, and no outsider any the wiser.

Only this time, while the client buggers off, baggie in

her hot, little fist, and Lil' Aran sprints away, Brutus stoops to tie his shoelace.

Again, no real issue, but, through the high-powered binoculars, Barcode couldn't see nothing wrong with the laces in the first place. They sure didn't seem loose to him.

First time it happened, Barcode didn't think nothing of it. After all, no self-respecting crewman would allow his brilliant, white laces to go slopping in the puddles, but seven deals later, same thing happened, this time with the other shoe.

Once was all right, twice maybe, but it kept happening. Over the course of two hours, Brutus tied his laces five fucking times.

The big guy either hadn't learned to tie his laces proper, which meant they kept coming undone, or he had another reason to fiddle with his sneakers.

Yeah. Another reason, right enough.

So fucking simple. When Barcode first sussed the shortfall, he'd credited Brutus with more brains. He expected the bastard to hand off the stolen money to an accomplice or an unwitting stooge. Maybe even hide it under a rock for a pickup in the middle of the night when even the hardest-bitten junkies crawled into their shitholes, and the Tribe had shut up shop for the day. He didn't expect something so blatant. How long did the fucker think he'd get away with it for?

So simple and so stupid.

A fiver here and a tenner there, but over a week, it would mount up. In the two months since Top Man gave Barcode the pitch, the fucker coulda syphoned off fucking hundreds.

Plain, old, sleight of hand—or rather of foot. No

accomplice. His fucking shoe! How careless to have missed it for so long.

Jesus fuck.

Barcode chewed his thumbnail down to the skin.

Disrespect.

Brutus was dissing him. Laughing at him.

For Brutus to treat Barcode that way showed more than greed. It showed contempt. Contempt for the Tribe and, worse still, contempt for Barcode.

Brutus is gone. End of.

Barcode crawled backwards along the roof and retraced his steps through the garden.

———

BARCODE TIMED HIS APPROACH SO LIL' Aran was heading towards the furthest point on his ride but before making his turn. The rider would be far enough away not to interfere if he was working the scam with Brutus, but close enough to act as witness and confirm Barcode didn't plant the cash.

No point taking chances.

"Hey, blood," Barcode called, smiling as he loped along the lane towards the pitch. "How's it hangin'?"

He waved with his left hand, keeping his right tucked tight against his side.

Brutus, as wide as he was tall, nineteen stones of pure beef—and a bucket load of it between the ears—looked up. The thief's eyebrows shot up.

His smile was as forced as any TV presenter Barcode had ever watched.

"Hey, blood. You early, man. Weren't expectin' you for a couple hours."

Yeah, and that's the whole point, fucker.

Brutus ripped the beanie from his head and used it to shoo away a mealy-mouthed, shit-for-brains regular who couldn't pay the full fee. The yellow streetlight shone on Brutus' polished dome.

Barcode stopped at arm's length and pushed out his left fist—the sign things were cool. They bumped. All sweet and friendly, like.

"Thought I'd come see how shit was hangin'. Apart from that dickwad"—he tilted his head towards the disappearing, failed customer—"how's trade?"

Brutus pulled the beanie back on and tucked his head into his shoulders. "Cold as fuck out here, man. I'm thinkin' we should relocate the store. Maybe we could take over one of them houses and set up shop in the warm and the dry." With his chin, he pointed at the street behind Barcode.

Taking care not to show Brutus his back, Barcode turned sideways and observed the row of houses running across from the alley, the closest had the garage he'd just been using. Above the fencing, the terrace stretched away and stopped when it reached the more expensive, semi-detached homes closer to the High Street. Each house showed lights. Each were lived in.

"Good idea, Brutus. Whose house we gonna occupy? How 'bout number fifteen? Yo' Auntie Grace live there, right? You reckon we gonna set up in her front room? And what happens when the bacon come a-callin'? You'll be holdin', and the riders won't have time to scoot nowhere. Nah, this shit's what we do, and this here station's where we stayin'."

Brutus lowered his head even more. He shuffled from one foot to the other, all nervous.

"Wazzup, man? You need the toilet?"

"Nah, freezin' my ass off, innit."

The runt, Barcode's real-life cousin, Lil' Aran, stopped outta earshot, balanced on his pedals, flashing his pure, bike-handling skills. Looked like he could tell something were off and didn't want no part in it.

Smart boy.

Any time now, Lil' Aran might be due a promotion, despite his youth.

Barcode pointed to the rider. "What's happenin' with Lil' Aran?"

As expected, Brutus turned to look.

Barcode stepped back a pace, grabbed the handle of the baseball bat, and pulled it from the deep pocket his Auntie May had sewn into the lining of his parka. He swung a hard uppercut, stepping into the blow—adding his full body-weight to increase the power of the swing.

The fat end of the bat landed between Brutus' legs with enough force to crush his dick, and take the rascal clean off his feet.

Brutus screamed, doubled over, and crumpled to his knees. Slowly, he toppled forwards to land face first in a grimy puddle. Barcode smiled at the effect of the under-hand blow, surprised he could generate so much power.

"Man, that's gotta hurt bad," he said, resting the fat end of the bat on the back of Brutus' neck. The blow had knocked the beanie clean off of the thief's head, and it floated on top of the puddle. "I can't tell if you pissed yo'self, or if that damp patch in yo' kecks is blood, blood. You feel me?"

Barcode flashed a glance up the alley. Lil' Aran's jaw dropped. The rider planted a foot on the ground to stop himself toppling.

To add to the bad vibes, a hard, cold rain started dropping. Before long, it poured down with all the force of a power shower. Spluttering, struggling to breathe, Brutus tried to pull his head clear of the water, but Barcode wasn't having it. He planted a foot into the middle of Brutus' back, forcing him down hard. Bubbles frothed around the drowning fucker's head. His arms and legs thrashed.

Barcode let him splash and buck for a count of twenty before releasing the pressure and stepping away.

Brutus exploded outta the water and rolled away, coughing and spluttering. Gagging like a bitch. He scrambled away on his thieving butt and fetched up against the rusted, chain-link fence, where he curled into a tight ball, face creased in hurt, eyes closed.

Yeah, now you know what pain feels like, blood.

"W-What the f-fuck you do that for, man?" he squeaked.

Barcode was impressed the fucker could speak at all after the crunching blow. Musta had balls of steel. Mashed steel now, though. Barcode couldn't hold back a snicker. He signalled with the bat for Lil' Aran to come as witness, but the rider didn't budge. Couldn't blame him none. Musta been scared shitless, thinking Barcode had totally lost his shit.

"Take off them sneakers," he ordered Brutus, speaking loud enough for Lil' Aran to hear.

When the fucker didn't move, Barcode ran the head of the bat along the fence above Brutus' head. It made an aggressive rattle and meshed well with the splashing rain.

The crumpled man turned his head up and rain sluiced into his pained eyes. "What? What you say?"

"You hear me, blood. Kick off them sneakers 'fore I drop you, fucker."

Still twitching and shivering, the big man's shoulders

tensed in realisation. "You ... you trippin', blood. Had too much product. You bust my balls and tell me to—"

Brutus screamed again as Barcode slammed the bat down on the top of his shoulder. The satisfying crunch of a shattering collar bone buzzed up through the handle.

Barcode yelled, "Shut the fuck up, you mutha!" and raised the bat high, holding it aloft but not completing the downswing. "Lil' Aran, come here, cuz!"

The young rider shook his head. "No way, man. You flipped."

Breathing hard, as much to steady his nerves as from the exercise, Barcode lowered the bat slowly and rested it on Brutus' bad shoulder. The thief squealed.

"Nah, lil' man. Things is cool. Come here, I need you as a witness. You safe from me, unless you part of it."

"Part o' what?"

"The thievery."

Lil' Aran sat up straighter in the saddle. Rain ran down his face and dripped off his chin like it was pouring out the spout of a teapot.

"You know me, BC. I ain't no t'ief!" he shouted above the whistling wind, the driving rain, and Brutus' groaning and crying.

"So, do as I tell you. Come here and rip off this fucker's sneakers!"

Lil' Aran paused a moment, considering. He threw a glance at his escape route, then looked at Brutus before pushing down on the pedal. The bike edged closer, not gaining much speed.

"Hurry, man. I's gettin' soaked here."

The rider pedalled harder, throwing up spray as the low-slung bike splashed through the growing pools of filthy water. Five metres away, he skidded to a sideways stop, jumped off his ride, and propped it against the fence. Then he approached the newly made cripple.

"Take off his sneakers."

Brutus raised his head to stare at Lil' Aran, "Don't touch me you mutha—"

Another scream cut off Brutus' cuss as Barcode pressed the bat harder into the smashed shoulder.

"Who give you permission to speak, fucker? Go on, Lil' Aran. Let's see what he hidin' inside them flashy Pitch Blacks."

Brutus tried to scrunch away but, crowded by Barcode on one side, Lil' Aran on the other, and tight against the fence, there wasn't nowhere he could squirm to.

Lil' Aran squatted in front of the fallen soldier and looked up at Barcode. "Okay if I takes out my cutter? Don't wanna mess with wet knots."

Barcode nodded. "Go for it, cuz."

The little rider pulled out a butterfly knife and flicked it open like he'd practised in his bedroom for hours. Musta been studying Gerard, the smooth-talking, French Heavy, but he didn't get the action quite so slick.

Lil' Aran sliced through the laces and ripped the right sneaker from Brutus' foot.

Using his fingertips, the rider fished inside the soft cuff. They came out with a bunch of crumpled banknotes. Lil' Aran gasped and shook his head.

"How much he got in there, cuz?"

Lil' Aran smoothed out the paper and sorted them into tens and fives. He counted them slowly. "Thirty-five quid."

"Check the other shoe."

The rider repeated the process.

"Fifty-five. That's ... er," he said, scrunching up his eyes to work the maths.

"Ninety, cuz," Barcode said, saving him the work. "He got ninety quid stuffed into them sneakers."

Lil' Aran stood and brushed water and gravel from the knees of his jeans. "Where'd he come up with that cash, BC?"

"Fucker's been rippin' off the Tribe. I been watchin' him for the last couple hours."

Brutus shook his head. "Nah, man. You got it all wrong. I'm clean. That's my stash. I put it there for safe keepin'. Honest."

He released one fist from his crushed junk and held it up to Barcode, hand open, begging.

Barcode sniffed, turned, and strolled away, all cool, like. Lil' Aran followed, stuffing the paper into his backpack. He collected his bike, and walked alongside Barcode.

"You just leavin' him there, BC?"

"What you want me to do?"

The rider shrugged. "Kill the fucker? He'll run, right?"

"Nah, lil' man. He ain't runnin' nowhere with bruised nuts and a smashed shoulder."

Barcode stopped walking and turned to face the pool of light. Somehow, Brutus had pulled himself to his feet. He leaned against the fence, hunched over, unable to stand straight. Barcode doubted the fucker'd be able to stand straight for weeks.

"I ain't killin' no one. That up to TM, not me."

"You sure, BC?" Lil' Aran asked, still looking up, blinking the rain outta his eyes. "I'll back yo' action."

"Thanks, cuz, but I's sure. Way I see it, TM's gonna send a posse o' Heavies to Brutus' crib. If he there, they likely do the job for me. If he gone, *no problemo*. He'll turn up soon enough. My job's to push product and take care o' business. Not my place to dish out punishment without orders. Me? I's just a foot soldier, cuz."

For now.

Chapter Two

Friday 19th February - Afternoon

Brooke Street, Walthamstow, London, England

Lara Orchard hugged Ryan Kaine's arm as they strolled through the neighbourhood, taking their time, chatting about nothing in particular. Her warmth permeated the sleeve of his light jacket and all was good, at least for the moment.

They picked their way along uneven pavements, dodging potholes, cracked paving slabs, and litter. Plastic wheelie bins with yellow, green, and brown lids, most full to overflowing, added extra obstructions to their leisurely progress.

Little kids on bikes weaved between the parked cars, narrowly missing the few scurrying pedestrians. Low-quality graffiti daubed most of the vertical surfaces, many including the purple tag, "PRT", inside the outline of a skull without a jawbone.

Shame, but hardly surprising.

Rubbish piled high in every open space. Mouthy kids smoked cigarettes and stared either blankly or threateningly —it was difficult to tell the difference when most had dead eyes.

"Those lads remind me of the Elbow song," she said.

"Who?"

"Elbow, the group. They remind me of the Elbow song, *Lippy Kids*. I'll play it for you sometime. You'll love it."

Kaine blinked as a gust of freezing wind watered his eyes. "I'm not much into music these days, but I'll give anything a chance."

They continued strolling, acting like a pair of tourists in no particular hurry, relaxed in each other's company.

Kaine took in the area with nothing more than a fleeting glance. For her part of the conversation, and mainly for show, Lara chatted away, describing what she saw in low tones. As the man, he did little more than grunt and add a few words in an effort to show her he was listening.

Brooke Street ended at a T-junction with Green Lane, which was anything but green and looked nothing like a lane. They stopped and made a big show of checking their bearings. Terraced houses in an even worse state of disre-pair, and separated by the occasional alleyway, stretched out on each arm of the "T". In the distance, one of the rows ended in a small corner shop. How it stayed open and who it served in such an uninviting neighbourhood, Kaine couldn't tell, but the light showing through the large window confirmed it did. They turned about-face and retraced their steps along Brooke Street.

A disused and overgrown children's playground took up a large corner plot, its equipment rusted, wooden slats broken, the grass overgrown with weeds, and the whole area strewn with drug paraphernalia.

A slow, five-hundred-metre walk later, they reached what used to be Glenmore Davits' house, Number 60. Darwin Moore owned it now, having inherited from his grandfather a few weeks earlier.

End-of-terrace, pitched roof, two storeys with an attached single garage. Postage-stamp front garden, untended. The garage had a black, up-and-over door. It was pitted with rust, dented from previous attacks, and smeared with the same PRT tags of gang ownership. The front door wore a similar spray job. It bore cracked and filthy window lights and a bruised and battered lower panel, which looked as though it had been kicked in and repaired more than once.

A concrete wheelchair ramp, complete with dull, metal railing, formed a five-metre bridge leading from a modified front porch to the raised pavement. An addition paid for by the local council, according to their detailed research.

Lara brushed a strand of windblown, auburn hair from her face. Her makeup, skilfully applied to mask rather than enhance her youth and beauty, added a decade to her age and covered the healthy-looking and natural suntan in a pale foundation.

They crossed to the other side of the street and strolled past a front garden filled with black, plastic bin liners, many overstuffed and bursting. One of the bags moved. A rat the size of a sausage dog broke into the open, sniffed the air, and scurried into a discarded pizza box.

Lara turned to face him. "Remind me why we didn't simply drive past and scope the place out."

Kaine smiled. She knew exactly why a drive-by wouldn't work, but he answered anyway, maintaining the pretence of a gentle conversation.

"A strange car driving slowly through these streets would stand out like a frogman at a banquet. We'd draw too much attention. As it is, we're hardly inconspicuous. Now, tell me what you're thinking."

She paused before responding.

"I've a feeling young Darwin Moore is struggling and really does need our help."

"What makes you say that?"

"I didn't see a 'For Sale' sign outside Number 60. Why would anyone actually choose to live in a dump like this?" she asked.

Kaine shrugged. "Who knows. Maybe the neighbours are nice. Sense of community. Memories. Whatever. It's not our job to force people to do anything they don't want to. Okay, let's get a chivvy on. We need to find somewhere local to stay overnight."

Somewhere clean and warm, for preference.

They increased their pace slightly, reached the end of the street, and turned left along Baker Rise, heading towards the main shopping area on the High Street about half a mile distant.

A right turn took them onto Lower Street and past Denny's Grill, a greasy spoon that offered all-day breakfasts and emitted an enticing aroma of grilled bacon, fried eggs, and chips.

"Hungry?" he asked.

She shrugged, said, "Not really, but I could force down a cuppa," and dragged him into the welcoming warmth and humidity of the near-empty café.

They found the most secluded table in the corner and

didn't have to wait long to attract the attention of the big man standing behind the serving counter. Close-cropped, grey hair, clean-shaven, and over six foot tall, the man had a barrel chest, thick arms, and was a great deal thicker around the waist. He wore a surprisingly clean, blue-and-white-striped apron and greeted them with a welcoming smile.

"We don't do table service here, mates," he said in a strong, Scottish accent, his voice deep and loud, but friendly. "Come and order, and I'll gi' ye a shout when it's ready."

Kaine stood and leaned close to Lara. "Fancy a Full English?"

"After that huge breakfast on the ferry, are you serious?" she answered keeping her voice down. "I'll have a pot of tea and a scone, thanks. Butter, but no jam."

Still close, and speaking quietly, he said, "Lesson number seventy-one for today, my dear student. In the field, you never know when your next meal will present itself. Take advantage of any opportunity to refuel."

Lara sighed, slipped out of her coat, folded it neatly, and draped it over the back of a nearby plastic chair. "We're in London, not the Hindu Kush or the Kalahari Desert. Tea and a scone will do perfectly well, thank you, William."

He winked, sidestepped between two closely spaced tables, and headed towards the serving counter. As he arrived, Kaine unbuttoned his coat.

The Scotsman nodded and waited for Kaine to read the menu. No surprises. The standard offerings for a low-rent café. Apart from the ubiquitous breakfast, Denny's provided sausages, battered cod, burgers, bacon—all served with chips, peas, and curry sauce—and an assortment of filled sandwiches. A menu sadly absent near their villa in France.

Kaine returned the nod and tried a smile. "Are you Denny?"

The man sighed and all but rolled his eyes. "Nah, mate."

Kaine allowed his smile to widen. "Bet you wish you had a pound for every time someone asked you that, eh?"

Not-Denny's shoulders dropped a little, and a twitch of his lips could have been mistaken for either a grimace or a weak grin. The faded tattoos on the man's forearms told of a lifetime spent at sea, and suggested he might be worth cultivating as a source of local intel.

"Too right, matey. I could've retired to the Costa del Money, years back. Right now, I'd be soaking up the sun rather than standing here developing sciatica and growing varicose veins. What can I get for ye?"

"Pot of tea for two, a buttered scone, and a Full English, please."

"Black pudding?"

"Sounds good to me." Kaine hadn't eaten a savoury blood sausage for years.

"It's an extra quid," Not-Denny said, pointing to the menu on the chalkboard over his shoulder.

"That's okay, don't mind pushing the boat out now and again. And make that two scones, two squares of butter, and a pot of strawberry jam."

Kaine's largesse raised a real smile from Not-Denny. "Last of the big spenders?"

"That's me. Taking my good lady wife around our potential new neighbourhood. You never know, we might become regulars in your fine mess hall, Chief."

Not-Denny's hard won half-smile turned into a quizzical frown. "Yeah, that's right. Chief Petty Officer. How'd ye guess? Ye've had some time in?"

"A few years."

"Officer?"

"No, mate, I—"

"Don't tell me," Not-Denny interrupted, "ye *worked* for a living, right?" He laughed at the old military joke.

Not heard that one for a while.

Kaine joined in with the laughter, surreptitiously throwing a quick glance at Lara, who'd buried her nose in the glossy magazine she'd picked up on the ferry. Trying hard to blend into any crowd, she wore her baggiest clothes, covered her gorgeous, auburn hair with a big, woollen bonnet, and wrapped a thick scarf around her neck. To complete the matronly look, she balanced a pair of horn-rimmed glasses—with non-prescription lenses—on the end of her nose. Kaine still saw her as completely stunning, but the fact that Not-Denny had barely given her a second glance confirmed the power of her disguise.

"Chief Petty Officer Jellicoe. Welcome aboard, mate," Not-Denny pushed out his open hand and they shook hard and fast.

"William Griffin, Bill. Pleased to meet you …?"

"My name's Philip. And no, afore ye ask, ma friends dinnae call me 'Prince', as in Prince Philip. They call me—"

"Don't tell me, Joshua, right?"

Kaine's new friend's bellow turned the heads of all five customers in the café, including Lara's.

"That's right, mate. This here Joshua"—he jabbed a thumb into his barrel chest—"won the battle of Jericho all by himself." Still laughing, he half-turned again, dropped three teabags into a large pot, and filled it with boiling water from an urn beside the sink. "What service were ye in, mate?" he asked.

"Marines."

As Kaine learned early in his time as a fugitive, one of the basic rules of creating undercover legends was to stick as close to the truth as possible. This made learning the details of the false career easier and, as a legend builder, Corky stood a class apart, as did Corky's competitor, Sabrina.

Ever since Kaine and Lara had been forced into hiding, Sabrina and Corky, their volunteer IT gurus, had competed to provide them with evermore detailed legends, both as individuals and as a couple. They'd also provided the full ID and all the paperwork needed to drop into character—passports, driving licences, health papers, and everything else imaginable. Each of the legends came fully supported by detailed background information, education, habitation, friends and social background, and all the historical data going back at least two generations. With finances not being an issue for Kaine and his team, the only limitation to their ability to change backgrounds happened to be his and Lara's facility for absorbing the facts needed to pass muster in an intensive interview—should they ever be subjected to one.

They had spent the drive north through France and the nine-hour ferry crossing from St Malo in Brittany to Portsmouth, boning up on their Griffin personas and testing each other's knowledge.

Apparently, Lara had always wanted to be an Elizabeth.

"Not sure I fancy being a William," he'd responded, adding, "Make sure you call me Bill, not Willie."

She'd chuckled. "Wouldn't dream of calling you Willie. Don't want to draw anyone's attention to it."

They'd been driving the dual carriageway into St Malo at the time, and he'd almost run out of the lane.

"What was that?"

She'd blushed. "Sorry, I meant ... I wouldn't want to

draw anyone's attention to you, not … you know what I meant."

He'd twitched the steering wheel to centre the car in the lane and built up speed again. Luckily, the motorways in northern France weren't as busy as those in the UK or they might have run into trouble. Literally.

"Is that what they call a Freudian Slip, Mrs Griffin?"

Lara batted off his question with a flick of her hand and a delightful frown.

"Men! One-track minds, the lot of you."

"Steady on, Beth. I wasn't the one referring to nether regions. I hope you're more selective with what you say when we reach Walthamstow. Things could get a little embarrassing otherwise."

Despite the need to concentrate in the café, Kaine couldn't stop himself smiling.

Not-Denny, Joshua, perked up at Kaine's revelation.

"Commando, eh? I thought ye guys were all giants who could pick up cars wi' yer bare hands and chomp on rocks for yer breakfasts."

Kaine shook his head firmly and added a theatrical sigh. "Yeah, true enough. I used to be over six foot tall, but the training wore me down to the nub."

A laughing Joshua set a large mug and a smaller cup and saucer on a tray with the teapot. Then he added a milk jug and sugar bowl. "Been out long?"

Kaine frowned in question. "How did you—"

"In ma day, no' many serving marines could get away with a mop o' hair that long. Mind ye, the bootie's standards have been slipping for years." The CPO added a wink to show he was still kidding.

Kaine scratched his beard. "Thought I'd let it grow out. See what it looked like. Bloody annoying and scruffy. If I had my way, I'd search out the nearest barber, but the missus likes it and ... well, you know how it is with women." He added the last part *sotto voce*.

"Aye, I know. Got to keep 'em happy, right enough. Where were ye stationed last?"

"RM Tamar, Plymouth," Kaine said. That much information, he could deliver without appearing too loose-lipped.

Joshua nodded sagely, leaned closer, and whispered, "1 Assault Group?"

Kaine shrugged and added a noncommittal, "Perhaps." Any serviceman would understand his reluctance to talk.

"Had a unit from 1 Assault aboard *HMS Sheldon* last time we shipped out to Malta. Good lads, the lot o' them. Hard as nails."

"Yep. Tungsten tough," Kaine admitted, digging a knuckle into his right hip and grimacing, "but this marine turned out a little brittle."

"So, how long ye been out?"

Kaine's defence mechanism rippled. Joshua might just be a friendly sort, but it never paid to be too open with strangers and Kaine didn't want too much information flowing around the neighbourhood.

"A few months, but ..." Kaine tapped the side of his nose with an index finger. "I don't want to be rude, but can't talk about it. You understand?"

"Oh, yeah, aye. 'Course." Joshua pushed the tray towards Kaine. "Understood. Mum's the word. So, I'll give ye a yell when yer grub's ready."

"Thanks, Joshua. Really looking forward to it."

Kaine picked up the tray and walked it back to their table, favouring his left leg slightly.

"Made a new friend, I see," Lara said, stirring the tea in

the pot and checking its strength—a little too weak for Kaine, but just right for her, judging by the colour.

She filled her little cup, added a splash of milk, ignored the sugar.

"CPO Philip Jellicoe," Kaine said, "Joshua to his friends. Really chatty. Maybe too friendly, but he's probably the type to know what's happening hereabouts."

"I suppose you'd like me to ask Corky to run a background check?"

"Don't see why not. Jellicoe's an unusual name. Shouldn't be too hard for our friendly 'information acquisition specialist' to run him to ground."

Lara took her mobile from her handbag. "You really think it's necessary? After all, we might not be here long."

Kaine lifted the teapot and gave it a swirl before pouring. The dark brown liquid flowing into his pristine mug looked perfect. "Probably, but there's something about this place ... a bad smell."

"What, in the café?"

"No, Denny's Grill is spotless. Nothing more than I'd expect in a place run by an old salt." He added milk to his tea and took a sip.

Pretty damned good, and way better than the French restaurant staff could manage on the ferry.

He raised the mug to the watching retired CPO and dipped his head as a sign of appreciation. For his part, Joshua smiled and carried on prepping Kaine's breakfast. Despite not being overly hungry, the aroma of frying bacon made Kaine's mouth water. Yep, he could certainly manage a plate of English grub.

"So?" Lara asked, gently pushing.

"The neighbourhood's ... I don't know ... wrong. Last time I felt something like this was in Helmand."

Lara raised an eyebrow. "That serious?"

"You think I'm nuts?"

"Oh no, I felt something similar myself. Outside, I was uncomfortable. It felt as though we were being watched, and not in a good way. Didn't want to say anything in case you laughed at me. Women's intuition and all that."

"Never. I happen to take intuition seriously. It's helped me out of many a tight situation."

"And I happen to believe in Ryan Kaine's sixth sense," she said, keeping her voice low. "What do you want to do next?"

On a signal from the counter, Kaine stood and leaned closer to Lara. "Next, I'm going to fetch our food and enjoy what I expect to be an excellent second breakfast. After that … we'll see."

"You're not sending me home," Lara said—a statement, not a question.

"We'll see."

"No we won't. You'll never leave without checking on the target, and I'm staying right here until you do."

"Elizabeth Griffin, you are impossible."

"Yes, and you know I'm right."

Kaine frowned all the way to the counter and all the way back with his heaving tray. Lara *was* right and they both knew it.

Despite their frosty silence, Kaine's breakfast was delicious and, although she'd claimed to have no appetite, Lara ate both homemade scones, which also looked delicious. She did ignore the jam.

Lara finished first, pushed her empty plate away, and refilled her cup. "Are we having our first real argument?"

"Yes."

"After thirteen years together, and twelve of them married?"

She'd clearly memorised her legend well. His mood lifted.

"Are you going to throw the way I treated your late mother in my face again?"

Lara pulled a tissue from her handbag. "You were horrible to her. And all she wanted was the best for her daughter." She dabbed her eyes with the tissue, playing her scene to the max.

"Darling," Kaine said, reaching for her hand, the one holding the mobile, not the crumpled but dry tissue, "I'm sorry. Your mother was a wonderful woman, even though she thought you'd married beneath you."

Lara sniffed, raised her voice to a plaintive whimper. "Maybe I should have married Peter Lancaster when I had the chance. He made regional manager at the bank last year. The man's far more successful than you ever were."

Kaine released her hand and leaned back. "You've been in touch with your old flame?" he bellowed. "What the hell, Beth. Why don't you go to him then? Maybe he's the right one after—"

"Oh William," she said, reaching for his hand, "that's so not fair. Aunt Marjory keeps in touch with Peter's mother, and she's the one who told me about his promotion. Haven't spoken to the man for years and years. I've never once regretted my decision, you silly, silly man. At least, not before today." She murmured the last part.

Kaine leaned close again, lowering his voice to match her whisper. "Okay, okay. Enough showing off your acting skills. I'm convinced. We're going to shelve this particular conversation until later, when we're alone. Meanwhile, do you mind dropping Corky a line while I go smooth things over with my new buddy?"

She piled the plates and cutlery onto the tray. "Yes, William. If you say so. You're the boss."

He shook his head in apparent frustration and grabbed the tray. "That'll be a first time in this marriage."

Lara's half-hidden smile made Kaine's heart lurch. He limped the tray to the counter and slid it across, fixing a hangdog expression to his face. "What do I owe you for the grub?"

Joshua rang up the bill and Kaine handed over enough cash to cover it. "Keep the change, mate. Food was delicious. By the way"—he threw a glance towards Lara, who was still tapping away at the screen of her mobile—"sorry 'bout that."

"Don't worry, mate. Been divorced twice. I know all about marital strife."

"Poor woman's still getting used to having me under her feet, twenty-four-seven. It's the longest we've been together since the wedding, and house hunting is always fraught."

"Ye looking for a new billet?"

Kaine shrugged and scratched at his beard, playing his part. "We'll lose our married quarters in a couple of months. The West Country's okay for a holiday, but a bit quiet, you know? Bloody expensive to buy a place and precious few decent houses for rent, too. At least not at the prices we can afford."

"Yeah, far worse in London though."

"Tell me about it. Bloody shoeboxes we've seen in the past few days claiming to be luxury apartments, doesn't bear thinking about."

"Where've ye been looking?"

"All over. Started out west and headed east, chasing the lower prices."

"Why Walthamstow? Not exactly the go-to place if yer looking for the nightlife. To be honest, the place is a craphole."

Kaine shrugged again. "Why not Walthamstow? We put a pin in the map and this is where we ended up. You never know, by the time we find something we like and can afford, we might end up in Canvey Island."

Joshua laughed. "Ye ask me, Canvey Island's no better'n Walthamstow."

Never having visited the place in question, Kaine simply nodded along, keeping a hopeful smile in place. "Don't suppose you can recommend a decent place for us to stay overnight. We were going to head for the nearest Premier Inn, but if you know somewhere better and closer ..." He let the sentence trail off and scratched at his beard again.

"Actually," Joshua said, raising a finger in the air, "I might well do. Give me a sec and I'll see if ma old mate, Bernie, has a room. Nah, there's no need for that old-fashioned look, mate. Bernie Halfpenny runs a decent little hotel 'round the corner on the High Street. Keeps the place clean and tidy, if not exactly shipshape." He took note of Kaine's questioning look and added, "Bernie's an ex-squaddie, but don't let that put ye off. He's good people. There's off-road parking, too, if ye have a motor. Won't break the bank, neither. 'Specially if I can twist his arm and get him to offer ye mate's rates."

"Thanks, Joshua. Beth and I appreciate your help. But, before you do that, can we have a refill?" Kaine asked, pointing to the teapot.

Joshua did the business and replenished the milk jug.

"There ye go. Just gi' me a sec and I'll get back to ye,"

Joshua said before turning his back and unhooking the land-line from its cradle on the wall beside the till.

Kaine returned to the table and poured while updating Lara on his chat.

"Makes sense," she said, taking what seemed like a reluctant sip. "If I know anything about military men, our Joshua will be a mine of local information."

Kaine watched as their host chatted into the phone and received payment from the remaining customers. Joshua noticed Kaine's interest and smiled, adding a thumb's up.

"Looks like we have a bed for the night."

"Good. Hope it's not too downmarket."

"We can make do for one night if it turns out to be a dive."

Kaine and Lara nursed their teas, waiting in silence for Joshua to end his call.

"There ye go," he called, replacing the handset and wiping his hands on a spotless dishcloth, "everything's arranged. Double bed, wi' colour TV, sixty-five quid a night. Sound good?"

Kaine glanced at Lara, who nodded, and he said, "Sounds perfect."

"Excellent. Ye'll no' be disappointed. By the way, that price doesn't include breakfast, but Bernie's place is only 'round the corner and ye can eat here. We're open at five bells ... that's oh-six-thirty"—he said to Lara—"and don't close 'til late."

Lara smiled her thanks—not that she would've needed an explanation of ship's bell times. Kaine had explained it to her once a few months earlier, and she had an excellent memory.

Kaine made a show of scanning the café.

"Since we're the only customers left, care to join us for a chinwag?"

Joshua rubbed his hands together. "Don't mind if I do. Need to take this great, big weight off o' ma pins."

He paused long enough to fill a huge mug with black coffee, stirred in three heaped teaspoons of sugar, and joined them at an adjacent table to give himself plenty of elbow room.

"Anything ye particularly wanted to know?" the CPO asked after taking a surprisingly delicate and silent sip.

Still holding her cup over her saucer, Lara turned to face him.

"Well, actually, there is."

"Shoot."

"Bill and I have just taken a stroll around the area," she started, hesitantly. "We noticed there were a number of houses for sale on Baker Rise and Brooke Street, and I've just been looking at the prices." She held up her mobile by way of explanation. "Not bad for this area. What do you think?"

Joshua made a face that looked like he'd bitten deep into a rotten apple.

"Well now, lass. If ye want some advice, steer well clear. I wouldn't buy a house anywhere along there."

Here we go.

Kaine leaned closer and rested his forearms on the table. "Why not?"

"That's Tribe territory."

"Tribe?"

Joshua nodded, his expression solemn. "Ye saw all those purple PRT tags?"

Simultaneously, Kaine and Lara nodded.

"They mark Palmerston Road Tribe territory. Most decent people steer well clear o' the area if they can."

"Why?" Kaine asked, his interest well and truly piqued.

"Street thugs and drug pushers, the whole area's infested wi' the wee basta—beggars. 'Scuse my language, Mrs Griffin. They're led by a real enigma …"

Kaine and Lara spent the following forty minutes pumping intel out of a first-class gossip and top-notch story teller. The elderly seaman only stopped when his next customers arrived in a flurry of activity, a burst of jovial chatter, and letting in a blast of freezing air.

———

THE CHATTY CPO proved true to his word. Bernie's place, The Rushington Hotel, turned out to be exactly what they needed. Although small, it stood on the corner of Lower Street and the High Street, around the corner from Denny's Grill, and within a gentle, twenty-minute stroll of the target's house.

Clean and tidy, low key, and with off-road parking for their hire car, the Rushington couldn't have been any more perfect. Joshua's "mates rates" proved to be a forty-percent reduction on the standard, low-season charge for a double room. While money wasn't an issue for Kaine and Lara, their alter egos, Bill and Beth Griffin, were ever so grateful for the generous discount, and they made sure to thank Bernie profusely when they signed in.

As a standard precaution, and before unpacking, Kaine checked the room for bugs—both living and electronic. He found neither. Thankfully, the place had been scrubbed hygienically clean.

By the time they'd finished discussing the plan of action

for the morning and settled in front of the TV to watch the late-evening news, they were pretty close to exhaustion.

At 22:30, Lara's mobile buzzed with a long text from Corky. His initial research threw up nothing problematic related to Joshua, and he promised to keep digging.

Not long afterwards, Lara fell asleep in Kaine's arms. He stared at the ceiling, listening to the wind howl and the rain attack the double glazing, stewing. How was he going to protect Lara from herself?

If half of what Joshua had told them turned out to be true, and not simply the overblown hype of an old salt, Lara shouldn't be anywhere near Walthamstow. In fact, she shouldn't be within a hundred miles of the Tribe, let alone within a half-hour walk of their turf.

Under any other circumstances, he'd have left her at the villa under protective guard, but his go-to guys, Rollo and Danny, were currently otherwise engaged.

Neither he nor Lara should have been in the UK, but Kaine was honour bound to help Darwin Moore, or at least find out how the young man was doing since his grandfather's accidental death.

His *apparently* accidental death.

For the rest of the night, Kaine studied the patterns on the ceiling made by the headlights of cars driving past on the street outside, unable to decide what to do for the best. He hated it.

Indecision weakened him, and it put people in danger.

Chapter Three

Saturday 20th February - Lara Orchard

The Rushington Hotel, Walthamstow, London, England

With her hair pulled back into a savage and unflattering bun, and wearing a dowdy, dark grey trouser suit and minimal make-up, Lara prepared herself mentally for the upcoming meeting. The first with their potential new "client", and her first as mission leader.

She and Ryan stood in the hotel foyer and he, ever the gentleman, helped her into her heaviest overcoat. As well as the nondescript and inexpensive shoulder bag, she carried a woollen hat and scarf to protect her from the biting wind and sleet that would greet them the moment they stepped outside.

"Ready?" Ryan asked, keeping his voice low.

Poor man looked as though he hadn't slept much.

More a worrier than a warrior.

"I think so. Darwin Moore's a university undergraduate. How hard is this likely to be?"

Ryan—looking as plain and inconspicuous as he ever could in a short coat, dark trousers, walking boots, and cloth cap—gave her an encouraging smile. The uncorrected contact lenses changed his eyes from warm brown to pale green, and the difference it made to his overall look was striking. Trimming his beard and darkening his longish hair to remove the grey streaks at the temples completed the transformation. No one would recognise him from the wanted posters. In fact, Ryan's closest military friends would struggle to identify him in that getup. Still, she couldn't help but worry, especially when he walked around in broad daylight. Anything could happen—they could bump into anyone outside.

As far as they could tell, Ryan's enemies were still on the lookout for him, and there may still have been a massive, underground reward on his head.

He could have chosen to stay out of sight, abroad and safe. After all, he had access to plenty of cash. Heck, he could buy a small Caribbean island and still have plenty left over to live extremely comfortably for the rest of his life. He was taking a terrible risk to keep helping the members of The 83, and she both loved him for it and was terrified of the potential consequences.

Fair enough that no one could defend himself or protect Lara better than Ryan, but he was only human. If the police ever caught up with him, even the resourceful Captain Ryan Liam Kaine wouldn't last long in prison.

Though he and Lara had proof positive of his innocence, if they made it public, it would take months, years even, to clear his name through the courts. In the meantime, he'd likely be held on remand in an open prison and would probably face terrible danger from inmates eager to make themselves rich on the back of Ryan's death.

"It shouldn't be too difficult, but I don't like involving you in—"

"Ryan ... sorry, Bill," she interrupted, mentally cursing herself for the slip. "We've been through all this 'til we're blue in the face. Let's move on, shall we? Darwin Moore might be okay. If so, we can sort out the financials and head back to the villa, back home, this afternoon. Alternatively, he might need our help, in which case, that's what we're here for, isn't it? Until we actually speak to him, we'll never know. I mean, his grandfather might not have told him about the money or The Trust."

Ryan snapped his mouth closed on his response as an elderly hotel guest descended the stairs. The man excused himself, and they stepped aside to allow him access to the dining room. Ryan pointed her towards the exit and, chivalry itself, opened the door to let her through first.

"After what Joshua told us, we need to be prepared for all eventualities," he said unnecessarily. "And Corky did confirm everything the old warhorse said."

The chill air caught in Lara's throat and she took the time to pull on her hat and wrap the scarf tightly around her exposed neck.

Sufficiently protected against the elements and from the anticipated gallery of surveillance cameras, Lara sighed. "Any more clichés to pitch in my direction, Bill Griffin?" she asked, the breath condensing around her head.

His warm smile melted a little of the growing frost.

"Sorry, but this is our first actual joint mission and … well, I'm concerned."

"So am I," she said, closing the slight gap between them and hugging his arm.

He pulled on a pair of leather gloves and clamped her hand to his arm, protectively. They descended the steps from the hotel and turned left, retracing their steps from the previous afternoon. Lara leaned against his shoulder, giving anyone who cared to look, the impression of a loving, middle-aged couple out for a gentle, morning stroll.

On Lower Street, directly across the road from them, Denny's Grill beckoned.

"Breakfast?" he asked.

"No, thanks," she said, shivering, but not just against the cold. "I'm too nervous to eat. Can we leave it for later?"

He smiled and squeezed her hand. "Not a problem. Nerves are good. Used properly, they'll keep you alive."

"Everything's an opportunity for training, isn't it?"

Ryan nodded, but said nothing.

They reached the end of Baker Rise and turned into Brooke Street.

Not long now.

Lara had insisted on helping and needed to hold herself together to do it. A rumble in her tummy had nothing to do with hunger. Use the nerves, Ryan said, and she would.

"You have all the necessary paperwork in that huge shoulder bag?"

She nodded. "Of course. Three different sets, depending upon what we find and how we want to proceed."

"Good. How are you going to open?"

She faltered a step, but he held her arm pinned against his and they carried on. "We went through this last night."

41

"Humour me."

"Why?"

"I've been doing this sort of thing for a while, but this is your first time at the coalface. Humour me, please."

"You want me to get my head in the game, right?"

While Ryan surreptitiously took in the area as they walked, she repeated the initial opening they'd worked on the previous night.

Cars parked on both sides of the road formed a slalom barrier to the oncoming traffic. Rows of Victorian-era, terraced houses crowded in on them, growing more dilapidated the further from the shops they walked.

Lara cast a glance up. Most of the street lights were broken. "This place will be badly lit at night."

"Not the nicest place to live I've ever seen, but certainly not the worst either. There's plenty of money in the pot to help young Darwin, assuming that's what he wants."

"Bill," she said, "he's a second-year undergraduate with mounting student debt. We're going to make his life so much better."

"Should do, but there's no telling how people are going to react to such news. Might take some time for him to come to terms with it. He probably won't believe us at first."

"Which is why I have all this paperwork."

"Good," he said, with a certainty Lara couldn't feel. "Today should be a piece of cake then."

For once, she couldn't tell if he was being ironic.

Since leaving the hotel, he'd been distant, deep in concentration. She'd seen him in full operational mode a few times, and knew the signs. At work, he was a different man, cold, intense, dedicated to the safety of those under his protection, and tough. Really tough. A man she still trusted completely but barely recognised from the one with whom she shared the quiet times. A man who would kill, and had killed, to save her and himself, but only when there was absolutely no alternative.

Apart from the very occasional passing car and a scurrying pedestrian or two, the north end of Brooke Street seemed deserted.

"Keep chatting. Make things appear normal. Damn ..."

His voice trailed off, and an increased tension in his hand on her arm made Lara take notice. "What's wrong?"

"Nothing. Just keep moving."

"Ryan," she whispered, ignoring the error, "what have you seen?"

Still smiling, Ryan whispered, "Those guys are paying altogether too much attention to us."

Lara followed his gaze. Fifty metres ahead, on the opposite side of the street, three young men gathered in the entrance to an alleyway formed by the ends of two terraced rows. They acted as though they owned the street. All three wore baseball caps, brightly coloured, hooded jackets, jogging pants, and expensive-looking trainers. They carried lit cigarettes and stood in a cloud of blue-grey smoke. Scowling, they faced Ryan and Lara, mumbling from the sides of their mouths. The slightly built one on the right flicked ash into the bushes at his back and said something Lara couldn't hear, but the one in the middle, a huge man with wide shoulders, a shaved head, and night-black skin shook his head.

"Nah. Chill, man," he said, his voice booming "They ain't the bacon."

"What do you want to do?" Lara whispered.

"Ignore them and keep going," he said, swapping places and forming a barrier between her and the trio. "Anything else would be inflammatory."

"But standing between them and me is okay?"

Ryan shrugged. "Only to be expected for a gallant husband who wants to protect his beautiful wife."

"Me, beautiful, in this getup?" she said after swallowing hard. "William Griffin, you are such a smooth talker. No wonder I fell for you all those years ago."

"Yep, that's me," he said, smiling but not taking his eyes from the group near the alley. "Mr Smooth, but you'd be beautiful in a potato sack."

A skinny kid on a tiny bicycle, dressed in the same unofficial uniform as the others, emerged from the alleyway behind the threesome and squealed to a rubber-burning, rear-wheel-skidding halt. With their attention taken by the new arrival, the three turned away and formed a four-person huddle.

"Notice their scarves?" he asked.

"Yes, dark purple. Members of the Palmerston Road Tribe, you think?"

"No doubt. They don't look all that scary, but those are just a street crew. Point men. There'll be dozens of them all over the area. According to Joshua, confirmed by Corky, the leaders are older, more savvy. Not averse to violence either. The police investigated a couple of stabbing deaths in the area last year and dealt with a few minor riots."

Lara nodded. "Yes, I know. I was there yesterday, remember? In Denny's Grill, listening. I heard what Joshua said."

"Just making conversation. Confirming you know what we're dealing with here."

"Don't worry about me. I can take care of myself," she said, more in hope of convincing herself than Ryan, who would never agree to that particular statement.

Two houses later, they reached Number 60.

"Here we go. Ready to play Mother Christmas?"

Lara smiled. "Of course. Are you ready to play one of my elves?"

He laughed. "Happy to, my darling Beth. Let's go."

Ryan stood a half-pace behind, assuming a passive but supportive role, and Lara rapped on the badly scuffed door. Behind the panel, the knock echoed through an empty hallway.

No response.

They waited.

The time on her watch read a few minutes past ten. Maybe a little early for a weekend visit to a university student.

She rapped on the door again, this time a little harder. Once more, the knocking echoed and there was no answer.

A shadow moved behind her as Ryan edged closer. She turned. The largest of the men from the group, the leader, stood in the middle of the road, legs apart, arms folded over his massive chest.

"What you want with Darwin, wo-man?" he demanded in a deep voice, close to a growl.

Behind him, two of his cronies watched with keen interest, but stayed in the mouth of the alley, making no attempt to approach. They obviously felt their extra-large friend didn't need any help on the intimidation front. The little one on the bike looked away, chewing on his lower lip. Lara took a closer look. The cyclist couldn't have been more than ten or eleven, definitely not yet a teen. Why did his parents allow him to mix with the older ones? Such a desperate shame.

Damn it, Lara. Concentrate.

Ryan adjusted his position, attempting to block her view of the men, but she leaned to the side. Unless they were armed with more than words, Ryan wouldn't need her, but she'd help if required and if she could. Well, at least she knew enough not to stand in his way.

"I ask you a question, wo-man," the big one taunted.

Oh dear. Here we go.

Ryan dropped his arms to his sides and flexed his fingers in readiness for action. So protective. He and Lara were only here at her insistence, and she couldn't let this get out of hand.

Lara took a pace to his side. Ryan shot her a warning glance, but she nodded and added a smile that hopefully showed more confidence than she felt.

"Do you know Mr Moore, sir?" she asked.

The two men near the alleyway snorted. The thinner, shorter one, who wore his cap backwards, shouted, "Hear that, Barcode? She call you 'sir'. When you ever been a 'sir'?"

Barcode shot his friend a glowering expression that made the youth snap his mouth shut and stare at his feet.

"You shut yo' mouth, Dylan, or I'll shut it fo' you. The wo-man's showin' me respect. Maybe I oughtta make all my posse call me sir, too. Yeah?"

Dylan kept his head lowered, but raised his eyes. "Aw, BC. Ain't no reason to be like that. We shows you respect alla time, bro."

"What you think, Rhino?" Barcode asked the second man.

Dylan's buddy shrugged, but kept silent. Of medium height like Ryan, the one called Rhino was stocky. He had dark skin, and bore a jagged, grey scar on the left side of his neck. He held his head tilted away from the scar as though displaying it as a badge of honour. Alternatively, it could indicate damage to one of his cranial nerves. Either way, his stance was intimidating. Not a good look for a young man, and it didn't exactly show him as a caring soul.

Barcode flicked his fingers at his "posse" and turned his attention to Lara, deliberately ignoring Ryan. "What you say, wo-man?"

Ryan formed fists. Despite the need for them to remain inconspicuous, Barcode had no idea how close he was to being embarrassed—painfully—in front of his deadbeat crew.

She leaned closer to Ryan, making her intention clear.

"I wondered whether you knew Mr Moore? We understand he lives here."

"You mean Sweet Darwin, the scholar?" Barcode asked, showing another deep sneer.

"Yes, he's the one. You wouldn't be him by any chance, would you?" Lara said, even though the big, angry man looked nothing like the photos on Darwin Moore's university ID card or his driving licence.

Lara didn't want the local hooligans knowing she and Ryan had access to information they shouldn't have.

Barcode barked out a derisory laugh. "Nah, wo-man. Do I looks like I need to go to school? Do all my learnin' on the streets."

"Might help you with your grammar, son," Ryan said.

He sounded calm and conversational enough, but Lara knew better. Ryan was seething.

"You talkin' to me, old man?" Barcode growled at Ryan, stomping nearer, growing ever closer to what, for him, would be an unexpected and intense embarrassment.

Things were deteriorating fast.

"Maybe you need to clear out your ears, son," Ryan said, his delivery gentle but uncompromising.

"Say what, you short-ass muthafucker?"

"Mind your language. There's a lady present."

Calmly, Ryan took three steps towards the loudmouthed fool and they faced each other, standing only a few metres apart.

Barcode, shaking with eye-popping, muscle-rippling anger, had a full ten centimetres of height and reach on Ryan, and maybe thirty kilos of brawn. The younger man couldn't possibly have known it but, even with the help of the two idiots near the alley, they were still hopelessly outmatched.

"I don't see no 'lady'," Barcode growled. "I see a be-atch hidin' behind a dwarf, muthafucker."

Ryan straightened. "Whereas there's much to be said for maternal love, young fellow," he said, "you need to learn some manners."

Even though Ryan had his back to Lara, she could tell he was smiling through the words.

Barcode, nostrils flaring, blood vessels on his neck and temples distended, raised a warning finger in the air. "See here, old man. This here's *my* turf, and you ain't welcome. You just found yo'self a whole world o' pain."

Lara, a pacifist at heart, should have been terrified but, for some reason, she felt calm, confident in Ryan's reading of the situation. He'd never overreact or knowingly lead her into danger.

Ryan shot a quick glance at her, and she shook her head as emphatically as possible. He nodded in return, the ghost of a smile stretching his mouth and thinning his lips, before turning to face Barcode once more. He took another step closer and said something so quietly that, despite the relative silence around them, Lara couldn't make it out. Next, Ryan dipped a hand into his pocket, pulled out his wallet, and flipped it open. He added a few more near-silent words, and their effect on the bully were instantaneous.

Barcode peeled back his lips into an evil grin that could have passed for a snarl, shouted, "See you later, old man," dipped his head, and turned away. He marched back to his posse, gathered them to him, said something low and guttural, and pushed Dylan into the darkness of the covered alley. The rest followed.

Ryan remained where he was until all three young men and the kid on the bike were lost to the shadows before breathing out.

"Interesting welcoming committee," Ryan said, his smile now real and aimed right at her.

"What's in the wallet, and what did you say to make him back down?"

"Tell you later. Shall we try again?" He pointed to the door behind her. "This time, knock even louder. Students can sleep through a rock concert, and it is a Saturday morning. No telling how late he was up last night, bopping."

"Bopping?"

Ryan hiked an eyebrow and shrugged. "Or whatever the younger generation gets up to these days."

"Oh dear, Bill Griffin's fifty-three, not seventy," she said quietly, before returning to the door.

Chapter Four

Saturday 20th February - Morning

Brooke Street, Walthamstow, London, England

Kaine relaxed a little. Instead of buckling under the pressure, Lara had handled Barcode's aggression with calmness and confidence, as he knew she would.

Her bright, hazel eyes shone with intensity and, in spite of her dowdy disguise, the woman oozed pure class. Lara Orchard was, and always would be, way out of his league. Anyone who said he was punching above his weight couldn't have been more accurate. She was, without doubt, far more than he could ever have hoped for in a life partner.

Had they met in a different life, she probably wouldn't have spared him a second glance. On the other hand, if he hadn't exploded into her life and taken her away for her own safety, they would never have met in the first place.

Kaine nodded his encouragement.

"On you go."

She leaned forwards, rapped on the weathered door with her gloved fist for the third time, and waited.

They stood back from the door and turned towards each other.

God, she was so beautiful. Kaine swallowed hard. To think of the trouble he'd dragged her into. He needed to put things right. But if he did that, if he closed the loop, proved his innocence, and removed the bounty on his head, he'd probably lose her forever. He'd argued the point with himself and with Rollo ever since taking Lara to the relative safety of the villa. Even if he published the evidence to prove his innocence, it wouldn't automatically mean the evil men would cancel the contract on his life. It wouldn't necessarily guarantee Lara's safety, either. He'd made enough enemies through the years, and there were plenty of evil men in the world who'd be happy to use Lara to get to him.

Beneath his old-fashioned cloth cap—chosen to age him at least ten years—his hair flapped in the wind, fluttering against his ears and the back of his neck.

"Bill, we need to think about getting you a haircut, or a comb," she said, still playing the wife to the hilt.

She didn't mean it, about the hair. In the quiet safety of the villa, she'd complimented him on the unkempt style many times.

Though they faced a low-risk meeting, there were always potential dangers, as the run-in with Barcode had shown. On top of everything else, he could be recognised at any time, and then they'd be in real strife.

For the whole of his adult life, Kaine had kept his

scrambled hair military short—number four on top, number two on the sides—but since his fall from grace, he'd been forced to let it grow long and woolly. Usually the colour of aged molasses flecked with salt, it matched the full beard for colour and scruffiness. On the rare occasion he glanced in the shaving mirror these days, he barely recognised the aging, whiskered face staring back at him, which was, of course, the whole point. The occasional but judicial use of coloured contact lenses, or glasses with non-prescription lenses, helped him keep under the radar during his brief but regular trips in the field, which was fine by him.

The beard had taken months to bed in enough to stop driving him nuts, but his hair had recently grown over his ears and he'd discovered a new annoyance and new decisions to make. Should he comb it back, or let it fall where it pleased?

"You're dead right, Beth," he answered, then lowered his voice to little more than a murmur. "Given the chance, I'd hack off this mop in a heartbeat. I look like a ruddy vagrant."

"Nonsense. You're rather distinguished. I really like the soft look. Much less the military officer."

He frowned, adding a grunt for good measure.

Lara shook her head, said, "Let's give this one more go, shall we?" and hammered on the door again.

A muffled, "Hang on a second. Be right with you," from deep inside the house made Kaine stand to attention.

Game on.

"Finally, we appear to have woken the dead."

Footsteps thumped loud on stairs with bare treads. The noise echoed off walls and bounced around behind the front door, indicating an open space with no carpet.

A chain rattled, a lock snapped, and the door screeched open to reveal a slightly built and clean-shaven man of multiracial heritage. Horn-rimmed glasses, corrected for short-sightedness, partially hid a narrow face beneath a tightly cropped head of jet-black hair. Despite the evident rudeness of his awakening, the man was smart-looking and presentable.

Intelligent brown eyes behind the glasses narrowed as the young man studied first Lara, then Kaine, and finally fixed back on Lara again.

Apparently satisfied they were neither a danger nor Jehovah's Witnesses, Darwin Moore opened the door fully and stood back.

As expected from the hollow echo of shoes on wooden treads, the floorboards were bare, the hallway empty of furniture, and the walls partially stripped of paper. The place looked prepped and almost ready for redecoration, but the build-up of dust in the corners and the cobwebs on the ceiling suggested it had been ready for quite some time.

"Can I help you?" the young man asked, his accent nondescript, and his tone educated.

"Mr Moore, Darwin Moore?" Lara asked, offering a professional smile. She showed him a badge identifying her as an official of The 83 Trust, a charity with very little public profile, but hundreds of millions of euros at its disposal. "I'm Dr Elizabeth Griffin, and this is my husband, Bill. We represent—"

"Sorry, Dr Griffin," the young man interrupted, raising the hand that wasn't holding onto the edge of the door. "I'm a student. As you can see"—he waved the hand in an arc behind him and stood sideways on to let them see— "I'm a little strapped for cash right now. Can't really offer a

53

donation, but I wish you well in your endeavours. Now, if you'll please excuse me …" He offered an apologetic smile and started to close the door.

"No, Mr Moore," she said, continuing to hold up the ID badge, "we're not looking for donations. Exactly the opposite, in fact. May we come in, please? It won't take us long to explain, but we'd rather not do it outside in the street. We have some confidential matters to discuss and the neighbours don't appear too friendly."

"Neighbours?"

"Yes," Ryan said, leaning forwards. "An unpleasant young man going by the rather colourful handle of Barcode."

Darwin's pained expression told Kaine their target had crossed swords with the thug in question.

"Oh," he said, simply. "Best to steer clear of him and his friends. They aren't a pleasant bunch." His gaze lowered to take in the damage to the lower panel of his front door.

"Might we come in?" Lara repeated, more insistent.

Darwin shook his head. "No, thanks. Whatever you're offering, I can't use. Now, I have some coursework to do. Big assignment next week, you understand. Thanks, but—"

"We're here because of what happened to your mother, Elise."

The door opened fully again. Darwin stood in the doorway, feet apart, one hand still holding tight to the inside handle, the other clenched into a fist.

"What about my mother?"

"She was one of the unfortunate victims of Flight BE1555, yes?"

The young man raised his head and nodded.

"Yes," he answered, barely loud enough for Kaine to hear.

"A terrible thing. We are really, dreadfully sorry for your loss, Mr Moore," Lara continued, professional but gentle.

Darwin's jaw muscles tensed. "That bastard, Ryan Kaine, murdered my mother months ago. And I've since lost my Pops. Leave me alone, will you?"

Kaine swallowed. It wasn't the first time he'd heard the accusation, and it probably wouldn't be the last. Every time someone said something similar, his guts churned, but he couldn't argue the matter. His finger *had* been on the trigger of the rocket launcher. To Kaine's undying shame, he *did* end eighty-three innocent lives. One of them, Elise Moore, Darwin's mother, and Glenmore Davits' daughter.

"Mr Moore," Lara continued, "we understand your position, but ... the charity we represent was formed to offer its support to the families of the victims. Support in any way we can. Financial ..."

She let the word hang in the air. Usually, the mention of financial support was the equivalent of "Open Sesame" to the people they talked to on a regular basis.

"Not interested." Again, the door started to swing shut.

"Last month, we contacted your grandfather, by letter. Did he tell you?"

The door stopped moving. She'd finally piqued Darwin's interest. His eyes narrowed again, this time in suspicion.

"No. What did the letter say?"

Lara patted the handbag hanging by a strap from her shoulder.

"I have a copy in here, Mr Moore. May we come in, please? I promise you, this won't take long."

Darwin read the time on his wristwatch, an old-fashioned, wind-up analogue with a steel case and scratched glass. A family heirloom, inherited from his grandfather perhaps. He stepped aside and pointed them along the hallway.

"Okay, then. You'd better come in. Keep your coats on though. The central heating hasn't kicked in yet."

Chapter Five

Saturday 20th February - Lara Orchard

Brooke Street, Walthamstow, London, England

Darwin Moore led Lara and Ryan part way along a narrow, poorly lit, and chilly corridor, into a cramped and even colder front room.

"Please sit," Darwin said, pointing to the two-seater sofa situated in the bay window that was facing the street.

Ryan wouldn't have felt comfortable with his back to a window, and she wondered whether he'd be able to stay deep enough in character to overcome the reluctance.

Darwin bent at the knees and threw the switch at the side of an old-fashioned, three-bar, electric heater. Nothing happened until he knocked the side above the switch, and the lower bar started to glimmer. The young man held his open hands to the weak, red glow.

"Blooming thing's a little temperamental, I'm afraid," he said, embarrassment clear in his voice. "The radiator's blocked, and I tend not to use this room in the winter."

Shivering against the chill but trying to hide it, Lara perched on the front edge of a grubby sofa that had seen much better days. Some of its seams had split, and the leather was cracked and worn thin with use. The breath condensed around her head in much the same way as it had done outside.

As expected, Ryan crossed to the window and peered through the net curtains, which would once have been white, but had yellowed over time. While Lara and Darwin studied each other in silence, Ryan stood, stiff and alert for a full thirty seconds before relaxing and turning to face the room.

"That was ... interesting," Ryan said. He chose an uncomfortable dining chair, whose slightly elevated position enabled him to see both Lara and Darwin, who had dropped into the only other upholstered chair in the room —a single wingback. From his post, Ryan could also take in the view through the window. "You clearly know that young ... fellow, Barcode?"

"He stepped into your business?" Darwin asked, his voice rising in pitch.

Ryan tilted his head to one side. "He tried to."

"You faced him down?" Darwin added, surprise showing on his youthful face.

"Couldn't simply stand by and listen to him insulting my wife. To be honest, I was really rather terrified."

Ryan lowered his head, trying to make himself appear as worried as he professed. Lara wasn't buying it, but people who didn't know him, people unaware of his skills, might easily have been taken in. Foolish people regularly mistook Ryan's average height and slim build for an absence of physical prowess. If they pushed him too far the wrong way, those same people were often made to regret their stupidity and their mistakes.

Ryan was slow to anger but implacable in his reaction to thugs and bullies.

The frown lines on Darwin's brow deepened. "I can't see any bruises on you. How did you make him back down?"

"Nothing I'm proud of."

"Is it a secret?"

Ryan studied the nails on his left hand and whistled silently, a study in nonchalance. "I simply asked him to reconsider the error of his ways, and ..."

"And?" Lara asked, desperate to know how he'd sent the bully packing without resorting to violence.

"...showed him my passport card."

"You did what?" Lara demanded, sitting up straight.

Ryan took out his wallet and flipped it open to the clear, plastic window to reveal a perfect—and valid—Irish passport card. His photo graced the left-hand panel, and the official harp hologram stood out clear on the right. Ryan's index finger held the wallet open, "accidentally" covering the *Éire/Ireland/Irlande* script along its upper edge.

"You scared him off with a passport?" Darwin asked, his frown deepening even further.

"Well," Ryan said, wincing a little, "I did tell him I was a member of the National Crime Agency, investigating gang crime in Walthamstow. I also asked him if he'd like to accompany me to Scotland Yard to answer a few questions."

After a silence long enough for Ryan to return the wallet to his pocket, a high-pitched and infectious belly-laugh erupted from Darwin's throat. "You scared off Barcode with a passport? Ha! That sod's vicious, but I didn't think he was thicker than mud. Who'd have thought he'd fall for that?"

"Well, I, er … imagine he'd have recognised a standard police warrant card, no doubt having seen a few in his time. Which is why I opted for the National Crime Agency. They tend to keep a lower profile than the Old Bill. I didn't think he'd have much of an idea what their IDs look like."

"You just made my day," Darwin said through the rippling laughter. "Can't wait to tell the neighbours." He wiped his eyes with the heels of his hands.

Ryan shrugged and threw out one of his disarming smiles. Lara exhaled and allowed her shoulders to relax.

A few moments later, Darwin's laughter faded into a sigh.

"Priceless," he said. "Okay, enough of the frivolity. What do you have for me?"

Again, Lara fished the wallet out of her shoulder bag and handed across the rather impressive-looking ID card, which had her title, name, and "The 83 Trust" emblazoned across the top. She'd designed the crest and the logo herself, and was more than pleased with the result. Every piece of information on the card was valid, from the address and contact numbers on the back, to the UK registered charity number on the front, below Lara's photo.

"As I said on the doorstep, Mr Moore, my name is Dr Elizabeth Griffin and, as you can see, I represent The 83 Trust. My husband, Bill, is here as my assistant and—clearly—my bodyguard." She paused to give Ryan the chance to apologise again, but he just smiled and waited.

"You mentioned financial matters and a letter you sent to Pops … er, my grandfather?"

"He didn't tell you about it?"

Darwin pursed his lips. "No. I hadn't seen him for a couple of weeks before he … passed. Don't always have the time to visit. In fact, I hadn't seen him since Christmas. I … I really miss the old guy."

Lara nodded in empathy. Ryan cleared his throat.

"What did it say in the letter?" Darwin asked.

"It introduced The 83 Trust and outlined our aims and objectives."

"Which are?"

Lara took a breath and launched into the well-rehearsed spiel, being economical with the details, but not with the truth.

"The 83 Trust is an official charity set up under UK regulations with the specific aim of supporting the families of the unfortunate people who died when Flight BE1555 crashed into the North Sea last year."

Darwin thumped the arm of his chair with the side of his fist. "It didn't crash. It was shot down by that madman, Ryan Kaine. The evil bastard killed my mother!"

Ryan's lack of physical reaction gave nothing away, but Lara knew how much the young man's words must have hurt.

"There happens to be some confusion over the exact sequence of events, but—"

"Ryan Kaine is scum. Pure and simple," Darwin growled, making fists.

Ryan closed his eyes momentarily before staring through the window again, the only outward sign of distress being a slightly increased blink rate.

My darling man.

Lara skirted the tension and continued. "The letter also contained a banker's draft to the value of nine thousand, nine hundred, and fifty pounds."

"What?" It was Darwin's turn to straighten in his chair.

"That's right, Mr Moore. The Trust sent your grandfather a banker's draft for nearly ten thousand pounds."

"Really?"

"Yes."

Darwin slumped into the back of his chair and blew a silent whistle.

"Sounds too good to be true and as Pops used to say, 'If it sounds too good ...'"

"I can assure you, Mr Moore, everything is completely above board. We are registered with the Charity Commission and are totally scrupulous. You can go online, or call the commission helpline to confirm our credentials. As we explained to your grandfather in our letter of introduction, The Trust was set up to help the families of the victims of that terrible event."

"What did Pops do with it? Did he cash it in?"

"We have no idea, Mr Moore. The point of a draft is the drawer can't tell if or when it is cashed, since the money has already left the account. We only know that your grandfather, Mr Glenmore Davits, signed for the letter on"—she read from the letter, pretending not to have remembered the date—"Wednesday, the thirteenth of January."

"Two days before he ... before he passed."

"Exactly."

"You surely don't think the money had anything to do with Pops' death, do you?" Darwin's expression showed utter distain. "That's just ridicul—"

"We're not suggesting anything of the sort, Mr Moore."

"Pops was an old man. He fell. Hit his head. An accident. The police agreed. So did the coroner."

"Mr Moore," Ryan said, his deep voice silencing the young man, "all we're here to do is make sure that you are financially secure. That's all. We have no other purpose. The police investigation is over and none of our concern."

"But the money. Might the police consider it a motive?"

Lara met Ryan's eye and he shook his head.

"Mr Moore," she said, "as my husband noted, we have nothing to do with the police or their investigations. If you choose to contact them with this new information, that is your right. We can provide you with copies of all the paperwork to give them, if you wish."

Darwin nodded slowly, taking the information aboard.

"Okay, okay. Thank you. I'll … think about it. Please do. I mean, please give me the papers."

Lara handed him the thin file. He glanced at the folder and placed it on the coffee table at the side of his chair.

"So, there was no sign of your grandfather having cashed the draft?" Ryan asked.

Darwin looked up at him, mouth open, eyebrows arched, and confusion and shock written large in his wide eyes.

"Didn't see anything in his bank account other than his pension payments and the usual standing orders, direct debits, and the like. I'm still waiting on probate, but I don't expect the estate to be worth much. Far as I know, he doesn't have any life insurances. All I'll end up with is this knackered house."

"Have you been through his things?" Lara asked. "His papers, I mean. If you find it, the bank draft will still be valid. We only raised it a month or so ago."

"Yes, yes. I've been through everything. There was no sign of a letter from the ... what was it again?"

"The 83 Trust."

"Strange name ... ah, wait. I see. Eighty-three people died on that plane, including ... including my mother."

In the corner, Ryan stared through the window, checking the street for signs of their unwanted friends.

"That's it, exactly, Mr Moore," she confirmed.

The young man's shoulders rounded. He lowered a hand, twisted a knob on the side of the heater, and the middle bar slowly turned red. In the growing silence, the only sound in the room came from the ticking of the clock on the mantelpiece over the open and unlit fire, and the crinkling of the second bar on the heater. Although glowing bright and burning through untold units of electricity, the heat thrown out by the pitiful thing did little to drive the cold from the room.

Ryan's gazed flickered from the window to Darwin and back. He never seemed to relax. The pressure on him during his frequent missions must have been unbearable. Eventually, it would surely take its toll. When they'd finished in Walthamstow, she would force him to take a holiday. They both needed a real break. A holiday together.

Eventually, Darwin took a deep breath.

"Darn it," he said. "I could have used that money to help pay for the funeral, and ... the house renovations. Let alone my student debts."

Lara leaned forwards. "We might still be able to help, Mr Moore."

"Really?"

"Eventually, we will be able to recover the money. All we need is a signed and notarised letter from you saying you never received it nor cashed it in. The Trust will handle the rest. We'll also make other funds available to you in the interim."

"Bloody hell! You will?" This time, his brown eyes shone with relief and excitement.

"Yes, Mr Moore. We will," Lara said, managing a gentle smile. "There are funds enough to cover all eventualities. As I said, our benefactors have been rather generous."

Ryan cleared his throat gently. "Mr Moore, Darwin, do you drink tea or coffee? I think we could all do with a brew, don't you?"

The young man looked up at Ryan. "There are some teabags in the kitchen, but no coffee, milk, or sugar. I haven't had the chance to shop. Only arrived home late last night."

"It's a little warmer in the kitchen, too, I imagine?"

"Don't bet on it," he said. "If I told you I don't feel the cold much, would you believe me?"

"Not really," Ryan said, smiling.

Lara stood and squeezed the young man's thin shoulder. "Darwin, you can afford to use the central heating now, I promise you. Where's the thermostat?"

Darwin shook his head. "The boiler broke down last winter. Damned heating hasn't worked properly for years. It's one of the reasons I didn't visit Pops as often as I should have. College digs aren't all that impressive, but at least the bloody heating works."

Ryan dug a hand into his pocket and withdrew his mobile. "We'll soon have it fixed. I'll search for a local plumber. Can't have one of our clients living in a freezing-cold house, can we, Beth?"

"No, Bill. Indeed we can't."

WITH ALL THE gas rings on the cooker burning and the electric oven set on full—despite Darwin's initial reluctance —the small kitchen didn't take long to climb from sub-arctic to sub-tropical. Ryan spent the subsequent few minutes regulating the burners to make the temperature bearable, and he soon had the place much more homely.

Lara filled the kettle and Darwin pointed her to the tea caddy.

"I prefer coffee," he said, gloomily, "but I ran out last week."

"You said you were out of milk, too?" Ryan asked and, when the young man nodded, he added, "We passed a shop on the way here. I'll pop out and pick up a carton while you and Beth deal with the paperwork. Mind if I borrow your front door key?"

"There's a spare on a hook in the hall. Help yourself. Here"—Darwin dug a hand into the pocket of his jeans and pulled out some loose change—"for the milk and stuff."

Ryan shook his head. "No need, Mr Moore. I think we can stand you some provisions. I'll be right back. Beth, can I have a quick word, please?"

Lara threw the switch on the kettle and followed Ryan from the room. Once in the hallway, he leaned close and whispered. "Won't be long, love. Keep young Darwin occu-pied. I'll lock the door behind me. Don't open it to anyone else."

"Did you see anything through the window?"

He nodded. "Couple of minutes after they toddled off, one of Barcode's cronies returned. He tried to keep out of sight, but he's not exactly the stealthiest creature I've ever seen."

"Which one, Dylan or Rhino?"

Ryan smiled, leaned in, and gave her a peck on the

cheek. "Never miss anything, do you, love?" He lifted the keys from the hook placed at waist height for ease of access to a man in a wheelchair, and selected the Chubb key for the front door lock. "Our spy is the squat one with the ugly scar on his neck, Rhino."

Lara cupped his cheek with her hand. "No point in telling you to take care, I suppose?"

Ryan tutted in mock reproach. "Dear, dear. You know me, love. I always take care."

She sighed. "Yes, sure. Just don't go looking for trouble, understand?"

"Me? Never. I'm just going out for some milk and bickies."

He turned and left, locking the front door behind him. She ducked into the front room and stood back from the window to make sure no one from outside could see her.

Ryan strode the five paces along the wheelchair ramp to the gate, opened it, and turned left, heading away from the shops they'd seen on the way from the hotel.

The moment Ryan was out of sight, Rhino emerged from his ineffectual hiding space in the partial gloom of the alleyway and headed off in not-so-subtle pursuit.

"Just going out for some milk and bickies?" Lara muttered to the empty room. "Ryan Liam Kaine. Always the joker."

In resignation, she returned to the kitchen. Tea didn't make itself and Darwin Moore seemed as though he needed the company of a friend.

Chapter Six

Saturday 20th February - Morning

Brooke Street, Walthamstow, London, England

Kaine spotted the scarred thug the second he broke cover.
Either Rhino was the worst tail in the world, or he didn't
care about being seen. Most likely the former, although
neither option mattered to Kaine, who took his time and
almost sauntered along the pothole-infected and heavily
cracked pavement.

Within a few paces of leaving Darwin's house, Kaine
pulled out his mobile. Without allowing his attention to
roam from his reconnaissance, and taking note of each
house, garage, alley, and garden on Brooke Street, Kaine
plugged in the earphones and hit a combination of keys to
activate the secure line. Kaine had no idea what time zone

Corky occupied, but he seemed to require little sleep and, more often than not, answered Kaine's call within a few rings.

"Whatcha, Mr K. How you diddling?"

"Hi, Corky. I take it you've been nice and busy for the past thirty minutes or so?"

"'Course, Mr K. Updating the database as we speak. You'll have access to the files in a couple of shakes."

"Find much on Barcode and the others?"

Kaine shortened his stride and slowed. The reflection in a nearby bay window showed the scarred man on the other side of the street matching his pace, step for step. Kaine increased his stride length again, picking up speed, trying to keep Rhino off guard.

A row of terraced houses ended in the patch of scrubland they'd identified the previous day as a kiddie's playground. The grass hadn't been cut in ages and brambles made access not far off impenetrable to anyone not under the influence of a recreational drug of some description. He turned right along Green Lane, walking past another row of two-storey terraces.

"There's not much out there, Mr K," Corky said, to a background music of surf breaking over coral. "Barcode's a small-time thug, by the looks of it. Nasty piece of work, though. A few years back, the Old Bill questioned him about the disappearance of a tattoo artist, but nothing came of it. Plenty of rumours but no actionable evidence. Right now, the geezer's a middle ranker in the Tribe. Corky's uploaded what police intelligence has on all of them. Precious little worthy of the name 'intelligence', Corky might add."

Kaine stopped in the lee of a tall garden wall, and leaned one shoulder against it, facing the road. Poor Rhino didn't have a clue how to react and simply dropped to one knee, pretending to tie a shoelace. Kaine smiled at the top of the squat man's head.

"Mrs Griffin and I will go through the files when we have a moment. Meanwhile, what can you tell me about the one going by the name Rhino?"

Corky's chuckle rattled down the line. More surf crashed against coral. It sounded idyllic, but Kaine imagined it was little more than a recording.

"Rhino's small potatoes," Corky said, the chortle slowly dying. "Muscle without much of a brain. Real name is Damian Baines. Twenty-two years old. Locked up for an eighteen-month stretch in Wandsworth prison. That's where he picked up his nasty scar. Apparently, the dozy beggar don't know enough to tread careful around the neo-Nazis. Earned an early parole for good behaviour, would you believe? Father's dead. Mother lives in Brighton. His girlfriend, Ariel Danby, is thirty-five weeks pregnant with their first baby. She's booked in for an ultrasound scan next week.

"While Corky's at it," he continued, "Rhino's address and family details are in the files Corky just sent you in an email, and also added to the database."

"Thanks, Corky. As usual, you've done a truly wonderful job." It never hurt to heap praise on their information goblin.

Corky laughed again at Kaine's tribute. "Yeah, you're damn right there, Mr K. Corky's a pure genius. Shedloads better than that second-rate French bird what ain't around much these days. Any idea where she is, by the way?"

"You can't find her?"

"Nah," he answered and rushed to add, "Not that Corky's been trying too hard, mind."

"In that case, she clearly doesn't want to be found. Not that second-rate then, is she?"

"Yeah, yeah. Touché, Mr K. You got ol' Corky there. Anyhow, next time you talk to her, tell her Corky said, 'Hi', yeah?"

"Will do, Corky. Do I detect a little techie 'hero worship', or is it jealousy?"

"Jealous? Corky? Not on your life, Mr K. Corky's never jealous of nothing. Certainly not of a Frenchie who doesn't do much."

Kaine smiled. "Methinks thou doth protest too much."

"Huh?"

"Shakespeare, Corky. You may have heard of him."

The IT guru snorted.

"Corky don't have much time to brush up on culture when he's always running errands for you, Mr K."

How the man had found the information so quickly, particularly Ariel Danby's medical details, was beyond Kaine. All he knew was the hacker volunteered his services and refused to take a penny piece for his troubles. Although, a man with Corky's highly marketable, not to mention dubious, skills wouldn't find it too difficult to earn an honest—or a dishonest—crust, he chose to help Kaine gratis. And for his part, Kaine was more than happy to utilise Corky's undoubted talents, especially since their alternative, Sabrina, couldn't always make herself available to help.

Kaine marvelled at the way the two IT experts sparked off each other, often battling to dig deeper, react faster, and provide better information than the other.

Since being dubbed a terrorist and a murderer, Kaine had plenty of reason to appreciate the support of so many brave individuals. None more so that the little, round-faced, and bearded information collector.

"Fair comment, Corky. You'll keep digging, though?"

"'Course, Mr K. What you gonna do?"

"I promised Darwin I'd contact a local plumber. Now seems to be as good a time as any."

"A plumber? Righto, Mr K. Tra."

Corky ended the call and Kaine ran a quick internet search. He only needed five minutes to convince the first business that answered his call to take the Trust's money. Such was the pulling power of big bucks.

After sealing the deal, he tugged out the earbuds, rolled up the cable, and dropped the phone into his pocket.

Low clouds scudded across the sky, pushed by a scything, winter gale. The forecast promised more rain that afternoon and the dark grey, woolly blanket overhead seemed to confirm it. Kaine turned up the collar on his jacket and resettled the flat cap on his head.

Time to move things along. He'd been away from Lara's side long enough.

Kaine pushed away from the wall and crossed to Rhino's side of the street, picking up the pace. Behind him, Rhino hurried, struggling to keep up.

Three hundred metres later, he reached the crossroads with Boothe Avenue. The area he'd walked through had become more and more downmarket, the houses even less well-maintained. To his left, the avenue extended through a broken-down industrial estate, heading towards Palmerston Road. To his right, it ran towards the High Street that was Walthamstow's town centre. Straight ahead, Green Lane stretched on, flanked by more terraces, some two-storey, others townhouses, all in various states of disrepair.

He turned left along the avenue, heading through a grim-looking Bernville Industrial Estate. Warehouses and workshops, each more dilapidated than the next, reached out on both sides. Some were occupied, most were shuttered and the businesses closed permanently. The recent economic downturn had clearly hit small businesses hard.

It took him ten minutes' hard marching to reach the end of Boothe Avenue and its junction with Palmerston Road.

Kaine stopped at the edge of the pavement, removed his cloth cap, and scratched his head. He turned, looking left and right, apparently lost.

Over one hundred metres to Kaine's right, on the opposite side of the road, stood a large, grey building surrounded by a black-and-rust, wrought-iron fence. Double gates in the centre of the fence barred the way to a set of five steps which led up to the covered porch of a once-grand entrance. The portico housed a pair of solid-looking double doors. A sign chiselled into the keystone above the entrance read "Palmerston Road School"—the HQ of the Palmerston Road Tribe.

What had once been a proud centre of learning, and before that, a stark, Victorian workhouse, now stood in a sorry state of disrepair, with boarded windows, cracked and missing roof tiles, and broken gutters and downpipes.

The area surrounding the school building looked more like a prison compound. It appeared to be the only building in the area still occupied, and the only one to have received a fresh coat of paint since the turn of the millennium. The woodwork on the doors and ground-floor windows wore the same garish purple as the PRT tags.

Cars were parked nose-to-tail on both sides of the street. Most were rust-spotted and long overdue a terminal visit to the wrecker's yard, but the ones parked close to the compound stood out as shiny and clean—and expensive.

Cigarette smoke billowing around the entrance portico spoke of guards and lookouts.

Kaine spent no more than a few seconds to take in the scene.

He'd seen enough of Palmerston Road for the moment. Depending on what happened with Darwin, he'd return that evening for a closer inspection, a real scouting session.

"Darn it," he said, loud enough for Rhino to hear, before turning about-face and retracing his steps.

On seeing Kaine reverse direction, Rhino's step faltered. He looked up, first at Kaine, and then over Kaine's shoulder towards the school, clearly unable to make a decision.

Kaine closed the thirty-metre gap quickly and stopped five paces away from his scarred follower.

"Damian, what the hell are you doing, man?" he asked.

Rhino's stare alighted on Kaine, then flicked all around him. Fear and confusion worked their way across his dark face.

"What—?"

Kaine drew two steps closer.

"We shouldn't be meeting in the open like this. What the hell's wrong with you?"

Rhino frowned, shook his head, and opened his mouth to speak, but Kaine interrupted again.

"You know our agreed meeting place and time," he hissed, "and this most certainly isn't it."

The scarred man shook his head again, as though trying to clear away some cobwebs. He formed fists.

"That's right," Kaine said, nodding encouragement. "Throw a punch, but make it look good. Use real anger."

Rhino obliged, but telegraphed his move so far in advance, Kaine could have had a cup of tea while waiting for the wind up.

With both fists raised, held in front of his chest in a sad parody of a boxer's stance, Rhino lumbered forwards, stomping his left foot ahead of the right. He threw a wild, roundhouse left. Kaine parried with his right forearm, side-stepping inside the blow.

A stiff-fingered jab driven hard into Rhino's left armpit ended things quickly. The squat man spun, toppled, and hit the pavement hard enough to knock the wind from his lungs. Rhino gasped, desperately trying to recover. His legs jerked, heels digging into the pavement in an attempt to scramble away from the unexpected danger.

"My dear chap," Kaine shouted, dropping into a squat beside the fallen thug, "you must have tripped."

Kaine pressed an index finger into the side of Rhino's neck, where the scar peeked out above the collar of his hoodie. To any spectator, it would have looked as though Kaine were checking the man's carotid artery for a pulse. To Rhino, the finger digging into the pressure point nestled in the notch between the mandibular ramus of the jaw and his earlobe, would have felt like a cattle prod delivering an electric pulse of excruciating pain.

He yelped and struggled to pull away.

"No, no, no," Kaine said, adding enough pressure to his index finger to make Rhino squeal and stop moving. This time, Kaine spoke so quietly, only Rhino would hear. "Stay right where you are, Damian, old sport. Struggle any harder and what 'Adolf' Smith did to you in prison will seem like a paper cut. Understand?"

Rhino's eyes widened, and he grunted something totally incomprehensible.

"Sorry. Didn't quite make that out, Damian, old chap. But I'll take it I have your undivided attention. Yes?"

A blink and a second grunt confirmed Kaine's inter-pretation.

"Good, good. Now, you'll have to trust me on this, but if

I add a few grams more weight to this pressure hold, you will stop breathing, permanently. Do you believe me?"

"Y-Yes."

"Good." Kaine eased the pressure a little, and Damian closed his gaping mouth.

"Excellent," Kaine continued. "It would be such a pity if you weren't around to take care of Ariel and the little one."

The brown eyes widened again, the capillaries in the whites standing out clear against the young man's darkly greying skin.

"Yes, Rhino, that's right. We know all about you."

"W-who are you?"

"Never mind about that. I may explain at some stage, but for now, just listen to me and behave yourself," he whispered, before adding more loudly, "Oh dear, we're making a bit of a spectacle of ourselves here, aren't we."

Kaine released his hold completely, stood, and offered Rhino his hand. "Here, let me help you up, old sport."

Reluctantly, Rhino lifted his arm. Kaine grabbed his wrist firmly, pressed a knuckle hard into the man's radial pressure point, and yanked him to his feet.

Rhino grimaced and tried to free his arm, but Kaine held the grip for another five seconds before letting go.

Breathing heavily, the beaten man hugged his temporarily paralysed arm to his chest.

"W-What the fu—"

Kaine held up a silencing finger. "This is a public place. We don't need to swear."

Rhino tore his stare away from Kaine and flicked it towards the school.

Kaine shook his head. "Don't even think about calling

to your buddies for help. If you do that, I'll have to kill you. Understand?"

The gang member's shoulders sagged. He lowered his eyes and nodded. "Y-Yeah, I unnerstan'."

"Good, good."

Smiling warmly, Kaine stepped closer and raised an arm. Rhino flinched.

"Don't worry, old chap. We're just two old friends, shooting the breeze."

Kaine draped his arm around the stunned man's shoulder. Rhino buckled under the weight, and Kaine's smile didn't falter.

"Whatcha want wi' me?"

"Nothing, Damian. Nothing at all." He stiffened his arm and pulled the man closer. "You and I are the best of buddies. We're going to have a little chat, and come to an understanding, okay?"

Fear and doubt fought for supremacy in the gang member's eyes.

"Okay?" Kaine repeated, almost growling the word.

Rhino nodded. "Yeah, right."

Kaine pointed back the way they'd come. "We're heading back to Brooke Street. There's a little patch of scrub we can use for a private chat. A place where we won't be disturbed."

Together, they turned. Kaine removed his arm and allowed his captive to lead the way.

"That's it, Damian. This will all be over soon."

Rhino faltered, and Kaine encouraged him forwards with a double-knuckle jab in the kidney—a gentle one.

"You gonna kill me?"

"That depends on you, Damian. We'd rather not, but that option is definitely available to us."

Rhino's broad shoulders seemed to wilt inside his heavy coat. His eyes started to tear and he sniffled. "W-Who you workin' for?"

"I'll ask the questions, Damian. You answer them honestly and you might just live long enough to welcome your new baby into the world."

Damian stiffened and looked around as though fearing others were close. "How you know 'bout me and ... Ariel?"

Kaine glanced about him, making sure they were alone, before clapping the man across the back of the head.

"What part of, 'I'll ask the questions,' don't you understand, Damian? How we gather our information is not for you to know. Suffice to say, you aren't the only Tribe member we're talking to right now."

Kaine smiled behind Rhino's back. Making things up on the fly wasn't his preferred option, but spreading discontent within the ranks of the opposition had worked plenty of times in the past. Besides which, messing with the bad guys' heads could be fun.

———

BEHIND A THICKET of brambles and overgrown shrubs, which Rhino kindly agreed to break through—under Kaine's gentle encouragement—they found a rusted and heavily damaged playground roundabout.

"Take a seat, Damian, old chap. This really shouldn't take very long."

Head bowed, Rhino perched on the edge of the roundabout. The wood cracked and screeched under his muscular weight.

Kaine stood over him. Intimidating. Waiting for the man to make his inevitable second move. The painful but superficial damage he'd inflicted on Rhino during their earlier dance would have worn off quickly and, depending on the gang member's state of mind, the rapid recovery might conceivably have wiped away the memory of how easily Kaine had taken him down. The squat man might still fancy his chances in a rematch.

"Here's how this is going to go," Kaine started.

Head still bowed, Rhino stiffened. He roared and launched himself from the roundabout, his powerful arms outspread, hands clawing for a target.

Kaine sidestepped the clumsy attack but left his leg outstretched. Rhino tripped, somersaulted in the air, and slammed, feetfirst, into the frame of a swing. Once again, he collapsed and lay still, breathing hard.

"Bloody idiot. Will you never learn?"

Kaine stood back from the young man while he recovered slowly. This time, he didn't offer any help as Rhino climbed groggily to his feet and stood, swaying slightly. Once again, he hung his head in defeat. After a short time, he staggered back to his original place on the roundabout, and stared up at Kaine through cowed eyes.

"Are you prepared to listen now?"

Rhino nodded, but kept silent. He sat, shoulders rounded, fists clamped between his legs. A crushed and beaten man. Kaine hadn't broken into a sweat. If only all his battles could be so easy.

"Who's in charge of your posse? What do you call it, the Tribe?"

Slowly, Rhino raised his head. He stared at Kaine through questioning eyes. "You don' know?"

"Of course we know." Kaine pulled a notepad from his pocket and flicked through its pages. They were all blank, but Rhino wasn't to know that. "Think of this as a test.

Give me any wrong answers, and I'll end this interview. I'll give you one guess as to what happens then."

Rhino stayed silent.

"I said, you have one guess!"

"You kill me?"

Kaine sneered and tilted his head to one side. "Don't be silly. We almost never resort to killing people. But you are learning the seriousness of your situation. Our preference is to proceed along the legal route. We'll make sure you go down for a long time and you know what that means for your partner and your unborn child. It will be so sad. Will Ariel be able to cope on her own without your emotional and financial support? If not, I'm sure we can arrange for your child to go into care. It'll be a crying shame, but probably better for the nipper in the long term. Don't get me wrong, Damian, we don't like seeing innocent children suffer, but if that's what it takes to clear the streets of scum, well … so be it."

Kaine smiled sadly and allowed the threat to hang in the air.

The tears flowing down Rhino's cheeks and his trembling chin indicated how effective the mention of his family had been. Kaine almost felt guilty at his actions, but the more effectively he could intimidate his opponents, the more quickly he could complete his mission and return Lara to the safety of the villa.

"Who runs the Tribe?" Kaine repeated.

This time, Rhino's response was immediate and comprehensive.

––––––––

BY THE TIME he terminated the interview, Kaine knew as much about the Palmerston Road Tribe as he needed. He'd both confirmed and added to Corky's extensive briefing notes.

"Thank you, Damian. That wasn't too hard, now, was it?"

Once again, the squat man lowered his head and fell silent.

"Now, my friend, you have two choices."

The head jerked up. Once again, the eyes carried a question. They also contained fear.

Kaine held up the index finger of his right hand. "Choice number one. You can go tell your Top Man all about how a middle-aged fart beat you into the ground, twice. You can also tell him how you spilled your guts and how much that same old fart now knows about the Tribe's operations and where it sells its product." Kaine paused, waiting for the implication to sink in.

"Or …" he said a moment later.

"Or?" Damian asked, his expression pleading.

Kaine smiled again. "Or you can be our second inside man."

"Second?"

"That's right, Damian. You can do what your other friend is doing and help us."

"What friend? You got to someone else?"

"Indeed we have, old chap. We like to hedge our bets. Call it our due diligence."

"Who?"

"Ah, now that would be telling. Wouldn't it?" Kaine answered, allowing his grin to widen.

Divide and conquer, one of the oldest strategies in

warfare. Kaine had used the concept many times in the past with great success. No reason it couldn't work again.

"You won't know who's working for us, and neither will he. Yes, it is a 'he'. Remember this. If you tell us something different from our other inside man, we'll know about it, and then all bets are off. Understand?"

Damian dipped his chin.

"Say it!" Kaine barked.

The man stiffened, looked up, and said, "I unnerstan'." He took a short breath, opened his mouth, and snapped it shut again.

"Show me your phone."

"Huh?"

Kaine snapped his fingers. "Come on. I won't ask again."

Damian dug in his pocket and pulled out a latest-generation smartphone. He offered it across, but Kaine refused it.

"Good. Very impressive. It'll do very nicely."

"What for?"

"How good's your memory for phone numbers?"

"S'all right. Why?"

Kaine recited his burner number and instructed Damian to repeat it.

"One final thing, Damian."

"Yeah? What."

"Do right by us and you won't only stay out of prison long enough to see your baby born and take its first steps, you might even earn enough to work your way out of this life."

"Really?" A glimmer of hope shone in Damian's expressive eyes.

"Assuming you do want an 'out'?"

He nodded as enthusiastically as his neck scar would allow.

"Yes, Mr Griffin. That I does."

"Good, Damian. Good. I'm looking forward to watching you earn it."

As Kaine turned to go, Damian raised his hand as though he were a student in school trying to attract the attention of a teacher.

"Yes, Damian? What is it?"

The younger man winced as he stood, looking more uncomfortable than he should have done. "I-I wanna tell you somethin', but ..."

"But what?"

"You ain't gonna believe me."

"Try me, Damian. What do you have to lose?"

Damian straightened and looked Kaine in the eye for the first time. He delivered his information and was right, Kaine didn't believe him, not for one second.

Without adding a comment, Kaine parted company with the scarred man and returned to his original mission— the supply run. This time, he made sure no one followed him.

Chapter Seven

Saturday 20th February - Midday

Brooke Street, Walthamstow, London, England

Thirty-five minutes later, Kaine returned to the house, armed with milk, sugar, assorted packets of biscuits, and an almond-topped fruit cake.

"Not sure whether you eat cake, but this looked rather enticing," he said to Darwin. "You can do a proper shop later."

Darwin's smile spoke for him. He seemed overwhelmed by the events of the morning and appeared happy to give Lara and Kaine free rein in the kitchen.

Once safely ensconced around the kitchen table, tea and coffee sipped, and fruitcake partially demolished, Lara turned to Kaine.

"Bill, did you manage to find a plumber?"

"I did indeed, dear. Local firm. They'll be here first thing this afternoon, ready and will—"

"Are you serious?" Darwin asked, pausing in the middle of refilling their cups. "You've actually convinced a plumber to come here at a moment's notice? I'll believe it when he gets here."

Kaine grinned. "Darwin, old chap, you'll be astonished how amenable tradesmen can be when you use the magic phrase, 'Money's no object.'" He tapped the side of his nose.

Doubt crossed the young man's face. "Central heating costs a fortune to fix and to run. The ten thousand pounds you promised me won't last long—"

"Darwin," Lara interrupted, "The Trust will pay for the work and the materials. We will also cover all the running costs. You have no reason to worry."

Darwin shook his head in disbelief. "Are you people for real? This is all too much. Things like this don't happen to the likes of me. No matter how much money you promise, there's no way a plumber's gonna come here. The neighbourhood's a no-go area to most. You saw what it's like outside. Not far off a war zone."

Kaine considered breaking the full news about Darwin's share of the Trust's millions. The kid needed to know just how much his life was about to change, but he'd already had more than enough to take aboard for one day. He had the rest of his life to absorb the good news. It didn't all have to happen in one morning.

"You could always move," Lara suggested.

"What? I'd love to, but who's going to buy this house? Nobody, that's who. Not with that lot infesting the area." He shot a glance towards the front of the house, the implication clear. Both he and his grandfather had been terrorised by the Tribe.

Kaine's jaw muscles worked beneath the beard he hated.

"You have no need to fear anything from Barcode and his crew. I promise," Kaine said, forcing a cold certainty into his delivery. "They're nothing but a bunch of cowards."

"It's not just Barcode," Darwin said, reaching out for his drink, but seemed to change his mind when his outstretched hand rattled the cup in its saucer. "He's just one part of the gang that owns the whole area. He runs the streets around here. It's not safe to go walking. Not even in broad daylight."

"What about the police?" Lara asked.

"Police!" Darwin spat out the word like a curse. "They come around now and again to sweep up the riffraff. 'Operation Clean Streets' they called the last one. Made the local TV news and the papers, but did sod all in the long run. They arrested and cautioned a few Tribesmen, but only the lowest on the totem pole. Then they released them again to do the same thing.

"Cosmetic, it was. Made the policewoman with the shiny buttons on her uniform look important for a while. Maybe earned her a promotion, but the attention didn't last long. Same as always. The little people are soon forgotten."

Kaine stood and took a breath. "Not always, Darwin. Not always."

"What's that you say?" the youngster asked, arching his neck to look up.

"The little people aren't always forgotten," Kaine repeated.

Darwin curled his upper lip. "Oh yes we are."

Kaine shook his head emphatically. "One way or

another, things will change, Mr Moore. You have our word."

Lara shot Kaine a sideways look of admonishment, a look that said he shouldn't make promises he might not be able to keep. She was right. Of course she was right, but he couldn't help himself.

The anonymous tipster who'd entered Darwin's details in to The 83 website and asked for their help—whom Corky later identified as local resident, Primula Johnston— had turned out to be dead right. Bad things *were* happening to people in Walthamstow. However, before Kaine could back up his words and offer Darwin a more detailed explanation, the handle to the letterbox rattled.

"Who's that now?" Darwin asked.

Kaine checked his watch. "If I were a betting man, I'd say our plumber has arrived. Would you like me to let him in?"

"A plumber. Yeah, right!" Darwin snorted in disbelief. "More likely to be Primula, the next door neighbour, poking her beak in. She'll be desperate to know who you are and what you want with little, old me. It's either Primula, or Barcode and his buddies back to check on your … passport. Those thugs can't afford to lose face to a couple of whiteys —if you'll pardon the expression, Mrs Griffin."

"Don't worry about me, Darwin. I've heard plenty worse."

"All the same, Mr Griffin. Take care when opening the door, right?"

The letterbox rattled again. This time louder. The flap screeched and a voice called, "Mr Griffin? This is Brian Able from Able Heating Supplies. Are you in there?"

Not for the first time that day, Kaine watched Darwin Moore's jaw drop.

Kaine smiled and winked before turning to answer the door.

"Be right with you, Mr Able," he called.

He opened the door to what looked like a teenager in a boiler suit so clean it couldn't have been anything other than brand new. Lettering embroidered across the chest of the garment introduced the wearer as a "Senior Heating Engineer" from "Able Heating Supplies Ltd", the third entry on Kaine's Google search. The line beneath the name read, "Willing and Able", this one in cursive script. On the doorstep at his feet, stood a fancy-looking, black, plastic clipboard balanced atop a metal toolbox.

The lad smiled, grabbed the laminated ID card hanging from a lanyard around his neck, and held it up for Kaine to read. The words "Brian Able, Senior Heating Engineer" and the subsequent academic letters seemed to confirm its claim.

"Mr Griffin?" Brian Able asked.

Kaine nodded. "That's me. Thanks for being so prompt." He added a welcoming smile.

On closer inspection, calling the plumber a teenager had been a little unnecessary. The sandy-haired, blue-eyed man on the doorstep had one of those faces that could have placed him anywhere on the age range spectrum, from fifteen to thirty-five. Small and lithe, he could also have passed for a middle-distance athlete.

"You spoke to my father. He handles the commercial side of the business. I'm growing the domestic contracts. At least, I'm trying to."

"Pleased to meet you, Mr Able—"

"No, no, Mr Able makes me sound like my dad," the lad interrupted, smiling enthusiastically. "Please call me Brian. Mind if I come in?"

"Certainly, Brian. Please do."

Kaine stepped aside and pointed towards the kitchen.

"The householder, Mr Moore, is down there, at the end of the corridor."

Brian picked up the clipboard and the toolbox, and stepped over the threshold. As they passed in the hall, Kaine held out his arm as a barrier.

"My wife, Elizabeth, will be project manager and Paymaster General. Mr Moore has had a bit of a shock today. Treat him gently."

Brian winked and added a conspiratorial smile. "Always treat the customers with respect, sir. Shall I get on with it?" He jiggled his shoulders. "Blooming parky in here."

"The boiler's broken. Hence the need for a plumber."

"So my dad said. Any idea where the boiler's hidden?"

"None whatsoever. You'll have to ask Mr Moore."

Chapter Eight

Saturday 20th February - Lara Orchard

Brooke Street, Walthamstow, London, England

"So?" Lara asked when they were finally alone in the front room, cradling large mugs of tea, which steamed heavily in the chill air. Within two hours of its ignition, the ancient, electric, bar heater had finally given up the ghost.

She spoke softly, but loud enough to be heard over the knocking and clattering from above their heads. True to his word, Brian Able had cracked on with the work. He'd found the recalcitrant boiler in an airing cupboard in the third bedroom, identified one of the fundamental issues—a seized pump—and was hard at work trying to fire it up with a temporary patch.

The strange-looking clipboard he'd arrived with turned out to be a plastic-covered computer tablet with a built-in, laser measuring device. He'd used it to calculate room sizes and work out thermal loading and material requirements. With the same tablet, the highly competent plumber accessed his firm's warehouse, confirmed they had the required parts in stock for a complete refurbishment, and worked out a total price for the job. Without reference to Darwin or Ryan, Lara accepted the quotation on the spot, paid the deposit money by bank transfer, and offered a five percent bonus for Brian's prompt arrival—to be paid on completion of the job.

The entire quotation and ordering process had taken less than an hour. As a demonstration of plumbing in the Internet Age, Lara couldn't fault it.

While the whole central heating system needed replacing with a modern, energy-efficient upgrade, Brian had offered to try to make emergency repairs on the existing hardware since he and his team wouldn't be available to start the project until halfway through the following week.

After their impromptu breakfast, Darwin had taken his leave and scooted upstairs to attack some coursework. Or so he claimed. Although, how anyone could study with such a commotion running in the background, Ryan said he could not understand. Lara's response, about today's youth being able to multitask and study while listening to their iPods, "unlike us old fogies," drew engaging laughter from the student on his way upstairs. Ryan suspected Darwin was more likely taking time to call all his college mates and share his good fortune.

The minute they were alone, she rounded on Ryan.

"So?" she repeated, quietly.

"So … what?" Ryan asked, giving her a look that attempted wide-eyed innocence, but failed miserably.

She sighed, having none of it. "That shop we passed is only around the corner. It shouldn't have taken you the best part of forty minutes to pick up a few groceries. Spill."

"Can't hide anything from you, can I?"

"Why would you want to? Come on, stop prevaricating."

"Five syllables? You know I get confused if a word contains more than three."

"William Griffin!" she said, delighted she'd managed to keep in character even when scolding him. "I'm warning you."

"Okay, Beth. My bad. You saw Rhino following me?"

She nodded. "Of course. The man couldn't have made it more blatant."

"Yep. Amateur hour. The fool wouldn't have lasted five minutes on patrol as a real scout."

"And?"

"And … young Rhino and I had a rather interesting chat. Very helpful, he was. Far more sociable than you might imagine—after an initial awkwardness."

She peered closely at his face. "Don't see any bruises or abrasions. I take it *young Rhino* isn't as tough as he thinks he is?"

"No, I'm afraid Mr Damian Baines is a bit of a wimp. All bluff and bluster. A real cry baby, in fact."

She frowned. "You didn't need to hurt him too badly, did you?"

"Of course not. At least, nothing permanent. Damaged his pride, mainly. But I'm sure he'll recover. I'll ask him how he's feeling when he calls."

"Come again? You're expecting him to call?"

Ryan nodded, still playing the innocent. "As I said, Damian and I came to an arrangement. We swapped numbers. Well, at least I gave him my mobile number. I already had his."

"Corky got back to you? That was quick."

"Actually," Ryan said, "I contacted Corky, but he'd done his usual, excellent, data-mining job."

"Care to tell me all about it?"

"Happy to, my sweet." His smile made Lara warm inside. "After introducing myself to the delightful father-to-be, he was only too glad to answer a few questions. In fact, he turned out to be most illuminating."

Ryan gave her a reasonably full account of what he called his "minor altercation" with the man carrying the disfiguring scar. She held off interrupting him until the part where he and Rhino reached the playground before breaking into his flow.

"If Rhino and Barcode are the worst they have to offer, the Tribe shouldn't cause us too many problems."

"*Us?* What do you mean, 'Us'?"

"We're a team, *Mister*. And don't you forget it."

"You're starting to sound a little trigger happy, Ms Orchard." Ryan whispered Lara's real surname and made his best efforts to scowl. Again, it didn't work too well. Captain Ryan Kaine might have been able to scare his men and terrify his enemies, but he could never intimidate Lara. No way. She already knew him too well.

"We're staying well out of this mess," he continued. "All we're doing here is making sure Darwin Moore is worthy of his share of the money. We'll fix his house, set him up for life, and maybe encourage him to move to a safer area.

That's all. We can't cure the whole world's ills, my darling wife."

Lara shook her head, and set her jaw firmly.

"Don't you dare try to give me any of that bull. Glenmore Davits' death is suspicious, and you know it."

"Perhaps."

"And you plan to investigate, don't you?"

"Perhaps," he repeated, breaking eye contact.

"Good. You can count me in."

"Whoa there, girl. Climb down off that high horse. You're not getting involved in any of this."

"And how do you propose to stop me? Unless you intend to send me back to the villa—alone and unprotected. Is that your plan?"

She watched the internal debate playing across his face. He tried hard to be enigmatic but, again, it didn't work with her.

"I was thinking about maybe taking you home"—her stomach still fluttered whenever he referred to his French safe house as "home"—"and wait until Rollo gets back, but …"

"But?"

"There's always Northamptonshire. I thought you might enjoy spending time at the farm, and I know Mike would be delighted to see you again. It's been a few months—"

"And I'm guessing you're about to mention the horses, right?" Lara interrupted. Sometimes, Ryan could be so transparent.

He scratched at his beard. Funny how it only seemed to irritate him when she challenged his plans.

"Well, you do keep telling me how much you miss that big, dark stallion."

Lara nodded, said, "Mike's okay, but I miss Dynamite even more," and added a salty grin.

"Oh dear," he said, sighing deeply. "That's so beneath you."

"Sorry, couldn't help myself. Anyway, you know I love Mike and his farm's a delight, but I'm staying here." She paused before adding the clincher. "Besides, you know I'm safer with you looking after me."

His slow nod and the accompanying drop of his shoulder indicated defeat. The wonderful man rarely lost in battle, but would happily give ground to her in their minor skirmishes.

"Okay, you win, but you must keep your head down. Agreed?"

"Yes, I promise to do as you tell me. But everything's going to be fine, right? After all, how dangerous can a low-rent street gang be? You can handle a few teenage kids, can't you? Your real challenge will be not to hurt them too badly. After all, you've already put the fear of the Almighty into Damian Baines."

Ryan leaned forwards and cupped her hand in both of his. He held it firmly.

"It's not as simple as that, love. Until last year, the Tribe *was* small fry. A minor, local irritation. They kept pretty much below the police radar and were little more than a bunch of thugs pushing a few baggies of cannabis on street corners."

"So, what happened last year?"

"They got organised. Became more professional."

"How so? Rhino told you something interesting? More than was in Corky's dossier?"

Ryan frowned through a nod. "A little."

"Care to elaborate?"

He gave her a pained expression, and she pulled her hand away.

"Okay, okay. You win," he said, leaning back in his chair. "Most of this is in Corky's notes, but Damian added some background. Early last year, the Tribe's previous leader, a twenty-something called Hooper, did a runner. Left his flat in the middle of the night and disappeared. Ran out on his girlfriend and their son, too. At the time, the boy was only eleven months old."

"Sounds suspicious. Did anyone call the police?"

"No. These people don't want anything to do with the authorities. Anyway, shortly after Hooper's disappearance, the Tribe's next in line, Second Man, was arrested after a random police stop and search found a couple of baggies of heroin in his backpack. According to the crime lab, the baggies had the guy's fingerprints all over them. The drugs had a street value of nearly twenty-five grand. More than enough to charge him with trafficking."

"Okay, that's serious."

"Of course, Second Man claimed the drugs had been planted. Swore he'd been set up by the police."

"Such a surprise."

"Yes, indeed. Well, he screamed his innocence all the way through the trial. It didn't help though. He ended up being sentenced to seven years for conspiracy to supply Class A drugs."

Lara offered a little shrug. "If you live by the sword. He gets no sympathy from me. I hate pushers."

"Me too," Ryan said, nodding, "but there may be some truth behind the man's claims of innocence. According to Damian, the Tribe never used to touch serious drugs. They pushed a little weed and offered 'protection' to some of the neighbourhood's corner shops.

Small scale, nothing serious. At least that's what Damian says."

Lara raised an eyebrow. "Is he seriously suggesting police corruption?"

"The Tribe thought that at first, but not these days. During the trial, the whole Tribe and their WAGs, all seventeen of them, picketed the courthouse every day, claiming they were being stitched up. The police kept moving them on until the protests fizzled out."

"You said, 'not these days'. What happened to change the Tribe's direction?"

"A new boss took over. A new Top Man. After that, things turned serious."

The pale sunlight flowing through the window brightened the eyes behind Ryan's coloured contacts, lightening the green and making them almost translucent.

"In what way 'serious'?" she asked, already suspecting the answer.

"The new Top Man brought in a fresh command structure, including a new Second Man by the name Demarcus Williams. He acts as the prime enforcer. He brought in a few others, too. All hard men from outside the area. And I mean 'men'. Damian said the new guys—he called them the Heavies—were a few years older than the existing gang members. Adults. They intimidated the younger members. Threatened. Cajoled. Bribed. In the end, they hospitalised any who tried to stand up to them or leave the Tribe. In short, they frightened the original Tribe members into submission.

"In business terms, it could be classed as a hostile takeover. Currently, the original members are being used as little more than street-facing gofers. They don't have a say in how the Tribe is run. Quite sad, really. Don't you think?"

She shook her head. "Not at all. A bunch of thugs is a bunch of thugs. They pretty much get what they deserve. So, I suppose your plan is to pay the latest Top Man a social call? Going to show him the error of his ways and encourage him to toddle off and leave the good citizens of Walthamstow in peace … after asking him what he knows about Glenmore Davits' death?"

"Ah, you make it all sound so easy. However …" Ryan grimaced.

"Oh dear. Does there always have to be a 'however'?"

"Apparently so, love. It seems that no one's ever seen the new Top Man. Nobody has any idea who he is or what he looks like. For all anyone knows, Top Man might even be 'Top Woman'. Stranger things—"

"What?" Lara stiffened. "That's ridiculous. How can anyone run a street gang without being directly hands on?"

"That's what I asked my new friend, Damian," Ryan added, cracking a wry grin.

"And he said?"

"Top Man, or rather, TM, communicates indirectly, through Demarcus Williams and the other Heavies. Whenever he talks directly to the Tribe, he uses a TV monitor attached to the wall of their clubhouse. The image is pixilated and the voice modulated electronically. As I said, no one knows who TM is, but the guy seems to know everything that happens in the area."

Ryan stopped talking, maybe to allow her enough time to absorb the information, or maybe to start making plans in his head that didn't include her. No way was she going to let that happen.

After draining the last of her cooled tea, Lara nodded, almost to herself.

"Okay, simple enough. We follow this Demarcus

Williams chap, until he leads us to TM. Then you can use your … subtle powers of persuasion. Alternatively, we can involve the police—indirectly, of course. Wouldn't want anyone recognising you."

He sighed. "Hell, girl. There you go using 'we' again. It's not going to happen. I'm working this alone."

"Ryan," she whispered. "Stop being so damned … stubborn. If you won't let me help, at least wait until we can bring in Rollo, or Danny."

"We've already discussed this. Rollo's on the other side of the world, and Danny's otherwise engaged. I can't keep butting into their lives like this. They need a break, too."

"What about Slim and Larry?"

"They're currently in Las Vegas. Apparently, they're planning to invest some of their hard-earned money gambling and watching the dancing girls. The rest, they'll waste on trivialities."

Lara closed her eyes and tutted her disapproval. "And you tell me off for my poor sense of humour. Surely there are others you can call?"

He held up his hands in surrender. "Okay, okay. It's short notice, but I'll see who's available. In any event, whoever I call, it's likely to take a couple of days for anyone to reach us."

"Meanwhile, you'll keep safe?"

He placed a hand on his heart. "Of course. Until I have some backup, I'll keep nothing more than a watching brief. I'll even try to do it remotely, through strategically placed surveillance cameras."

"Promise?"

"Promise." He raised his hands to show her his uncrossed fingers. "In the meantime, young Damian Baines will be my ears on the inside."

"Sure you can trust him?"

"Don't be daft. Of course I can't trust him."

He smiled disarmingly, but her expression must have given away more anxiety than she intended, and his smile quickly faded. "Not funny, Ryan. Not funny at all."

"Sorry, lass."

"You will be, *Mister*."

"Ooh, scary."

Ryan grinned and held up his hands in mock surrender, and everything was good again.

"Good. Anyway, you're right," he said. "I can't just sit back and do nothing. Especially when our original good intentions might have led to Glenmore Davits' so-called accident."

"Sending him the banker's draft, you mean?"

He nodded. "Glenmore might have told someone about it."

"The neighbour, Primula Johnston?"

"Well, she did send that anonymous tip to the Trust's website. Which is what led us here in the first place," he said, lowering his voice even further and shooting a quick look at the door when the noises above their heads stopped suddenly.

"There's no such thing as 'anonymous tips' with someone like Corky on the case," Lara said, matching his volume.

"Which reminds me," Ryan said, easing smoothly to his feet, "it's about time someone visited the ever-so-helpful Mrs Johnston."

Despite their agreement, Lara couldn't help worrying.

Even though Ryan was, without doubt, the most competent and resourceful man she'd ever met—her late and equally wonderful husband included—he was still only one man. Surely he didn't think he could take on the whole Tribe single-handedly and come through unscathed?

He knew very little about the full scope of the Tribe's operations or their numbers. This new revelation about a mysterious TM pulling the strings behind the scenes with the help of a bunch of goons, made the issue significantly more dangerous.

After receiving the email from Primula Johnston, Lara was the one who'd insisted they visited London together right away, and she had to shoulder most of the blame for whatever happened. She shouldn't have encouraged Ryan to check on Darwin Moore in person. In the safety of their French hideaway, things had seemed so straightforward. Visit London and find out why one of The 83—a crippled, old man with no family apart from a grandson in university —passed away, apparently by accident. What could be so simple?

Yet, here they were, in the middle of danger again.

The moment Ryan learned that Glenmore Davits' death might relate to the money, and that Darwin Moore lived in what might well have been a war zone, at least part time, she'd known what he'd do.

Ryan would never allow the situation to continue unchecked. Oh no, not Ryan Kaine, who had vowed to spend the rest of his life protecting The 83.

Even though he tried to hide his guilt from her, she could see it in his eyes and sense it in his dreams. When they lay together in the dark of the night, she'd feel his body tense, and she'd listen to his ragged breathing as he relived the moment in his sleep. The moment he pulled the trigger that ended the flight and killed all those innocent people.

Poor, dear Ryan.

From his position by the window, Ryan flinched.

"Hello," he said, "if I'm not mistaken, here's our anonymous informant."

"Who, Damian?"

"Not unless he's taken to wearing drag. This will be the neighbour, Primula Johnston. Saves me a trip next door."

The letterbox handle rattled, the lock on the front door clicked, and the door opened.

"Hello, Darwin?" a woman's voice called out loud and bright. "It's only me! I've let myself in."

Upstairs, towards the back of the house, Darwin's bedroom door opened and his heavy footsteps moved along the landing.

"Come in, Primula. I'll be right down. Go straight through to the kitchen. We'll have a coffee."

Footsteps clattered along the hall to the kitchen, and the door closed.

Lara jumped up. "How do you want to play this?"

"With a straight bat, love. Let Darwin take the lead and introduce us if he likes. If he mentions the Trust and Primula wants to admit emailing us, all well and good. If not, we can talk to her later. Independently."

Ryan opened the sitting room door and allowed Lara into the hallway first, but only after having checked it was safe. Damian, wearing a clean sweater and jeans, and a slightly annoyed expression, skipped down the stairs. He stopped when he reached the bottom step.

"This'll be fun," he whispered, glancing towards the kitchen. "A word of warning. Apart from being a busybody and a total fantasist, Primula Johnston is the biggest gossip in the known universe. By now, every person on the street will know I have visitors. They'll also know a plumber's working on my boiler. Treat everything she says with a large bucket of salt, and please ... no talk of the money." He tapped the side of his nose. "I don't want the whole world knowing my business."

He hurried through to the kitchen, brushing past Lara in his haste. She and Ryan exchanged telling glances and followed him down the hallway.

"That answered one of our questions," Ryan whispered. "This should prove interesting."

Chapter Nine

Saturday 20th February - Lara Orchard

Brooke Street, Walthamstow, London, England

The bulbous and voluminous Primula Johnston filled the kitchen, practically sucking all the air out of the room when she spoke. The woman sat at the table, teacup in one hand hovering over a saucer held in the other, trying to drag information out of a reluctant Darwin. No one witnessing the event would ever have called her subtle.

Darwin introduced her as a wonderfully helpful neighbour who would run little errands for his Pops, which included grocery shopping and the like.

"Oh yes," she said between delicate sips from a cup which never seemed to empty, "my husband and I like to do our bit for the less fortunate amongst us, y'know. Glenmore was such a lovely man. Suffered terrible bad wit' his hip and back, but rarely complained. Not like Mr Lubbock at Number 37. Oh dear me, no. Why, only last week, he—"

"Pops was really grateful for all your help, Primula. As was I, of course. He wouldn't have been able to survive without your support, especially when I left for college."

When she smiled, her cheeks bulged, her eyes narrowed, and her crow's feet extended to her ears. She'd entered the house wearing a hat and a heavy coat, and kept them on, despite the rising heat in the kitchen.

"That was our pleasure, dear. And"—she looked over her glasses at Lara and Ryan—"who, might I ask, are your friends?"

"Dr and Mr Griffin are here from … The 83 Trust. They just wanted to make sure I'm doing okay since Pops … you know."

Primula Johnston's beady, little eyes opened, and the cup trembled in her hand. She centred the cup on the saucer and lowered them both to the table.

"The 83 Trust? Oh, how excitin'. You received my message, then?"

Ryan shot a look at Lara that said, "Over to you," and she took the lead.

"Your message?" she asked.

"Yes, dear. I typed it into that lil' box on your website. Suggested you investigate Glenmore's passin'."

"You did what?" Darwin demanded, raising his voice and displaying real annoyance for the first time.

If Primula noticed Darwin's irritation, she didn't let it show. The woman had the thickness of skin any pachyderm would have been proud of.

"Yes, dear. Didn't I tell you?"

"No, Primula. You didn't."

"Musta slipped my mind."

"Why on earth did you do such a thing?"

"Well, y'know. Wit' all the trouble we've been havin' aroun' here. ... with that Barcode fellow and the Tribe ... Glenmore was worried for his life."

"He was?" Lara asked.

"Yes, Glenmore tol' me about how Barcode kept hangin' aroun' outside his door. In the alleyway. Sellin' his drugs. Glenmore wasn't a happy man. Not at all. Kept shoutin' at Barcode to move away."

"Did you have any specific reason to contact the Trust?" Lara asked.

Primula shuffled in her chair. "Well, not as such. But since he died just after gettin' that registered letter, it got me to thinkin'."

"Thinking what, Primula?" Darwin asked, clearly struggling for patience.

"Well now. Two days after receivin' a suspicious letter ..."

"Did Pops tell you what was *in* the letter?"

Primula's bloated face crumpled. "No, but—"

"But nothing, Primula. Your imagination's running wild again. Remember the time you claimed to have seen a UFO, only to discover it was a police helicopter?"

Primula frowned and tucked in her chin. "Looked like a flyin' saucer to me. Bright light in the sky. Hoverin' over all the houses—"

"That was its searchlight, Primula."

"Anyone can make a mista—"

"But you called the police and the BBC," Darwin gasped.

"Like I said. Anyone can make a mistake. But wit' Glenmore dyin' shortly after gettin' that letter, that wasn't no mistake."

"Nothing but a coincidence, Primula."

Darwin looked from Lara to Ryan. His exasperated expression seemed to ask, "See what I have to put up with?"

A double-rap on the kitchen door made them all turn.

"Yes?" Darwin called.

The door opened and the plumber stuck his head through the gap. "Hi, sorry to disturb. Can I come in?"

Lara remained seated at the table beside Primula, and Ryan huddled into a corner near the pantry, trying to remain inconspicuous. Darwin stood and beckoned the plumber into the overcrowded room.

"Come in, come in," Darwin called. "Any news?"

Primula looked as though her birthday had arrived early. Her grin was almost wide enough to split her cheeks. Surprisingly she kept quiet, absorbing every exciting morsel of information.

Brian Able pointed towards the ceiling and cocked an ear. In the silence, an anaemic rattle interspersed with the occasional bubbling pop reverberated through the floorboards.

"That boiler's older than my dad and nearly as obsolete," Brian started, grinning widely. "Never worked on anything so decrepit, but … as you can hear, I've managed to coax some life into her. To be honest, I'm not sure I should leave it running, but this house is freezing. I've given it a quick health check. No apparent problems with the exhaust gasses, they're venting to the outside, but … well, there's no telling how long my patch is going to last. I'll hang around for an hour until the system reaches temperature, just to make sure the thermostat—"

Upstairs, after a heavy thump, the rattling stopped, replaced by a hissing gurgle.

Brian shouted, "Darn it," spun around, and dived back out through the door again. His footsteps thumped up the stairs and, with her eyes, Lara followed the clomp of work boots crossing the bare boards above their heads. Moments later, the hissing slowed and eventually turned into the regular drip-drip of water filling a bucket.

"Oh dear. That sounds terminal," Ryan said, unnecessarily.

"Perhaps you should stay in a hotel until the heating's been fixed," Lara suggested.

"A hotel!" Primula spluttered. "How's he gonna afford that? He's a student, y'know!"

"It's all right, Primula. I'm only here weekends. I can cope with a little cold."

"Nonsense, boy. Why don't you come stay wit' me and Albert. We got a spare room since Petunia moved in wit' her … her woman friend."

Primula's sneer and the air she sucked between her teeth made her disdain for Petunia's choice of lifestyle perfectly clear.

"No, no," Darwin said, the words gushing from his lips. "That's really a very generous offer, but I'm comfortable here. Really, I am. It's only for a few days a month. The college dorms will fill in the rest of the time. Thank you, but no."

Ryan saved Darwin's further blushes by saying, "I'll ask young Brian if he knows where to source some electric space heaters." He turned towards the door. "Beth? Why don't you carry on chatting with Darwin and Primula while I pop upstairs and have a word with the plumber? Then I'll go fetch the car from the hotel, to save you having to walk back in case it rains."

He winked at Lara, nodded to Primula and Darwin, and closed the kitchen door behind him.

Minutes later, water from the bucket emptied into the toilet and the cistern flushed. A short while after that, Brian Able returned to the kitchen, an expression of defeat etched into his youthful face. Toolbox and electronic clipboard in hand, he stood in the open kitchen doorway.

"I guess you know what I'm going to say?" he asked Darwin.

Lara could just make out Ryan hovering near the front door, ready for a rapid escape.

"Knackered?" Darwin suggested.

The plumber nodded. "'Fraid so. Main combustion chamber is corroded and the electronic interface is bugg— uh, shot. Not worth spending any more time or money on it, I'm afraid. Best I can do is pop back to the warehouse for some temporary heaters. Won't take me long. Be back inside the hour."

"Good idea," Lara answered. "The quicker we get some real heat into this place the better. You'll be able to start the installation on Wednesday?"

"As promised, Mrs Griffin."

"And how long will the job take?"

The young plumber's eyes scanned the screen on his tablet.

"Not easy to tell for certain. We'll have to remove and replace all the old pipework and the radiators before laying the new kit. Probably best to allow at least a week, maybe a fortnight." He cast his eyes along the hall, looking towards the front door.

"The place will be a building site," he said. "Any chance you can find a place to stay awhile, Mr Moore?"

"Never mind about me, Mr Able. I'm sorted during the week."

From her seat at the table, Primula Johnston's eyes lost some of their sparkle, but the woman had plenty to tell her listening circle and it was clear she had no real intel to help Lara and Ryan.

The aged chatterbox had nothing to offer but the rampant speculation of a vivid imagination in a bored mind.

Chapter Ten

Saturday 20th February - Early Afternoon

Brooke Street, Walthamstow, London, England

Kaine followed the plumber out of the house. If anything, the wind had freshened since his dance with Damian, and a light rain had started to fall. He pulled up the collar of his jacket, tugged the zip all the way up to his scarf, and jammed the cap tight down on his head.

"Won't be long," Brian said as he slid behind the steering wheel of a late-model Ford Transit. "Can I give you a lift anywhere?"

"No, thanks, Brian. I need to stretch my legs and get some fresh air."

Brian guffawed. "Fresh air? In London? Good luck

finding any of that. You might as well suck on the tailpipe of a double-decker bus for all the good this stuff's going to do your lungs. Still, I'm hardly helping with this big, gas-guzzling Transit. Saving up to buy an electric van, but they're so damned expensive. Need to grow the business first. Catch you later, Mr Griffin?"

Kaine touched the peak of his cap. "Be seeing you, Brian."

The plumber fired up his van and pulled away, heading south along Brooke Street, towards Baker Rise and, eventually, the High Street. Kaine set off in the same direction, keeping a leisurely pace, and maintaining full awareness of his surroundings. Despite his confident responses to Lara's questions, there was no telling how Damian or Barcode would react to Kaine's presence.

In truth, he felt exposed and unarmed. Kaine could probably handle untrained, knife-wielding, young thugs easily enough if they attacked one at a time, but he had no idea how many punks he might actually face. And he had Lara to protect, not to mention Darwin Moore. No doubt about it, he needed a proper weapon, and he knew exactly where to source one.

Since long before his life had turned to crap—with the definite exception of finding Lara—he'd maintained a safe house in London, a place no one knew but him, Lara, Rollo, and Danny. He'd inherited the renovated cellar in a back street of Camden from a distant relative and had sold it to a shell company he'd registered in the Channel Islands under an assumed identity. The shell company paid the utility bills and the council taxes. Since taking ownership, he'd done very little to the apartment. The decor was post-war functional, but the building was secure and, with Rollo's help, he'd installed a large gun safe and had stocked it with emergency supplies, including cash, identification papers, and various pieces of military equipment which included small arms.

Apart from a brief stay with Danny, he hadn't really visited the place since the evening before turning the tables on Sir Malcolm Sampson, former head of Sampson Armaments and Munitions Services Plc, and current occupier of one of Her Majesty's prison cells. Kaine could still feel the impact of the beating he suffered at the fists of Sir Malcolm's primary stooge, Adam Akers, but allowed himself a satisfied smile as he recalled the way Akers had earned his new moniker, Pinocchio.

The fastest way would be through the underground, but travelling via public transport carrying an unlicensed firearm and other military ordnance was begging for trouble. Some of London's larger travel hubs had been fitted with metal detectors, and the recent epidemic in knife crime had encouraged the Home Secretary to update the police's powers of stop and search. News bulletins confirmed that the Metropolitan Police were not exactly shy in utilising this new power, nor were they renowned for the efficiency of their targeting process. Suffering a random stop and search was a sure-fire way for Kaine to end up inside, and once in the tender embrace of the authorities, his life would be over, both figuratively and actually. He was under few illusions. He'd be unlikely to survive even a brief stint in lockup.

Although possessing incontrovertible proof of his innocence—provided in Sir Malcom Sampson's own words—Kaine was still in danger. Powerful people wanted nothing more than for Ryan Kaine to vanish, permanently. If his death ensured that situation, no one in authority would shed any tears.

On top of everything else, if Kaine placed the evidence

in the public domain, the tax man would insist he return the millions he'd liberated from Sir Malcolm's slush fund in return for clemency. Kaine wasn't about to do that. He'd taken the money with the express intention of supporting The 83, and he'd be damned if he'd let it be used to pay Sir Malcolm's back taxes.

On his way to the hotel to pick up the hire car, Kaine passed a number of pedestrians, none of whom he recognised, and none who presented a challenge. The Tribe's foot soldiers were clearly reluctant to face the chill wind and rain of a wintery afternoon in London's fair city.

The shower increased in intensity, and Kaine doubled his pace. Steady at first, the drizzle soon built into a heavy downpour, drumming on his cap and soaking into the shoulders of his light coat. He should have brought the brolly.

Kaine turned left into Baker Rise and broke into a jog. The hotel was less than a mile away, but he'd be completely soaked and frozen by the time he reached the place. It would teach him to step out of the house unprepared.

He jogged into Lower Street and hurried along, side-stepping shoppers part-hidden under brollies and hopping over the growing puddles. Up ahead, a bus stop offered a brief respite from the deluge. He ducked under the awning and waited for the worst of the weather to pass.

Three people, hunched against the cold, noses buried in their smartphones, waited for the Number 91. According to the digital display attached to a nearby lamppost, the bus would arrive in three minutes. A mother pushed a baby buggy into the bus stop. Kaine smiled at her. She blanked him.

Fair enough.

Kaine's mobile vibrated. He dug a sodden hand into his

coat pocket and pulled out the phone. A text message filled the screen from an unknown number.

You wife in danger. Need help now.

Apart from Lara and Corky, only one person knew that particular burner's number—Damian Baines.

Shit.

Without further thought, Kaine dived back out into the driving rain, his heart hammering.

With feet barely touching the pavement, he retraced his steps at a sprint.

Nose-to-tail cars blocked Lower Street. Pedestrians obstructed his path. He buffeted, collided, barged.

"Excuse me!"

"*Hey, what the fu—*"

"Sorry, mate!"

"*Bloody hell—*"

"Excuse me!"

"Sorry!"

As he made the turn into Baker Rise, the traffic cleared and the pedestrians dispersed. He sidestepped someone yelling into a mobile, and jumped into the middle of the road. Breathing hard, legs driving, arms pumping, he sprinted past a slow-moving taxi, an SUV, a panel van, a hatchback.

Car horns blared. Drivers yelled.

A motorbike filtered between the cars, hogging the central gap, head-on. It stopped, headlight flashing as Kaine slid past.

He had fifty metres before the turn onto Brooke Street. Only fifty metres …

His lungs burned, his legs aflame.

Lara. What if they'd hurt her? What would he do?

Don't go there, Kaine.

He sprinted on.

The rain stopped suddenly.

He splashed through puddles. Dodging the traffic, he screamed right onto a deserted Brooke Street, increased his pace. The houses blasted past. Number 32 … 40 … 54.

There, up ahead on the left, Number 60! Still at full pelt, he dug a hand into his pocket for the key.

"Lara!" he screamed.

Hell. Wrong name. Wake up!

Hopefully, no one heard.

"Beth?" he yelled.

After vaulting the low, wooden gate, he climbed the ramp in two long strides, slip-slid to a stop, and paused at the door long enough to jab the key into the lock and crash through into the hallway.

"Beth!"

He raced along the hall and barged into the kitchen. Darwin and Primula turned as one, shocked to see him.

"Where's Beth?" he yelled, panting hard.

"What's the matter?" Primula asked.

"My wife, where is she?"

Darwin pointed towards the front door. "She popped out to the corner shop for some—"

"Shit," Kaine shouted, turning and heading out again. "Why d'you let her go?"

The young man's response was lost in the crash-rattle of the front door slamming shut.

Kaine darted back out onto the path. Despite the panic during his mad dash, his mind raced through the options. If Lara had headed towards the shop near the High Street, he'd have run past her, therefore … which way?

Which way? Which bloody way?

Still breathing hard and sweating through heavy, wet clothes, but recovering fast, Kaine stood still, trying to think.

The corner shop? Which corner shop?

Raised voices cut through the quiet—taunting, mocking, laughing.

Voices. Young men.

Where?

Away to his left. Well away at the far end of the street. Three hundred metres, maybe more. Near the ruined playground.

Kaine hurdled the front gate and scrambled towards the noise.

Oh God, no. Please no!

A pale sun broke through the heavy clouds. Damp air cooled his face and hair. Sometime during his sprint, he'd lost his cap. There, in the distance. At the end of the terrace, a narrow alleyway, Crease Cut. Figures moved. Circling.

Corralling.

Kaine dug deeper into his reserves, ran faster. Faster than ever, but time slowed. He'd started running through treacle.

Lara, surrounded by three men, raised her arms, backed away.

"Beth? Beth!"

Facing the men, she backed up against a wooden fence. Nowhere left to go.

Kaine screamed again.

"Leave her alone, you bastards!"

Only a hundred metres away, but it might as well have been a kilometre. The biggest of the three, Barcode, grabbed Lara's arm.

He was too late.
Too damned late.

Chapter Eleven

Saturday 20th February - Lara Orchard

Brooke Street, Walthamstow, London, England

Lara pulled on the handle to the front door. Swollen by the lack of paint and the damp atmosphere, it stuck tight against the jamb. She tugged harder and the door burst open, nearly bopping her on the nose for her troubles.

Idiot.

Smiling in embarrassment at nobody, she glanced back towards the kitchen, but the closed door confirmed neither Darwin nor the irritating neighbour, Primula, had seen. His apologetic voice and her wailing confirmed they were still too engrossed in their discussion to have noticed her error.

Lara stepped outside, into the cold and wet.

To close the door properly, she slammed it and the noise

reverberated through the hallway. If Darwin insisted on staying in the house, they'd offer to upgrade it for him. She'd ask Ryan to authorise a total rebuild, and he would agree. Of course he'd agree. On top of that, Ryan was bound to know someone reliable in the building game. Former shipmates. That was how it worked with the military. People knew people who knew people. If not, their resourceful quartermaster, Rollo, would know where to source decent workers.

In her haste to leave the embarrassing spectacle in the kitchen, she'd wilfully ignored Ryan's instructions, but a quick trip to the nearest shop with a pharmacy for some headache pills and more groceries surely wouldn't be a problem.

Darwin had pointed her in its direction.

Which way did he say? To the left, away from the High Street.

Lara pushed through the gate. Rusty hinges screeched. Another item to add to the repair list—Darwin needed a new front fence and gate. She turned left and hurried along with the wind and rain at her back.

The time of day, together with the inclement weather, meant Brooke Street was pretty much deserted. Lara weaved in and around the puddles, keeping her head bowed and shoulders hunched. The rain increased in force. February in London, a far cry from the windswept but milder weather they enjoyed on the Aquitaine coast. Damn it, she should never have ventured outside without an umbrella. They had one in the boot of their hire car, but she'd forgotten to bring it out with them that morning. She'd remember for tomorrow.

Still, it didn't really matter if she got wet. A little rain wouldn't hurt her. In fact, she rather enjoyed being close to nature. It made her feel alive. The only thing better would be if Ryan were there with her.

"Hey, wo-man. Where you goin' all on yo' own?"

The voice, from the side and slightly ahead, crashed into her thoughts. Lara stopped. Jerked up her head. Three men appeared from a narrow, muddy, side alley. One she'd completely missed.

In the middle of the three, Barcode stood a head taller than the others and slightly to the front. Once more, the leader.

To Barcode's left, stood a skinny, white youth, little more than a teenager. He wore a sodden denim jacket, jeans, and filthy trainers. Bare-headed, the kid's lank hair hung to his shoulders. His brown eyes stared at her from a face that revealed little emotion.

The third, his acne-scarred face as expressionless and disinterested as the skinny one's, but much wider and darker, hung back from the others, slouching under a purple baseball cap. Tribe colours. Hands stuffed into pockets and leaning against a rickety wooden fence, he presented no immediate danger.

Barcode's tone bled aggression. He took a single, swaggering pace towards her. Confidence written all over his handsome but brutish face. She was alone. Defenceless. Without Ryan at her side.

Barcode allowed his arrogance full rein.

"I asked you a question, be-atch. Answer me."

Lara scoped the area. Out in the open. No one in view. Houses crowded in all around, but the closed doors and blank windows offered no immediate sanctuary.

Lara, you idiot.

She'd been such a fool. How many times had Ryan told her never to let down her guard? Even here, in London, in broad daylight, she should have been more careful. Ryan was going to be so disappointed in her. She was disappointed enough in herself.

Stupid woman!

She pulled in a breath, and fought the urge to scream in rage and fear. No, that would likely enrage Barcode, put him on his guard when she needed him overconfident. So what if she were on her own? She wasn't helpless. Oh no, she wasn't helpless at all.

Her heartrate jumped, and she swallowed down the nerves.

Poor Ryan. He'd lost so much, but he damn well wasn't going to lose her, too. Not today.

Barcode took two more self-assured strides forwards. Slow and certain, he was playing with her. A tomcat with his prey—his terrified mouse. Two metres separated them. Slightly more than arm's length. He stared down at her. Intimidating. Smirking. Flashing milk-white teeth.

If she ran, he'd catch her in seconds. With a greater start, she'd be able to outpace him. No doubt. The man was big, muscular, but she had endurance and pace. In France, Ryan had drilled the fitness into her. They trained for hours, covered miles, raced along the dunes near the villa, swam miles in the Bay of Biscay. Yet, there she stood, up close to danger, with no means of outrunning her attacker. She backed up, edged to her right, away from the alley, closer to a slatted fence.

Barcode's smirk grew wider.

The two behind him, Skinny and Acne, shared a glance before closing on their leader, staying wide to encircle her. They paid more attention. Their interest increasing.

Despite her daggy clothes, Lara was a woman, apparently helpless. To them, she presented an opportunity for amusement. A way to pass the time on a wet winter's day.

She may have allowed herself to wander into danger, but this wasn't over.

Remember your training, Lara. You can do this.

Danger and anger forced the adrenal glands to release their payload. Adrenaline flowed through her system. Her heartrate doubled, pumping blood faster through her system. Muscles warmed, preparing for action. Her breathing rate increased, oxygenating the blood, driving fuel into the voluntary muscles.

Time slowed to a crawl.

The pupils in Barcode's brown eyes narrowed, his nostrils flared. He licked his lips. The sneer reappeared. Bared teeth showed pink gums, moist with saliva. A ravenous animal.

Acne snickered. Paying even closer attention to their prey.

Skinny hesitated, apparently reluctant to join in the hunt.

Lara backed further away, sidestepped again. Now fully at her back, the fence offered protection, no one could get behind her, attack her from the rear.

Barcode lunged and grabbed Lara's right forearm. He hooted in triumph.

Time slowed further. Her moves came easily, practised. Automatic.

Without conscious thought, Lara made a quarter turn, rotating away from the attack. Simultaneously, she placed her hand on top of his, locking the powerful man's wrist against her own. She lifted her arms straight up in front of her face as though raising a sword, and stepped through the arch formed in Barcode's twisted back.

Barcode's arm bent at the elbow, it had no choice.

He squeaked in surprise, his balance gone, the whole of his weight resting on the fulcrum formed by Lara's wrist-lock. For a briefest moment, he teetered on one leg, the other dangling out in front, waving in mid-air.

She took a shuffle-step forwards, extended out, and cut down and away with her arms in a sword-slicing motion.

Barcode howled, flew backwards through the air, and landed in the middle of the pavement, head, arms, and ankles slamming into the concrete. Air whooshed from his lungs. The back of his shaved head cracked against the paving slabs. The skin split, and blood spurted through the gash.

During the two-second manoeuvre, neither Skinny nor Acne had time to move. They stood still, slack-jawed, arms hanging loose at their sides.

In the distance, someone shouted.

She backed away from her attackers, splitting her attention between the downed and bleeding Barcode, and his ineffective backup crew, remaining aware of their every move. Her heart rate slowed and along with it, her breathing.

Another shout. A man's voice. Pounding, splashing. Approaching from behind.

More? God no!

Arms up and held out in front, Lara turned sharply to her left. Keeping Barcode and his crew in her peripheral vision, she faced the new danger head on.

Things were escalating beyond her control but she wasn't giving in. Not now. Not ever.

Ryan!

Her Ryan sprinted towards her, his face livid, his expression furious.

His impending arrival seemed to release Acne and Skinny from their inertia. They scrambled towards Barcode, helped the thug to his groggy feet, and half-carried, half-dragged him into the dark recess of Crease Cut. Beaten and humiliated, only Barcode cast a backwards glance.

"I'll be back, be-atch," he mumbled while the blood ran down the back of his head and dripped into the hood of his cream-coloured jacket.

Ryan threw a strong arm around her shoulder. "Better bring your sister to hold your hand, little man! So much as look sideways at my wife again and you can kiss your arse goodbye."

Skinny and Acne struggled to keep Barcode from tumbling to the ground.

Chapter Twelve

Saturday 20th February - Lara Orchard

Brooke Street, Walthamstow, London, England

Lara watched the three would-be assailants scurry away along the muddy lane and fade into the damp gloom.

"'Kiss your arse goodbye'?" she said, looking into Ryan's flinty eyes. "What sort of a threat is that?"

"All I could come up with on the spur of the moment. Sorry. Next time, I'll have something prepared."

As Ryan held her, the shakes arrived. Lara recognised them as the inevitable reaction, the aftermath of the adrenaline rush. She gulped in the air, trying to fight the twin sense of fear and euphoria.

She'd beaten a huge beast of a man in an even fight, using nothing more than movement, balance, and surprise.

How was that possible?

Ryan lifted her up and pulled her into a tighter hug.

"Lara," he whispered into her ear. "Are you okay?"

She struggled, forcing him to lower her to her feet. He held her at arm's length, hands gripping her shoulders, dividing his attention between checking her for injuries and making sure the Tribesmen didn't recover enough to launch a fresh attack.

Relief took over. Relief mixed with pride.

"Did you see, Ryan? Did you see? Those self-defence sessions at the villa worked. They actually worked!"

She practically shouted the words. Full of herself. The power chugging through her felt awesome. She raised both hands in a "high ten", but rather than responding and basking in her success, he frowned and left her hanging.

"They're getting away, Ryan. Heading towards the industrial estate. Let's go finish them off. C'mon. You and me. We can do it together."

Ryan frowned, shook his head, and said, "Idiot."

With that single word, Lara lost her high. It exploded out of her as though he'd popped a balloon with a pin.

"What? What did you say? Didn't you see? Didn't you see what I did?"

Still frowning, jaw set hard, he nodded and said, "I saw," before taking her wrist, almost as fiercely as Barcode had done. Ryan pulled her away, heading towards Darwin's house and safety. She had to jog to keep from falling.

"Ry—Bill, you're hurting me."

Ryan looked down at his hand, frowned as though in surprise, and released her wrist.

"Sorry," he muttered and slowed his pace.

Once back at his side, she took hold of his forearm, forcing him to stop or drag her over.

"Bill, what's wrong? Didn't you see what I did?"

He stopped. Fists clenched, jaw muscles bunching beneath his beard, Ryan closed his eyes and let out a long breath through flared nostrils. She'd rarely seen him so agitated, and never had it been directed towards her.

Finally, he opened his eyes again and stared into hers. Soft eyes, that could be so loving and warm, glistened with anger and tears.

"I saw it. *Shiho-nage*. Aikido's four-directions throw. Executed perfectly, I might add." He spoke with forced control, his tone flat when she expected him to be impressed and congratulatory.

"So, what did I do wrong?"

He stepped close, reaching out to hold her hand in both of his. This time, his grip was tender, gentle, but his hands trembled.

"Bloody hell, girl, haven't I taught you anything?"

"Now you're worrying me. What's wrong?"

"What's the first rule of self-defence?"

Realisation hit with the force of a slap to the face. She lowered her head.

He released her hand and stood sideways-on to her, keeping a wary eye open for attackers, as she should have done.

"It wasn't a rhetorical question, Lara. Answer me."

"The first rule of self-defence is to avoid dangerous situations in the first place. Fighting should always be the last resort."

He pulled her into another tight hug that made breathing difficult. After an age, he unwrapped his arms and held her slightly away again. Tears, real tears, formed at the corners of his eyes. For a man like Ryan Kaine to cry indicated how much she meant to him—and confirmed how badly she'd messed up. Lara's vision blurred in sympathy and her throat constricted so tightly she found it impossible to swallow.

"When I saw you throw that big thug, my first reaction was to cheer and shout, 'Go get him, girl,' but to think of you in danger in the first place turned my stomach. You shouldn't be here. It's too dangerous. Anything could have happened. They might have been armed." He pulled her close again, and his chin grazed her cheek. "Think of all the knife crime around here. For God's sake. People have died, love. What were you thinking? Why did you leave the house?"

She squirmed around enough to kiss him.

"Sorry, Ryan," she said, remembering to whisper his real name. "I really am."

"You have no idea how terrified—"

She leaned in and kissed him again.

"...terrified for you, Lara," he mumbled. "Can you imagine how that feels?"

Wait a minute. Oh no you don't!

She gritted her teeth, wriggled free of his arms, and punched his chest harder than she meant to. So hard, pain bloomed in her fist. If it hurt Ryan, he didn't show it.

"Yes, I can imagine exactly how it feels. Too bloody right, I can, *Ryan Liam Kaine*! Every single time you go on a trip without me!" Even though she whispered his name and checked the area for eavesdroppers, she spoke with the venom of someone who knew both sides of the argument.

They faced each other on the pavement and the world fell silent. Even the wind seemed to die and leave them in a vacuum. While she looked at him, studying his anguished expression, Ryan still split his attention between her and their surroundings—never at rest, always on guard. He took full responsibility for the safety of everyone he cared for. It was one of the reasons she loved him so much.

"For pity's sake, Lara," he whispered at last. "What the hell am I going to do with you?"

"Forgive me for being an idiot?"

She leaned in again and kissed him once more. This time, his shoulders relaxed.

"Okay, you win. I forgive you."

Ryan sighed. He took her hand and turned towards Darwin's house but she held him back. "I can't go back there for a while. It's too awkward."

He glanced up ahead and then behind. The frown returned. "Why? What happened?"

"That bloody woman, Primula Johnston. Such a busy-body. Simply wouldn't stop trying to wheedle information out of us. Eventually, Darwin lost patience and asked her to leave. He also asked her to return the spare key. He argued that, since his grandfather no longer required her help, she wouldn't need access to his house. Well, you can imagine her reaction."

"A wailing and a gnashing of teeth?"

Lara nodded.

"Pretty much. She started with, 'After all I did for your grandfather!' and continued with, 'What have I done to deserve this treatment?'. And on, and on. For goodness' sake, the woman's squeaking voice could shatter glass. I just couldn't stand it any longer. Had to leave. Ryan," she said, staring deep into his eyes, "I really am sorry for lowering my guard. It won't happen again. I promise. Forgive me, for real?"

He let out another world-weary sigh.

"Suppose I'll have to, won't I."

"Yes," she said, then added, "You will," and ended the topic.

"You were heading to the shop?"

"My excuse to leave was a headache. I told Darwin I needed some painkillers. He pointed me to the nearest shop with a pharmacy which is … the other way." She stopped and jabbed her finger towards Green Lane, away from Number 60.

"Well," he said, sticking out the crook of his arm for her to hold, "we'd better do just that, then."

They reversed direction. Walking hand-in-arm and, much more centred, Lara felt the need to talk.

"What are you doing here, anyway? I thought you were heading back to the hotel for the car?"

He told her about receiving the text from Damian Baines.

"You didn't consider it might be a trap?"

"Of course I did, but … what else could I have done but act on it? Was he one of the three who attacked you? I couldn't make out the other two who dragged Barcode away."

"No. Rhino—Damian—wasn't one of them," she said and described Skinny and Acne, adding, "They did nothing but crowd me. Barcode made all the moves, but … well, you saw what happened."

Ryan nodded thoughtfully but otherwise didn't respond. She allowed him to mull things over until they reached the junction with Green Lane, then he paused.

"What are you thinking?"

He glanced at her, but maintained his vigil. "Looks like I was wrong about our friend, Damian. Seems as though we might be able to use him after all."

"Use him for what?"

He squeezed her hand and pulled her closer until they were walking shoulder-to-shoulder.

"I'm afraid I have a little confession to make," he said, giving her a pained expression."

"Well, you know what they say. Confession is—"

"No, no, no. Please don't say it."

"Say what?"

"Don't say, 'confession is good for the soul'."

"Why not?"

"You know I hate clichés."

"Yes, but I like them. Nothing wrong with the occasional old saying, if it's relevant. However, moving on. What, dear William, do you have to confess to your long-suffering wife?"

He grimaced and let out another sigh, this one deeper and longer than the other.

"Well, I didn't quite tell you everything Damian said during our little *tête-à-tête* this morning."

Tightness developed on Lara's forehead but, this time, she tried not to frown. "Ryan Kaine," she whispered, "you said there'd be no secrets between us." She added the hint of a smile to diffuse any tension.

"Lara Orchard," he answered, equally as quiet, "operational necessity sometime requires me to hold certain intelligence from my operatives."

"Your operatives? I'm nothing but an 'operative' to you?"

"When we're in the field, yes," he said, adding a smirk. "A very special one, though."

Lara closed her eyes for a moment then shook her head slowly, allowing him to lead the way. He remained silent as a woman pushing a pram rushed past, quietly soothing her baby—a six month old with pale skin, fair hair, and striking blue eyes.

"Being serious for a moment," she said, once mother and baby were far enough away, "why hold out on me?"

"To be totally honest, I didn't believe a word the man said."

"Which was?"

"Damian said he wasn't actually going to attack me. Apparently, he only followed me because he wanted to talk."

"And you didn't believe him?"

"Would you have?"

She tilted her head. "Doubt it. So, he was following you for a chat? What about? The latest football results, perhaps?"

"Nope," Ryan said, shaking his head again. "According to Corky's research, Damian's an Arsenal fan. We don't have anything in common. As you know, can't stand the Gunners, me."

"Bill, stop dragging this out. What did the man say?"

"Apparently, when Barcode ordered him to follow me, Damian decided to wait until we were out of sight before offering to help me close down the Tribe."

"Really?"

"It's what he said. Unfortunately, I engineered our little meeting before he had the chance to approach me. At least, that's what he claimed."

Lara lifted an eyebrow.

"I can see why you didn't believe him."

A gust of wind blew Ryan's wavy hair across his face. Lord, he was handsome. Even though he claimed to hate the new look, the beard and long hair suited him. It softened the tough, military edge.

"Exactly. And that's why I gave him my burner number. I wanted to offer him the chance to prove his mettle. It seems he's done just that."

She nodded. "Agreed."

"I'll have to work out a way to thank him properly for the warning."

He pointed ahead, towards a busy corner shop on the other side of the road, a hundred metres distant. It doubled as a grocery store, a pharmacy, and an off-licence. Sales posters decorated a large display window. Beneath a single door with pristine, red paintwork, a sign read "Mamet's Groceries – Open All Hours". Lara smiled at the association to the old sitcom and wondered whether Ryan would understand the reference.

"Not far now. Keep your eyes open," Ryan said, keeping his voice down. "We might bump into Arkwright and Granville."

His words answered her unasked question and she allowed her smile to grow.

After another brisk walk, they reached the shop and Ryan stopped.

"What next?"

"You buy some tablets for yourself, and a few more groceries for young Darwin," he said.

Although he returned her smile, his eyes kept scanning the neighbourhood. She took it as her cue and copied him.

In the distance, at the far end of the street, something dark and green stood out against the grey tarmac, the red brickwork, and the slate-black of the roofs. The same something stirred in the easing wind. Could it be vegetation battling to survive in the middle of one of western Europe's most polluted cities? Anybody's guess.

As she took in the scene, the sun broke through the

clouds and did a great deal to lift her gloom. When had she turned into such a misery? Perhaps it was the after-effects of her incident with Barcode. Either way, for Ryan's sake, she needed to snap out of her sudden dark mood.

He broke the spell. "The coast is clear. I'll wait here. By the way, if you see a pack of trail mix in there…"

"I'll pick one up for you, but I will check the sell-by date first."

He nodded. "You know me so well."

She pushed open the shop door and entered a dark Aladdin's cave of knickknacks and treasures, and the mouth-watering aroma of curry spices.

———

BY THE TIME she returned to Ryan, armed with the tablets, trail mix, an apple, and other assorted goodies, he had his mobile in hand and was sliding a thumb up the screen.

"Have you decided what to do with Damian?"

Ryan shrugged. "Not exactly. I'll discuss the options after I meet him this evening. Need to hear what he has to say first."

"Something else you didn't tell me?"

"Not guilty this time." Ryan flashed her the burner. "I've only just decided to invite young Damian for a drink. Fancy joining us?"

"Try stopping me."

His eyebrows jumped up. "After seeing what you did to that monster, Barcode, not likely, love. You scare me to death."

She jabbed him in the chest with a finger. "Quite right, Mister. And don't you forget it."

"Not me, wife. Never going to happen." He leaned

closer and whispered, "I think you're wonderful, Ms Orchard."

For the briefest of moments, Lara's heart seemed to stop beating.

"And," he continued, "until I know the lay of the land and have formed a battle plan, I'm not letting you out of my sight again. No arguments."

Ryan cared so much for her. It was clear that her brush with Barcode had upset him badly.

"What if I need to visit the powder room?" she asked, trying to make light of the episode.

Ryan stiffened and fixed her with his temporarily green eyes. The twinkle had gone, nothing but serious calculation remained. This was his "game face". No doubt about it. She'd seen it so many times before. He was in calculation mode.

"This isn't a joke, Lara. You might think you're equipped to protect yourself, but you aren't. Not fully. Back there, with Barcode, you were lucky. Really lucky. You took that big bugger by surprise. Next time—if there is a next time—he'll be on his guard." He grabbed her by the upper arms, his grip tight, almost painful. "I'm not having you in danger. If it comes to it, I'll join you in the bloody 'powder room' and stand outside your stall while you do your business."

He closed his eyes and the crushing grip eased. She leaned against him again, soaking up his warmth.

Lara wanted to fold herself into his arms and absorb his strength. She didn't want to admit it, not even to herself, but after the initial euphoria of dealing with Barcode and facing down the other two, fear had leached in. She could barely stop herself from breaking down into a puddle of terror. Only the worry of what such a breakdown would do to Ryan enabled her to hold herself together.

His jacket was wet and cold on her cheek, but she didn't pull away.

"You're soaked."

He shrugged. "That's what happens when it rains."

"You need to change your clothes or you'll catch your death."

"A little damp won't hurt me. I've been wetter." He released her and turned to face the way they'd come. "We need to check in on Darwin and head back to the hotel. I want to prep for our meeting tonight. A swift change of clothes, pick up some hardware, the usual."

"Hardware? Are we heading to Camden?"

He nodded. "We need some clothing for night-time operations. Just a sec."

She stood and watched as he pecked a text message into his mobile using his thumbs, slowly.

Ryan did most things supremely well—especially the physical stuff—but social media and civilian tech happened to be two significant weaknesses. She wanted to type for him, to hurry things along, but he wouldn't have appreciated her offer. For all his skills and wonderful traits, Ryan was still a man, after all.

He reread the message and hit send.

"Where are we meeting him?"

He held up his mobile and showed her the text, addressed to Damian Baines.

Meet tonight.
Allenby Reservoir, Hard Lane roundabout.
00:15.
Come alone. Unarmed.

"Allenby Reservoir?" she asked. "I thought you didn't know Walthamstow?"

"I don't," he answered, "but while you were picking up those groceries, I took a wander around the place. Scouting the area."

"How could you have done that? You didn't move from outside the shop."

He gave her one of his rare smiles and her heart melted anew.

"Satellite maps are wonderful things, Mrs Griffin. I've flown over the locale, virtually. Allenby Reservoir is the only decent open space around here for miles. I'll be able to see him coming from a long way off. Make sure he's alone."

"And me?"

Ryan looked her up and down, appraising, not admiring.

"You're not that much smaller than me," he said. "You'll look good in my lightweight body armour and battle fatigues. The colour will suit you."

"What colour is it?"

"Black."

The colour of mourning.

Lara wished she hadn't asked and prayed it wasn't an omen.

Chapter Thirteen

Saturday 20th February - Night

Allenby Reservoir, Walthamstow, London, England

23:17

Cosy and protected from possible heat-sensitive imaging by an ultra-lightweight, thermal blanket, Kaine raised the field glasses to his eyes and focussed on the roundabout. The single working streetlight lit the scene in a dull, yellow glow. The minor road leading from the Hard Lane round-about to the reservoir's main entrance gate remained completely free of traffic.

The reservoir was surrounded by chain-link, metal fenc-ing. Clearly, it's owners, London Water, didn't encourage overnight ramblers on the footpath surrounding their deep puddle in the middle of London. The dangers were self-evident. Muddy slopes dotted with brambles, trip hazards, and a few million litres of open water offered plenty of natural risks.

The guardhouse protecting the main gates stood dark, unoccupied. What had once been a twenty-four-hour, manned security operation had succumbed to the financial strictures of the age. Security had been outsourced, handed over to the private sector. Currently, a private security company provided an intermittent and sub-standard patrol of the area.

In the two hours since he and Lara had scaled the fence and taken up their surveillance position on the inside edge of the "doughnut"—a raised mound encircling the lozenge-shaped, artificial lake—a Group-16 security van had made a single desultory circuit. The rain, which had been intermittent all evening, chose that moment to start up again, encouraging the solitary guard to remain in his van. He hadn't even stopped to check whether the main gates were still locked.

Pitiful.

At his side and dressed to kill, literally, Lara blended into the darkness so well, if he hadn't seen her slide into position beside and behind him, he would hardly have known she was there. As expected, his light battledress fitted her reasonably well. Head-to-toe in black, and with night-time, camouflage makeup, she wore the look well. Lara hadn't even complained when he insisted she pull on the Kevlar ballistic vest, which was enhanced by ceramic chest and back SAPIs. When Kaine explained it meant "Small Arms Protective Inserts", Lara had frowned and threatened to hit him with the vest, hard enough for a few of the "darned SAPIs" to leave bruises.

Of course she knows what that means, idiot.

Even though the whole assembly weighed more than fifteen kilos, not far off a third of Lara's total body weight, she didn't make a peep.

A wonderful, brave, and beautiful woman. It killed him to place her in danger again, especially after he'd done that very thing the moment he tumbled into her existence.

Despite the life he currently led, a life outside the law and vilified as a terrorist by the media and the public at large, Lara Orchard was the single good thing to come out of the whole sorry mess.

His guts still roiled from the memory of Lara having to defend herself from Barcode's cowardly attack and all its potential ramifications. What would he have done if she'd been hurt? Kaine shook the thought from his mind. It was not the time to dwell on the negative. He needed his head to stay firmly in the game.

At some stage, Barcode would pay for laying a hand on her. By God, he would, but the payback would have to wait. Not for long, though. Not for bloody long.

When Lara had emerged unscathed from the tussle, he'd wanted nothing more than to pick her up and carry her to the hotel. Once there, he'd have packed their bags and headed for home. If not for a certain Glenmore Davits and his questionable death, and for his grandson who'd also suffered intimidation at the hands of the Tribe, Kaine would have done exactly that, but the situation had forced his hand.

Kaine's vow to protect The 83 was absolute, and he'd as soon lose an arm as willingly break it. Glenmore Davits had been a member of The 83, and Darwin still was. Kaine needed to clear Darwin's neighbourhood of its vermin. Which meant he'd have to wipe the Tribe from the map.

Walthamstow would have one less street gang, one less source of drugs, and one permanently crime-free district. Some of the Trust's millions would see to that, even if it meant he'd have to hire a long-term security team. It wouldn't be Group-16, though. Certainly not that bunch of amateurs.

Once again, Ryan Kaine was going to war—as he had so often in his life. This time, the only differences were that he had made the declaration, and he would define the rules of engagement.

Before the first skirmish began, he had two objectives. First, he needed a way to protect Lara. If he was going to bring down a small and lightly armed, but close-knit, enemy force, he couldn't do it while he had any concern for her safety. Second, he needed to gather as much intel as possible.

Hopefully, Damian Baines would cover the second requirement, which was the reason they were lying on the rain-dampened ground in the middle of London on a bitter February night.

To fulfil objective one, he required the help of a former colleague.

———

23:53.

"See anything?" Lara whispered, speaking for the first time since they'd settled down after having climbed the fence and tramped the three hundred metres to the best observation point in the grounds.

Her warmth pressed against his hip, offering comfort and confirmation of her safety. He'd placed her on his left, away from the Hard Lane entrance, protecting her from any potential danger. The camouflaged, thermal blanket crinkled and squeaked under her movement.

"Yep."

"Care to elaborate?"

"He arrived fifty minutes ago."

Lara stiffened. "Damian?"

"Yep."

She wriggled upwards, to the leading edge of the thermal blanket, drawing closer to his ear. "And you didn't bother telling me?"

"Nope."

"Why not?"

"Didn't see the need."

Her frustrated grunt made Kaine grin. She was acting exactly the way he expected—like a raw recruit on her first operation behind enemy lines. Tense, keen, and needy. Desperate for information. Desperate to feel as though she was being kept in the loop.

Time to go a little easier on her.

"I'd have told you when he arrived, but you were fast asleep."

"What? Darn it, Ryan. I wasn't asleep. How could I sleep out here on this frozen mudpack?"

"You're on a waterproof bedroll under a high-tog thermal blanket. Height of luxury, girl. Compared to some of the patrols I've been on, this bivouac rates as highly as a room in the Hilton."

An elbow dug into his ribs gently. "Idiot. I wasn't asleep. Too bloody uncomfortable to sleep."

"Your snoring nearly spooked young Damian, and he's nearly three hundred metres away."

"Ryan Liam Kaine, I do not snore!" she hissed.

"Yes, you do. It's a cute, little rumble followed by a sigh

and a tiny burble ...." He allowed the happy thought to trail off.

"Bloody hell, Ryan. Where is he?"

"Over there, by the main gates. See him?"

"No. What's he doing?"

"Waiting for us."

"How on earth——"

"Lara, you know the rules. Pipe down, Marine."

"Rules, *schmules*. We're not under fire, and you're not the boss of me."

She spoke so gently Kaine could barely hear her despite the fact she was close enough for her breath to warm his ear.

"Silly girl. Yes, I am. At least out here. Now pipe down."

Movement beside him in the darkness—or at least as dark as London would ever manage—told Kaine she'd raised her smaller, lighter, night glasses. More squirming told him she hadn't found her target. Without altering his scan of the target area, dimly lit under the halo of the single streetlight, he leaned against her, jogging her arms and spoiling her unsuccessful search.

Just because things were deadly serious, didn't mean he couldn't have a little fun.

"Ryan. Stop that," she breathed.

"Stop what?"

"Damn it. Sometimes you're nothing more than a big kid!"

"Oh no I'm not. Take that back or I'll tell teacher," he whispered.

Another soft harrumph made him smile again.

"Where is he? I don't see him anywhere."

Kaine gave her a few more seconds to search before answering. "See the Ford Focus by the guard house?"

More movement and the rustle of cloth scraping against cloth.

"Got it. The windows are dark and the engine's off. Is he inside?"

"Nope."

"Ryan, for goodness' sake."

"As soon as Damian arrived, he climbed out and ducked into the shadows. Take a line from the front of the car and follow the track around to the right until you come to that big hawthorn bush at the edge of the pool of light. See it?"

She swung her binoculars.

"Uh, yes. Got it."

"Look up and to the right, in the darkness. See the intermittent red glow? Our man with the scar's having a crafty ciggie. That's his third in less than an hour. The man smokes too much. Won't do anything for his lungs. Got him now?"

"Yes," she breathed excitedly. "I see him." More movement at his shoulder confirmed Lara's nod. "Hope he doesn't smoke around his pregnant fiancée, or the baby when it arrives."

That was his Lara, the perpetually caring medic.

"Not our problem."

"It'll be a problem for the poor kiddie," she said with a little more volume.

"Lara, keep your voice down or he'll hear us."

"No, he won't."

"How so?"

"There's a stiff wind in our faces, taking sound *away* from Damian. I could probably shout at the top of my voice from here and he still wouldn't hear me."

Again, Kaine smiled.

"Good girl. You have been paying attention. Go to the top of the class."

"Ryan, sarcasm doesn't become you."

"Not sarcasm, praise."

The red glow from the cigarette grew bright, then disappeared.

"That's another ciggie finished," he said, checking his watch. 00:07.

Damian would soon be growing even more fidgety.

"Is he alone?" Lara asked.

"Looks like it. Didn't see anyone around before he arrived, and no one's turned up since. I couldn't see anyone in the car when he opened the door and the courtesy light popped on. Damian's clearly not trained in covert ops. At the very least, he should have turned off the interior lights before opening the door. And there's no way he should have parked in such an exposed place."

"He's being cautious, though."

"Yep. If he's going to be of any use gathering intel, he needs to be. The man will be in a dangerous situation. I'm guessing he's pretty terrified right now."

"Can't blame him. And you're certain no one's arrived since we've been here?"

Kaine smiled at another good question.

"Unless they're a damned sight better at night-time ops than our Damian, which I doubt, he's alone."

"Okay, what now? Are we going down there to him?"

"Nope. He'll be coming to us."

Kaine shrugged and the thermal blanket moved, allowing another knife blade of bitter air into their improvised tent. The meeting time approached, but he awaited a new arrival, one who was taking his time. But he wouldn't be long.

"I'll give him a call in a couple of minutes. Let's see what—"

The alarm—a rear-facing motion detector he'd installed as they arrived—buzzed in his ear.

Lara jerked.

"Ryan, oh my God. Look out!"

Chapter Fourteen

Saturday 20th February - Lara Orchard

Allenby Reservoir, Walthamstow, London, England

23:17.

Lying scrunched under the groundsheet on the edge of a reservoir in the middle of a rain-soaked, and freezing, London night gave Lara time to think about what had happened since she'd thrown Barcode onto his backside.

Had she really defended herself from the thug?

Wow. Who'd have thought it?

She'd been lucky. Surprise had been her ally, but … to think what might have happened if Ryan hadn't arrived in time. It didn't bear dwelling on.

When Barcode and his cronies surrounded her, and Barcode attacked, she'd simply reacted. Months of training had asserted itself and she threw Barcode in the same way she'd thrown Ryan and Rollo hundreds of times in their makeshift dojo in the villa.

In truth, despite Ryan's calm insistence that they practise the moves diligently, and despite his absolute professionalism and his expertise in the training, Lara never imagined aikido would work in the real world. But it had. By God, it had.

If she was being honest with herself, she worked so hard during their hand-to-hand-combat training sessions because she loved being close to Ryan. She loved being part of his life, and she loved the physical and emotional high she reached during their workouts. Although her life as a vet specialising in large farm animals kept her reasonably strong and fit, her present state of physical conditioning was a revelation. Currently, she sported a set of toned abs an Olympic heptathlete would be proud to reveal in skimpy race gear. The way Ryan studied her new body when he thought she couldn't see was anything but a professional appraisal. But he kept reminding her that the newfound physical fitness and her growing military skillset served one purpose and one purpose only—to keep her safe. To keep her alive.

"I can't always be there to protect you," he'd said more than once, "but I can give you the skills you need to survive if I'm not around."

Hell, she loved him so much. If things were different, they could even be happy together. Maybe, one day …

Lara, pack it in.

She couldn't afford to think that far ahead. She needed to concentrate on the now. Things were serious.

When Barcode's head had smashed into the concrete, euphoria had flooded through her. It took over. In that brief moment, she'd been powerful, unbeatable. If Ryan hadn't stopped her, she'd have chased the brute and his buddies down the narrow alley to give them the hiding they deserved.

Bloodlust.

She'd never felt it before and hell, it had been wonderful at the time. But, the comedown had struck like a physical blow and, within moments of Ryan's arrival, the reaction had set in. The fear hit. If she hadn't been able to defend herself from Barcode, she would have been badly injured, or worse.

The expression on Ryan's face—the anger, the hurt, the helplessness, the fear—brought the danger home in one hard, vicious, belly punch. In the hours since the incident, rather than protest against Ryan's ultra-close attentiveness—as she might have done before Barcode's attack—she latched on tight. Despite him staying so close it bordered on paranoia, Ryan's mere presence made everything better. It made everything feel safer.

For the rest of the day, Lara had relaxed into the comfort and warmth of his protection. Since the attack, he'd been true to his word and not let her out of his sight except when she needed the bathroom.

The afternoon and early evening had passed as something of a blur.

After dropping in to take their leave of Darwin, who'd finally managed to rid himself of the cloying Primula Johnston, they'd left him and Brian Able to discuss the upcoming works and collected their hire car.

From the hotel, they'd driven straight to Ryan's place in Camden. Traffic held them up so badly, the ten-mile drive had taken nearly ninety minutes, but the journey had been worth it. She caught a rare peek at Ryan's life before it had collapsed around his ears. Although being minimalist to the point of spartan, the small apartment must have been worth a fortune, given the location. When he'd inherited it, he wouldn't have received much change from three quarters of a million pounds, yet the bedrooms were so small they barely allowed space for a bed. The kitchen had clearly never been used for making anything more involved than a cup of coffee. Neat and tidy, and devoid of warmth or a woman's touch, it did boast a hidden, room-sized compartment, stockpiled with military equipment.

The flat was pure Ryan Liam Kaine.

During the four hours they'd spent in the safe house, Ryan outlined his plan for the evening's meeting with Damian, allowing her little time for questions or debate. He took her through the plan as though it were a military operation which, of course, it was.

Ryan was in charge and, for the moment, she was his subordinate. Even though she grumbled about it from time to time in a lacklustre attempt to make him pause, Lara secretly loved it.

Shortly after they'd reached Camden, he'd handed her a set of clothing big enough for a man two sizes larger than her taut, fifty-six-kilo frame, together with a ballistic vest that weighed nearly as much as she did. He also instructed her in the correct way to don it.

Good God above, the thing was heavy. Stifling, too.

"I'm boiling," she said after stepping out of the empty bedroom and giving him a twirl. "Can hardly move in this stuff."

Ignoring her ungrateful complaints, he stepped close and ran his hands all over her, checking for fit. He adjusted the location of the ceramic breastplate in the ballistic vest and stepped away, head tilted in appraisal.

"Well?" she demanded, offering another encumbered twirl.

"A half-decent fit."

"That's all you have to say?"

His serious expression softened slightly. "If this were the villa, I might have said something along the lines of 'you make the most beautiful soldier the world has ever seen'."

"So, what's stopping you?" she interrupted, reaching for the clasp of the belt that was cinched tight to hold up her trousers.

"This is neither the time nor the place." He pointed her back to the bedroom. "You can change into civvies for now, but remember how to fit that vest properly. It might just save your life."

A few hours later, when they parked their car out of sight in a dark lane and marched half a mile in the freezing cold, February night, she learned to appreciate the thermal protection the battledress afforded her.

She appreciated it even more when they climbed the fence surrounding the reservoir and he made her lie on a wafer-thin strip of plastic he claimed was a bedding roll specifically brought along for her comfort. He threw a light sheet of night-camouflaged material over her, instructed her to lie still, and then disappeared for fifteen minutes, leaving her alone in the pitch black. The only sound came from the wind whistling through the tall grasses and the incessant hum of nearby traffic. No matter what the time, London's arterial roads seemed never to be silent, and it was never, ever, totally dark. It didn't take her long to grow accustomed to the smell of damp and mud, and rotting vegetation, though.

Only about an hour.

"Where've you been?" she asked in a shocked whisper

after he returned and slid under the sheet alongside her, letting in a blast of air so icy it made her teeth chatter.

Once safely hidden beneath the cover, Ryan threw a switch and a dull, red glow bloomed on his chest. According to Ryan's earlier briefing, the torch was similar in wavelength to the light used in a photographer's darkroom and would enable them to see each other without being seen from a distance. It would also help maintain their naturally developed night vision.

"I've scouted the surrounding area—all clear—and set up a secure perimeter. Here, put these on."

He handed her a pair of earbuds attached to a device half the size of a smartphone.

"What am I listening for?"

"I've set up two PIR Em-decs—"

"What's a PIR Em-dec?"

With a pair of binoculars raised to his eyes, and scanning the main entrance to the reservoir, he smiled.

"*PIR Em-decs*—passive, infrared, motion detectors. Military grade. If anything larger than a fox or a badger crosses the beams behind us, they'll send an alarm through those earbuds and—"

"And if that happens?"

"You roll to the left and give me room to manoeuvre. Understood?"

She gulped and nodded.

"Say it out loud. What will you do if something triggers the alarm?"

She sighed before answering. "Roll left to give you room."

"Good. Rehearse the action in your head. Drive it into your brain so you'll react immediately."

"Ryan, is this really necessary? We're meeting a potential ally. Aren't you being a little paranoid? To be honest, you're scaring me."

"Good," he said, without lowering the binoculars. "If you're scared, your reactions will be faster." He held his breath for a moment before lowering the glasses and turning on his side to face her. "Although there's nothing to suggest we're in danger, and Damian's done right by us so far, we don't know his real motivation. Hell, Lara, he might be acting against Barcode so he can scramble up the Tribe's hierarchy. At this stage, we simply don't know. I didn't survive almost a decade in the SBS by lowering my guard."

He rolled back into his original position and raised the binoculars again.

"Besides," he added, apparently as an afterthought, "this is your first operation in the field. We've trained hard and you have great instincts and aptitude, but—"

"I get it," she said, "this is a training opportunity and we're in full operational mode."

"Yes, Lara. That's it exactly. Now, please let me concentrate. Snuggle down lower into the nest and listen for that alarm."

At that precise moment, the true seriousness of their ongoing situation hit home. This was a live operation. Ryan wasn't going overboard. He knew training only went so far, even if it was field-based and realistic. Ryan wanted to know how she handled herself during a real operation in case she really did find herself alone one day. He was preparing her for life without him, in case he didn't come home from one of his missions.

Oh God.

The breath caught in her throat and she stifled a gasp.

No matter how well-trained and competent he was, Ryan constantly placed himself in danger. One day, he might come up against someone he couldn't beat. Someone more skilful, better equipped, stronger, faster.

The realisation nearly made her burst into tears, but she held herself together, for Ryan's sake.

But the thought knotted her stomach, made her sweat. As instructed, she squirmed deeper under the thermal sheet, lay on her front, and rested her head in her hands. The earbuds blocked out some of the ambient sound and, thankfully, remained resolutely silent.

UNBELIEVABLY, she *had* fallen asleep, despite her denials. The warmth under the thermal blanket, the reaction to the day's events, the sound-deadening effects of the earbuds, together with the rhythmic thump of Ryan's slow and solid heartrate, had all combined to relax her. She'd actually fallen asleep on the inner edge of a man-made hillock over-looking a reservoir in the middle of a wintery and some-times rainy London.

Who'd have thought?

There was something to be said for lying next to the man you loved, feeling his comforting and protective pres-ence. Even in the face of danger, humans were social animals and needed the touch of a loved one.

The glowing tip of Damian's cigarette focused her attention on the present moment.

After Ryan's wakeup call, with minimal movement, she'd been running through her stay-warm routine. As Ryan had taught her, almost from the first day of their life together, she worked from feet to neck and down again, tensing and relaxing each major muscle group in turn. The routine warmed muscles and joints that had stiffened from the immobility of sleep and of lying still. After the exercises, if she needed to move quickly, her body would react instantly, and the risk of injuring cold tissue would reduce. The exercises had become second nature to her.

Preparation for action. Fight or flight, or both.

Ryan thought of everything. He trained her well and, as a consequence, she worked diligently. If he needed her fit and prepared for instant action, that's what he would get.

"And you're certain no one's arrived since we've been here?" she asked, looking through her binoculars at the glowing, red tip of Damian's cigarette.

Ryan took a little while to answer, keeping his deep voice low, despite the driving, buffeting headwind which tugged at the camouflage sheet and chilled her face. "Unless they're a damned sight better at night-time ops than our Damian, which I doubt, he's alone."

"Okay, what now? Are we going down there to him?"

"Nope. He'll be coming to us."

Ryan moved, letting another blast of cold air under the blanket.

"I'll give him a call in a couple of minutes. Let's see what—"

Humming!

An alarm buzzed in her ears—the motion detectors.

What? God no!

Lara jerked.

"Ryan, oh my God. Look out!"

Chapter Fifteen

Sunday 21st February – Lara Orchard

Allenby Reservoir, Walthamstow, London, England

00:12.

Instinctively, Lara rolled to her left, downhill. The camouflaged sheet wrapped tight around her, restrictive, clinging.

Heart pounding, she expected rough hands to grab her, a blade to stab, slice. A bullet's report. Tissue damage. Pain.

Panic seized her. Blind, unthinking panic.

The sheet tightened around her legs and upper body, limiting movement, pinning her hands to her sides. Helpless. She was helpless. The weight of her body armour made things infinitely worse. She kicked, scrambled, dug her heels into soft earth.

Ryan.

Where's Ryan?

Was he safe? He'd be the first target.

Stop struggling.

Think.

It wouldn't help Ryan for her to panic, to draw his attention away from the danger. He needed to concentrate.

Lara stopped fighting. Rolled further away, down the incline. The thin wrapping loosened, and the restrictive binding eased. She slipped her arms free of the sheet. Crawled out into the bitter air. Able to breathe, but still disorientated.

Ryan?

"Ryan," she whispered, forcing herself not to scream his name.

Lara threw aside the clinging, lightweight material, rose to one knee, and crouched low, minimising her target profile. Keeping below the top of the mound.

She'd rolled into the heavy, frosty darkness of the downslope. Damp coldness sliced into the back of her neck—the damp of millions of litres of water. The spangled, orange glow of London formed a halo above and around her. Up, on top of the mound, a black-grey blanket of night, and … movement.

Two figures, dark, silhouettes. Backlit by the dim glow of the night-time city.

They faced each other, crouching, side-stepping. Prepared to lock in a dance of death.

On the left, Ryan stood, arms outstretched as though in defence.

On the right, a man, the reverse image of Ryan, dressed in black, head covered. He circled to his left, turned his back to Lara, and moved closer to Ryan.

Seconds. She had mere seconds.

She scrambled forwards, leaped on the man's back, pummelling, gouging, kicking.

"What the f—?"

"Lara!"

A strong hand grabbed her wrist and tugged. The man she straddled dipped a shoulder. She flew through the air, head over feet, legs and arms flailing. She landed with a thump on the soft earth, winded but unhurt.

Again, she rolled, this time away from her attacker, away from Ryan, giving him room to act. Breathing hard, Lara scrambled to her feet, fingers gripping the long grass, using it for leverage. Up and on balance, she formed fists, ready to advance.

No one was going to hurt Ryan. No one. Not if she had anything to do with it.

"Lara, no! He's a friend."

The stranger backed two paces away, hands up. Movement at her side. Ryan's familiar shape and aura surrounded her.

"Ryan? What the—"

"Take it easy, Lara. This is Sergeant Blake. A former colleague of mine."

Holding her firmly by the upper arm, Ryan turned her to face the newcomer, who grinned, his white teeth glowing from a jet-black, smile-dimpled face.

"Evening, Doc," he said, pushing out a hand for her to shake. "The captain said as 'ow you weren't someone to mess with. Seems 'e was right. Nice to meet you at last."

His voice was deep, his accent local and strong. A Londoner.

Taller than Ryan by at least five centimetres, but of a

similar build, she finally recognised him from his dossier on file.

"Oh my God, Connor ... Connor Blake," she said, her voice hushed. "I'm so sorry. I thought you were ... Are you okay?"

The smile didn't falter, but he rubbed the back of his head through his dark green, woollen cap. "Nothing a week in a nice, warm infirmary on full pay wouldn't cure, Doc. Assuming you'll sign my medical chit."

"Maybe the *captain* can sign it. He's the one who didn't warn me you'd be sneaking up on us," Lara growled—couldn't help herself.

The wide grin faded a little and the dimples shallowed as Connor shot a glance at his captain.

Ryan coughed before saying, "I take it there's no one else around to concern us, Sergeant?"

"That's right, Captain. I've recced the whole area. There ain't no one 'ereabouts but the target."

"Excellent. Thank you. Good work. Would you mind giving young Damian a bell and inviting him up here for a chat? He must be feeling a little parky. And do it now, please. It appears the team's medic and I have some operational issues to discuss."

Ryan spoke, as calm as anything, clearly trying not to match the newcomer's smile.

Connor threw him a smart salute and nodded to her before turning his back on them and facing the main gatehouse. He dropped to one knee, pulled out a mobile phone, and started dialling.

Fists clamped against her hips, jaw clenched tight, Lara confronted him. "Ryan, what the bloody hell—"

He pressed a finger to his lips, pointed away from Connor and led her part-way down the hill towards the water, but she'd had more than enough. He'd been playing games at her expense. Embarrassing her in front of Connor. Why? Why would he do such a thing? Warmth flooded to her cheeks, her eyes moistened. As far as she knew, he'd never played pranks on a mission before. Whatever the reasons, his actions hurt and she wasn't going to let him brush her off this time.

Before they stopped walking, she opened up again.

"Ryan, this is far enough. Why didn't you tell me about Connor? That was so embarrassing."

Ryan stopped and faced her. He dropped to one knee, making sure he was well below the top of the ridge, and indicated for her to follow suit. She kneeled with him, her anger ebbing away when she read the seriousness of his expression, lit by the nightlight on his chest.

"Lara, this isn't a joke. You were brilliant. Your reactions were superb."

"A test? It was another bloody test?"

He shook his head. "Only in part. Despite all your training, I needed to know how you'd fare in the field. When Connor showed up, your reactions … they were perfect."

"Perfect! Are you mad?" Lara hissed, struggling to keep control of her confused and raging emotions. "I was terrified!"

"I know, love, but you didn't freeze. You did exactly as I instructed. You rolled away in the right direction, kept your voice down, and even attacked the poor guy—didn't expect you to do that, mind. Brave but foolhardy. You could have been seriously hurt."

She wanted to punch his arm, but such a loss of control would not have helped her state of mind.

"*He* could have been seriously hurt, you mean. I panicked, Ryan. I wasn't in any form of control. I was bloody well terrified out of my skin. That was a horrible thing to do," she said, the trembling in her voice evident, despite the enforced whisper.

Tears blurred her vision, but she wiped them away with her knuckles.

"My beautiful girl," he said, lowering his voice to a breathless whisper and pulling her close—close enough for her to absorb his warmth, "when I saw you tangle with Barcode this afternoon, it turned my stomach. It brought home how much danger I'd dragged you into, and it scared the crap out of me. And when you were in such a hurry to chase them into the dark alley … Love, I can't tell you often enough. This is not a game. This is deadly serious.

"If someone ever hurt you I'm not sure what I'd do to them"—he pushed her away and held her at arm's length, his expression cold and deadly—"but, it would be extremely violent, excruciatingly painful … and permanent."

Ryan's confession and the tears glistening in his eyes forced the remaining anger from her system as quickly as it had arrived. She cupped his cheek and leaned in for a kiss, but he straightened and backed away.

"Not here," he said softly, shaking his head. "Not in front of the men."

"The men?"

He nodded towards the top of the ridge. Connor had been joined by another man, this one squat and dressed in a loose, dark hoodie—Damian Baines. Both men looked down towards them, but as she and Ryan were in deep shadow, they probably couldn't make out much. No matter the situation, Ryan always seemed to be fully aware of his surroundings. His razor-sharp senses kept him alive in his horrific world of death and destruction.

"Sorry," she said, head lowered.

Ryan hooked a finger under her chin and lifted her head gently. He smiled. "No need to apologise to me, love. But do hold that thought. I'll explain everything after we've had our chat with Damian."

"Promise?"

"Yes. I promise. Okay, let's go. Our audience awaits."

He helped her climb the hill to the waiting men, where he shot out a hand to a flinching Damian and said, "Thanks for the warning yesterday afternoon. Most appreciated."

After the initial recoil, Damian straightened and took Ryan's hand briefly. Greeting over, a sheepish grin softened his expression, and he shot a hooded sideways glance at Lara. "Way I heard it, Mr Griffin, yo' wife weren't in as much danger as I thought. Seems she whooped Barcode's ass, real good. Whole Tribe's talkin' 'bout it. Laughin' they fool heads off, mostly."

"Nevertheless," Ryan said, his expression still serious, "Mrs Griffin and I appreciate your efforts. You've proven yourself worthy of our trust, and you're presence here— alone—adds further proof."

Damian raised a hand as though he were in class, wanting to ask a question. "One thing, though. I … don' really know how to say this."

"Speak up, Damian. You're amongst friends. Blake is one of my most trusted men."

Connor gave no reaction to the compliment, but his eyes kept scanning the surrounding area. Lara had never met the man before, but she had read his military dossier and, according to it and to Ryan's personal written appraisal, Connor Blake was the strong, silent, and depend- able sort. His present demeanour, standing quiet guard over them, confirmed Ryan's assessment perfectly.

With Ryan and men like Connor in her corner, Lara allowed herself to relax a little.

Damian tilted his head towards Connor and seemed to study him intently before continuing. "It's just that, Barcode don' react like most people. The brother's weird, y'know?" Rhino tapped his temple with an index finger. "Touched in the head."

"We know."

"Just sayin' you wanna watch out for him. Your woman"—he winced and shook his head—"sorry, I mean, Mrs Griffin. She ain't safe from him. Barcode won't take kindly to bein' dissed none. He'll be on fire to make up for what he lost, y'know? His respec'. Just sayin' is all."

Ryan patted a hand in the space between them. "We appreciate the warning. You can rest assured that young Byron—"

"Who?"

"Byron Codell. It's Barcode's real name."

"It is?"

Ryan nodded. "It is, indeed."

"Never knew. Don' look like no 'Byron' to me."

"Nonetheless," Ryan continued, "my wife is now under Sergeant Blake's protection and, if you think I'm tough—"

"I do," Damian interrupted, rubbing the side of his neck. "I really do."

Ryan's grin contained little mirth. "As I was saying, if you think I'm tough, Sergeant Blake makes me look like a wimp."

Lara didn't miss the shake of Connor's head, but since Damian was standing with his back to the sergeant, he wouldn't have seen the action.

"But to anyone who asks, Connor Blake is a distant relative of Glenmorc Davits, coming to pay his cousin Darwin a visit. Is that clear?"

Damian dipped his head. "Sure 'nough. Ain't no one gonna hear nothin' from me 'bout it. You can trust me on that one. Take it to the bank."

Ryan stepped a little closer to the scarred man and dropped a hand on his shoulder.

"You know, Damian?" he said, calmness and confidence clear in his tone, "I really think we can." He lifted his hand from the young man's shoulder and pointed towards the reservoir's main gates. "Now, since there's no one else around to disturb us, let's go find somewhere warm and bright for our conference, shall we? We passed a late-night café on the way here. If you fancy it, I'll stand you a latte."

He stepped back and, always on guard, allowed Damian to lead the way. Lara took up her position on Ryan's left side, and Sergeant Connor Blake assumed the role of rear gunner.

She'd rarely felt safer.

Chapter Sixteen

Sunday 21st February - Lara Orchard

The Café, Walthamstow, London, England

00:40.

After spending a large portion of the evening lying on the frozen earth, Lara reached The Café chilled to the core, rain washed, and unable to stop shivering. She expected to need time to acclimatise to the warmth of the place, but the aroma of freshly ground coffee and the internal glow of the drink itself, together with sticky buns—two *pain aux raisins*—soon did the trick. In fact, the high-calorie snack worked so well in generating internal heat, she struggled to stay awake, nestled next to Ryan in the most isolated corner of the cosy, little café.

Before committing to enter the place, Ryan had sent

Connor in for a quick reconnaissance. Once satisfied it was empty of customers, Ryan led them inside, where the heat and humidity caused Lara to melt into a bath of sweat under her heavy clothes. It also made the non-prescription glasses, which she wore to partially hide her hazel eyes, fog into opacity.

While they waited in the entrance area, Ryan strode up to the service counter. He entered into a private and lightning-fast conversation with the barista, a thin-faced man in his late twenties with swarthy, Mediterranean looks, and his slicked-back hair held in place in a ponytail.

Ryan had slipped the barista two fifty-pound notes from his wallet, and placed the order they'd agreed to in the car on the way from the reservoir—four large Americanos and a trayful of assorted pastries.

The barista turned away to work his coffee-making miracle and Ryan waved them inside, pointing to a booth in the farthest corner from the entrance. The booth was lined with bench seats surrounding a low table. Before sitting, Connor and Ryan removed the two high-backed armchairs that enclosed the booth making it a cosy, little enclave—chairs that would have blocked their sightlines.

Lara took her place in the corner, flanked by Connor and Ryan.

As usual, Ryan sat with his back against a solid wall within easy access of the nearest point of egress—in this case, a door at the side of the building which led to the toilets and the fire exit.

Ryan faced the main entrance, watching, always on guard. Connor sat at a right angle to Ryan, doing the same thing. Between the two of them, they had the whole coffee house covered. Despite the place being empty, Ryan would never lower his defences, not in public, and definitely not with Lara exposed to potential danger.

Lara loved Ryan for the way he protected her, and for the way he would risk his life or his freedom for anyone he saw as deserving. Even though she found it difficult to condone the way he'd deliver a terrible vengeance on anyone he considered worthy of the punishment, she grew more understanding of it the longer she spent in his world. She'd even grown to accept the stark necessity.

Ryan's moral certainty would beat any legal code ever written, and Lara trusted him completely.

The low coffee table separated her from Damian, who sat hunched and brooding. His eyes never settled, but darted left and right, and he wilted under Ryan and Connor's steely gaze. Damian still wore his heavy coat, the only concession he'd given the stifling heat being to drop the hood and lower the zip to half-way. The square man seemed impervious to heat, but allergic to light, if his slouched, cowering demeanour was anything to go by.

"Nice place," Connor said, dividing his attention between Damian and the entrance. "Cosy. You book it in advance, sir?"

"Yep. Mrs Griffin and I dropped in on the way to the reservoir. Armando normally closes at midnight since there's not much late trade in this part of town. I 'encouraged' him to stay open for a few hours." Ryan smiled. "He's a very amenable chap, is our Armando."

"Cost much?"

"Not really."

"I saw the century you gave 'im. Not much for a private party. Cushty."

"That was in addition to the four hundred I handed him up front."

Connor waggled his head from side to side. "Gotcha. A monkey's more like it for a private party in a place like this and in this area."

The quiet conversation continued, probably designed to relax Damian, until Armando arrived, carrying a tray filled with their order. He set it on the coffee table and palmed two more of Ryan's banknotes into his back pocket—these ones twenties.

"Thanks, Armando," Ryan said. "Do you have somewhere out back you can crash for the next couple of hours?"

The barista smiled knowingly and added a slight nod. "No worries, mate," he said, his Aussie twang stretching out the vowels. "Take as long as you like. Storeroom's got a bar fridge, a dunny, and a bunk. Give me a hoy when you're done, and I'll lock up after you."

Once Armando had disappeared through a door behind the bar, Connor turned his eyes on Damian and said, "Now that Armando Dundee's out of the way, mind telling me what's goin' on, sir? Your message was a little ... terse. 'I need your 'elp,' and some co-ordinates. You weren't never one for wasting your words."

A frowning Damian followed the conversation with barely hidden confusion. He didn't have a clue who Ryan and Connor really were, but seemed happy to let them take the lead, as long as they left any physical jousting out of the equation.

"You'll have a full briefing at base, Sergeant, but for now, we need to get down to business," Kaine said then pierced Damian with his sharpest stare.

Lara almost felt sorry for the shuddering gang member.

"For the benefit of Sergeant Blake, please repeat what

you told me when we first met. Leave nothing out. We're all friends here."

After a faltering start, and under Ryan's crisp encouragement, Damian outlined the situation with the Tribe's takeover by the enigmatic TM. He ended with, "Been a clusterfuck—er, a disaster from start to finish, it has. I woulda left the Tribe months ago if I thought I could make it out alive. Scared, I am. Somehow, TM gets to know everythin'. If he … If he finds out I've been talkin' to you, I'm a dead man. My shorty and the baby, too."

"So," Ryan said, "why the warning text yesterday?"

Truck headlights raked the café's windows, illuminating all but their shadowy corner. Damian jerked in his chair. His frightened eyes followed the vehicle as it turned right at a set of traffic lights, headed along the empty road, and disappeared into the night. He relaxed tense neck muscles before answering.

"What you said and what you did made me think you'd be as tough as TM an' the Heavies. Figured if I help you save your wo—er, Mrs Griffin"—he slid Lara an apologetic glance—"I'm thinkin' you'd remember and help me with *my* family."

The fact that Connor failed to react to Damian's use of her cover name—both in the café and at the reservoir—explained why Ryan felt he could trust the quiet Londoner. He was evidently quick on the uptake and able to hold his tongue when necessary.

"And how do you think I might do that, Damian?" Ryan asked.

"I guess you plan to take over the hood?"

"Do you?"

The gang member lowered his head and looked at Ryan through darkened eyes. "You don'?"

Ryan tilted his head. "You don't need to worry about my organisation's intentions towards the Tribe, Damian, old chap. Let's just say this. If you play it right by us, we'll do the same by you."

"Yeah?"

"You have my word. If you want to dig yourself out from under this mound of doggy do-do, I'll provide the shovel. And, as a parting gift, we'll even add enough shekels to help you start a new and comfortable life with Ariel and the little one."

"You will?"

"We will."

Damian cut Lara a sideways glance, then returned his focus to Ryan. "What I gotta do to earn the shovel and the coin?"

"Simple. All we need is your help to identify Top Man and—"

Damian almost dropped his mug onto the coffee table. He half-rose but stopped when Ryan raised a hand and pointed down.

"Sit!"

Damian dropped back into his seat and landed like a sack of spuds.

"You want me to finger TM? No way, man. Can't be done. No way. Too fuckin' dangerous. People who cross TM disappear when he want them to disappear. An' they only turn up again if him wanna make a statement."

"Don't worry, Damian. We're not asking you to do anything dangerous. We just need some intelligence. Information to help us take down the big player. Once we have the head of the snake in the bag, the rest will be a simple matter of logistics."

Connor leaned forwards, elbows on knees, chin resting

on his interlaced fingers, nodding his encouragement. If Lara didn't know better, he and Ryan might have choreographed their moves in advance.

For her part, Lara remained as still as possible, trying to keep her face expressionless, showing outward calm while her insides quailed. How could Ryan and Connor be so fearless? They were talking about taking on a gang with God knew how many members. Two men and Lara against maybe dozens of street thugs, and they had no idea how well they were armed.

No. What was she thinking?

Ryan would no more allow her into a dangerous situation than he would turn his back on Darwin Moore. He would most likely order Connor to protect her and take on the whole Tribe alone.

What was she going to do? How could she turn things around?

She'd call Rollo and Danny. Maybe they could talk some sense into Ryan. But no, who was she trying to fool? They'd never go against his orders. Every one of Ryan's old colleagues would do exactly what he asked of them. And worse, Ryan would never forgive her for interfering.

No, she'd have to think of another way. She'd help, no matter what the personal cost. But she'd have to do it without letting Ryan know anything about her interference. After all, she'd proved her worth against Barcode. She wasn't some weak-willed heroine in a Victorian-era novel needing to be saved by the devastatingly handsome leading man.

However, truth be told, Ryan Kaine *was* the devastatingly handsome leading man in her life. Eyes so brown, and a smile so warm. How she loved it when he smiled at her.

Yes ... this place is nice. Warm ... cosy ...

Her eyelids drooped, and she struggled to keep them open.

"I ain't no James Bond," Damian protested, snapping Lara out of her dream world and returning her to the relaxing warmth of the café. "I already tol' you, Mr Griffin, TM's untouchable. Don' even think Demarcus Williams know who the guy is. Leastways, that what the rest of the boys reckon."

Ryan nodded his understanding and paused for a moment before speaking again. "This comms link of his, how is it initiated?"

"Huh?"

"How does Demarcus Williams contact TM? And how does Demarcus know when TM has a message to deliver to the Tribe?"

Damian shrugged. "Hell if I know. Happens on dif'rent days of the week, but always at eight o'clock in the evenin'. I got no idea how TM talks to Demarcus or the other way 'round. Prob'ly by phone, but I ain't never seen them converse in private."

Connor spoke for the first time in ages. "You're certain Demarcus and TM are two different people? They ain't one and the same person, playing games?"

Damian paused for a moment, his frown deepening in thought. "Nah. I thought the same thing myself early on. But it ain't possible. The way everyone talks at the same time and answers TM's questions, it can' be a recordin' or nothin'."

"And Demarcus is always in the room when TM's on the monitor?" Lara asked, unable to keep out of the interrogation and needing to add her input to keep awake.

Ryan's brief nod told Lara it was okay for her to contribute.

Again, Damian shrugged and, again, his head tilted to one side as he did so. Without doubt, the serious scar tissue restricted free movement of his neck. It was clear from the way he resorted to turning his shoulders as much as his head when looking from Connor to Ryan, that his injury was causing significant discomfort. The evidence stood out clear and strong. Medical care in Her Majesty's custodial system left plenty to be desired.

If things worked out the way she hoped, and if Damian proved as helpful as Ryan clearly expected, maybe they could release some funds to provide reconstructive surgery. They had a long way to go before that could be a considera-tion, though.

"Nah," Damian said after a while. "Can't remember a time when Demarcus weren't in the room when TM were on the big screen. The boys and me think Demarcus and the other Heavies are watchin' the Tribesman and reportin' any trouble to TM after."

"See?" Ryan said. "You're already providing confirma-tion of the intel we've received from our other informant. That in itself makes you a valuable backup resource."

Connor's expression remained unchanged, but a slight catch in his breath confirmed he had no idea about Ryan's phantom, second, inside man. The minute they parted company with Damian, the three of them needed to have an in-depth discussion—a full debrief.

Lara worked hard to hide the smirk that formed when she thought of Ryan without his briefs. Hell. Her mind had started wandering—again.

God, but she was struggling to fight the fatigue. Really struggling.

How could Ryan stay so alert for so long? He'd been up since before dawn that morning. No, since dawn the *previous* morning, since it was past midnight and had already turned into Sunday.

She covered her mouth to hide a yawn.

Damn it, Lara. Stay awake. Don't let Ryan down.

For the first time since she'd seen Damian, his customary scowl softened. Compliments, it seemed, worked as well on gang members as they did on anyone else. Damian's shoulders straightened and he sat up taller in his chair.

"Hey, Mr Griffin, I don' know who else you got workin' for you in the Tribe, but they ain't no way as good as me. Ain't gonna get you as much info as me. If you promised him the same deal as you made me an' Ariel, he won't have the same motivation as me, neither."

Ryan leaned away and gave Damian another appraising stare. "And what makes you say that?"

Damian nodded and jabbed himself in the chest with a thumb the size of a baby cucumber. "I'm the only Tribesman with a family they care 'bout, and I know fo' sure your other spy ain't one of TM's Heavies."

"Okay," Ryan said, "that remains to be seen, but I can certainly give you the benefit of any doubt. You'll need to prove your worth, though, but if you do ..." He paused, apparently, for emphasis.

"Yeah?" Damian asked, leaning forwards.

"If you do, we'll make sure you and your family are set up for life. Relocation, new identities, financial security, the works. Think of it as witness protection."

"Really? You can do that? You a Fed?"

Ryan's extended sigh screamed exasperation. "Damian," he said, "this isn't the US, we don't have the Feds here. However, in our own small way, if we can't match their total resources, we can at least come close. So, are you in? Do you want the chance of a new life away from Walthamstow and the Tribe?"

Damian placed his palms flat on the coffee table. "Ain't nothin' keepin' me in this crap-hole 'sides fear and poverty. I don' got no family but Ariel an' the new baby."

Ryan smiled. "That's good, Damian. Really good. We have ourselves a deal."

"What I gotta do?"

"We'll start easy. When's TM's next transmission?"

"Tonight," Rhino answered, without hesitation.

"Twenty hundred hours?"

Damian scrunched up his face. "Er, yeah, s'right. Eight o'clock this evenin'."

The second answer took a little longer, and required him to convert military timing into civilian by subtracting twelve. In Damian they weren't exactly dealing with a man in possession of a lightning-fast mind.

"If you wants me to record the meetin' or take a photo of the screen, that ain't happenin', Mr Griffin. TM don't allow no one to use phones during a meetin'. If Demarcus Williams or any of the Heavies see us take out a phone when he on screen, the man caught gets a serious beatin'. A beatin' in front of the Tribe." He took a breath.

"First and only time it happened, they broke the boy's jaw an' one of his kneecaps. Poor kid ended up in hospital for three weeks. Lost both his front teeth, too. Walks with a limp now, permanent. One of the little ones. Only thirteen, answerin' a call from his mamma. Pitiful, it was. The kid was wailin' and screamin' for help." Damian swallowed hard and shook his head slowly.

Lara slammed the side of her fist on the table, unable to help herself, fatigue driven away by anger at the thought of a child being beaten senseless by a gang of fully grown men.

"None of you lifted a finger to help?" she demanded. "How many Heavies were there, compared with the rest of you?"

Damian lowered his head, seemingly in shame. "There was four of them in the Hub at the time, Mrs Griffin. All with clubs and knives. On top o' that, Demarcus Williams carries a gun. A chrome-plated semi-automatic. An' he ain't afraid to use it, neither. We all seen him shootin' rats in the courtyard out back overnight when the trains go past to mask the sound. Good shot … from what I witnessed. Cold fucker, he is, too. S'cuse my language, Mrs Griffin. The asshole loves to kill and hurt things. His eyes was shinin' when he was beatin' up the kid, too. Laughin', he was. Nah, we couldn't do nothin' to help him. I wanted to, though. Honest to God, I did."

Ryan covered Lara's right hand with his and squeezed a little, offering comfort and encouraging restraint.

"Okay, Damian," Ryan said, teeth gritted, lips a thin, stiff line, "I understand."

Lara understood, too. She understood the meaning behind Ryan's expression. He wasn't a man to let someone get away with attacking a child, not if he could do anything about it. She already knew him too well. In the previous fourteen hours, Ryan had marked three men for his particular brand of attention—Barcode for laying his hands on her, Demarcus Williams for leading the attack on a child, and Top Man for instigating the whole, sorry business.

Given her basic, pacifist nature, she almost felt sorry for the three men slated for Ryan's retribution. Almost, but not quite.

Damian took a deep breath. "That weren't the worst of it, though. Nah. TM was eggin' the Heavies on and cacklin' the whole time. The asshole's laugh sounded real strange through the electronics. Creepy, y'know? Like somethin' from an 'orror flick. Made me shiver, it did, and I've seen plenty of beatin's, both inside and outside of a prison cell."

He raised his left hand to finger the ugly scar, which stood out pale grey against his ebony skin.

"When they dragged the kid out, unconscious, TM called it a lesson we all needed to see. No one's used a phone in a meetin' since, and I ain't gonna be the one to start."

"That's pretty much what our intel is saying," Ryan said, pursing his lips, deep in thought. "We'll have to come up with a simpler, low-tech way of signalling when TM's making his transmission. All we need to know is when TM's online and when he's off again. One of our men will track his signal back to an IP address, and then we'll have his location and his identity."

Damian frowned and leaned back a little. "Whacha mean, 'low-tech', Mr Griffin?"

"Is there a window in the meeting room?"

Damian hesitated before replying.

"Yeah. The den used to be a school. A real old school. Back a hundred years or so. There's plenty of windows in the Hub. Used to be the main assembly hall."

"Covered or uncovered?"

"The windows? Yeah, they got thick, black curtains blockin' all the windows facin' the road out front and on one of the sides. The other side looks out over the railway lines. Nobody can see in for miles. An' they're covered with vertical blinds, y'know?"

"Okay," Ryan said, nodding and giving Lara's hand another squeeze, "I know how we can handle this. Don't worry, Damian. I'm sure we can do this without causing you any distress."

For the next couple of minutes, Ryan explained what he expected of Damian and made him repeat the instructions to ensure the young man knew his precise role.

"Okay now, Damian," Ryan said. "You've finished with your coffee, I see."

Ryan stood and rested a hand on Lara's shoulder when she tried to stand with him. She relaxed back into the stiff padding of the bench seat and took note of the way Ryan dismissed Damian at the end of the meeting. He was used to commanding men, and it showed in their responses.

Damian jumped to his feet with the speed of a jackrabbit. "Yeah, Mr Griffin. I's finished. And don' worry, sir. I ain't gonna let you down. I got this."

"Excellent, excellent. You won't mind finding your own way back to your car, will you? It's only a couple of kilometres. You know the way from here, right?"

Disappointment flashed in Damian's eyes, but he nodded meekly and headed for the exit. Halfway to the door, he turned and dipped his head to Connor and to Lara. "Mrs Griffin, I really did wanna help that kid, y'know. The kid with the busted kneecap, I mean. Hated watchin' it happen."

She returned his nod, but didn't otherwise respond. The powerfully built man turned, pushed through the door—the bell rang—and headed into the cold, wet night.

The second he disappeared past the window and around the side of the building, Ryan nodded to Connor, who jumped up and left the café through the fire exit.

"Ryan?" Lara asked, without feeling the need to elaborate.

Ryan smiled. "Not to worry, love. Connor's going to make sure our friend doesn't lose his way."

"You mean he's confirming Damian's not doubling back and trying to eavesdrop on our conversation?"

"My word, you are learning my moves, aren't you. I'm impressed."

She smiled.

I hope so, darling. I truly hope so.

Since the day they met, she'd been studying Ryan Kaine and his methods closely, trying to absorb everything that made him tick.

Like it or not, sooner or later, Ryan was going to need her help. And, when that day arrived, she wouldn't let him down. She would never let him down.

Chapter Seventeen

Sunday 21st February - Night

The Café, Walthamstow, London, England

01:35.

Kaine listened for movement from the room behind the serving counter. Nothing. The barista Connor had dubbed "Armando Dundee" hadn't woken to the tinging of the doorbell. It appeared as though Aussie baristas slept deeply.

"Fancy a top up?" he asked, pointing to Lara's empty mug.

"Yes, please, Ryan. It might help keep me awake."

He nodded. "You look exhausted, love."

"Gee, thanks. You do know just how to flatter a girl."

"You don't need any of my bull. It's been a long and tiring day. I'm in need of sleep, too."

"You are?"

"Of course."

"But you don't show it. You look as fresh as you did this morning, or was it yesterday morning? Damn it, I'm used to doing all-nighters at work, but this is different. I'm completely grey."

"Don't worry about it, love. I'm more used to the tension of an op than you are. That's all. Now"—he rubbed his hands together—"how about I fix you that drink while we wait for young Connor's return?"

"You know how to work one of those fancy coffee makers?"

"Surely you can't doubt my skills as a barista?"

"Certainly do. I've seen you in the kitchen, remember. It's like you're waging war on the crockery."

He placed the flat of his hand over his heart. "Ouch, you cut me to the core."

Lara smiled. Even though she was shattered and in the middle of an operation, she could still stir his heart.

Lara eased out of her seat and sidestepped her way around the far side of the coffee table, pausing only long enough to give him a peck on the cheek along the way.

"That was nice, but I was serious when I asked you not to do it in front of the men," he said, following her to the counter.

"Why not? Bad for discipline?"

"Nope. They'll all expect a kiss."

He shot her another smile, which she returned then started messing with the chrome-and-black device that wouldn't have looked out of place in the cockpit of a passenger jet.

After a few minutes, the machine spluttered out its creation and Lara filled fresh mugs. Armando Dundee had earned enough that night, he wouldn't baulk at washing a few cups. She added sugar to hers—she needed the energy boost—but left Ryan's unadulterated.

"Here you are, *Captain*," she said, playing the subordinate to perfection.

He took a grateful sip and thanked her with a smile and a nod.

They returned to the corner booth and she leaned heavily against him, leaving her cup on the table, untouched. He threw an arm around her shoulders and she snuggled tight. Seconds later, the steady rhythm of her gentle breathing told him she'd drifted into a deep sleep. He sat still, nursing both his coffee and his girl.

He stared at the top of her head and smiled. God, she impressed the hell out of him.

Since being forced to join him in hiding, Lara had treated everything from bullet wounds to stabbings. She'd even tended to the physical and psychological injuries suffered by Angela Shafer with more care and attention than any "real" doctor he'd ever met. In each situation, she'd reacted brilliantly. Her performance during medical emergencies could not be faulted. Her additional studies into the field of human medicine had certainly served the team and The 83 well. As things stood, Kaine trusted her skills better than some of the field medics who'd worked on him over the years.

On the one hand, her presence at his side gave him comfort, on the other it presented a huge challenge.

Rarely during a mission had he felt so on edge. He couldn't let anything hurt her, which was the main reason he'd summoned Connor. They'd worked together a number of times, and the former squaddie had always acquitted himself supremely well. On top of everything else, for this particular mission, his colour and his background as a born-and-bred Londoner made him a perfect addition to their small team. Connor wouldn't look out of place anywhere in the neighbourhood, and he would be perfect as Lara's personal bodyguard. A win-win all around, and one that would allow Kaine free reign to handle anything the Tribe could throw at him—at least in theory.

With Lara's sleeping weight pressing against his arm, he considered the upcoming mission. The Tribe wasn't a well-organised, military unit, or even a heavily armed and disorganised militia. They were, at worst, half a dozen paid men, the shadowy TM, and a bunch of unwilling kids who, if he believed Damian, had been forcibly co-opted into the fight. If he took out TM and the Heavies, in all likelihood, most of the Tribesmen would run and hide. A question mark hung over Barcode, of course, but Kaine had a special place set aside for the man with the ridiculous tattoo. A place of pain and deep suffering.

Despite the apparent weakness of his opposition, Kaine knew better than to underestimate them entirely.

One option would be to wait until he'd gathered more men around him, and that remained a potential alternative. If a direct assault on the Tribe's Hub proved too complicated or dangerous, he might well call in more support. On the other hand, any delay would extend Lara's exposure to danger, not to mention Darwin Moore's discomfort, and that of his neighbours.

For the moment, all his options remained open.

The first tasks on the agenda were to assess the full strengths and weaknesses of the opposition and identify TM. Only then would he be able to formulate a battle plan, making sure he and Lara remained undercover.

LARA MOVED UNDER HIS ARM.

"How long will Connor be?" she said, her words muffled by his jacket.

"I thought you were asleep."

"Just needed a little catnap," Lara slurred. "It'll tide me over until we're back at the hotel."

Lara pushed herself away and arched her back. She stretched an arm towards the ceiling and used her free hand to hide an expansive yawn. He passed across her mug of coffee.

She took a sip and winced. "Cold."

"That's hardly surprising. You've been asleep almost thirty minutes."

"Really?"

"Given me a dead arm, too," he said, flexing his fingers and working the life back into his hand.

"No sign of Connor?"

"He shouldn't be much longer. When he returns, I'll brief him on the situation and give him his orders."

"But he's here to help you take the Tribe down, right?"

"In part," he admitted. "He's damned good at his job, and I needed someone reliable at short notice."

"You know, I'm not a liability, Ryan," she said, setting the mug down on the coffee table.

He stiffened and straightened in his seat. "Where the hell did that come from?"

"Connor's here for my protection rather than as your backup, and don't bother denying it," she said, turning to face him, but leaning slightly away.

"I have no intention of denying it. Connor will be sticking to you like superglue."

She took a deep breath and let it out slowly. "While we're in the field, you should treat me like any other member of the team. You saw how I handled Barcode, and you did say you were impressed with my reactions at the reservoir. Was that bull—"

"Lara, stop right there." He reached for her hand, but she pulled it away. "Just because you dealt with Barcode that one time, doesn't mean you're ready for action."

"Ryan, the Tribe is nothing to worry about. They're nothing but a bunch of thugs. You and Connor will be able to take them down with one hand tied—"

"Please, Lara," he snapped, stopping her mid-sentence. "You know better than that. In a war, there's no such thing as 'nothing to worry about'. If I thought for one moment I could convince you to go home, I'd have you and Connor in the car and on the way to the ferry the minute he returned. But—"

He broke off when the fire exit door dinged open and Connor stepped into the room, dripping wet.

Kaine leaned close to Lara and whispered, "We'll continue this later," then turned to Connor and spoke up. "A little damp outside?"

"Pissing it do—" Connor shot Lara an apologetic glance. "Sorry, Doc. I mean it's 'ammering down out there."

Connor removed his hat and coat, draped the coat on the back of a chair, and shook the rain from the hat before dropping it onto the seat. He closed on the booth.

"Make yourself a coffee. There's a kettle and instant if you can't work the gizmo."

"Cheers, Captain. I'm freezing."

A few seconds later, armed with a steaming cup of sweetened, black coffee, the former army sergeant returned to his original seat. A cold wave emanated from his clothing.

Lara shivered and edged closer to Kaine, who wasn't about to complain.

After a loud slurp, Connor smacked his lips. "Nice stuff. Needed that."

"Anything untoward happen?" Kaine asked.

"Not a thing, sir. Geezer were good as gold. Kept mithering about the weather and 'aving to walk all the way to 'is car, mind. Didn't see 'im use 'is mobile, and I'll lay good odds 'e didn't notice me following 'im, neither. Not the most difficult bloke I've ever 'ad to tail. In fact, it was a piece of pi—er, sorry again, Doc. It was a piece of pie."

"Don't worry about me, Connor," she said, smiling. "I was married to a soldier, and I've been around military men —and farmers—long enough to have grown a thick skin in the face of salty language."

Connor lifted his head in acknowledgement. "Okay, Doc. I'll remember in—"

"Good," Kaine said, keen to get down to business. "I thought we might be able to trust our scarred friend, but—"

"Pays to be careful, though. Right, Captain?" Connor said. He took another swig, this one quieter, and nodded. "Yeah. Rhino seems a decent enough sort, I s'pose."

"Okay, I don't know about you, *Connor*"—he emphasised the sergeant's first name to make a point—"but *Dr Griffin* and I are in great need of some shuteye. Mind if we get down to business?"

"I'm all ears, sir."

"Good. Okay, from now until I call an end to this mission, we drop the normal, military protocols. No ranks, no bull. As far as the world is concerned, Lara is *Dr* Griffin, and I'm her devoted hubby. You'll be our employee."

Connor threw a thumb's up. "Okay, sir. Before we go on, can I just say I never believed what the media were saying 'bout you last year. Not for one second. The idea of you being a terrorist and a 'threat to the fabric of society' were total bollocks. When Q called me out of the blue last night, saying you needed my 'elp, I were only too 'appy to volunteer."

Lara's grip on his hand tightened.

"So, you *did* call Rollo?"

Kaine nodded. "Couldn't get hold of Danny, although I did try."

"What on earth could Rollo do from the South Pacific?"

"You'd be surprised at his resourcefulness. New Caledonia even has internet services these days."

Connor's eyes lit up. "Q's in the South Pacific? Bloody 'ell. What's 'e doing down there?"

"His new, French wife has a brother on the island," Lara answered for Kaine. "We thought it would make a nice, surprise destination for their honeymoon."

"Well, mount me and display me on the mantelpiece," Connor said, leaning back and shaking his head. "If someone as ugly as Q found someone to marry 'im, there's 'ope for us all. No wonder he sounded so knackered!" He ended with a chuckle and swallowed some more coffee.

"All right, enough of the jocularity," Kaine said, turning to Lara. "Before we left the villa, I called Rollo and asked him to check out the short-notice availability of everyone within shouting distance of Walthamstow. Top of the list was young Connor here." He tipped a nod towards the former army sergeant. "Earlier, while you were trying on your military fatigues, I asked Rollo to set things up with Connor and ... well, here we all are."

Connor dipped his head in recognition. "Like I said, sir. Only too 'appy to 'elp. I'm down with your payment structure, too. Beats working the doors at The Blue Tightrope for a living."

"The Blue Tightrope?" Lara asked.

The sergeant grimaced. "It's a sort of 'Gentlemen's Club'. In Soho, but there ain't many 'gentlemen', if you get my meaning."

"A strip joint?"

Again, Connor dipped his head. This time, he looked a little sheepish. "More like a lap dancing club, but without much in the way of dancing talent."

"I'd have thought you'd love the place," Kaine offered. "The ambience. The naked women."

"Nah," Connor said, shaking his head and avoiding eye contact with either of them, "the Tightrope's one of the worst gigs I've 'ad since leaving the army. Crap pay, lowbrow workmates who couldn't 'old a decent conversation to save their souls. And then there's the low-rent clientele, the sticky carpets, vomit, and all the coke-snorting in the toilets. You get the picture?" He paused to take another long sip of his drink, still with his eyes lowered. "And despite the watered-down drinks, we get more'n our fair share of drunks spoiling for a fight come kicking out time."

"Not too upset at taking a few days off then?"

"Not one little bit, sir," Connor answered, straightening his shoulders and looking up from his mug. "Q's call, couldn't've come at a better time."

"But?" Kaine asked.

"Sorry, sir?"

"I sense there's a 'but' coming."

Connor shook his head, but his pained expression betrayed an inner conflict.

"Out with it, lad. If I don't know what's troubling you, I won't be able to help."

The younger man squirmed in his seat. "Sorry, sir. It's just … well … 'ow long is this job likely to take? It's just that I'm on a zero-'ours contract, and if I don't turn up, I don't get paid. Bills to cover, you know?"

Kaine clapped the younger man on the shoulder. "Don't worry, Connor, I asked Rollo to transfer a month's pay into your bank account the moment you took the contract."

The former sergeant jerked to a seated attention. "You did?"

"Yes."

"A month's wedge?"

"That's right, and at our agreed rate."

"Bloody 'ell," he said, swallowing hard. "That's not far short of what I'd get from The Blue Tightrope in a year."

"Hopefully, this'll be the easiest, most boring contract you'll ever work. You'll be getting money for old rigging."

"'Ang on a minute," Connor said, his gaze flitting between Kaine and Lara. "'Ow can you 'ave added money to my account when I ain't never given no one my bank details?"

"We have our methods," Lara answered for Kaine. "I'm guessing you have the app on your phone. Why not check your account?"

Connor drained his mug before pulling out his mobile and, frowning in concentration, tapped on the screen, his thumbs flying. After a few moment's silence, he looked up, confusion and slight annoyance easy to read on his face.

"Bugger me!" he said under his breath. "'Ow the 'ell d'you manage that?"

Lara turned to Kaine. "Should we tell him?"

Kaine shot an appraising look at the former sergeant and dipped his head to Lara. "Connor's a new trusted member of the team, prepared to risk his life—"

"I am?" Connor asked in mock surprise, which transformed into a grin.

Kaine returned the grin. "If not, you can finish your coffee and take a hike."

"Okay, okay. I'm in!"

"As I was saying before I was so rudely interrupted," Kaine continued, a thin smile stretching his lips, "Connor's with us all the way, and he deserves to be read in."

"Okay, in that case, here goes. We have a Corky and a Sabrina," Lara said, a smile on her beautiful face, and laughter in her quiet voice.

"You have a who and a what now?"

Lara sat up and arched her back in another luxurious stretch. "Corky calls himself an 'information acquisition specialist', but Sabrina tells it like it is. They're both hackers and very good ones. World class, in fact."

"And these two work for you?"

Kaine nodded. "On a purely voluntary basis."

"They married?"

Lara laughed. "Corky and Sabrina married? Oh, that's priceless."

"Why's it priceless?"

Kaine fielded the question. "If you saw either of them, you'd know, but I doubt that'll ever happen. I've never even met Corky. At least, not in person. We video call now and again."

Connor sighed. "Not sure I like the idea of being on the radar of a couple of 'ackers, but ..., if you say they're good people—"

"We do," Lara confirmed.

"Then it's okay with me and my bank balance." Connor slipped his phone back in his pocket and placed the flat of his hands on the table. "Right then. Q said something about a babysitting gig. That right?"

Lara stiffened, but to her credit, managed to avoid making any comment.

"Pretty much," Kaine answered, nodding slowly, "but one of the clients can't know you're a minder or he's likely to kick up a real fuss. The other client does know, and she is probably about to scream blue murder at me."

Lara kicked the side of his foot. He ignored it.

Connor's expression relaxed into a gentle smile. "Care to explain, sir?"

Kaine paused. "How much did Rollo tell you about me and the mission?"

Connor shrugged. "Not much. Just said that you was innocent of the charges against you—which I knew anyway —and as 'ow you'd liberated a load of readies from the arsehole who was really responsible for the ... incident."

Kaine sighed. At least he hadn't called it a bombing, which counted in his favour.

"Q said I were likely to be operating under military conditions the whole time I were with you. Sounds good to me, sir. Whatever you need, I'm your man." He confirmed the statement by clapping a hand over his heart before returning it to his mug.

Lara leaned forwards in her seat. "That's all good to hear, but there's something I can't work out."

"And what's that, Dr Griffin?" Connor asked, the smile returning.

"How did you find us at the reservoir? It was dark and the place is huge."

Connor glanced at Kaine before returning his gaze to Lara. "Want me to tell her, sir, or would you prefer to do it yourself?"

Kaine took up the baton.

"When I called Connor, I gave him the approximate location and an ETA. The rest, I left up to him."

"How long did it take you to find us?" Lara asked.

"I saw you arrive and settle in," Connor answered. "Then I spent the rest of the evening searching the area for uninvited guests."

"You saw us arrive?"

"Sure did, Doc."

She twisted to face Kaine. "Did you know Connor was there all the time?"

Kaine nodded. "Yep. Saw and heard. He made so much noise I'm surprised you didn't spot him yourself."

Connor lifted a hand, index finger wagging towards the ceiling. "Now 'ang on a min—"

"To be honest, I almost reconsidered hiring him. It's a real shame when a highly skilled soldier loses his edge," Kaine continued, talking to Lara but looking at Connor.

"Come on now, sir."

"Connor," Lara said, "he's kidding again. Having fun at both our expenses. Aren't you, William!"

Kaine nodded, and said, "Okay, Sergeant. Here's what you need to know …."

He rattled off the bare bones of the situation. When he reached the part where Lara and Barcode tangled in the street, Connor laughed, said, "Good for you, Doc," and offered Lara a high five, which she took and then slid Kaine a smug side grin.

Kaine summed up with, "Until I tell you otherwise, you have two tasks."

"Only two?"

"Yes, but they're essential. The first is to protect Darwin Moore, without letting on that you're his minder. Okay?"

"I'll do my best, sir. And the second task?"

"Is to keep wifey here"—he jerked a thumb towards Lara—"out of trouble. Understood?"

Connor, serious again, nodded, and said, "Understood. You can count on me, sir."

I hope so, Sergeant.

"Meanwhile, if you don't mind my asking, what are *you* going to be doing?"

"Me, Connor?" Kaine said, eyes wide. "Nothing much. I'm going to unmask a gang leader, and take it from there."

After his announcement, Kaine allowed a short silence to develop. As expected, Lara was the one to break it.

"And how do you plan to achieve that task on your own, pray tell?"

Despite anticipating her question, it didn't make the answer any easier to find. Fortunately, Connor provided an opening.

"You're going to watch for Damian's signal in the window tonight, yeah?"

"And you'll have Corky monitor all the internet traffic in the Hub?" Lara added, before he could respond.

She caught on fast, but her expression said she hadn't forgiven him for forcing a "babysitter" on her. No doubt they'd have it out when they eventually reached the privacy of their hotel room.

Before the meeting, Kaine had been mulling over a few options, but their suggestions had helped make up his mind.

"By the way, sir," Connor asked. "What you planning to do when you identify this TM geezer?"

"That depends on who he is and how ... open he is to persuasion."

Lara reached for his arm but seemed to change her mind and dropped her hand to her knee.

"And if 'e's not? What then?" Connor asked.

"No idea. I'll address that situation when it ariscs. But," Kaine added, "the fact this TM character likes to remain incognito suggests he's a little shy. I might be able to use that."

"What about Demarcus Williams and the rest of the 'Eavies?"

"They're nothing but a bunch of second-rate thugs who get their fun by beating up kids. I doubt they'll put up much resistance."

"Ryan," she said, using his name almost inaudibly, "you're starting to sound complacent and that's worrying me."

"Confident, maybe. Complacent, never. Trust me, Lara. I know what I'm doing."

Yeah, right. Of course I do.

This time, Kaine did have his fingers firmly crossed, but hidden under the table.

Chapter Eighteen

Sunday 21st February - Byron Codell

Barcode's Crib, Walthamstow, London, England

Barcode woke from an interrupted sleep with a pounding head, a stiff back, stinging cuts and bruises, and in a stinking mood.

The naked ho on his left, mouth open, dribbled spit down the side of her face. Arm draped limply over his chest, she snored like a slobbering pig, and she slept with her eyes half open and rolled up into the back of her head, lost to the product.

In the night, she looked good, horny, desperate for some blow and willing to sell her ass for the product, but now ... a pug-ugly bitch, with no redeeming features.

He shook off her arm, threw back the creased covers, and took a daytime look at the skank.

Huge, drooping tits, flabby belly, but—her saving grace —a big booty. Massive it was, wide and ripe for pummelling, if only his head weren't thumping so hard that it seemed about ready to crack open like an egg.

The ho snorted. Blurred and bloodshot eyes opened fully and tried to focus on his face. Gave up and the lids drooped again.

"Got any more sugar for me, honey?" she slurred, snaking a hand towards his groin.

Slut made him wanna puke.

"Fuck off, ho," he snarled, slapped away the hand, and grabbed her by the throat. "You ain't worth no more o' my time. Dress yo'self and get the fuck outta my crib."

Woman gagged and tried to pull his hand away, eyes open wide, staring, fully focused. Scared for her life.

Fuck yeah!

He squeezed. Harder. Smiled.

Her eyes popped, tongue poked out from the foul-smelling, lipstick-smeared mouth. Garbled some words. Legs kicked, hands scratched. False nails tore the inside of his wrists, drawing blood.

"Fuckin' be-atch!" he roared and pushed hard, releasing his hold.

She fell off the bed in a sprawl of arms and legs, screaming, swearing. Spewing out garbled shit about his parentage.

Despite his throbbing head, he jumped from the bed breathing hard, sweating—and stood over the ho.

"You got ten seconds to get the fuck outta my crib, 'fore I slice yo' ass, skank."

She tore her eyes from his monstrous dick and gathered her clothes. Scraps of glittery cloth that wouldn't cover much of her black hide. The strappy bra hung on the post at the foot of his bed, where he'd thrown it in his hurry to get at the goods. Fuck knew what use it was to the ho. Didn't look strong enough or big enough to hold her mammas in place.

As she wobbled around the room, flabby, saggy, used, and abused, Barcode couldn't figure out how he'd managed to work himself up to service the bitch. Showed what anger, alcohol, and product would do for a man's performance.

The woman stuffed the bra into a tiny handbag, pulled on a dress no bigger than a T-shirt, and slipped her feet into a pair of strapless heels. She stood, tottering, looking from him to the door and back. The shiny, pimpled forehead creased into a frown. Cunning. Calculating.

Yeah. Here it comes.

Her head dipped, and she stared up at him, trying for seductive, but coming up like an animal on the prowl.

"Throwing me out into the cold without so much as a taste," she mumbled, "you ain't no kind of a man."

"Man enough fo' you last night, be-atch. Now fuck off outta here."

Her chin dimpled, tears started up in her bloodshot eyes in a pathetic attempt to look pitiful.

"You sure I can't have a little taste? I'll make it worth yo' while, Barcode. You can take me up the ass. I know you love the booty."

What she probably thought was a sexy smile made her look like one of them animals on a wildlife programme circling they prey. She lifted the back of her dress and twisted enough to expose a naked butt.

"C'mon, honey. You know you want it. A little blow for some of this. How 'bout it?"

She slapped a cheek, lifted her foot, and placed it on the chair next to his bed. Opening up to him.

For half a second, Barcode thought about taking her, but the throbbing head wasn't in the right part of his anatomy. He swung a leg and kicked her in the fat butt. She flew across the room, screaming, and crashed head first into the door.

Two strides forwards, he took a handful of her hair, opened the door, and threw the ho out onto the landing. Her shoulder crunched into the far wall and she slid in a heap to the thin carpet. Barcode bent down, picked up the handbag, and threw it in her face.

"I's gettin' dressed now. You still here when I come back out, I'm gonna mess you up, bad. You hear me, be-atch?"

"You ain't no kind of a man!" she screamed, gathering up her bag and using the handrail to pull herself to her shaky feet.

"You already say that, ho."

Fully upright, but balancing unsteadily with one hand grabbing the handrail and the other flat against the wall, the ho filled her lungs, which made her tits swell to the size of overripe melons.

"An' I meant it, limp-dick! Couldn't hardly feel you inside me you was so damn small."

Barcode snarled and took one pace towards her, stepping out into the hallway in all his butt-naked glory.

Who cared if the neighbours saw him through the uncovered hall windows? They'd see the ho was lying about his equipment. All the other sluts in the hood could testify to his size and his prowess. Legendary, he was. A stallion. All the girls told him so.

The ho cowered away.

Still spewing her lies to anyone who'd listen, she staggered and stumbled down the stairs, the four-inch heels making her life difficult. Halfway down, she toppled, nearly fell, but caught herself on the handrail. Seconds later, she fumbled with the locks on the front door, opened it up, let in a gust of freezing, rain-filled air, and tumbled outside.

She left the door wide open to the elements, but fuck it. Ain't no one in the hood gonna break into Barcode's place. His crib was safe. No one would dare, and he wasn't about to head down the stairs, naked, to close the door. He'd do it later, after getting dressed.

Another blast of glacial air hit his bare skin. He shivered, pecs bunching and bouncing, and looked down. Shit. Cold didn't do his boy any favours. One glance at the not-so-big man and the hookers in the hood would maybe change their minds.

Barcode turned, ducked into his room, and pulled on some warm threads.

Fuckin' head.

Wouldn't stop throbbing. Painkillers might help since the product wasn't cutting it. Needed a little trip to the pharmacy.

A pharmacy?

Barcode smiled to himself as an idea worked its way into his aching brain.

Yeah, that'll do it.

An idea to help push him to the top of the pile. An idea to make him stand out to TM and the rest of the Tribe.

And he needed to make a statement to prove he wasn't no wuss after what the pasty-faced bitch had done. Had to prove it to himself as much as anyone else. At the same time, he'd let off some steam.

He'd had more than enough of standing in line, bowing and scraping to the man—assuming TM was a man. No way of telling with all them electronics hiding his face and his vocals from the Tribe.

What was up with that, anyway? Why hide away from your people? No adulation that way, and without the hero worship, what the fuck was the point? Money and power didn't mean squat, not unless you could flaunt it.

Once dressed, Barcode stood still and admired himself in the mirror built into his closet. The power of black.

Black Converse, black jeans, black polo shirt, black puffer jacket, black baseball cap with a silver star logo. The cap hurt where it dug into the wound on the back of his head, but he'd survive. The cap hid his injury from the world, added shadow to hide his face from the surveillance cameras, and completed his black-on-black look.

Man, he was fine. Wore his threads with style.

Without pulling his eyes from the hunk in the mirror, Barcode fastened his zip, pulled it halfway up, and rubbed his hands together. He smiled, teeth flashing white in the mirror.

Time to "borrow" a car, head out for some meds at the Three Ps, and have himself a little fun.

———

PARTHAK'S PARKSIDE PHARMACY, a small, family-run shop on a back street five miles from Walthamstow, stocked exactly what he needed—super-strength ibuprofen. He even paid for the packet of ten and a small bottle of water to wash them down. No profit in thievery if it drew attention outside Tribe territory.

He kept his black leather gloves on and paid in cash. No point leaving clues or drawing attention to himself. The baseball cap did its job of hiding his face. Early on a

Sunday morning, the shop had been empty, except for the middle-aged pharmacist who served him. Small, pointy-shouldered, and quiet, the man barely even look at Barcode.

Excellent.

Almost like he planned it.

On the way back to the car, he downed three of the full-strength tabs and drained the water bottle. Fuck knew how long the meds would take to work, but it couldn't happen fast enough for him. Apart from making him irate, the headache was fucking with his vision. Blurred it was. So blurred, he nearly ran up the ass of a black cab that stopped suddenly to unload a passenger. Cabbie's foul language and the slur he cast on Barcode's lineage nearly made him change plans.

It wasn't beyond the realms of possibility for Barcode to follow the cabbie all day, waiting for the chance to run the fucker down the first time he get outta his ride. If he hadn't already made up his mind to wreak havoc on an enemy, Barcode woulda done it, too. Cabbie would never know it but, that day, he happened to be one lucky, toilet-mouthed, white dude. On the other hand, Barcode had a shit-hot memory for faces and numbers, and had taken careful note of the black cab's licence plate.

One day, Cabbie's luck would run out.

Yeah, one day.

His car, a gutless, old Fiat 500, lifted from an unmanned NCP carpark using a thin, steel lever and a screwdriver to unlock the ignition, wouldn't win no races. The little, green fucker wouldn't turn many heads, neither. But it was perfect for Barcode's purposes.

Perfect.

He'd parked on double yellow lines across the street

from the pharmacy, but didn't expect to wait long, not in *Parksiders'* turf.

Sure enough, twenty minutes after he'd swallowed the tabs, and five minutes after the fucking things finally started to ease his hurt, the random targets revealed theyselves.

'Bout Goddamn time!

Three jacked-up assholes wearing hoodies and showing Parkside Crew colours—bandanas in snot green and puke yellow—turned the far corner, heading towards Parkway Shopping Centre. Their backs to Barcode, they was the only ones on that side of the street. A bus lane, yellow lines, and loading bays kept the street clear of parked cars, too, which was why he chose that particular spot, and that particular pharmacy from the get go.

A hundred metres and sliding further away.

Smiling, heartrate rising, Barcode studied his prey.

Assholes wore the same "uniform"—dark green parkas, blue jeans, and white trainers—and walked with a swagger that shouted out they confidence and smugness. None looked around. None sensed danger. The tall one near the kerb wore a black beanie, and the two smaller ones wore baseball caps, one green, the other white. They jostled each other, laughing and joking. Having a great time.

Not for long, dickheads.

The one in the middle elbowed Beanie Boy, who lost his balance and staggered into the road. A cyclist in the bus lane yelled a warning. Beanie Boy jumped back onto the pavement, helped by his buddies. They all laughed and jeered at the stupid fuck on the town bike, who dropped his head, hit the pedals hard, and rode through the next set of lights on amber. Car horns honked. Lycra-man disappeared into the distance.

Time for some jollies.

Barcode twisted the screwdriver and held it on a full turn. The engine took longer to get going than his last shorty. The motor didn't exactly purr, but it did hold steady, eventually. The fuel gauge were near empty. Didn't matter a damn, though. Wouldn't need to run much longer.

Like the excellent driver he always were, Barcode checked the wing-mirror before cruising into the slow-ass traffic. The lights turned again and the traffic stopped.

Barcode kept the Fiat in first, left foot hard down on the clutch, right foot on the brake.

The Parkside trio made the crossing and strutted towards the shopping centre. Two hundred metres and getting further away.

The lights turned green and the cars ahead moved off. Barcode allowed a gap to grow between him and the slick motor in front, a BMW 3 Series—midnight-blue with tinted windows. A real beauty she were. A motor to kill for.

Behind Barcode, the driver in a filthy, white van grew antsy, sounded his horn, and flashed his headlights a couple times. Barcode threw him the finger and waited.

More angry horns blared.

Barcode bided his time.

Green.

Wait for it.

The fucker in the van threw open his door, leaned out, and started hollering.

Ahead, the flasher on the BMW indicated left. The car turned and drove off. The other cars in Barcode's lane crawled further along the High Street. The gap between them and his Fiat grew.

Still green.

Wait.

Barcode released pressure on the brake and let his foot hover over the gas pedal. The Fiat rolled slowly forwards.

Van Man popped back inside his cab and slammed his door.

Still green.

Wait.

Amber!

Barcode stamped on the gas. The engine screamed and the Fiat burned rubber. The car crossed the line as the lights turned red and Barcode's foot hit the floor.

Beanie Boy reacted first. He turned. Blue eyes in a white face stared wide. His mouth opened in a scream that were drowned out by the engine.

Barcode yanked the steering wheel, entered the empty bus lane, and aimed the car dead centre.

People screamed. Horns blared.

His mates scattered, but Beanie Boy took the full force of the Fiat.

The steering wheel juddered in Barcode's hands as bones turned to powder under the impact of rusty steel and rubber. More screams. Another yank on the wheel and he was back in the bus lane, gathering speed.

The Fiat sideswiped a big-assed Ford but Barcode kept the pedal to the metal. In the rear-view, bodies thrashed and a splash of red tagged the grey pavement.

Two minutes later, Barcode, still laughing his ass off, slowed and turned left into a quiet side street.

A minute after that, he found an empty disabled bay outside a derelict shop and parked. Keeping his head down and turned away from any street cameras, he climbed outta the Fiat, and grabbed the empty water bottle from the passenger seat. Then he took a circuit around the car to inspect the damage. Apart from the smear of blood, some hair and shit on the bumper, and a slight dent, Beanie Boy hadn't caused the Fiat much damage. Car's owner could count himself lucky. Beanie Boy couldn't.

Barcode chuckled, stuck the bottle into his pocket to bin later, and headed for his crib. He slouched his shoulders and added an extra roll to his walk. Soon as he found a dark alley, he'd duck inside and reverse his jacket to show off the bright, red lining. It didn't hurt to confuse the people watching the all-seeing surveillance cams.

Man, what a blast!

He hadn't felt so good in a long time. One sure-fire way to clear a throbbing headache.

Who need ibu-fuckin'-profen?

Chapter Nineteen

Sunday 21st February - Byron Codell

Palmerston Road School, Walthamstow, London, England

After an urgent summons from Demarcus Williams, Barcode stepped into the near-empty Hub with his heart thumping hard and fast. His throat were as dry as the snatch on the fat ho from last night, his hands were sweating, and his head had started thumping again from cracking it on the pavement.

Although nervous as fuck, he was still buzzing from the action. Man, he loved taking out them Parksiders.

Almost better'n sex.

Soon as he smoothed things over with TM, he'd get his

own back on the skinny, white bitch who'd knocked him flat on his ass and made him look like a moron.

Assuming it were possible to smooth things over with TM.

Assuming he made it through the next couple hours.

Fucking bitch flipped him like he was a burger on a griddle. How she do that, tiny as she was? All skin and bone. No meat on her. Damn near flat-chested and fuck-all booty. Caught him unawares is what happened. By surprise, but he'd give her a good seeing to before killing her. No one made Barcode look stupid and lived long after. Back when he were a kid, all them years ago, the ink-man tried to do it, and look where that got the fucker.

The bitch would die—painful and slow. After that, he'd take care of the wiry, little fucker she were married to.

No one dissed Barcode and got away with it.

No one.

Second Man greeted him from behind a desk with his usual, arrogant snarl. Barcode lowered his gaze. Looking Demarcus in the eye would be seen as a challenge. Not the time. Not the place. One day it would happen, but not this day.

The buzz of the Hub had died the moment Barcode stepped through the doorway. In the hallway outside, two of the Heavies—the big one with the squinty eye who carried a baseball bat, and the fat one with the shaved head—patted him down like Five-O before letting him inside. As though he'd ever try a frontal attack on Demarcus Williams in the Hub. Did these people think he stupid?

Nah. If Barcode were going to make a move on Demarcus, he'd do it sneaky. Wait 'til the big, tattooed fuck was alone and unsuspecting. He'd catch the mutha outside, down a dark alley, and shiv him in the kidney. Asshole would die slow that way, painfully. Bleed to death from the inside.

Yeah, that would be the way to do it, but Barcode needed an alibi. Not for the bacon, but for TM. He'd wait until Demarcus was alone. That's when he'd do the meat-head. Not in the middle of the fucking Hub with five armed guard dogs, five armed Heavies.

The fuck-off, big TV screen hanging on the wall behind Demarcus, the one TM used to deliver his instructions, were blank. Dark and menacing, but blank.

Thank fuck for that.

Last thing he needed was to hear TM's electronic voice taunting him about being butt-fucked in public. Nah, that ritual humiliation would occur at the usual call time, eight o'clock. He had a while before that happen.

Maybe he'd catch up with the skanky bitch before the evening meeting. And he'd be sure and take snapshots with his phone of the way he took his revenge before dropping her beaten and bloody corpse into the Thames. A good dumping ground, the river. Washed away all the forensic evidence. Sometimes it washed the corpse out into the Channel, never to be seen again. Confuse the Feds. That were the point. Worked before, with the ink-man, and it would work again.

The monitor on the wall was huge. Like a cinema screen. Thank fuck it was dark.

Barcode swallowed and kept his head slightly lowered.

Play the part, man. Play the part.

The big TV and all the computer screens made the Hub look like a for-real centre of operations and impressed the fuck outta the rest of the Tribesmen, but not Barcode. Took a lot more than shiny computers and big screens to impress him.

Still sneering at Barcode, Demarcus snapped his fingers at a Geek sitting behind one of the computers. The big monitor blinked on, revealing a detailed street map of the hood. The same Geek tapped a couple keys and added all the pitches to the map. They appeared in different colours —green, amber, and red. Barcode's three pitches were flashing an ominous amber. Not good.

Shit.

He knew exactly what the flashing and the colour meant. His position as crew leader was up for discussion. One of his team were making a move, and Barcode had a good idea which one. A weasel with zit scars all over his ferret-face.

Demarcus Williams, the musclebound and bald fuckwit, climbed to his feet and lumbered around to the front of his desk, chest pumped and elbows rounded out, like a strutting silverback gorilla. Two of the other Heavies, Delinquent and Gerard, stood close by, ready to jump to Demarcus' defence. Would they really take a bullet for Demarcus Williams or TM? Maybe one day Barcode would find out.

Demarcus sat his big, fat butt on the front edge of the desk and waited in silence for the sign of respect. Barcode obliged the fuckwit with a nod and waited. It didn't take long.

"Wh'appen yesterday?"

Demarcus' deep voice boomed around the room, bouncing off the painted brickwork. The pencil-necked Geek in the corner stopped typing. His fingers hovered over the keys, but he pretended not to listen.

Barcode spewed out his rehearsed answer. "Path was muddy, man. I slipped and fell."

Demarcus sucked air through his teeth. "You slipped?"

"Yah, s'right. I slipped. Muddy in that lane. Been rainin'

hard and my old trainers got no grip. Bought myself a new pair, look." He lifted a foot to flash his jet-black Converse All Stars. "Tread's better on these babies."

Second Man sucked through his teeth again and pulled his flabby lips back into a sneer. Dissing him. Dissing Barcode. Asshole.

"That not the way I heard it went down."

"What way you hear it, Mr Williams?"

Yeah, he'd be *Mister*, for now. Wouldn't be forever, though.

Demarcus tilted back his head and looked down his nose at Barcode.

Dis me now, fucker. We see what happen later.

"Way Benjie tells it," Demarcus growled, "you was smacked down by a white woman who weren't no taller than my mammy. Benjie said you ended up flat on your face with the woman's boot up your ass."

Barcode rounded his shoulders and puffed out his chest, copying Demarcus Williams' stance, but not overdoing it.

"Benjie a liar. Let him come tell me to my face!"

"Benjie!" Demarcus called over Barcode's shoulder. "Come tell us all what you saw!"

Benjie, the shit-faced weasel who shoulda had Barcode's back, slid into the room from the outside hall where he'd been skulking. He was all apologetic and shy, like—until opening his mouth.

"Yes, Mr Williams? What I do for you?"

Second Man pointed to the floor at his feet. "Come here. Tell Barcode what you tol' me earlier."

Benjie shuffled forwards, unable to look Barcode in the eye. The weasel doing what he did best, being all weasel-like, packing no guts. He stopped in front of the big man, shoulders stooped, head lowered.

"I only just told you what I saw, Mr Williams."

Demarcus bunched his fists. The knuckles cracked. "Tell it again. Now!"

Hang-dog, Benjie shot a whipped look at Barcode. He made his shoulders slope so much, like he thought the blame would slide right off the fuckers.

"We was mannin' our pitch, mindin' our business, like we always do, Mr Williams. Near that old playground at the end o' Brooke Street. By Crease Cut, y'know?" He nodded at the map on the screen. "We just go where TM tell us to go. We do good trade there, Mr Williams. People know when an' where to come for they gear, y'know?"

"Quit the bullshit, Benjie. TM knows where you was."

Demarcus flashed a glance at the big screen as though he thought TM was behind the glass, listening, even though the monitor displayed nothing but the street map. A shiver rolled down Barcode's spine.

Fuck. Is TM listenin'?

"TM got spotters making sure his crews are where they s'posed to be and doing what they s'posed to be doing," Demarcus said. "And he's got me and my team to enforce it. Tell your tale 'fore I gets angry."

Benjie nodded a few times, like he was a pigeon pecking at some seeds. Pathetic, it was.

Pitiful.

"This ... white woman ... come out the old cripple's house," Benjie said, stammering and hesitant. "A real betty, she was. Y'know, a looker despite her bein' so old. An' she walk towards us, headin' somewhere. For the shop maybe. Made the mistake o' lookin' at us direct, y'know. Give us eye contact. It seem like she were dissin' us. Least that's what Barcode say. If I remember correct, he say somethin' like, 'That bowl o' fresh cream's dissin' you and me, Benjie'. At least that the way I remembered it. That right, Barcode? Ain't that what you say?"

Barcode stared the weasel down but couldn't openly lie. It was pretty much exactly what he did say, and Petey would back up Benjie's words. Instead of lying, Barcode jerked up his chin in agreement.

"S'right," he added, all confident. "I say that."

"What was she like, this 'betty'?" Demarcus Williams asked Benjie.

"Old, Mr Williams. In her thirties, easy. But built, y'know? Nice rack an' chassis. She move well, like all rollin' an' slinky. Not much booty, but if you likes them small an' racy, she weren't at all bad."

"W'happen next?"

Benjie piped up again. "Barcode say we should slap the be-atch into place. Teach her some manners."

Demarcus speared Barcode with one of the accusing looks he used to scare the Tribesmen, but Barcode wasn't so timid. Didn't scare so easy. After all, the big Heavy wasn't TM.

"That what you say?" Demarcus asked.

"Somethin' like that," Barcode answered, staring at Benjie, the turncoat weasel.

Benjie continued, looking at his feet. Clad in Nike Airs they were. Cheap and nasty. Benjie got no class or style. Never had. Never would.

"So," Benjie said, looking up at last. "Barcode step outta the cut an' onto Brooke Street." He pointed to one of the three pulsing, amber lights on the wall monitor. "Stand in her way, he did. Wo-man try to walk around him, but Barcode kept gettin' in her face, y'know? They was dancin', like. You know, like on that show on TV?"

Benjie mimed a ballroom dance, a waltz or something.

Demarcus grunted, but Barcode couldn't tell if the ugly mutha was amused or angry.

"And then?" Demarcus asked, looking at Barcode, not Benjie.

"An' then Barcode went to grab the betty's arm. Well, Mr Williams. Next thing I know, she doin' this kung fu type shit. Y'know, all arms an' legs an' twistin' an' turnin'. Then, Barcode's flyin' through the air an' landin' on his butt. Squealin' like he broke somethin'. Man, it was somethin' to see."

Benjie whirled his arms in the air and spun around like he'd just had a bad hit of angel dust. When he faced Demarcus Williams again, Benjie lowered his head and stopped giggling.

Still focused on Barcode, and with a face dark as thunder, Demarcus asked, "That right, Barcode? That what happen?"

How the fuck could he answer that?

Barcode still didn't know how the bitch put him on his back. His elbow, shoulder, and butt still hurt from the tumble, but the cut on his head was worse of all. Still saw stars from it.

Next time, he promised himself. Next time he saw the fucking ho, she were going down. All the way down to Hell where she belonged.

If he admitted to Demarcus Williams the old bitch had put him on his ass, he'd lose face. Worse still, he'd lose his pitches. No way could he let that happen. He'd waited months for the promotion and wasn't gonna give it up easily.

Barcode stood taller, looking down on Benjie, but being careful not to crowd Demarcus Williams. He shook his head and spoke all quiet.

"Mighta look that way to this fool, but like I told you before, Mr Williams, I slipped. She backed away, and I lost my footin' when reachin' out fo' her. Like I told you, it were them damn, ol' sneakers. Won't happen again. Hell no."

Demarcus glanced at the screen before fixing his thunderous expression on Barcode once again. The big mutt still threw out evil vibes, but at least he didn't draw his piece, or call on any of the other Heavies to sling Barcode from the Hub. He'd seen it happen once and it didn't end up too well for Linus, the poor fucker who got slung out. Nobody never seen or heard from Linus again. Rumour said he'd fetched up at the bottom of a canal somewhere, and Barcode didn't wanna end up the same way.

"So, why didn't you get up and teach her a lesson?"

"Her old man arrived, shoutin'," Benjie spouted, all excited again. "Ran at us like he ain't carin' who we was. I mean, me and Big Robert and Barcode, the three o' us was all a head taller than the little guy, and he came flyin' at us like he didn't give a shit. Like he was packin' heat, Mr Williams. I thought it best to burn rubber 'fore things turn ugly. Big Robert and me help Barcode outta the mud and we blurred."

"Little guy? Describe him."

"Old, pasty-faced dude, pushin' forty. Shaggy, dark hair and bushy beard. Skinny, but wiry, y'know. Man, could he shift. We didn't make it far 'fore he reach his missus. What with havin' to carry Barcode, and all."

Barcode took his turn to growl. "Fuck. There you go again, dissin' me to Mr Williams alla time. I told you I slipped. Hit my head, you mutha."

Barcode leaned closer to Benjie, all intimidating, but the little fucker ducked behind Demarcus, acting like a kid grabbing his daddy's trouser leg. Hiding. Scared.

Demarcus Williams elbowed Benjie in the ribs. The weasel backed away.

Barcode bared his teeth.

That put him in his place.

"What time this happen?" Demarcus Williams asked, clearly not forgetting the reason for all the ructions.

"Right after we break for food," Benjie spouted, stepping out from Demarcus Williams' shadow, rubbing his ribs. "I guess it a little after two, Mr Williams."

"In daylight?"

"Yes, Mr Williams."

"What the fuck? You threatened a civilian in daylight?"

"No, Mr Williams," Barcode said, jumping in before Benjie could dig him a deeper grave. "We just markin' our territory, man. You know what it like when the honkies move in. There goes the hood."

The old joke had the effect Barcode was aiming for. Demarcus' sneer turned into a smile and he nodded.

"That it does, that it does, but in future, you remember TM's rule. Keep the local action quiet or the bacon is likely to get all pissed and business is gonna take a hit. You unnerstan'?"

He held out his fist. Barcode relaxed a little and pushed out a fist of his own for a bump, but Demarcus Williams cracked him over the knuckles hard, like he were trying to break bones.

Barcode clamped his teeth together, desperate not to cry out. Fuck, it hurt. He could almost feel the hand swelling, but he didn't look down. Didn't rub the skin, neither. Couldn't show weakness. Not now he was so close to climbing outta the brown stuff.

Demarcus sniffed. Scanned the Hub with beady, brown eyes that landed on the Geeks. "What the fuck y'all doing?

TM ain't paying you to sit there with your thumbs up your asses. Get on with your work."

Once the Geeks started tapping, Demarcus turned and headed back to his desk. He dropped into his seat and sneered at Barcode. One gold tooth glittered in the low light.

"What we gonna do with you?" he asked, pointing Barcode into the chair opposite and waving Benjie away like he was swatting at a fly.

Barcode sat and waited, throat still dry, and the bruised hand throbbing.

The gold-plated phone on Demarcus Williams' desk buzzed. The big bastard snatched it up off of the desk and hit the connect button. He listened for a bit without speaking before disconnecting the call and lowering the phone to the desk. He stared at the glittering case, nostrils wide, breathing deep. The mutha seemed upset. Demarcus picked up the phone again and twiddled it between his fingers. Eventually, he dropped it back onto the desk.

Finally drawing his eyes from the phone and fixing them on Barcode, He stood, prowled over to one of the Geeks, mumbled something in the little fucker's ear, and returned to his chair. Geek hit a couple of keys and the three amber lights on the big screen behind Demarcus' head stopped flashing.

Barcode started breathing again. He waited for them to turn green, but they stayed amber.

Demarcus spoke again. "TM give you a reprieve. Said the only reason you're not about to be lying next to dear, old Linus is you done good work up to now. An increase of eleven percent since you took over your patch. TM give me some wiggle room with you, Barcode. You feeling me?"

Even though the big screen only showed the street map,

TM was definitely watching and listening to what went on in the Hub. Barcode nodded to himself. For the first time, he had certain proof the boss kept eyes on them all. Barcode tucked away the information in case he needed it for later.

Knowledge was power, assuming you understood how to use it properly.

Barcode nodded again, this time towards the big man behind the desk. "I'm feeling you, Mr Williams."

"Good, but it don't mean you coated in Teflon. TM putting you on probation. Y'unnerstan'?"

Sure, I understand, asshole.

"Yes, Mr Williams. I got it. Is there anything else?" Barcode eased up and outta his chair.

Demarcus Williams waved him back into the seat. "As it happen, there is. TM tell me he know how your mind works."

Barcode frowned.

What the fuck now?

"He does?"

Again, the gold tooth glinted inside the wide mouth. "Yeah. He say you prob'ly intend to go do something nasty to the woman who slapped you down."

"Aw hell, Mr Williams, I tol—"

"Yeah, yeah, you slipped. That what you say, but TM reckon you be planning to go nuclear on the woman, and he don't want that."

"That right?"

"Yeah, that right. TM say if a white woman like her gets hurt or goes missing, it'll bring us some attention we don't need right now. The bacon don't mind us squabbling amongst ourselves so much. They hardly even bother investigating our little rumbles with the other gangs no more, not unless one of us ends up on a slab. But if a white woman get herself murked, it'll kick up a shitstorm. TM say we don't need the Feds or media people taking an interest in our business right now. Get it?"

Barcode dipped his head in a reluctant nod.

"Yeah, yeah. I get it."

The fuck I do.

Demarcus leaned closer, his chair creaking under the weight of all that muscle and bling. As he pointed a finger at Barcode, the big, gold rings—that acted like knuckledusters in a rumble—gleamed. "TM tell me to make this part totally clear. You do not touch the white woman. If she so much as stub her toe, TM's gonna have me take it outta your hide. And you know what, Barcode?"

"What's that, Mr Williams?"

"Taking a strip outta you would give me great pleasure. I haven't dished out a decent kicking for ages. I'm getting rusty, and I hate that. Something about you make me itch, Barcode. You ambitious. I can see it in your eyes."

Barcode kept silent, and he didn't react.

These ambitious eyes will be the last thing you'll ever see, asshole.

The gold phone rang again. Demarcus Williams picked it up and listened for a few seconds, staring hard at Barcode.

"Really?" he asked, before adding, "Yes, TM. Right away," and ending the call.

The mutha dropped the phone on the desk again. It rattled for a while before stopping. Barcode enjoyed the way the gold caught the light. Flashy.

Sweet. Gonna have me some o' that.

"Well, now," Demarcus said, "for some reason, TM like you. He say you got balls. That right?"

Barcode narrowed his eyes, scratched his chin, and thought for a bit.

Where you goin' with this, asshole?

"I ask you a question, Barcode. Do you have stones?"

"Yes, Mr Williams, I got stones."

"Good," Demarcus said, smiling like it meant something important, "because TM got a task for you."

Barcode's senses prickled. Whatever TM had in mind probably weren't going to be good for him. Barcode knew he'd have to pay for the reprieve somehow, and this didn't sound cool.

Demarcus Williams levered himself outta his chair again and stood tall, trying to crowd over Barcode. "Come with me, you."

The big mutha turned and swaggered towards the door leading to the old kitchen. Barcode followed, doubting he was about to be offered afternoon tea and crumpets.

Fuck. Look lively, man. This shit's serious.

Chapter Twenty

Sunday 21st February – Byron Codell

Palmerston Road School, Walthamstow, London, England

The door opened into a long corridor. Second Man led him past one marked "Kitchens" and past three others before opening the fourth and pushing into a small, dark, and windowless room the size of a cupboard. He threw a switch. Fluorescent lights flickered before glowing white. Harsh.

Dark green tiles halfway up the walls, cream paint above. Grey, steel table stood against the far wall, and a pair of chairs faced it, backs upright and the seats hard. No cushions.

Fuck.

He didn't need no hard chairs given his butt and back still hurt so bad from smacking the pavement.

Barcode had seen better-furnished police interview rooms.

What's up?

On top of the table, a big-assed computer screen blinked on and TM's blurry outline appeared, shimmering against a white background.

Oh shit.

Barcode stood in the open doorway, hesitant.

Run. Fucking run!

Demarcus Williams shot out a hand and grabbed the back of Barcode's upper arm, digging his sharp fingernails into his armpit. Hurt like a knife cut.

TM's silhouette moved.

"*Don't make a liar out of me, Mr Codell,*" TM said. The quiet, electronically distorted voice prickled the hairs on Barcode's neck.

"I-I won't, TM."

"*I told Mr Williams you had balls. Was I right?*"

Barcode swallowed. Demarcus pushed him deeper into the room and forced him into the chair on the right. The Heavy released Barcode's arm and dragged the empty chair further from the table, setting it between Barcode and the door. In the way. He sat, crossed his arms, and leaned back, never taking his eyes off of Barcode.

"*I don't like repeating myself, boy.*"

"S-Sorry, TM?"

"*Do you have balls?*"

"Yes, TM. I got balls. I got huge balls."

"*Good, good. See, Mr Williams? I told you he had the stones.*"

The feet of the metal chair screeched on the concrete floor. "You did, TM. But, if you'll forgive my saying so, this prick need to prove it. From where I's sitting, it look like the fucker's about to shit his pants."

The head of the shadow on the screen tilted to the left. *"Not fear, Mr Williams. I'd call it a man revealing a healthy desire for self-preservation. What do you say, Mr Codell?"*

"I'd never disagree with you, TM. I's confused, is all," Barcode said, his voice dry.

Confusion, fear, and anger mixed to screw Barcode's guts into a tight knot. What the fuck had he crashed into? That white bitch had a lot to answer for. Didn't matter what TM's orders were, he'd find a way to make her pay.

"Confused? I can understand that. In your position, I imagine I'd feel the self-same way."

"Thanks, TM," Barcode answered, happy to hear his voice sounding more confident, despite the twisting in his guts.

"After what happened with Brutus—"

"You know 'bout Brutus?"

"Don't you dare interrupt me, fool!" TM's amplified voice echoed off the shiny walls and rattled inside Barcode's ears so loud it hurt. Made them ring, and he were only just starting to get over the damned headache.

Things were racing outta hand. Barcode shot a glance at the door, then at Demarcus Williams, who sat in his chair, smiling and shaking his head as though he was reading Barcode's mind.

"I know everything," TM said, this time with more control and not so loud. *"Who do you think made Brutus disappear?"*

"Sorry, TM. I thought he run off after I give him that slappin'."

"Why didn't you come to me when you discovered he'd been ripping me off?"

So, TM really did know everything. How were that possible?

Barcode sat up straighter, ignoring the pain the seat was giving his butt. "Sorry, TM. Didn't want you thinkin' I couldn't handle my crew."

Again, the dark head on the screen dipped. "*I thought that might be the case, which is why I gave you a pass on acting against Brutus without securing my permission first. It's also the reason you're on probation rather than fertilising the local allotments.*"

TM's laugh and Demarcus Williams' snorting grunts didn't do nothing to untie Barcodes knotted innards.

"*To be perfectly honest,*" TM said after letting his laughter fade, "*I was thinking of offering you a promotion for acting on your own initiative. There will always be a place in my organisation for people with resourcefulness and intellect. Unfortunately, your lack of judgement with the white woman yesterday has rather brought into question your long-term position in the Tribe.*"

Fuck, what could he do to turn this shit around?

"How can I earn back yo' trust, TM? I'll do anythin'."

"*First you have to prove yourself. Would you like to demonstrate your loyalty to the Tribe?*"

Barcode ducked his head. "Yeah, yeah. I'd like that, TM. I'd like that lots."

"*I imagined you might. Keen, are you?*"

Barcode ignored Demarcus' second derisive snort. One day, he and the bastard would face off, and that day wasn't so far away.

"Yes, TM. I's keen."

"*Once again, you talk a good game, but can you walk the walk?*"

"Try me, TM. What you want I to do?"

"*When was the last time you ran into the Parkside Crew?*"

Fuck, did he know that, too? How could he? He couldn't know. No one knew who murked Beanie Boy apart from Barcode. He'd been careful, told no one. Hadn't even boasted about it to his crew.

"The Parksiders?"

"Yes, those disrespectful gentlemen who keep trying to muscle in on my turf. When did you last do anything to hurt them? Standing orders are to discourage them from setting foot in my hood. What have you done to support that lately?"

Could he risk fessing up?

If TM knew already and he denied it, Barcode would find himself in an even deeper pile of shit. Other side of the coin, if he claimed credit for murking Beanie Boy without proof, TM could accuse him of lying. Bragging didn't mean nothing without proof. Which way to go for the best?

Shit. Go for it, man. Show him your stones.

He sat up straight in his seat, coughed to clear his throat. "Did you watch the news this lunchtime, TM?"

"Always."

"You know that hit-and-run over by West Green? Took out three Parksiders."

"What about it?"

Barcode dug a thumb into his chest. "That were me. I done that!"

"Bullshit," Demarcus Williams snapped. "You don't have the smarts to get away with something like that."

Barcode spun in his chair and faced the ugly fucker down. "It was me, I tell you! Stole a car, drove over to West Green, and bided my time 'fore I pounced."

"You can prove that statement, I suppose?"

"Well, I didn't take no pictures or show my face to the security cameras, but I can give you all the details and tell you where I stole the car from and where I dropped it off after the doin'." He tapped a finger to his temple. "Got it all up here. Good memory, me."

"*Okay, Mr Codell. Give Mr Williams the specifics. I'll ask one of my contacts in the local constabulary to confirm your claims. In the meantime, I'll take your word on the matter. But*"—the mussed-up shape on the screen moved again, a shadowy hand came up at the side, index finger wagging—"*if you're telling falsehoods, it won't go well for you. I don't take kindly to liars. Especially people who try lying in order to ingratiate their way into my good graces!*"

Barcode had to work hard to understand what TM were saying. He spoke so posh, with all them stupid, long words.

"It the truth, TM," Barcode said, with total confidence. "On my mother's life. I swear it."

Barcode sighed and lowered his eyes in what he hoped was a display of honesty.

The figure on the screen moved again and the hand disappeared.

"*Okay, assuming you're telling the truth, you'll have no trouble carrying out a little errand I have planned for you for later tonight.*"

Barcode turned again, the seat of his trousers squeaked on the hard chair. It sounded like a fart, but it weren't embarrassing. Not much.

Demarcus stared back at him, the expression on his bearded face hostile and mocking.

"*Do this one little thing for me, Mr Codell, and I'll forget all about yesterday's incident with the white woman. Furthermore, I'll double the size of your turf and your crew. What do you say?*"

"Yes, I'll do it."

"*Even though you don't know what I'm asking?*"

"I's happy to do anythin' you wants, TM. Anythin' at all."

Second Man growled. He leaned forwards and rested his huge forearms on his thighs.

"*Do you have anything to say, Mr Williams?*"

"Yes, I do, but I hesitate to interrupt you, TM."

*"Pray continue, Mr Williams. You know I'm always highly inter-
ested in receiving your valued input."*

Why did TM have to speak like one of them news-
readers off of the TV? So posh, Barcode found it hard to
understand what the fucker was getting at. Some of what
came outta the scrambled figure's mouth sounded real
sarcastic. Mostly, Barcode just nodded, took it all in, and
planned to work it out from memory later, when he wasn't
so rushed. This particular conversation would be one of
those that needed revisiting. Good job his memory were up
to it. Barcode didn't like being taken for a fool.

Demarcus Williams smirked at Barcode before talking.

"In my opinion, this dipshit"—he jabbed a finger at
Barcode—"just lied to your face. I wouldn't trust him to run
out and buy me a coffee. Fucker doesn't have the nerve or
the brains for what you have in mind. Why not let me and a
couple my men do the deed?"

Barcode clenched his fists and clamped his teeth
together hard.

Fuckin' asshole. I'll show you.

Wouldn't be that long a wait, neither.

*"Mr Williams, I thank you for your considered opinion. You make
a good case for the prosecution. What have you to say in your defence,
Mr Codell?"*

Fuck, the man on the screen were making out they was
in a courtroom now. Shit was getting even deeper.

"Whatever you need, TM, I can do it," Barcode said,
leaning towards the screen, pleading. "Just try me. Barcode
won't never let you down."

"That remains to be seen." The shadow's head tilted to one
side again and the screen fell silent for what seemed like
hours before TM spoke again. *"Mr Williams, after due consider-*

ation and despite your eloquence, I am *going to give Mr Codell the opportunity to prove his worth to me and to the Tribe."*

Barcode smiled at Demarcus Williams, who dipped his head towards the screen.

"If you say so, TM," the big fucker said, still eyeing Barcode with contempt.

"I do indeed, Mr Williams."

Barcode returned Demarcus' stare.

Soon, very soon, TM's right-hand man was going to regret speaking trash about Barcode in public. Big as he was, the asshole weren't unbreakable. Beanie Boy found out how well the human body stood up against a moving car, even a little shit-box like the Fiat 500. How would Demarcus Williams handle a BMW 5 Series rammed up his ass?

After a five-second stare down, Demarcus sniffed and flapped his hand. "Sorry for the interruption, TM."

"Not to worry, Mr Williams. As I said, I value your counsel. Now, let us proceed with the matter in hand. Mr Codell, I imagine you know the location of the Parkside's original clubhouse? I don't mean the one they're using these days."

What the fuck?

"Yes, TM. It's … halfway down Lowland Road, West Green. Backs onto the park, right?"

Demarcus lifted an eyebrow and nodded. What was that, respect? If so, it weren't before time.

"Very good, Mr Codell. You see, Mr Williams? Our young friend isn't at all as ignorant as you suggested."

"Seems that way, TM."

Barcode didn't rise to the bait, but mostly kept his eyes on the screen.

"Some valuable information has come into my possession. It would appear that one of my suppliers is offering the Parksiders preferential

terms on their latest collection. I don't like that. Don't like it one little bit. It's not at all conducive to the wellbeing of my overall business strategy. Whereas I'm all for capitalism, and I am a massive supporter of free enterprise, I don't like being undersold. Do you follow me, Mr Codell?"

Despite not having a Scooby, Barcode nodded.

"Yeah, TM. I's followin' you right 'nough."

After all, he couldn't have Demarcus Williams being proved right.

"Good, good. Very good. So, in the face of this blatant affront to our business arrangements, we need to teach both the Parksiders and the suppliers a lesson. Wouldn't you agree?"

Again, Barcode nodded.

"Yeah, that's right, TM. They needs teachin' a lesson."

"However, it wouldn't be prudent to upset the supplier with a flagrant act of aggression, would it?"

Why didn't he just get on with it and say what he wanted?

"No, TM."

"That's right, Mr Codell. Such a brazen act of aggression might be counter-productive. You see, for the Tribe to remain financially secure and, indeed, thrive, we need an uninterrupted supply of product. Upsetting this particular supplier might not be the most prudent course of action. In fact, we are in the middle of some rather delicate and protracted negotiations. With this in mind, if the Tribe was seen to be acting, shall we say, precipitously ..."

Although Barcode pursed his lips and nodded his understanding, he had no idea what the blurred-out dipshit were banging on about. He just needed the bottom line. What the fuck did TM want him to do?

"...it might not pan out the way I want it to. So, all that being said, we can't go in mob-handed and risk revealing ourselves. Oh no, that would never do. We need to be more subtle. We need to disrupt the

Parksiders' supply chain without risking damage to the delicate negotiations, or my expansion plans. And that's where you come in, Mr Codell."

Barcode swallowed. Bugger were finally getting to the point.

'Bout fuckin' time.

"What you need, TM?"

The shadow moved again. *"Over to you, Mr Williams."*

Demarcus shifted in his seat. He reached into his trouser pocket and pulled out an envelope. "Can you read?"

What the fuck?

"What you say?"

"I ask if you can read, dickwad."

"'Course I can read! What you got there?"

Demarcus offered the envelope, but when Barcode reached for it, the fucker snatched it away, leaving him with a handful of air.

"Mr Williams, stop playing with him. You're being rather cruel, and extremely childish."

"Sorry, TM. Couldn't help meself," Second Man said, pushing out the envelope once again.

When Barcode made no move to reach for the paper, Demarcus had to stand and place it right into his open hand. Win to Barcode. Loss to the big fucker with the beard and the shaved head. The one who looked like someone had stuck his head on upside-down. Stupid mutha.

"Inside that envelope, you will find the time of the drop and a few other details. You already know the exact location. This information is all you need to make the interception."

Barcode started tearing at the seal of the envelope.

"Read it later, Mr Codell. I have other things to do."

Barcode jumped to his feet. Couldn't leave the stinking room fast enough. Not only was Demarcus big and aggres-

sive, the fucker reeked of stale sweat. Why the fuck couldn't
he stand under a shower now and again?

Barcode held the envelope up to the screen before
stuffing it into his pocket. "Won't let you down, TM. Me
and my crew will be all over this."

*"No! You don't understand at all! This has to be handled with
caution. Under no circumstances do you tell anyone about this. You need
to work alone. The instructions will tell you how it must be done. And
don't forget to burn the paper after you've read and memorised the information. You must not leave a trail. Do I make myself clear?"*

"Yeah, yeah. Clear as glass, TM."

Barcode nodded again, swamped by the thoughts
whirling around in his head. What the fucking hell had he
let himself in for?

*"See you make it happen, Mr Codell. I am counting on you. The
whole Tribe is counting on you. Now run along. Mr Williams and I
need to discuss some other business. Don't worry about the details of
this afternoon's liaison with the Parksiders. I'll take you at your word,
for now. And you have no need to attend tonight's meeting either. Since
your private enterprise won't take place until overnight, I'm sure you'll
want to reconnoitre the scene and consolidate your plans."*

"Right on, TM. You can trust me. I ain't gonna let you
down."

"As you keep insisting. Now, away with you."

Holding his breath against the foul stink, Barcode
slipped past Demarcus Williams and dived outta the airless
room. The door slammed closed behind him, but not in
time to shut out Demarcus' rumbling laughter and TM's
electronic cackle.

What's their fuckin' game?

Barcode rushed along the corridor, retracing the earlier
route. When he re-entered the Hub, he slowed and rolled
through the place, taking his time. Every eye in the room—

not that there were many—were focused on the back of his shaved head and he didn't wanna give off the vibe he'd been scared shitless.

Once through the main doors, he shifted gears, keen to open the envelope and read the instructions that were supposed to be inside, although he wouldn't have been surprised to find nothing more than a blank piece of paper. He half-expected to be met outside the building by Heavies wielding knives and baseball bats—or worse.

Once through the front door and out in the cold, early-evening air, he tensed, waited, and found nothing but an empty street and a light drizzle.

He pulled up his hood and headed for home but couldn't avoid the nagging feeling he'd just been played.

Chapter Twenty-One

Sunday 21st February – Demarcus Williams

Palmerston Road School, Walthamstow, London, England

Demarcus flexed his arms and tensed his abs, enjoying the way his biceps bulged and his six pack rippled, instilling fear into the minions. Tribesmen were terrified of him. As they should be. Since he and TM—whoever the fuck the fancy-talking bastard was—had taken over the Tribe, they'd ruled the little assholes with terror. Fear worked on so many levels, especially with the young, sweet ones. The innocent, little beauties. Boys, girls. Didn't matter a damn to Demarcus, they all tasted just as sweet.

He took two deep breaths. Had to keep his needs in check. One slip would end him. TM paid well but kept him on a short leash. Who knew what the invisible mutha would do if Demarcus gave in to his urges so close to home.

No, the Tribe's babies were off the menu, for a while.

One day, Demarcus would discover TM's identity. Then he'd take his rightful place at the top of the totem pole. But, while the money kept rolling in and his physical and emotional needs could be met by adults—barely old enough to drive, but adults just the same—he'd take his time. He and his men would take their orders from whoever gave them and grow rich on the easy pickings.

The uppity snot, Barcode, might prove problematic over time, but for now, the fool would carry on being useful, especially if he pulled off the takedown like TM ordered. Fool would do his shit and Demarcus and the rest of the men would keep their hands clean. If Barcode fucked up and got caught—by the Feds or the Parksiders—and the shit hit the spinning blades, they'd all be free and in the clear.

Despite being nothing but a rippling shadow, TM had smarts. No doubt about that. He knew how to plan and what moves to make. In a few short months, he'd turned a bunch of amateur street thugs into a profitable concern. Sure, Demarcus and the men helped, but TM made the plans. Branching out across county lines and using cuckoo's nests had been genius, apart from the shit that had gone down in Southend. Still, shit happened and Demarcus and the boys had cleaned up the mess easy enough.

TM had it right. Time had come to start over. Cuckoo's nests were too profitable to ignore for long. This time, they'd work the background better.

Demarcus checked his watch. A little after seven thirty. Nearly time to let in the squirts.

"Red," he called, "open the doors. They been hanging outside in the cold long 'nough."

The red-headed Irishman exposed his gap-toothed grin, but stayed where he was, sitting in an upholstered chair in the corner, soaking up the heat from one of the new big-assed radiators.

"Ah now, can't we let the feckers suffer a wee bit longer? You gotta love seeing the little people shivering and huddling close to each other. Makes me old heart glad, so it does."

"You, Red, are an evil man. Pull your Mick finger out. TM's going to be online soon. We don't want to keep him waiting, do we?"

Red gave Demarcus "the look", the one telling him what he really thought of TM, but he knew better than to voice his opposition inside the Hub. Or anywhere in the hood, come to that.

TM had an uncanny ability to gather information and understand how best to use it. Somehow, the fucker knew everything that were going on. It was useful. Hugely profitable. But worrisome, too.

Demarcus looked down and flexed his fingers. Long hours in the gym pumping iron every day gave him a ripped bod and strong hands. He looked good. Felt good. *Was* good.

He closed his eyes and listened to the hot water flow through the central heating pipes and click through the radiators. How the ancient system kept working in this part of the school when the rest of the building was falling apart around their heads, no one knew. The plumber was good, damned good. A sure-fire miracle worker. It didn't pump out too much heat, but it made the Hub and the few rooms close to it, including the library, habitable. Just.

Demarcus checked the time again—coming up to a quarter to eight.

"Red, get the fuck moving, asshole!" he barked the order, loud and sharp.

The wiry Irishman wiped his nose on the sleeve of his sweater, unpeeled himself from the chair, and shambled slowly towards the main doors. He was nothing but bony knees, skinny arms, and sticking-out elbows. For the millionth time, Demarcus wondered what made TM hire the fucker in the first place. He hadn't seen the filthy, Mick pig do much of value.

Red couldn't fight worth a damn, and he couldn't handle a knife like the Frog, Gerard. But he could read a wiring diagram. A sparky, the guy had set up all the screens and run out the internet cables.

No, not a fighter, Red looked more like a trolley boy or a barista than a terrorist.

A Mick terrorist? Really?

Maybe Red knew how to handle explosives, too. That would answer the question. Ah well, TM knew what he was doing.

Prob'ly.

Red unbolted the doors and worked the key in the lock and the fuckers—the sweet, young things—hurried in.

Chapter Twenty-Two

Sunday 21st February - Early Evening

Palmerston Road, Walthamstow, London, England

19:47.

As with the previous night, a bitter, driving rain hammered down on Kaine's back and legs. This time, with Lara safely in the hotel and under Connor's close protection, Kaine could relax into his task a little more easily. Not that he could ever fully relax when on duty.

He adjusted the aim of the laser mic, trying to improve the sound quality, but the scraping of feet on wooden floors and the mumbled chatter of a few dozen youngsters, mostly male, made the detail difficult to identify and the conversations impossible to follow.

Useless.

Kaine powered down the mic and set it to one side. He tweaked the focus on his field glasses, bringing the target window into greater clarity. The vertical blinds remained in place, unmoving, backlit by the brilliant white of fluorescent strip lights.

A bleep in Kaine's earpiece indicated an incoming signal.

The state-of-the-art, bone conduction comms kit was a recent addition to their communications arsenal, provided courtesy of Rollo, the team's Quartermaster. The device's prime benefits being silent operation, minimal interference on the reception from ambient noise—an absolute boon for battlefield operations—and the hyper security of the scrambled wireless transmission.

He tapped the earpiece into activation.

"Alpha One receiving. Over," he whispered.

"*Whatcha, Mr K. How ya diddling?*"

Gritting his teeth, Kaine shook his head slowly. No matter how hard he tried, he could never instil proper radio protocols in their hacker, but he wouldn't give up the attempt. He had to tread carefully, though. Corky was, after all, a volunteer who could disappear from the grid any time he chose—as could every one of his team. Even though they worked with Kaine and gladly accepted the generous fees and bonuses he provided, they mainly did so out of a rather humbling loyalty.

"*Alpha One* receiving you full strength. *Over.*"

"*Yeah, right. Good oh! What's happening your end?*"

"TM's transmission's about to start. *Over.*"

"*Yeah, okay, Mr K. Corky's not picking up nothing of interest on his end. In fact, he can't find no internet traffic within one hundred metres of the gaff ... Corky means 'the Hub'. On top of everything else, mobile phone activity in the building's just stopped. Er, ... over.*"

It seemed as though the Tribesmen were obeying the standing orders.

Excellent.

During his earlier recce, Kaine had studied the area surrounding the Tribe's HQ.

A ninety-metre-wide strip of scrubland, dissected by multiple railway lines, separated him from the rear of the four-storey building. The commercial estate close to the Hub stood dark and empty, the warehouses and workshops being occupied only during the day. Some were boarded up and derelict. Most of the streetlights remained dark, broken. At night, the industrial zone pretty much turned into a wasteland.

Beyond the radius of Corky's predicted internet and comms blackout, rows of terraced houses radiated away, some running east to west, others north to south, some of their windows lit yellow, indicating occupation. Further away, the active streetlights and the rainbow of colours— moving headlights, the occasional flashing blues of emergency vehicles, multi-coloured shopfronts, bars, and restaurants, showed a city in movement, a living, breathing city.

The heavy rumble of life.

The rear of the Hub, with its back-lit windows, stood in the centre of a well of darkness. The only immediate sign of activity. If there was a metaphor somewhere, Kaine couldn't find it.

"Alpha One to Control, it's pretty quiet here. Should be easy to identify TM's signal and piggyback it all the way to his location. Over."

"Yep, right. That's Corky's plan. Got all his considerable resources focused on that one bit of real estate. Corky won't let you down, Mr K. You don't never need to fear on that score. Er, … over."

"Stand by, Control. Alpha One, out." He tapped the earpiece into silence.

Kaine checked his watch. 19:59.

Not long now.

He settled under the meagre shelter offered by a dormant thorn bush and tried to ignore the rain dripping from his cap and running down the back of his neck. The more he aged, the more difficult he found it to cope with the discomfort of lying in the open on a winter's evening. The Good Lord alone knew how long he could go on this way. Not that he had much of an alternative.

There!

Movement through Kaine's field glasses caught his attention. A strip of material twitched in the bottom right corner of a window. The dark silhouette of a fist revealed itself. Slowly, the thumb extended and then the hand disappeared.

Damian's signal!

Kaine tapped the earpiece once.

"Alpha One to Control, are you receiving me? Over."

"Corky's receiving you right well, Mr K. Any news?"

Kaine gritted his teeth. Corky may well be one of the best hackers in the world, but he might also be the planet's most annoying human being.

"Alpha One to Control, signal received. Repeat. Signal received. Over."

"You certain, Mr K?"

What the hell was going on in Corky's head? Kaine took a breath before answering.

"Confirmed, Control. I received the signal ten seconds ago. You should be seeing a transmission right now. Over."

"That's interesting. Real interesting. Okay. Give Corky a minute, will you? Be right back. Control, out."

Kaine frowned and shook his head again. The fact Corky had used the correct radio termination signal, not only confirmed he knew the protocol, but that he deliberately avoided using it to annoy Kaine. It also indicated that Corky was distracted, maybe even irritated.

That was the first time Corky had ever displayed anything other than supreme confidence. Normally, the man was self-assured to the point of arrogance.

Frowning, Kaine settled back. This was likely going to be an even longer night than he'd been expecting.

Chapter Twenty-Three

Sunday 21st February - Damian Baines

Palmerston Road School, Walthamstow, London, England

19:51.

Damian "Rhino" Baines trembled as he entered the Hub. Once upon a time, he liked the homely vibe of the place, except in winter when it used to be damp and freezing cold, but not no more. Nowadays, despite the heat thrown out by the new rads, he hated the place.

Way back, when he first joined the Tribe, the Hub were safe, a place for the bros to hang out. At least it had been better than the shitty home life he'd suffered with the drunken, fist-throwing, bum of an old man and a useless, addict of a mother. Back then, the Hub were a sanctuary where he'd meet his buddies, share some brews, split packs of ciggies, spark up some spliffs, and chill. So what if they sold a few baggies of weed to line they pockets? Nobody got hurt. At least not often, and not bad.

That were back in the days of the first Top Man.

Sure, the Hub had been a shithole back then. Dark, dirty, no power, cold as fuck, damp, but it were *their* shithole. A place to hang, a place to chill, a place of safety. But now … fuck.

It look better. That was for sure. Shiny, almost clean, and bright with its electrics and its internet. In the far corner, where the Geeks sat doing who-the-fuck-knew-what, the place look like the *Enterprise*, for fuck's sake.

Damian touched the ugly scar on his neck. Damn thing never let up hurting. Stiff and painful, the thing cut his moves and made him look like a freak. Give him the rotten nickname, Rhino, too. Fucking disrespect weren't easy to live with. Even the little kids used it, but he couldn't blame them. When the new TM give him the nickname, making it official, Damian weren't in no position to argue. Whatever the new TM say became Tribe law. If Damian ever grew a pair and stepped outta line, the Heavies would stamp on him.

Led by the creepy fucker, Demarcus Williams, the one who look funny at all the young ones, the Heavies would have their jollies. Damian probably wouldn't survive, and then what would happen to Ariel and the little one who weren't even born yet?

The Griffins offered him a chance. A slim chance maybe, but Damian's only hope of finding a way outta the mire. Didn't matter if he believed Mr Griffin or not, Damian didn't have no option.

'Tween a rock and a hard place.

Surrounded by the other Tribesmen, excited and chattering like the ignorant fools they was, Damian shuffled into the outer edge of the Hub, keeping his head down, trying to stay invisible.

Demarcus Williams and the spineless Irishman, Red, eyed them all as they piled through the main doors, making sure no Tribesman were stupid enough to ignore the rules about phones. Occasionally, they'd stop one or two apparently at random. Demarcus mostly stopped the younger ones and patted them down. Some of the little girls, he'd take extra time over. He'd feel between they legs, cup they snatches, squeeze they butts. On the surface, he make it look like he were checking for contraband, but Damian knew better. The older, longer-serving Tribesmen knew better, too. But Demarcus were protected by TM and the other Heavies, and there weren't nothing nobody could do about it. Damian hated being helpless. Hated the fucker, Demarcus Williams, too. Hated him with a fire.

Once they all filed into the Hub and stood in rows in front of the screen—no one were allowed to sit during TM's briefings—Demarcus shut the doors and took his usual place alongside the monitor. Red guarded the door, and other Heavies, Gerard, Crabapple, and Delinquent, spread out around the walls, making sure they had a good view of what went down.

Damian scanned the faces in the crowd. Everyone were present. No, not everyone. Barcode weren't nowhere to be seen. Strange. The arrogant bastard had been toadying up to the new TM ever since the Tribe come under new management. Tattooed wanker fancied himself a "made man". Fancied himself as one of the elite. When TM give Barcode his own patch and crew, the creep started swaggering around the place like the Queen had invited him to a garden party at Buck House.

Fuckin' asshole. Where he at?

Not like Barcode to go AWOL when there was asses to kiss and assholes to lick.

He'd love to know where Barcode had gotten to, and, given what happened with his wife, Mr Griffin might be interested, too. Unless the middle-aged man with the bad-ass moves had already punished Barcode for trying to strongarm his wife. Now that event, Damian would really like to witness.

Oh yeah. I'd love to see Barcode take a can of whoop-ass from soldier boy.

Damian ain't forgotten the world of pain Mr Griffin laid on him with a single lightning-quick, finger jab. Again, he rubbed the area above the scar. The electric shock hadn't lasted long, but while it did, he were frozen, totally at Mr Griffin's mercy. Despite that, the man hadn't taken advantage. Instead, he helped Damian to his feet, walked him to a quiet place, and listened to his tale.

No idea who the white man really were—definitely not the filth—or what he really wanted, but Mr Griffin already give him a bundle of cash money. He'd also offered Damian, Ariel, and the baby a future, and Damian were planning to grab the opportunity with both hands and run with it.

He worked his way to the edge of the crowd and closer to the wall overlooking the railway lines.

Demarcus Williams, the creep, read the time from his big, gold wristwatch and silenced the crowd with a howled, "Shut up!" then hit the power button at the bottom of the big screen.

Rude bastard.

The kids was excitable, no need for being nasty. Terrorising little kids weren't never cool.

Behind the creep, the screen flicked on bright. The familiar, black outline against a white background hardened.

"Good evening, Tribesmen. It's so good to see another excellent turnout. Makes my heart glad. I take it you are all in tip-top form and awaiting your instructions?"

The Tribe mumbled something.

"I asked you ungrateful people a question!" TM shouted, the weird voice rising to a roar. *"Are you ready for your instructions?"*

This time, the response were louder, more concerted, but still ragged.

"Yes, TM!"

"Good, good. Now, let's get down to business …"

With everyone's attention on the bullshit spewing from the speakers, Damian edged closer to the corner window. Still facing the monitor, smiling and nodding along with the rest, he stuck his hand behind his back, and slid it through the nearest hanging strip. He stuck up his thumb, held it for a count of three, and pulled the hand back, sticking it in his pocket.

To his right, Red's eyes narrowed, stared right at him. After a while, Red shifted his gaze to Demarcus Williams, and then focused back on Damian.

What the fuck?

Sweat poured outta him, his hands shook, and his gut clenched. He hadn't been so terrified since facing the posse of skinheads on the inside. The bastards had worked him over, big time. Left him with the shit-ugly scar that ruined his looks and his life. He thought everything had ended until Ariel smiled at him from behind the counter at the chemist. He'd only gone in to collect the cream that made the thick tissue on his neck slightly more bearable. Not much, but enough to make a difference.

His beautiful, gentle, and lovely Ariel.

The first time they met, she looked at his scar with sympathy, not disgust. Then she smiled at him again. Later, on their first date, she ask him about it, where and how he got it. He'd hesitated before answering, but even then, Damian knew she were the one. If he wanted Ariel in his life—and he did—no way could he lie about nothing. Not never. Even though she mighta taken fright and run away screaming, Damian gave her the whole, sorry tale. But she didn't run. Instead of bolting, she stayed. She even helped apply the medicine every day in the places he couldn't reach so easy.

Damian fingered the scar again. When he sweated, the skin around the edges stung like a mutha. He wanted the meeting over so he could get home. Home to Ariel.

Red turned his head towards Damian again. They eyes met, locked. Red sneered, rolled his head, and lifted a hand to tug his earlobe. Was he taking the piss at Damian's scar or was he sus?

Had he seen the signal?

Shit.

What were he gonna do?

Play it cool, Damian. Play it cool.

Red didn't see nothing. He didn't.

"...*stepping up the Tribe's profile in the area,*" TM said, his rhythm quickening. "*I'm putting plans in place to smite our enemies.*"

What the fuck were the asshole cracking on about?

Concentrate, Damian. This shit's important.

Whatever TM was spewing, however ridiculous, Damian needed to remember it for his report to Mr Griffin.

If there were any hope for the white man keeping his word, it would only work if Damian proved useful. A few banknotes here and there wouldn't do no good in the long run. Damian needed a new life and a new identity for his family, and the only way to get it would be through Mr and Mrs Griffin. There weren't no other choice.

Helplessness weren't a good feeling.

"You might have noticed one of the Tribe is missing this evening," TM said, pausing while most of the Tribesmen looked around them.

Some frowned and whispered out the side of they mouths, but Damian and the rest of Barcode's crew nodded. They noticed all right. Lil' Aran—Barcode's cousin and only real friend—even had tears in his eyes. Probably thinking of how the Heavies had taken Barcode out permanent, like, on account of Mrs Griffin kicking his butt. Lil' Aran would be the only one to miss the tattooed mutha if he had fallen foul of TM's rage.

Would serve him right, though. Damian wouldn't be wasting no tears for the loss of that murdering scumbag.

"That's right. Mr Codell is not with us today," TM continued, *"but don't worry, he hasn't been punished. Oh no. At this precise moment, Mr Codell is working through a mission for the Tribe. He's putting himself in great danger for the cause, and I applaud him."*

The blurry shadow on the big screen moved and hands appeared above its head, keeping in full view. He started clapping. The Heavies joined in immediately and encouraged the Tribesmen to do the same with threatening stares. The newer ones didn't need too much encouragement and added whoops and hollers to they wild applause. The older ones, the original members of the Tribe, were less keen.

After allowing the applause to die down, TM continued. *"If his mission is a success and, since Barcode is a resourceful indi-*

vidual armed with good intel, I'm sure it will be, it will provide a serious blow to our nearest enemies, The Parkside Crew!"

He practically screamed the crew's name and brought new and spontaneous applause from the Tribesmen. Damian had to give TM a grudging respect for the way he handle the crowd, but there weren't no doubt, he hadn't finished. The hands appeared again, this time on either side of the blob of a head. They patted the space alongside where his ears might be, making a "calm down" move, but he kept quiet until the noise were gone completely.

"And that's only the start," he added. *"By the time we've finished, the Parkside Crew will be destroyed!"*

More howls of delight. More back slapping and applause.

TM carried on rousing the rabble for another few minutes before restoring order and starting in on what he called "the housekeeping".

FOR THE FOLLOWING hour or so, TM summed up the previous week's performance of each crew and each pitch in turn. He went through his usual intimidation, mocking, threats, encouragement, bribery, and promises of future riches.

He ended each rant with specific instructions to each team leader and ordered Gerard, who were now sitting behind one of the desks, to hand out product and envelopes. That part of the process always reminded Damian of the movies he saw as a kid where working men would get they pay in cash and in brown envelopes on Friday afternoons ahead of spending the weekend blowing it all in the local boozers.

When TM first started doling out the cash this way, Damian half-expected to have tax and national insurance payments taken out. But it didn't work like that. Each team leader received his team's cash to divvy up as he saw fit. No even-handed profit sharing for the Tribesmen.

Fuck that.

Things couldn't go on, they had to change.

"*Right now, where is he?*" TM said, the darkened head moving as though scanning the faces in the crowd. "*Ah, there you are, Rhino, my man. Why are you skulking back there in the corner?*"

Damian flinched.

Oh Jesus, what now?

The crowd of white and black faces, Heavies included, turned towards him. His mouth dried. Couldn't swallow.

"*It's not like you to be so shy. Step forwards, Rhino, dear fellow.*"

Damian blinked under everyone's stares.

Move. You can do this!

He threw back his shoulders as best he could against the stretch of the scar and stepped to the side of the front row.

TM boasted he knew everything, saw everything.

Shit, no.

The signal. The bastard seen his signal to Mr Griffin.

"*That's right, Rhino. Step forwards.*"

Silence fell. An ominous silence.

"Y-Yes, TM?" he managed, his voice little more than a squeak.

"*Since Barcode is away on … other business, I'm going to hold onto your team's payment until next time. We need to ensure the correct protocols, don't you agree?*"

Relief flooded through Damian, but he tried not to show it. Maybe he *would* see Ariel again. He'd maybe even live to see the baby born.

"Er, yes, TM," he said, nodding. "We all needs rules. They keep the Tribe strong."

He parroted the words TM used to end all his transmissions. They almost sounded like a prayer.

"But can you operate without product?"

A trick question?

"No, TM."

"As you happen to be Mr Codell's deputy, you'd better step up, then. Collect tomorrow's supply from Gerard. It wouldn't do to let the customers down, now would it?"

Damian bobbed his head in agreement, said, "Er, no, TM. Right," and turned away from the screen.

He hurried to the desk to collect his crew's package from the solid, white man with the smarmy French accent. The skinny Geek at the table next to the cashier's desk weighed a brown-paper package, typed something into his computer, and handed it to Gerard, who passed it across.

Damian felt the weight of one day's supply. Five hundred notes' worth of blow and a couple hundreds' worth of grass weren't heavy. He stuffed the bundle into the inner pocket of his jacket and strolled back to his position by the window. He needed to be ready to make the end-of-show signal, but couldn't make it obvious. He wanted to rush, but couldn't risk drawing any more attention to his moves. TM's transmission didn't usually last long after he'd dealt out the packages and delivered his last words.

With TM's final rant underway at last, Damian leaned his back against the wall alongside the window. Not long now.

"That's it until tomorrow, when I'll be calling for volunteers for the next County Lines run. I'll also be looking for another cuckoo team," TM announced. *"Remember this. If I don't have enough volunteers, I shall be running a raffle. Now, go and make the Tribe richer. But*

remember … it's a dangerous world out there. Be careful and remember to obey the rules. We all need rules, as they keep the Tribe strong."

The dark head dipped and the screen turned black. End of transmission.

As the Tribesmen relaxed and started buzzing, Damian lowered his head.

Thank fuck for that.

He'd gotten away with it. Only one more thing to do. A simple thumb's up sign and he were done, maybe for good.

Slowly, he edged to his right, sliding his left hand behind his back. His fingers found the straight line of the window and touched the blinds. With his right hand, he fingered the scar on his neck, with the other, he gave the sign.

Done. He were done.

"What the fuck was that!" Red screamed from across the room, pointing at Damian.

"What?" Damian said, terror flooding his system, weakening his bladder.

He nearly pissed himself.

"You rattled the blinds. A fucking signal," Red shouted, reaching into the pocket of his cargo pants and rushing forwards.

"No. I didn't. Didn't do nothin'!" Damian raised his hands in surrender.

Around him, the Tribesmen scattered, clearing space for Red and the rest of the Heavies.

Jesus, fucking Jesus.

Demarcus Williams met Red in the middle of the room. With Frenchie still in charge of the inventory, the other two Heavies, Crabapple and Delinquent, covered the doors, knife and baseball bat up and ready for action.

Lockdown in full swing.

Damian stood still. With no hope of making a run for it, he checked the faces of the Tribesmen, but none was about to eyeball him. He were alone. Totally alone.

"I saw it," Red said, loud, definite, accusing. "You did the same thing when TM started speaking."

The big screen blinked into life again, and the shadow reappeared.

"*Explain yourself, Mr Doohan,*" TM's electronic voice demanded.

Doohan? Red's name was Doohan?

Did it matter?

Oh shit.

"Sure thing, TM," the Irishman replied in triumph. "When you started speaking, Rhino rattled the blinds over there. Did the self-same thing when you signed off just now, so he did."

Damian was fucked. Not a chance, but for Ariel and the baby he needed to try.

"No, TM. Scratchin' my back, I was. Got aches and pains. You know, on account of …" He touched his fingers to his neck.

"*Wait. I'll check. Hold him still.*"

The screen turned blank once again. Before Damian could say anything else, before he could move, Demarcus Williams and Crabapple swooped in and pinned both arms behind his back.

No point struggling. They had him tight.

Demarcus leaned closer. His foul breath warmed Damian's cheek.

"I'm gonna enjoy this, fucker," he whispered. "Haven't had much exercise this week. Need some target practice, too. Stops me getting rusty."

While Crabapple held still, Demarcus tightened his grip on Damian's forearm and levered up hard.

His shoulder popped. Burning fire tore through his body. He screamed. Couldn't hold it in. He stood on tiptoes, trying to relieve the pressure. Blood pounded in his ears, beat through his shoulder.

"No, please. Stop. Stop!"

The whisper returned. "Before you die, you gonna tell me who you was signalling. The Parkside Crew? The Hall-gate Mob?"

"No, please. I-I weren't signallin' to no one. H-Honest."

Sweat leaked outta Damian. Poured from him. Fire torched his shoulder and arms, and the wrist Demarcus twisted with near enough force to snap bones.

"Then, after we fuck over the Parkside Crew, or whoever, I'm paying a little social visit. Ariel and I is gonna get better acquainted."

Damian screamed. Lost it completely.

"You bastard! No! Leave her alone!"

Blind panic took over.

He bucked, fought the agony. Struggled. Kicked out, aiming for shins. Missed. Only succeeded in increasing the fire in his shoulder.

Jesus, no!

His vision swam, dimmed, faded to grey.

"*Stop!*"

The monitor brightened and Demarcus' grip on Dami-an's arm loosened but didn't break. Fire still pulsed through his shoulder, but the pressure eased and he dropped to his feet, panting hard.

"I-I didn't do nothin', TM. Nothin'. Honest, I didn't."

The image on the monitor changed to a video of the Hub taken from high up, above the main monitor. In the bottom right of the image, a figure wearing a dark blue jacket, Damian, leaned against the wall beside one of the windows. A time at the top showed 20:02:05 and counting.

Right behind the figure, one of the blinds rippled.

Damian tried to swallow, but couldn't find the spit.

The image froze and the screen split in two. A second video appeared beside the first, looking the exact same. The new video rolled forwards, the clock ticked on. After ten seconds, the same thing happened to the blind and the video stopped moving. The only real difference between the two stills were the time. The second clock registered 21:49:19.

Demarcus Williams whispered in his ear again. "Looks clear enough to me, fucker. Say your prayers."

His quiet, ugly laugh turned Damian's stomach inside out. He tried to catch the eye of his crew, and of the other Tribesmen, but no one met his gaze. No one were coming to his rescue.

He was totally and utterly fucked.

TM's silhouette emerged in the top corner of the monitor.

"*Anything to say for yourself before I pass sentence, Rhino?*"

"I didn't do nothin', TM. Scratch my back is all."

"*Not good enough,*" TM said, his voice calm, almost sad. "*Mr Williams, Mr Cox, take him away. Find out all you can. Don't forget to film it for me. You know how I love home movies.*"

With the images on the screen standing in frozen proof, Demarcus Williams and Crabapple dragged him across the floor.

Damian, panicked and desperate, kicked and screamed the whole way outta the Hub.

Chapter Twenty-Four

Sunday 21st February - Evening

Palmerston Road, Walthamstow, London, England

21:58.

Kaine tapped the earpiece. "Alpha One to Control, are you receiving me? Over."

He waited.

Come on, Corky. Where are you?

After eight long seconds, he repeated the call.

"*Oh, just a sec, Mr K,*" Corky responded, offhandedly. "*Be right with you.*"

Annoyed, Kaine couldn't help grinding his teeth at Corky's demeanour. In his head, Kaine counted to five—the most he could manage. He breathed long and hard.

"*You still there, Mr K?*"

"Alpha One to Control, yes, I'm still here. Over."

Kaine relaxed his jaw muscles. Teeth grinding did the molars no good at all, and it made talking difficult.

"*Ah, bonzer.*"

Bonzer?

Surely the hacker wasn't still trying to convince Kaine he was based in Australia? No matter, Kaine had no intention of trying to identify a location for the extremely useful but massively annoying hacker.

"Alpha One to Control, I received the termination signal at 21:49. Over."

"*Ten to ten. Got it.*"

"Any news for me? Over."

"*Yep, sure have, and its real interesting, Mr K. And by the way, there ain't no need for all this 'over and out' military bull. These here are closed comms. No one is ever gonna be earwigging these conversations. No way.*"

He coughed out an aggravating, little chuckle before continuing.

"*Corky and the Q designed this state-of-the-art techie stuff for our radio chats. Targeted, full-encryption protocols, multi-site, and random signal generation and receipt. Completely and utterly secure, it is. The only way anyone's gonna hear what you says is by creeping up on you and listening hard. And from what Corky knows about you, Mr K, that ain't likely to happen. Not in this lifetime. Is Corky right?*"

Kaine pulled in a deep, cleansing breath, wiped the rain from his face, and tried not to answer with a string of expletives. He left swearing to the ignorant and poorly-educated. Mostly.

"Security of messages is not the main reason for following radio protocol, Control. When the caller says 'over', it's the signal for the recipient to … oh forget it. Why did you say 'interesting' just then? Over."

"*Well now, Mr K, that there happens to be the million-dollar question. Corky said it were interesting, because, for the past two hours, there has been no signal leaving or entering the Hub. Is that interesting enough for you?*"

What?

Kaine blinked more rain from his eyes.

"Repeat that, Control. Over."

"*You heard Corky right, Mr K. Nobody in that building were using no comms equipment. No mobile phones, no landlines, and no satellite signals. Nada. Zilch. Rien.*"

"Are you certain? Over."

"*Totally, Mr K. Ever since you laid this little challenge on Corky, he's been digging into the techie setup inside the Tribe's lair. They've got a real smart system over there, but not smart enough to block out dear, ol' Corky.*" Again, he chuckled before continuing. "*They got all the goodies. Corky means a landline with PXB, VPN, satellite, two-way radios, you name it. Hell, they've even got a mobile phone mast on their roof. And, through that, they have powerful and instant access to every licenced carrier in the UK. Corky's been monitoring their comms for the past … little while. Ain't no worries on that score. But, from the time Rhino gave you the start signal, to the moment you got the termination signal, there weren't no comms traffic in that there building. Guaranteed.*"

"Okay, Control, I understand. Over."

"*You know what this means, Mr K?*"

"Yes, Control, I rather think I do. Over."

"*Yep, that's right. TM's using a hardwired, closed-circuit system to talk to the Tribe. The dingbat's inside the school! Corky can't piggyback on the signal, 'cause there ain't no signal to piggyback on. Only way Corky could give you any pictures or sound is by physically splicing into the cables, or by planting his own cameras and mic inside the school, and no way that's happening. Corky ain't no cat burglar.*"

"*However, come to think of it, Corky does know one particular*"

*geezer what might be able to help. This geezer, Corky's mate, owes him
a favour or two. Yeah, and he'd probably be happy for a little excitement about now, what with his new baby making his life so boring and
all. Want Corky to give him a shout?"*

The pause in Corky's rant gave Kaine the only indica-
tion his question wasn't rhetorical.

Kaine didn't relish the idea of having one of Corky's
potentially unreliable and unvetted "mates" sticking his nose
into The 83's business. After all, Kaine was a fugitive, one
of the UK's top ten most wanted. The last thing he needed
was to allow a total stranger to join the team. Someone
who, for all Kaine knew, would hand him over to the
authorities at the drop of a five-pound note.

"Alpha One to Control. Thanks all the same, but I'm
not sure that will be necessary. I have my own idea of where
to take this. Over."

*"Yeah, Corky's been giving it some thought, too. What you gotta do
is sit on that building with Rhino at your side, and watch people leave
through the front or back door."*

Kaine nodded. "My thoughts exactly. Over."

*"Why don't you set up a couple of video cameras front and back,
and do it remotely? All you gotta do is get Rhino to tell you which
bugger weren't actually inside the Hub when TM was gabbing. Then
you'll twig who he is. Is Corky right, Mr K? You bet your life he is. Er,
… over."*

Corky had a point, but Kaine could see a major flaw in
the hacker's logic.

"Alpha One to Control, how many exits are there?
Over."

"Just the two, Mr K. Just the two. Over."

"Are you certain? Over."

*"Corky's always certain. Main entrance at the front, and the back
door you're looking at right now. They can't climb out no windows on*

account of all them security bars. By the way, those bars is a real fire hazard, you know? Health and Safety nightmare, you ask ol' Corky. No wonder the authorities condemned the building all them years ago."

"Control, did you find any architect's drawings of the school and, if so, can you send them to me? Over."

"'Course, Mr K. Mind you, they aren't exactly up-to-date. Thirty-odd years old, but they'll give you an idea of the basic layout. Doubt the Tribe will have made any major structural changes to the place, neither. Leastways, Corky ain't been able to find no record of tunnels being built in the past year or two. Don't mean they haven't, though. But it ain't likely."

"Do you mind emailing me the blueprints anyway? Over."

"On their way, Mr K."

"Thank you, Control. Over."

"You is real welcome, Mr K."

Kaine took a moment to think.

"You still there, Mr K?"

"I'm still here, Control. Over."

"Yeah, thought you were. As it happens, while we've been chatting, Corky's been texting with his mate. He's read about you and hates the way you was set up as the bad guy. Says he'd love to help if you ever need it."

"Damn it, Corky!"

"Steady on, Alpha One, old chap," Corky said in a surprisingly accurate, plummy accent. *"That's hardly the correct comms protocol, don't you know. Over."*

"Control, I sincerely hope we never meet in person. I'm pretty sure I'd end up losing my ... Stand by, Control. Something's happening. Alpha One, out."

The rear door to the school crashed open, and a rectangle of white light burst into Kaine's field glasses, momentarily blinding him. Kaine blinked twice to remove the orange after-image.

The rear door swung closed and movement-activated floodlights situated on the rear wall high above the exit exploded into life.

Three men stood out sharply under the lights.

Or rather, two of the men stood. The third swayed like a drunk at pub-emptying time, struggling to keep his feet, while his mates held him upright, preventing him from face-planting onto the concrete. Only it was clear they weren't his mates and they weren't trying to help.

The one in the middle was begging them to let him go. Pleading. His sobs echoed around the courtyard, bouncing off the three crumbling walls and spilling across the gap to where Kaine lay in the bushes.

Kaine trained his binoculars on the prisoner and adjusted the focus, but, with his back to the powerful flood-lights, the man was nothing but a black silhouette, uniden-tifiable.

Two against one. Bad odds.

Someone was about to take a serious beating.

The large individual on the right—shaven-headed with a full and bushy beard—aimed a brutal kick to the groin of the one suspended in the middle. He screamed and curled into a foetal ball. The captors released his arms and the victim slowly sank to the ground. He ended up on his knees, bent double, awaiting his fate, crying and begging for mercy the whole time.

The attackers stepped away and started circling their victim, promising a slow and painful death.

Hell!

"Alpha One to Control, are you seeing this? Over."

"Nah, there ain't no surveillance cameras in the area for Corky to tap into. Why? What's happening?"

Kaine gave Corky a blow-by-blow account of what he was seeing.

"Okay. Whatcha gonna do?"

"Nothing. Can't afford to show my hand yet. These people are drug dealers and thugs. They know what to expect. Deserve all they get. Alpha One, out."

Kaine cut the comms link and concentrated on the scene playing out below and fifty metres away.

The downed man looked up, shoulders hunched, one slightly higher than the other, head tilted a little to one side.

His head swivelled awkwardly left and right, the shoulders moving at the same time, as though head and shoulders were welded together. With one hand raised to protect his head, the victim twisted at the waist, and the light fell on his bruised and bloodied face.

Damian!

Chapter Twenty-Five

Sunday 21st February - Evening

Palmerston Road, Walthamstow, London, England

22:06.

Kaine dropped the binoculars. With the courtyard's lights shining, he could see well enough without them.

So much for standing by and watching two drug dealers dispensing punishment to one of their own. Damian Baines had been acting on Kaine's instructions, which meant, *de facto*, he was one of Kaine's people. His responsibility.

The two attackers continued circling. Every so often, one would dance forwards and aim a kick at Damian's head, but deliberately fall short or wide. The next flying boot might not miss. The next one might land, prove fatal.

Psychological torture mixed with the physical. An old and dirty trick.

And all the while, Damian begged for his life, while the other two laughed.

Kaine had seen the method used before. Twice in the past, he'd fallen victim to something similar. Similar, but worse, more professional, more extensive. He retained the mental and physical scars as reminders. Even though these men were amateurs, the effect would be pretty much the same.

Sickening.

He pulled the SIG P226 from its holster and confirmed the load. Fifty-five metres in the rain. Not the easiest shots he'd ever taken, but not totally outside his operational parameters. But at such a range, he couldn't be certain of where he'd hit. He could aim to injure them, but any error in judgement or movement from the target could make the shots fatal.

Despite having no love for drug pushers or bullies, he couldn't act as public executioner. He wasn't sure the two men deserved to live, but nor could he be certain they deserved to die. Kaine didn't have the legal or moral authority to pull the trigger.

Bugger.

Kaine rolled down the woollen ski mask to cover his face and started forwards. He slithered through the long, sodden grass.

Moving through the dark towards the light, he didn't need to take too much care, he only needed to keep his noise down. The Heavies were having too much fun mocking and torturing their prey. Their attention was on their victim, not the surrounding wasteland.

Amateur hour.

No matter how secure they felt, the Heavies should never have left their flanks unwatched, unprotected.

Thirty-five metres.

With every metre gained, the margin for error improved, but not by much.

The building behind his targets, with its walls full of unprotected windows and at least one room filled with kids, wouldn't prove much of a defence for a through-and-through. No, he couldn't risk taking a shot. Reluctantly, he slid the SIG back into its holster and secured the retaining strap.

He angled to the right, taking a circular route, keeping away from the lights.

The larger man with the beard stopped walking. He stood at right angles to Damian, who had to twist awkwardly to see him. The bearded man's partner mirrored his movements, stopping on Damian's other side and standing with his arms crossed. Icy rain soaked his thin top, plastering the material to his skin and making it steam, but he didn't seem to mind. Apparently, too wrapped up in his business to notice.

"Who were you signalling, asshole?" Beardy asked, shouting over the driving rain.

"No one, Mr Williams. Scratchin' my back, I was. Like I t-told you in … in the Hub."

Beardy—probably Demarcus Williams, one of the Heavies—danced forwards. This time, his kick connected with Damian's ribcage, whose scream couldn't quite muffle the crack of breaking bones. Two, maybe three ribs at least. Damian collapsed, coughing.

Such an injury could puncture a lung.

Shit.

Kaine scrambled to his feet. Raced forwards.

"Your turn, Mr Cox," Williams ordered, through his laughter. "See if you can match that."

Cox made a movement forwards, then stopped, looking in Kaine's direction. His mouth dropped open and he raised a hand, index finger pointing.

Kaine reached Williams first. In one blinding movement, he snapped out a fist, landed a vicious rabbit punch to the big man's left kidney, and kept moving.

By the time he hurdled Damian's crumpled form, Cox still hadn't had time to finish raising his arm. His slack-mouthed face registered shock.

Kaine's straight jab splintered the man's nose. Cartilage crunched and blood exploded. Cox screamed, stumbled backwards. His hands flew up in protection, exposing a rounded gut.

Close in, Kaine threw a flurry of belly punches. Cox covered up, tried to dodge the blows. He bent double then screamed as his damaged face connected with Kaine's rising knee.

Slowly, Cox toppled sideways. His face hit the concrete in a sickening crack of splintering teeth and fracturing facial bones. He lay still, poleaxed, arms splayed wide, legs crossed at the ankles.

A howl and movement from the side and slightly behind made Kaine dive to his left. He somersaulted to his feet, doubled back, and crashed into the legs of a slowly recovering Williams. The big man's knees buckled, forcing him to the ground.

Breathing hard, Kaine regained his footing.

Williams, lying face up on the concrete, moved his right hand, scrabbling at his side, searching for something. A weapon?

Kaine booted him in the ribs.

Williams howled, coughed. He hugged his chest, the weapon forgotten.

Kaine stepped close to the gagging, spluttering creature. He crouched, searched Williams' pocket and found a snub-nosed revolver, a Smith & Wesson Model 442. Compact and lightweight, designed for concealed carry. Small but power-ful. At short range and in the hands of an expert, the .38 could be accurate and highly effective.

Groaning, Williams tried to roll away. Kaine dropped his knee onto the man's damaged chest.

Williams groaned. Pink spittle flew from his mouth. He stopped moving and Kaine eased off his weight a little.

"Ain't pleasant, bein' kicked in the ribs. Is it, arsewipe?" Acting on the fly, he offered what he hoped was a half-decent, East End accent.

Save for the slight rise and fall of his chest, Cox remained motionless. Damian writhed on the ground where he first fell. Struggling for breath, in dire need of hospital-isation.

Kaine had to move things along.

Built without an internal lock, the S&W 442 was hardly the safest handgun on the planet. He thumbed the release lever, broke open the chamber, removed the bullets, and dropped them into his pocket.

Williams turned his head, breathing heavily, but with difficulty. "Who … who the fuck are you?"

Behind the ski mask, Kaine smiled. "I is the guy what's just kicked your fat arse, dickwad." Kaine winced internally at his use of the vernacular. "Tribe's been gettin' uppity lately, and we's 'bout ready to close you down."

"Who are you?" Williams repeated.

"You know who we is."

"Parkside?"

"Nighty night, arsehole."

Kaine snapped the 442's empty chamber closed, reversed the gun, and clubbed the handle to the back of Williams' head with enough force to stun, but not enough to crush the skull—unless he had a particularly weak one. Not that it mattered too much.

Williams' eyes rolled up to the back of his head and he flopped backwards, groaning gently. He'd wake with a screaming headache at the very least, concussion maybe. But he would wake.

Inside the Tribe's building, more lights bloomed.

Kaine rolled Williams onto his side and lifted his chin to open the airway. He scrambled across to Cox and placed him into the recovery position, too. There would be no deaths on Kaine's heavily laden conscience that day.

He hurried to where Damian—on hands and knees—was still struggling to breathe. Wet burbling noises confirmed Kaine's initial diagnosis. The young man's eyes bulged in fright. Suffocation was a real possibility. Drowning in his own blood. A terrifying thought.

"Damian, you'll be okay. Try not to panic. Try to breathe slowly. Easy for me to say, I know."

Choosing the uninjured side, Kaine eased a hand under Damian's armpit and helped him to his feet.

"Come on, son," Kaine said, pulling the youngster's arm around his shoulder as gently as possible, trying to ignore Damian's grunt of pain, "let's get you to hospital."

Struggling under the young man's weight, Kaine shuffled away, heading for the side of the building, with Damian groaning and breathing wetly.

Keeping his eyes and ears open for a flanking attack, he hit the side of his head with his palm. No time for finesse.

"Alpha One to Control, are you receiving? Over."

"Corky's here, Mr K. Heard the lot. Worked out what happened. Impressive. You really kicked arse. Over."

Kaine panted under the load. "Thought I'd powered down the comms link. Over."

"So you did, Mr K, but Corky has a built-in override. He heard everything. Bad language and all. Naughty, Mr K. Over."

"Control, Damian's in a bad way—"

"Yeah, Corky heard. Not to worry, the ambulance is on its way. Should be on the corner of Boothe Avenue and Green Lane in about five minutes. Over."

"Excellent. Directions to the RV point would help. Over."

"Keep going as you are, turn at the end of Palmerston Road, and head for the bright lights. You're within seven hundred metres. Over."

"Thank you, Control, you are a genius. Over."

"Now tell Corky something he don't know, Alpha One. Hey, Corky's getting the hang of this radio lingo. Did you notice? Over."

"Yes, Control. I noticed and it's appreciated. Over."

"Do Corky one favour though, Mr K. Over."

"What's that, Control? Over," Kaine asked, gasping. Damian weighed a ton.

"Work on your Cockney accent, will ya? You sounded worse than Dick Van Dyke in Mary Poppins. Over."

"Will do, Control. I promise. Alpha One, out."

Everyone's a bloody critic.

Chapter Twenty-Six

Sunday 21st February - Evening

Palmerston Road, Walthamstow, London, England

22:14.

Kaine struggled under Damian's almost-dead weight.

In the brightly lit courtyard, they were hopelessly exposed. The blinding light from the floodlights made them stand out like targets on a firing range. He needed dark, the edge of the radiance.

Pity's sake, move, man.

He strained under the heavy load, stumbled, corrected his hold on the injured, groaning Damian, and trudged forwards. One foot in front of the other. Gasping.

"Blimey, Damian. Are you lugging ... lead weights around in your pockets?"

Damian coughed gently. "Don't … make me laugh … Mr Griffin. I's hurt bad."

They stumbled on the uneven path. Kaine's legs almost collapsed beneath him. Damian grunted and slumped more heavily against him. He practically had to take the whole of the powerful young man's weight, and his back spasmed from the struggle.

Sweat mixed with the driving torrent. Salt-laden rain-water stung his eyes and ran into his mouth. He spat it out. Breathing heavily, he shifted the burden higher onto his shoulders and struggled onwards.

As if in sympathy, the rain eased a little, changing from tropical downpour to heavy drizzle.

"Stay with me, Damian. Not far now, son. After the medics fix you up, you can find your new home. Anywhere you fancy. You deserve it. Abroad even."

"Th-Thanks … Mr Griffin," Damian rasped, "I-I didn't … tell them nothin'. Really, I …"

"I know, son. Save your breath. We're not far."

They finally reached the threshold of the blessed darkness. A heavy door crashed open behind them, and another light added to the glare.

"*Stop them, you morons!*" an electronic voice screamed. "*Stop them!*"

TM?

It had to be TM.

Kaine stopped and turned. At his side, Damian's wet cough sounded worse, even more worrying. He propped the young man against the school's rear wall, deeper into the blackness.

"Damian, can you keep going?"

"I-I think so." He grimaced, eyes creasing in pain, the scar tissue standing out pale against his dark skin.

Kaine gave him the directions and ended with, "Good man. I'll catch you up. Go, go, go."

With one hand pressing against the wall for support, Damian staggered away. Slowly. Painfully. He needed time to reach the ambulance collection point, and Kaine planned to provide it.

Kaine turned to face the courtyard and stepped out into the edge of the light. Scanning the scene, he stood his ground in the driving rain. Feet shoulder width apart, left arm held loosely at his side, right hand resting on the butt of his SIG, the holster's retaining clip unfastened. He was ready for anything. Alone against the Heavies. Four or five against one, maybe. He'd survived worse odds, and he only needed to hold off the enemy for a few minutes.

Not a problem.

Three Heavies in large, hooded coats strode out in to the light—one wide, one slim, and one slightly stooped and with thinning, red hair. The one with red hair bent over Williams, trying to wake him. The slim one did the same with Cox.

"Five thousand pounds to the man who drags that Parkside piece of shit into the Hub! I want to see the fucker's face when you kill him."

The two Heavies jumped to their feet. The one who'd remained standing—a white man with a deep suntan, a strongly handsome face, and short-cropped, fair hair—grinned.

"Delinquent, Red, and I will be happy to oblige, TM," he said. Given the circumstances and the downbeat location, the man's strong, French accent couldn't have been much more incongruous.

"Don't just stand there, Mr Coulthard. Go grab the fucker. And don't forget Rhino. I want him, too!"

The Frenchman, Coulthard, smiled. White teeth bright

against the tan, the glint in his blue eyes betrayed ... what, excitement? His breathing rate increased in depth and speed, and the exhaled air around his head condensed into a misty hood.

Delinquent, a shaggy-haired, light-skinned man with a youthful face, stepped alongside the Frenchman. The other one, Red, held back a little, hiding in their shadows.

Delinquent's lips stretched into a cruel sneer. "Look at the scrawny fucker just standin' there, bold as brass. Why he wearin' that ski mask, d'you think?"

"The coward is too afraid to show his face," Coulthard answered, loud, taunting.

"What d'you reckon he waitin' for?"

Coulthard shot his partner a withering glance. "Is it not self-evident? The fellow wants to give Rhino time to escape. It does not matter. Rhino will not get far. Are you ready to collect your share of the reward money?"

Delinquent nodded. "Let's go kick his—"

At his feet, Cox groaned. His arms moved, hands clawed the concrete, trying to roll himself onto his back. Failing.

Demarcus Williams still hadn't moved.

Delinquent pointed to his fallen buddies. "How he do that, d'you reckon?" He had to speak up over the rain sluicing in the blustery wind.

Coulthard shook his head and clapped Delinquent on the shoulder. "The coward must have taken them by surprise. He no longer has that advantage, *mon ami*."

The Frenchman started forwards, swaggering towards Kaine, who remained motionless, sizing up the opposition and finding them wanting.

After a momentary hesitation, Delinquent fell into step

beside and slightly behind his leader. The one called Red sidestepped to his right and hung back, watching, waiting.

"Don't look like no coward to me," Delinquent said. He spoke under his breath, but loud enough for the wind to carry the words to Kaine. "Cowards run, and this guy ain't runnin'."

Coulthard shot him another look, this one revealed pure derision. "Who is the coward here, *putain*?"

The Heavies closed the gap to ten metres. Kaine released the SIG's handle and covered both the gun and its holster with the tail of his jacket. He had no need for a weapon with these clowns. He raised his right arm, hand open, fingers up, a policeman halting traffic.

The moment Kaine moved, Red froze, shock and fear written in his bulging eyes and his trembling chin. His eyes scanned the vicinity, searching for danger, and he started nibbling on his lower lip.

"Hold it right there, arseholes," Kaine said, his tone clear, decisive.

Coulthard halted. Delinquent bumped into the side of him and mumbled an apology. Coulthard's furious scowl cut twenty percent from his "movie star" looks.

Kaine bared his teeth in a sneer and continued to speak harshly. "I gots one question for you, dickhead. Answer it proper and you might survive the night wiv all your teeth still in place."

Delinquent frowned in confusion. He shot the Frenchman a sideways glance before returning his gaze to Kaine.

Red stopped his lip-biting, but it only made his trembling chin more obvious.

Coulthard's answering grin returned the looks scale to a full-wattage, one hundred percent, Hollywood leading man.

He dug his right hand into the pocket of his jeans and pulled out a pearl-handled butterfly knife.

The Frenchman disengaged the knife's safety catch with his little finger. Lightning fast, he flipped the top handle to expose the blade and flicked his wrist to rotate and close the two halves of the handle. Simultaneously, he turned side on, slid his right foot forwards, and raised the razor-sharp blade, pointing it at Kaine's throat.

Kaine opened his eyes wide, nodded in false appreciation, and clapped his hands three times, slowly, derisively.

"Nice work, Coulthard. Pretty impressive, that. Looks like you been practisin' that move for hours. Prob'ly in front of a mirror, yeah?"

Delinquent's eyes gaped wide. He stared at Kaine as though he'd lost his marbles. He'd undoubtedly seen people faint clear away at the sight of Coulthard's silky method of opening a butterfly knife.

For his part, Coulthard growled, his face darkened, and a vein bulged on his forehead. It looked close to popping. This time, he turned from Hollywood action hero to snarling beast.

Leading with the outstretched knife, the Frenchman moved forwards, keeping his right foot ahead of the left, in a shuffling, sliding dance of aggression.

Kaine smiled, balling his right hand into a fist, but keeping it behind the left and a little lower, awaiting his moment.

Coulthard screamed and lunged, aiming for a body strike. Stainless steel glinted under the floodlights.

Kaine shimmied and ducked right, stepping inside the thrusting blade. Keeping Coulthard between himself, Delinquent, and Red, he twisted and shot out his right hand, first knuckles of the index and middle fingers extended. The knuckles connected with the soft tissue inside Coulthard's exposed right wrist, crushing blood vessels and pinching the nerve bundle. Still circling, Kaine followed up with a left-handed, clubbing blow to the same target.

Coulthard screamed. The knife flew from his limp, paralysed hand, clattered to the concrete, and skittered out of the ring of light and into the darkness.

Kaine danced back and away, maintaining his balance, keeping a safe distance.

Delinquent stood still, mouth open and eyes bugged wide enough to pop.

Apart from shaking his head and opening his mouth, Red didn't move. Again, his chin dimpled.

Coulthard trembled and stood, cradling his damaged wrist against his chest with his good hand, his eyes betraying shock and fear. And pain.

Resorting to first defensive position—left arm held out in front of the right, left foot leading, maintaining good balance—Kaine raised his left index finger.

"Sorry 'bout that, Coulthard," Kaine said with no hint of real regret, "but I don' like wankers wiv flashy knives. They piss me right off."

"*Merde, mon poignet,*" the Frenchman spat. "My … my wrist—"

"Tough titties, arsehole. What you gots there is a crushed median nerve and mashed carpals, I reckon," Kaine said, scrunching up his face in mock sympathy. "Trapezium and trapezoid, to be exact. Maybe the scaphoid, too. Doubt you'll be usin' the hand again for a while. Deffo have to forget that fancy move wiv the silly, little knife. Shame that, innit. Maybe try practisin' wiv your left hand? Can't do no worse."

"*Qui est-tu?*" Coulthard gasped. "Who are you?"

"Ne'er mind that, Coulthard. My name ain't gonna do you no good."

He slid half a pace closer.

Delinquent backed away.

Without looking where he was going, Red shuffled backwards. He tripped over one of Cox's trailing legs and fell in a heap, cracking his head on a raised piece of concrete. He squealed, scrambled to his feet, and took off running away from the school and into the night.

"Oops," Kaine said, still scanning the area in case some interlopers chanced their arm while he was being kept occupied. "No stomach for a rumble? Shame. An' I were just gettin' warmed up, too."

Delinquent leaned forwards at the waist, as though making ready to attack.

Kaine pointed at him. "Stay right where you is, sunshine. One more move outta you and I might lose my rag."

The baby-faced Heavy swallowed hard and raised his hands in submission, but otherwise, stayed locked in place, balancing on the flat of one foot and the ball of the other.

"Right," Kaine said, smiling again and reverting to his original conversational style. "Now I gots your full attention, I'll ask my question. You ready?"

Pale and sweating, Coulthard stared at his damaged, trembling hand. It stood out light against the dark jacket. The wrist had already started to swell.

Delinquent stood mute, gawping at the Frenchman's back.

"By the way, that weren't the question, but you can answer it. You bozos ready?"

He danced two paces forwards, flicked Coulthard's

damaged wrist with his middle finger, and returned to his safe distance.

Coulthard screamed, jerked away, fell. He continued screaming as his backside and elbow hit the concrete, jarring the wrist once more.

"*Non, s'il vous plait.* Stop," he pleaded. "Ask your question. If possible, I will answer."

"Gerard, no," Delinquent warned, "TM's gonna—"

Kaine silenced him with a raised index finger and a quick shake of the head.

Coulthard glowered at Delinquent and grimaced as he used the elbow to push himself into a seated position, in the middle of a dirty puddle. "My hand. *J'ai besoin d'un docteur.* Ask your … question, *monsieur.*"

"It's very simple. Did you kill Glenmore Davits?"

Coulthard's gaze lifted from his mangled wrist and met Kaine's steady glare. Confusion compounded his pained expression.

"*Quoi?*"

Kaine repeated the question, adding a little more volume and speaking more slowly.

Coulthard closed his eyes for a moment longer than necessary for a blink. When they opened, the pain remained but the confusion had deepened. Still sitting in his growing puddle, he shook his head.

"*Qui?* Who?"

"Glenmore Davits."

Recognition slowly dawned. The Frenchman's mobile face failed to hide his emotions.

"*Le vieil homme*, the old man … in the wheelchair?"

"Yep, he's the one."

Coulthard's instant and plaintive, "No, *monsieur*. Please believe me. I-I did not kill the old man," made Kaine inclined to believe the Frenchman, whose bluster had disappeared the moment his butterfly knife hit the concrete. "In fact, *monsieur*," he continued, "*les keufs*, the police, they say it was an accident. The old man fell and hit his head, *n'est-ce pas*?"

"What about you?" Kaine asked, ignoring the Frenchman's question and turning his attention to the youth.

Delinquent shook his hands in front of his face. "It weren't me. No way. Why would I kill a cripple? No need. Like Gerard said, the bacon reckoned the old guy fell down the stairs. Shame an' all, but I didn't kill him, honest."

Kaine shook his head sadly and added a heavy sigh. "Trouble is, Delinquent, whenever I hears a moron say 'honest', it makes me think he's lyin' through his rotten teeth. Is you lyin'?"

The youthful-looking man shook his head vigorously. "No, no. I ain't lyin', honest … I mean, no. No way. I didn't do nothin' to Old Man Davits. In fact, I even liked the geezer. He had balls, y'know? Stood up to people, he did. Apart from him not bein' able to actually stand, like. But you know what I mean, yeah?"

Nerves were giving the kid verbal diarrhoea.

"Okay, let's say I believes you's telling the truth. Makes the next and final question even more important, dunnit?" Kaine said, adding a dramatic pause. "Who *did* kill Mr Davits?"

He waited. Neither Heavy made a move to answer.

Kaine stepped closer to the Frenchman and kicked him gently on the leg. "Coulthard?"

"*Je ne sais pas.* I-I do not know, *monsieur. C'est vrais.* It is true. This I swear," Coulthard answered and braced for another blow.

"Delinquent? What 'bout you?"

The younger man lowered his head and stared at Kaine through hooded and bushy eyebrows. "I ain't got no idea who'd wanna kill 'im, man. The old guy never did no one no harm. Mouthed off a bit about the way the area was goin' to hell an' all, but he weren't no danger to nobody. 'Sides, TM told us to back off the locals. More trouble than they's worth. Said it would bring the bacon down on our heads."

As if the man himself had been listening, the screech of electronic feedback echoed through the courtyard, bouncing off the brick walls and concrete ground.

"Are you three having a fucking picnic? No one killed the old man. At least no Tribesman did. Unless I sanction a death, it doesn't happen. Do I make myself clear?"

Kaine cast a look around for the microphone. TM couldn't have heard his quiet interrogation of the two Heavies from inside the Hub.

In the eaves above his head, a small, black box gave him his answer. He spoke directly towards it.

"Whatcha TM," he said, maintaining his low-brow accent, "I gots your undivided attention, yeah? Who is you?"

"Wouldn't you like to know."

"'Course." Kaine smiled behind his ski mask. "Yes, an' that why I's askin'."

"Why the ski mask, arsehole? Too scared to show your face?"

"Who's the pot an' who's the kettle."

"What?"

"Ne'er mind, arsehole. It ain't important. Thing is, I don't believes you. I reckon you does know who killed Glenmore Davits. An' y'know what? I's gonna find out who you is and where you live"—Kaine saw no value in letting on he knew TM's current whereabouts—"*and*, when I do, I'm gonna beat the crap outta you 'til you gives me the answer. I'll be takin' my time over doin' it, an' all."

TM's electronically manipulated laugh sounded maniacal. Which, presumably, was the intention.

"An' when we meet," Kaine added, "I'll be tellin' you my name, and showin' you why I needs the ski mask. I'll be off now. Cheerio."

Keeping a weather eye on Delinquent, Kaine moved closer to the school wall, heading for the outer edge of the floodlight's arcing beam.

A sash window on the top floor, third from the left and directly below the east chimney, screeched and slid upwards. The muzzle of a large-calibre rifle poked through the gap.

Kaine dived backwards into the darkness, rolling as he hit the deck and kicking up into a standing position. The crack of a gunshot exploded into the night. The bullet hit the concrete metres from where Kaine had been standing. Sparks flew and the bullet ricocheted harmlessly away towards the railway tracks.

"Bugger me," Kaine called from the deep shadows. "That ain't exactly sportin'."

"Fuck you, shithead!"

The muzzle wobbled and another explosion rocked the night. The bullet whistled into the darkness way to the left of Kaine's new position.

"Be seein' you, TM!" he shouted.

Sticking close to the brickwork, Kaine slipped away.

And sooner than you think, sunbeam. Much sooner.

Chapter Twenty-Seven

Sunday 21st February - Byron Codell

Palmerston Road, Walthamstow, London, England

21:52.

Barcode crept deeper into the shadows, biding his time.

The lights in the Hub shone bright in the darkness.

Even though Palmerston School was the best-maintained building in the crappiest part of the hood, the shithole still looked in danger of collapsing in on itself. On the other hand, most of the internal walls were solid enough, and dozens of builders' props held up the parts that wasn't. The shell was shitty and, apart from the daubs of purple on the woodwork, it looked as derelict as the rest of the street, which were the whole point. If a building stood out as new, it would draw attention to itself, which were the last thing TM and the Tribe needed.

If the bacon didn't take no notice, it were fine and dandy with Barcode, too. He had his plans and they didn't include the strong arm of the law.

For the millionth time, he checked his watch—nearly five to ten. TM would be winding up his bullshit soon enough, and Barcode could do his business in time to make the Parkside run. He'd be cutting things close, but if things went down right, he'd do the first deed, then the second, and no one would be any the wiser—least of all TM.

Barcode had TM's blessing for the second part, but not the first. Definitely not the first. The first part were totally for Barcode's benefit.

To pull it off proper, both actions had to be perfect. Fuck-all room for error. If he screwed either up, there'd be no way back. Barcode would be fucked up and fucked up good.

Sure, he coulda waited to deal with Weasel later, but doing the deed right under TM's nose were too sweet an opportunity to miss. In fact, it was fucking excellent. One act would balance the other—assuming he got them both right.

After another fifteen minutes' waiting, the school's front doors opened and the Tribesmen started filing out, pushed by two of the Heavies. The little ones was quieter than normal. Most often, they be bubbling after TM finished one of his bullshit speeches that were supposed to motivate the crews.

Normally, the younger Tribesmen would fuck off back to wherever they called home, high as kites on a touch of free product and TM's bullshit, but it weren't happening this time.

This time, they moved quiet and quick, either looking straight ahead or down at their feet. One of the softer ones, a sweet, young thing no more than twelve, were crying her little eyes out. A couple of the boys were pale. Something musta gone down in the meeting. Something serious. Fuck knew what, and Barcode certainly weren't about to step into the street and ask. No fucking way.

If he stayed put and listened, he might overhear something interesting but, if not, he'd find out soon enough.

As they all trooped past his hiding spot, one of the middling ones said something like, "Rhino's fucked."

Interesting.

It weren't like Rhino to stick his head out above the wall —not that he could do nothing like that since his neck were so stiff on account of the shit-ugly scar. But he had been acting weird since the fucking bitch had dumped Barcode on his butt. What had old scar-neck gotten himself involved in this time? Knowing Rhino like he did, it probably had something to do with his squeeze and the spawn she was about to fart out into the world. Fucker wouldn't stop banging on about "Ariel and the baby" this and "Ariel and the baby" that. The way Rhino had turned so soft all of a sudden twisted Barcode's melon, big time.

So what if the bitch was going to pop out a little Rhino? It didn't change nothing about the way the world worked. If anything, it should've made the scarred fucker work harder. If he did more graft and turned over more product, it would feed directly into his back pocket. TM and Barcode would be happy, Rhino would be happy, and, in turn, Ariel and the sprog would get fed and clothed.

That were the way the market worked. Meet the demand and turn a profit. Simple as fuck. Not necessary to complicate nothing.

"C'mon, Weasel," he muttered. "I don't got all evenin'."

The front doors opened again and the next load of Tribesmen spewed out, lit up by the lights in the entrance hall.

Yeah. There he were, the son-of-a-ho weasel, Benjie. Wearing a self-satisfied grin like he'd just seen something entertaining. There he was, standing in a huddle with Dylan, Spook, Lil' Aran, and the rest of Barcode's crew. Behind them stood seven others, the Loring crew. The crew what would merge with Barcode's after he'd jacked the Parksiders' delivery and collection. If TM stood by his promise.

Sherpa Loring, the leader of the crew, wouldn't enjoy playing second string to Barcode, not after leading his own crew, but he'd get used to it. He had to, or Barcode would tear him a new asshole—assuming TM didn't do it first.

The two groups merged at the top of the steps, stood around for a few seconds in a weird kinda silence, then separated. TM always insisted they spread out after leaving the Hub. Large groups of Tribesman walking the hood at night attracted attention. Separate quick and keep it quiet, TM ordered. And, for this coming task to work proper, Barcode wanted the self-same thing.

Loring and his people headed east along Palmerston Road and split into three units, each one slipping down a different side street.

Lil' Aran keyed the lock securing his bike to the railings and rode off without his usual cheery wave. The rest of Barcode's crew turned west and strolled away.

As they drew closer to his hiding spot in the bushes, their quiet conversation became easier to hear.

"...dunno, bruv," Benjie said. "Didn't see him do nothin'. You?"

Spook shook his head and scrunched up his shoulders against the wind and rain. "Nah, I were lookin' at the screen, man. You know how TM want us all concentratin' when he speakin'."

"Yeah, blood. An' with Barcode bein' away, he'll be wantin' me to let him know what went down. Me bein' Barcode's deputy, an' all."

Benjie? My deputy? Yeah, right. Up your ass, Weasel.

Three of the crew split off down Byron Street, leaving Benjie and Spook to walk on together. Wouldn't be long before they parted, neither.

Barcode spied the area, checked it were empty, and pulled up his hood before peeling himself outta his hiding spot. He followed the pair at a good distance, keeping real silent.

Two hundred metres later, Spook punched Benjie's shoulder, all playful, like, and ran up the steps to his parents' place. A shitty flat on the top floor of a tower block. Benjie threw him a jibe about being a "Mummy's boy", and carried on along Boothe Avenue, alone. As expected.

Perfect.

Barcode lengthened his stride and closed the gap. The timing needed to be exact. He aimed for silence, tried to stop his threads swishing together and giving the alert.

Up ahead, the cross junction with Green Lane neared, with its streetlights and brightly lit houses—no good for Barcode's plans. Before that, the unlit Pound Lane split off to the right.

He closed the gap.

"Hey, Benjie," he called. "Hold up, blood."

The weasel stopped sharp, spun around, and raised his fists before recognising Barcode. His arms dropped, but the fists stayed clenched.

"That you, BC?"

"Yeah, it's me. Chill, blood."

Benjie's fingers loosened and he leaned to one side, as though trying to see past Barcode.

"Wazzup, man? TM said you was on a special mission."

"I am, bruv. And I need yo' help. Come with me." Barcode pointed to Pound Lane. "TM got me spyin' on the Parksiders. We gonna jack they next shipment."

Barcode stepped past Benjie and ducked into the quiet lane, beckoning for the asshole to follow. Without looking to check Benjie were behind, Barcode hurried along the lane until the darkness were almost complete. He stopped and turned, waiting for the weasel to catch up.

"Who's 'we'?" Benjie asked.

"You and me, blood. I come up with a plan, but I need someone I can trust to back me up."

"You mean you ain't pissed at me no more?"

Barcode threw him a questioning frown. "Pissed at you for what?"

"For what I say to Demarcus Williams 'bout what happen with the betty. Sorry, man. Didn't wanna drop you in the shit none …"

Nah, 'course you didn't.

"…but, y'know what it's like when the Heavies ask a question and TM's prob'ly listenin'. Truth is needed, y'know?"

Barcode turned his frown upside-down and flapped both his hands in a sign of forgiveness.

"No worries, blood. We's cool. I'da done the same thing in your situation."

"Really? We cool?"

"'Course we cool. In fact, we downright chilly. Why else would I be askin' you to back my play against the Parksiders? You and me do this right and we be in real tight with TM. He promised me a promotion, and I'll be bringin' you along for the ride."

Benjie's shit-eating grin showed again, this time in relief as much as greed.

"You fo' real?"

"Sure I am, blood."

Still smiling, Barcode threw his arm around Benjie's shoulders and pulled him into a hug. He rubbed the top of his head before releasing him and pointing the way down to the far end of Pound Lane. "Now, blood. We in a rush. Need to be outside Parkside Hall 'fore the drop."

He started walking, hugging the right side of the pavement. Benjie hurried to catch him, pulling alongside and to the left.

"So, you gonna tell me what happened in the meetin'? Why all the dark vibes when you all left the Hub? Look like somethin' serious went down." Barcode spoke so softly, Benjie had to lean closer to hear.

At the same time, Barcode reached for the pocket sewn into the inner lining of his jacket.

"Aw, man. It were real weird. That Mick asshole, Red, accuse Rhino of signallin' to someone outside the Hub. Then the shit hit the fan, big time. TM show the act on the monitor and they drag him outta the Hub. Don't think we be seein' ol' Rhino no mo—"

Barcode threw his left arm over Benjie's shoulders, spun him around, and stabbed his belly with his favoured five-inch blade. He sliced up and in, and twisted it around.

Benjie's eyes opened wide and his expression, confusion mixed with terror, nearly made Barcode wet himself with glee.

"Didn't see that comin', did you? Hey, Weasel?"

Benjie's face crumpled. He doubled over, hugging his belly tight, and sank slowly to his knees. "You fuckin' bast—"

Barcode stepped to one side, grabbed the weasel's hair, and snapped back his head to expose a scrawny throat. Pressing hard, he moved away and slowly drew the blade's razor-sharp edge from left to right. Blood exploded in a pulsing, steaming flood. Air gurgled through a severed gullet.

Benjie's hands flew up from his belly and started clawing at his throat, trying to stop the flow. It wouldn't work. Nothing could save the fucker.

"Nobody fucks with Barcode, blood," he hissed into the dying weasel's ear, keeping well away from the spurting blood. "Ain't you learn nothin' since school, shithead?"

Barcode wiped his blade on Benjie's coat, slicing deep into the cloth. He released his iron grip on the fucker's hair, and Benjie slumped into a heap on the ground, writhing, kicking, spluttering.

For a moment, Barcode considered putting the fucker outta his misery by caving his head in with a running kick, but he stepped away. The asshole had turned on Barcode. Deserved all he had coming. Let him live out the last few remaining seconds of his fucked up existence repenting his sins.

Served the fucker right. Nobody rat on Barcode and get away with it. Nobody.

Quickly—more quickly than the fucker deserved—the wriggling, squirming, choking slowed, then stopped. Benjie Harrington weren't breathing no more.

Before turning away from the corpse, Barcode took a baggie from his pocket. He grabbed the button he'd taken from the jacket of the same Black Bear crewman who

289

"donated" his scarf to Barcode a month back, and pushed it into Benjie's lifeless hand.

As a kid, Barcode had spent hours in front of the TV, soaking up the lessons from all them forensics shows and documentaries. Research, he called it. Barcode knew it'd come in handy one day.

Whistling a jaunty tune, Barcode hurried away. He still had his main mission to complete that night. A mission that would cement his place as the Tribe's main mover and shaker, and give an internal alibi for Benjie's demise.

After all, not even TM would suspect someone who robbed the Parksiders' next delivery of murking one of their own at pretty much the same time. The stolen button would likely lead the bacon to suspect a turf war, and Barcode needed an alibi or his recent beef with Benjie might come back to bite him on the butt.

No one punished a Tribesman but the Heavies, and then only with TM's okay.

Ha! No one but Barcode, fuckers.

Chapter Twenty-Eight

Sunday 21st February - Night

Cambourne Cross Hospital, Leytonstone, London, England

23:25.

Kaine paced the brightly lit, but tired and slightly grimy, hospital corridor. With so much still on his plate, he could have done without the wait, but he wasn't about to leave his young charge alone.

He'd caught up with Damian soon after leaving the courtyard and helped him the rest of the way to the rendezvous. The ambulance reached the pickup point a couple of minutes after they did. The green-clad para-medics were quick and efficient. They strapped Damian onto a trolley, hooked him up to the usual array of machines, fed him oxygen through a facemask, and ferried him and Kaine, under blue lights, to the nearest A&E Department—Cambourne Cross Hospital.

The hospital's late-Victorian, redbrick façade gave it the appearance of a town hall rather than a place that dispensed medical care, but the bright lights at the entrance suggested a warm welcome.

A few metres from the entrance, hunched against the weather, a gaggle of smokers enjoyed their cancer delivery sticks in the white corona of a streetlight. Patients in dressing gowns and medical staff in warm coats polluted the air around them with a blue-grey fug. The bald irony of smoking cigarettes outside a place dedicated to the treatment of the sick evidently eluded these diehard holdouts to a habit once cherished but now largely scorned.

Braving the thick smog of toxins drifting towards them from the smokers, the paramedics rolled Damian through a set of double automatic doors.

Fortunately, Cambourne Cross had yet to fit a metal detector, so Kaine didn't have to ditch his SIG. Instead, he followed the team, watching for security guards armed with handheld detectors.

There were none.

The lead paramedic, a jolly forty-something with a roly-poly waistline that didn't look too impressive imprisoned within his green jumpsuit, gave a short overview of Damian's stats to a woman standing in the middle of the admissions hall and carrying a clipboard. From his notes, the paramedic read off heart rate, blood pressure, and oxygen saturation and suggested a possible "tension pneumothorax".

The admissions nurse, whose scrubs were as grey as her hair and as creased as her face, pointed them to the nearest empty, curtain-shrouded cubicle and turned to Kaine.

"Name?" she asked, delivering the question in a voice every bit as bored as it was tired.

"Sorry?"

"Name?" the middle-aged woman—Senior Nurse G Emmanuel, according to the nametag pinned to the pocket of the wrinkled scrubs—asked again. She barely looked up from her clipboard.

"Damian ... er, Damian Baines, I think."

"You think?"

"Yes, I think," Kaine repeated.

"Age?"

"No idea. Early twenties?"

The nurse's blue eyes attempted first to skewer and then to slice him open.

"What relationship do you have with the patient?"

"Madam, to what are you alluding?" Kaine asked, unable to resist placing a hand over his heart.

"Are you a relative or acquaintance of the patient, *sir*?"

Her enforced emphasis on the "sir" indicated her adherence to the hospital's standing instructions to be courteous to patients and clients at all times—according to the notice attached to the wall above Emmanuel's computer station behind the screen in the corner. Unfortunately, the notice failed to indicate the tonal quality required in the courtesy. A voice that could etch lines in bullet-resistant glass didn't fit the sentiment of the notice.

"Neither. I was just passing by and tried to help. By the way, the patient is conscious and lucid. The nurse will be able to take a case history, I'm sure."

"I am the admitting nurse, sir," she said, tapping the name badge with the top of her biro.

Kaine backed away from the cubicle and waved her towards it, saying, "Then please continue, Senior Nurse Emmanuel. I'll be here if Mr Baines needs me."

The nurse's expression suggested she thought the last thing her patient needed was a total stranger standing over him while he was undergoing medical treatment, even if said total stranger happened to be a Good Samaritan.

"Thank you, sir. You'll find a chair in the waiting area." She used her ballpoint to indicate the way past the entrance foyer and towards a part of the building that looked about as welcoming as a police drunk tank at Christmas, and just as heavily occupied.

"Is it okay to use my phone in here?"

The pen swung around to point to a sign on the wall behind his head. It had the outline of a mobile phone inside a red circle with a diagonal line sliced through it.

"So I have to brave the smokers' den?"

Without answering, Emmanuel turned her back to him and ducked behind the cubicle's curtain.

Kaine hurried outside, turned away from cancer corner, and finally called Lara, the paramedics having refused to allow him to use his mobile in the ambulance. Lara, of course, took his news with her customary calmness and, after listening in silence to his brief instructions, passed the mobile to her minder.

"Connor," Kaine started, "the doc needs to go out. She'll brief you on the way. Bring both her and Ariel Danby here to the hospital and don't take no for an answer. Don't give Ariel time to pack, either. She needs to travel light. Things are probably about to get hairy, and I don't want either Ariel or the doc out of your sight until you get here. Understand?"

"Yes, sir. Be there ASAP."

Kaine ended the call, returned to the internal corridor, and resumed his quiet pacing. Although he aimed for "worried friend", he was actually standing guard. TM would know the location of the nearest A&E and might order the remaining Heavies to finish Damian off. The weight of the fully loaded SIG—964 grams—gave him little comfort. He'd be hard put to imagine a scenario where he'd be prepared to fire it inside a hospital with flimsy partition walls.

———

THIRTY-FIVE MINUTES LATER—KAINE counted every second—an impossibly young-looking doctor finally arrived. He hurried from an area deep within the bowels of the antiquated facility. Muddy, brown food stains marked the front of his white coat—at least Kaine hoped they were food stains. The clean-shaven but bleary-eyed medic introduced himself as Dr Hamilton, Senior Doctor in Charge, failing to stifle a yawn as he did so.

"Sorry, sir," Hamilton said, yawning again. "I've been on call for thirty-two hours straight. But don't worry, the patient is in good hands."

Hamilton blinked hard, undoubtedly trying to swipe the fatigue from dry eyes. He dipped his head at Kaine in a tired, sympathetic nod and turned away to join Senior Nurse Emmanuel behind the curtain.

Inside the cubicle, their hushed conversation was so quiet and jargon-filled, Kaine couldn't follow it even from the other side of the thin, waterproof material.

Two minutes later, Hamilton reappeared, carrying a clipboard, his expression serious.

"As indicated by his stats and his history, I strongly suspect a tension pneumothorax," he announced, nodding thoughtfully. "I've ordered a CT scan to confirm the extent of the damage and to determine whether the patient needs emergency surgery."

He looked at Kaine almost for the first time since leaving the cubicle and smiled. "Not to worry though, sir. The condition is usually not life-threatening when treated in time."

Kaine nodded. Before he could ask how long the CT would take to organise, Hamilton spoke again. "The bruising around the patient's face, however …"

"Yes, Doctor?"

"Was there any loss of consciousness?"

"Not that I am aware of. He took a couple of kicks to the ribs, and a number of blows to the face, but I wasn't close enough to the incident to see it in great detail."

"I understand," Hamilton said, adding a note to his paperwork, "that you were just passing by?"

"That's correct. I'm just trying to help," Kaine said, eyes wide in an expression of total innocence.

"Would you be able to describe the assailants to the police?"

Kaine responded by closing his eyes to indicate deep thought, followed by a considered headshake.

"Sorry, Doctor. Whereas I'm more than happy to make a witness statement," he lied, "there's very little I can say to assist the police in their enquiries."

"I understand completely," Hamilton said, nodding and adding more notes to the form on his clipboard.

In the distance behind the medic, the entrance doors

opened to admit Connor, Lara, and a heavily pregnant woman he took to be Ariel Danby.

Lara craned her neck, searching the admissions foyer quickly before she spotted him and beamed. She pointed him out to Ariel and held the pregnant woman's forearm as they hurried along the busy corridor, shepherded by the reliable Connor Blake.

"Dr Hamilton," Kaine said to the exhausted medic, "if I'm not mistaken, this is the patient's partner. The lady alongside her is my wife, Dr Elizabeth Griffin."

Kaine made the full introductions, giving Lara higher accreditation than Hamilton, and basing her in Queen Elizabeth's University Hospital, Birmingham. The QEUH was well-known and highly respected, but far enough away for it to be unlikely for Lara and Hamilton to have ever met. As usual, Corky had thought of everything.

The young doctor displayed some irritation at the idea of having a senior consultant looking over his shoulder. After all, this was his turf.

"Oxygen sats?" she asked, after Hamilton repeated his initial diagnosis.

"Eighty-nine-point-three," he said and reluctantly passed her the clipboard when she held out her hand for it.

"Oh dear," Lara said, frowning as she flicked through the pages. "Not good."

"But the patient is holding stable."

"Yes, I see that. You're treating with oxygen?"

"Yes, Doctor."

"Very well. Needle decompression or chest tube?"

Hamilton shook his head. "Mechanical ventilation was not required and, as the patient is stable, I considered it prudent to wait for the CT scan before calling in a thoracic consultation. As you know, Dr Griffin, pneumothoraces can often heal themselves."

"Quite so, Dr Hamilton," Lara said, smiling gently. "However, we also know that, with trauma-induced pneumothoraces, other organs may suffer damage. And there's also the question of a potential head trauma. Have you considered ordering an upper body scan?"

Kaine didn't miss the condescension in Lara's smile. Nor did Hamilton. His youthful face reddened under her intense scrutiny.

Hamilton retrieved the clipboard and studied the place Lara pointed to on the top form.

"Yes, er … well. Under the circumstances, I suppose a full upper body scan might be the prudent option. Will you be here to review the results for … er, with me?"

Lara pulled back the cuff of her jacket to read the time off her watch and took the opportunity to glance at Kaine surreptitiously. She acknowledged his nodded agreement.

"Very well, Dr Hamilton. I can see you are rather busy. I'll be happy to stay for a few hours and offer whatever assistance I can provide. How soon can we move Mr Baines to radiology?"

The stiffness in Hamilton's shoulders eased and his grateful smile reminded Kaine of a puppy being stroked behind the ears. The only things missing were a lolling tongue and a wagging tail.

Hamilton added another note to the form and glanced at the throng of annoyed patients in the waiting area.

"As I said, Dr Griffin, I have already ordered the CT scan as a matter of some urgency. The porters will be here shortly to take the patient … Mr Baines to radiology. In the meantime"—he lifted the pager clipped to the pocket of his white coat—"if you'll excuse me, I'm needed elsewhere."

"Thank you, Dr Hamilton. You've been very thorough. I'm sure we shall see each other later."

The young man hurried away to minister to more people in urgent need. Lara leaned closer to Kaine and whispered, "Oh Lord, that was terrifying."

"Really? You were so impressive, I thought young Hamilton was going to pass out for fear of upsetting you."

"Ryan," she said, still whispering, "I've never actually impersonated a doctor before."

"You were magnificent. Wouldn't surprise me if Hamilton asks for your help with the rest of his shift. The kid looks ready to collapse under the pressure of running this place alone overnight. Take a gander at all those poor souls in the waiting area. Some of them look as though they've been here long enough to take root."

Ariel's soft crying from the cubicle drew their attention.

Lara left Kaine to duck behind the curtain, and he signalled Connor to guard their backs before following her into the cubicle.

Damian lay on a trolley, eyes closed, with his upper body elevated and turned slightly to one side, favouring the uninjured part of his chest.

Wires and tubes led from his torso and fingers to various machines on shelves either side of his head. A transparent, plastic mask covered his nose and mouth, fed from a tube connected to a port protruding from the wall. His breathing was shallow and rapid, his colour had improved slightly, and the scar appeared less aggressive. The wire from a plastic clip on the index finger of his left hand led to a silent monitor, and the orange numbers on the small display read "89.7%". A slight improvement in his oxygen saturation seemed encouraging, but Kaine had been in enough trauma suites to know the normal human range of pulse oximetry levels rested somewhere above ninety-five percent.

Damian's condition was serious and, although Kaine shouldn't have endangered the young man in the first place and guilt ate away at him for doing so, he knew exactly who to blame for delivering the actual punishment.

TM and the Heavies were going to pay for what they did to Damian, but not before Kaine learned the truth about Glenmore Davits' death.

Chapter Twenty-Nine

Monday 22nd February - Lara Orchard

Cambourne Cross Hospital, Leytonstone, London, England

00:33.

Lara stood beside Ariel, trying to offer comfort and support. For her part, the pregnant girl held Damian's unencumbered hand in both hers.

"Is he dying?" Ariel asked through the sobs.

"Not if I have anything to do with it," Lara answered, studying the machine readouts.

"Beth?" Ryan said, calling her by her false name, which she still found difficult to recognise.

Ryan seemed to fall into whatever role he took on as

though born to play a part. For her, things were much more difficult, they came much less naturally.

"Yes, love?"

"Can I have a quiet word, please?"

Lara squeezed Ariel's shoulder. "Give me a moment to speak to my husband."

Why did the idea of them being married still send a gentle shiver all the way through her?

"Please don't go, Dr Griffin." Ariel pulled her top hand from Damian's and placed it on the side of her distended belly. "The baby's kicking up a storm. I'm so scared."

Her wide, hazel eyes, which paled to light green under the harsh overhead lighting, stared up at Lara, pleading, terrified.

"I'll be right outside. Call me if there's any change in Damian's condition—or yours."

She followed Ryan, who signalled for Connor to join them and marched a short way along the corridor. He stopped out of earshot but within sight of the cubicle. They huddled in a tight group, to one side of the corridor. Ryan kept his back to the wall, his eyes roaming the area, on the lookout. He wore the peaked cap he always carried to hide from any facial recognition cameras, and kept his head lowered and his back hunched to change his stride pattern and alter his profile. Hanging around on the second floor of a busy hospital festooned with surveillance cameras would hardly be the first choice for a fugitive. The fact that Ryan had remained in place for so long revealed how honourable her "husband" happened to be.

She'd been with Ryan long enough to have an idea of his emotional state. Right now, he was controlled but seething. Damian had been acting on Ryan's instructions and was currently lying on a stretcher, fighting for breath.

That must have only added to his sense of moral outrage. On top of everything else, although they'd never actually met the elderly gentleman, Glenmore Davits had been a member of The 83 and, as such, was under Ryan's protection. He would not let Glenmore's murder, if indeed it was murder, go unpunished. Ryan would be planning his next few moves in advance, including delivering payback for Damian's injuries.

He turned to Lara, the anger in his eyes hidden from the world, but not from her.

"Are you okay to stay here tonight?" he whispered, looking first to her, and then to Connor. "Some unfinished business needs my attention."

Connor looked at her before answering. "No problem, sir. I don't 'ave nowhere else I'd rather be."

"You're heading back to Palmerston Road, aren't you," she whispered.

Ryan gave her the slightest of shrugs. "You know me so well."

"Damn it, Ryan," she said too loud, instantly grimacing at her mistake.

Ryan stiffened and stared at a passing nurse who threw a glance in their direction before continuing on her way. Only then did he relax.

Lara shot out a hand and grabbed his forearm.

"Sorry," she said, "that was unforgiveable, but"—she released her grip and lowered her voice—"for God's sake. You have no idea of the school's layout or how many people you'll be facing."

Ryan turned to Connor, glanced along the corridor, and nodded. Her bodyguard jerked up his chin, backed away a few steps, and positioned himself to be able to see both her and the cubicle.

She moved closer to Ryan but made sure not to restrict his view. "Please don't do anything reckless."

His expression softened. "My dear Dr Griffin, have you ever known me to do anything reckless?"

"Don't humour me, you ... you idiot. Every time you leave the villa, you're being reckless. For pity's sake, Ryan"—this time, she whispered his name—"you're just one man. You can't hold yourself responsible for everything bad that happens in the world. And you can't take on every evil that crosses your path."

He pulled her into a hug and spoke so gently into her ear, only she could possibly hear.

"Lara, I *am* responsible for what happened to Damian, and I *am* responsible for The 83—every single one of them. Nothing's ever going to expunge the damage I caused to those families, but I'm damn well going to spend the rest of my life trying to help them—however long that will be."

He tightened the hug so much she struggled to breathe before he relaxed his hold.

"We arrived too late for Glenmore Davits. I let him down, but I'll be damned if I ignore his death, and I'll be damned if I let Damian go unavenged."

Lara pushed against him and stared up into his eyes. Hard and dark green they were in his disguise, not the soft, milk chocolate she normally saw when he looked at her.

"At least take Connor with you."

Ryan shook his head emphatically. "No way. Connor stays with you. There's no telling what TM will do if he finds out where we've taken Damian. No. Connor definitely stays here."

"But—"

"No buts. That's my final decision."

Lara had seen his determined expression many times

before. No power on earth could change his mind. She released a heavy sigh.

"Listen," he said after they stared into each other's eyes in silence for a long while, "I promise to take care. Corky sent me the school's architectural plans, but I haven't had a chance to read them yet. All I plan to do tonight is study the plans, recce the place from the outside and maybe plant a couple of surveillance cameras. That's all."

"Really?"

He nodded and crossed a finger over his heart. "Consider tonight nothing more than an information-gathering exercise. Hopefully, we'll identify TM and move one step closer to ending this."

"And the one with the tattoo, Barcode?"

"What about him?"

"He's only a kid."

"A kid? He's in his twenties, love. And, according to the information Corky found on the police servers, that particular 'kid' has a record stretching back to when he was still a juvenile. He's probably responsible for at least one murder, and ..."

"And?"

"He put his hands on you," he said, his eyes darkening even further. "Young Barcode needs to be taught some manners."

"Ryan, he's no match for you."

He winked. "After witnessing the way you poleaxed him the other day, I tend to agree. On the other hand, he's a coward and a bully. Wouldn't surprise me if he had something to do with Glenmore Davits' death." He paused long enough to scan the corridor once more before continuing. "That 'kid', Barcode, hangs out on Brooke Street. We've witnessed that first hand. He could easily have seen what the postman delivered and decided to take it for himself. And even if he didn't, he might know what really happened. If I run into young Byron Codell, all I plan to do is ask him a few questions."

"Like a police interview, you mean?"

Ryan smiled and added a wink.

"Something like that, my angel."

Still smiling, he leaned in and kissed her forehead.

"You really mean one of your devious, Special Forces interrogations, don't you?"

Ignoring the question, he took her hand and led her to Connor, who straightened as they approached.

"You 'eading out now, Mr Griffin?"

"I am indeed, lad. You happy with your role here?"

"Yes, sir." He tapped his ear. "By the way, the bone mic the doc gave me is totally ace. I've been talking to your technician."

"Corky called you?"

Connor nodded. "Not exactly 'ot on comms protocol, but 'e seems to know 'is stuff."

"He does indeed. What did he have to say?"

"Nothing much. Just wanted to introduce 'imself. Complained about 'ow you'd gone off comms and 'e couldn't contact you."

Ryan shrugged to Lara and turned back to Connor.

"The reprobate has been giving me earache all evening." He patted a jacket pocket. "I'll put the earpiece back in when I head out. Couldn't take any more messages from a man whose prone to wearing loud, Hawaiian shirts."

Connor shot an enquiring glance at Lara. She shook her head and said, "Don't ask. You'll find out soon enough, I imagine," which seemed to satisfy Connor well enough and he faced Ryan once again.

"Your man told me to let you know 'e sent you some new intel. Apparently 'e uploaded it to the villa's server. Said you'd know what 'e meant. That right?"

"It is."

"Good," Connor said, fingering his left ear. "Neat bit of kit this. Totally silent reception. Wish we'd 'ad comms equipment this good in Kandahar. Would've saved no end of strife. Too expensive for the MoD's budget, I guess?"

Still maintaining his vigil on the corridor, Ryan smiled. "That little gizmo in your ear and all the equipment used to run it would likely buy you a small house in Leytonstone. Don't ask me where the QM acquired the components, he wouldn't tell me. And speaking of comms, for this operation, I'm Alpha One, Corky's Control, and the doc's Alpha Two. That makes you—"

"Alpha Three," Connor said, triumphantly. "Corky already told me."

"Did he, by God. I'm surprised he bothered. The man rarely uses call signs himself. Aha, here they are. And about time."

He nodded towards Damian's cubicle, where two young men in purple scrubs pulled back the curtains.

"That's my cue to stretch my legs."

Smiling, Ryan held out his hand to Lara.

"What's wrong?"

"I need the keys to the hire car."

"Connor drove. Ask him."

"Connor?"

Her minder dropped a set of keys into Ryan's hand. "'Ope you don't 'ave to chase no bad guys, or escape the 'bules. That bloody car couldn't pull the skin off a custard tart. Tip me the nod if you ever need a decent set of getaway wheels. You know, one with some real guts. A couple of car mechanics not too far from 'ere owe me a favour. They'll sort you out, no worries."

"That's okay, Connor. The little Peugeot's good enough. Inconspicuous. It stays below the radar."

"Nah," Connor said, "my guys could make a knackered, old Ford Focus run like a Ferrari F40, without changing the way it looks. Sweet they are, sir."

"I'll think about it next time we're in this neck of the woods."

He kissed Lara's cheek, said, "Take care, dear," and hurried away.

"No, you take care," she muttered to his back before facing Connor. "Okay, Terry McCann, let's go."

"Terry who?"

Lara suddenly felt very old and even more tired.

"A TV character from a few years back."

Connor bared his teeth in a brilliant grin. "Yeah, Terry McCann, ex-boxer turned minder to protect Arthur Daley and 'is missus, ''er indoors'. Just winding you up, Doc. Everyone needs a bit of a laugh now and again, right?"

"Please don't. There's a time and a place for … oh dear. This doesn't look good."

Forty metres away, at the far end of the corridor, a stern-faced Dr Hamilton was waving and trying to catch her eye. She tried ducking behind Connor, but it was too late.

Hamilton rushed towards her, right arm aloft, finger waving to the ceiling.

"You want for me to run interference, Doc? Before 'e calls security?"

"Of course not. He's just doing his job."

"I don't intend to maim the geezer, just delay 'im long enough for you to get going."

Although tempted, Lara stuffed her hands into her pockets and waited.

"Any idea what the penalties are for impersonating a doctor?" she asked.

"But I thought you *was* a doctor?"

"Connor, I told you this is no time for jokes."

"Sorry, Doc."

Hamilton practically skidded to a halt in front of them, panting, a thin sheen of sweat on his smooth forehead.

"Dr Hamilton, is everything okay?"

He shot a sideways glance at Connor, and his Adam's apple bobbed. "There's been some sort of a misunderstanding. You see, I've just this moment gotten off the phone to Queen Elizabeth's Hospital in Birmingham ..."

He swallowed again and took another breath.

Lara leaned to one side to look around the young doctor, expecting to see a pair of uniformed security guards at best, a pack of armed police officers at worst.

Ryan Liam Kaine, what have you dropped me into this time?

Chapter Thirty

Monday 22nd February - Night

Galton Street, Walthamstow, London, England

00:53.

Kaine parked far enough away from Palmerston Road to avoid running into any Tribesmen, but close enough to reach the car without having to indulge in an extended, town-centre yomp. He tugged his lightweight backpack, his Bergen's little sister, from the luggage area, pulled it onto his shoulders, and shrugged it into a more comfortable position. At a little under twelve kilos, the baby-Bergen weighed less than half the weight he'd normally have to carry when on manoeuvres.

Piece of cake.

He closed the tailgate quietly, activated the central locking, and scanned the area. As expected at oh-dark-fifty, the back streets of this part of Walthamstow were deserted.

Kaine settled the rolled-up ski mask on his head, wearing it like a fat beanie, and took a circuitous route towards the school.

He'd taken a few minutes to study the architect's blue-prints and that, together with Damian's earlier description of the inside of Palmerston School, confirmed that the building's current layout didn't differ much from the tech-nical drawings. The only major changes lay in the configu-ration of the Hub and a couple of the ancillary rooms behind it. The internal walls remained pretty much intact, only the rooms' usage differed.

He didn't expect too many difficulties in gaining access to the building, should the need arise. However, to begin with, his initial plan consisted of planting two or three cameras, hooking them up to Corky's satellite systems, and taking a low-key watching brief. At least, that's the plan he'd sold to Lara.

Whenever they identified TM, the plan would likely change at a moment's notice. In the meantime, he needed to be prepared for any eventuality, hence the baby-Bergen and its military payload.

Galton Street, one of many leading to the rail lines and flanked with dilapidated, terraced housing, stood dark and quiet, with most of its streetlights broken. Long, unlit areas of deep shadow made Kaine's job easy. Head down in case of private CCTV coverage, he strolled along at a relaxed pace, preferring not to draw the attention of any neighbour-hood watch schemes. Although, given the prevalence of riffraff and miscreants dealing drugs and spreading havoc, the existence of such a civic-minded group in the area seemed an outside bet at best.

More likely, he'd come under the watchful stares of gang members, dealers, and the local constabulary on one of its rare forays into Walthamstow's underbelly. However, given Corky's timely report on the state-of-play at the local nick, they were running a skeleton night shift, the Metropolitan Police having had its funding cut once again.

While clinging to the shadows without being obvious about it, Kaine turned into Rennie Row. Halfway along, he ducked into a narrow alley separating the back gardens of neighbouring streets. The smell of rot, damp, and stale urine stung his nostrils. He padded forwards until he reached the end of the alleyway then stopped in the shadow of an overgrown privet hedge and dropped to one knee.

Palmerston Road ran parallel to him—east to west—and the school lay some two hundred metres to his left. Opposite, a metal fence topped with vicious barbs restricted casual access to the rail lines, but would do little to prevent encroachment by a determined visitor. A visitor such as Kaine.

Once settled, he popped the comms unit into his ear and tapped it once.

"Alpha One to Control, are you receiving me? Over."

"Corky's here, Mr K. How you diddling?"

Kaine sighed.

Here we go again.

"I'm near the rail lines now. Over."

"Corky knows, Mr K. Been tracking your signal, remember."

"Any news from the hospital? Over."

"The patient is in the scanner as we speak, Mr K. Nothing visible so far, but they're starting at his head."

"You're watching the scan in real time? Over."

"Yep. Transmitting the scans to the doc's tablet in real time, too. The pictures are a bit small, but the doc says she's coping. In fact, she's

seeing the pictures before Hamilton. Want to know how Corky managed this magnificent technical feat?"

Kaine checked the time. 01:08. No need to rush. He had no intention of approaching the school before the bottom of the hour. According to what he'd learned from Damian, the building stood empty overnight, guarded only by the enhanced surveillance systems, and he needed to give the remaining Heavies and the Tribesmen plenty of time to bolt.

"Certainly, Control. Please feel free to enlighten me. Over."

"Well, it's like this, Mr K. The CT scanner is hooked up to the hospital's IT infrastructure, and Corky gained access with his usual ease. To be honest, the NHS firewall is a chuffing joke. Might as well not exist. If you ask Corky, the hospital's so-called Chief IT Security Officer wants locking up. Taking money under false pretences, he is."

"Control, please open a link to Alphas Two and Three. I'd like a blow-by-blow while I'm waiting. Over."

"Not possible while they're in the radiology suite, Mr K. Too much interference from the gizmos."

Corky wasn't making sense and it was giving Kaine a headache.

"Control, if that's the case, how can you send the scans to Alpha Two? Over."

"Good question, Mr K. Glad you're paying attention. Corky's having to use the hospital's LAN to talk directly to the doc's tablet. Ordinarily, Corky would use the hospital's IT system to piggyback the messages onto the web and transmit to the bone mic's infrastructure, but there ain't enough bandwidth, and the signal delay would make comms impossible. Get it?"

"Understood, Control. Thanks for the explanation. Over."

Kaine shook his head. He understood perhaps half of what the IT guru had said.

"*You is welcome, Mr K. Corky's only too happy to help spread enlightenment.*"

"Any news on the school? Over."

"*Nothing much. Corky's been keeping his eyes on the place.*"

"How are you managing that?"

"*Corky has his ways, Mr K.*"

"Control, have you been breaking into military satellites again? Over."

"*Not giving you no details, Mr K, but right now, there's an Igor in South Ossetia, who's scratching his head wondering why his pet satellite ain't responding to his signals.*" Corky's delighted chortle rattled down the line and made Kaine smile.

"*Tell you the truth, Mr K, it were really funny watching that bald arsehole with the beard leave the school. You know, the first one you smacked, Demarcus Williams. Man, what a mess. Wobbling all over the gaff, he was. Looked like he'd been in the boozer for a week. The other one, Johnny Cox, Crabapple, were even worse. The bozos had to pour each other into a taxi. So funny to watch. Like one of them gross-out teen movies when all the characters get blotto on a stag night.*

"*The French bloke managed to walk without help, but held his arm awkward, like. As for the geezer with the red hair and the wonky teeth … wouldn't surprise me if he's still running.*"

"Sounds like a real hoot, Control. Don't forget to send the recordings to the servers and to Damian's mobile. I'm sure he'll get a real kick out of it. Might help his recovery. Over."

"*Already done that, Mr K.*"

"Excellent. Any other news for me? Over."

"*Yeah. Corky's got a shedload of stills of Tribesmen leaving through the front doors. Running facial recognition on the dirtbags right now. Identification's coming in all the time. So far, no obvious candidates for TM, though."*

"I'd have thought satellites would be too high for you to run any kind of facial recognition. The angle would be wrong. And there's been a fair bit of cloud cover tonight. Over."

"Like Corky always says, Mr K. There's more than one way to skin a fluffy, little bunny rabbit."

Kaine smiled and shook his head.

"Control, I've never heard you say anything of the sort. Over."

"Funny that, Mr K. One of my most favourite expressions, it is. Honest."

There was the use of "honest" again. Something was off. Kaine couldn't help feeling Corky was hiding something, but he shook it off. If he couldn't trust Corky, he was in deep doo-doo.

Paranoia's a dangerous thing, Kaine.

"Keep working on it, Control. I'll be setting up some more cameras in the next hour or so. We need the whole area covered, Over."

"Right you are, Mr K. Unfortunately, there ain't no telling how many of the little scrotes slipped out the back way. Over."

"Yes, Control. I planned to install the cameras earlier, but circumstances changed. Over."

"Yeah. Not to worry. Corky reckons Damian's really grateful you stepped in when you did. Not sure he would've survived much more of a beating. ... Oh, hang about. Looks like the doc's just seen something interesting on the scan. Corky'll get back to you when he can. Corky takes it you don't have your mobile switched on, so there's no point in asking her to call you for a while. Over."

"No, Control, I'm in no immediate rush. Tell her to ring me. I'll power up my phone right now. Alpha One, out."

Kaine tapped the earpiece in an attempt to silence Corky's inevitable interference. He pulled out his phone, which had been synced to the bone mic's interface, and hit the power button. Breathing deep and slow, he waited.

And waited.

One of the occasional freight trains rattled past. In the distance, traffic rumbled its thrumming beat. The glow from London's millions of lights flooded the sky and bounced off the clouds in a mist of subdued colours. The time on his covered watch ticked slowly by. Only eight minutes since he last checked.

Still, he waited.

Three minutes later, his mobile buzzed, and he hit the green button.

"Hi, Beth," he whispered. "How's the patient?"

"Fairly serious. Three broken ribs and a two-centimetre tear in the lower lobe of his left lung. He's being prepped for emergency surgery right now."

"Damn. What are his chances?"

"The prognosis is good. In fact, this sort of surgery is pretty commonplace, and he's likely to make a full recovery. Damian's lucky you reached him in time."

"Not that lucky. I was the one who put him in danger in the first place."

"He knew what he was getting himself into. Don't go feeling guilty. There's no value in it."

Kaine smiled. Trust Lara to see things in the best possible light for him.

"Any other injuries? He took a hell of a blow to the head and was slurring his words."

"Nothing definitive showed up on the CT scan, but they're likely to keep him in for at least a couple of days, monitoring for compression and concussion. If you're happy to fund it, I'll book him into a private ward. It'll be more comfortable for him and Ariel. Easier to defend, too."

"He risked his life for us and didn't talk under pressure. As far as I'm concerned, that makes him one of the team. Of course I sanction the spend. How's Ariel handling everything?"

"She's coping really well, considering how far along she is. Wouldn't surprise me if we found ourselves flitting between the surgical recovery ward and the maternity wing before too long."

"And you? Any problems with the admin side of things?"

She laughed. "Bill, I don't know how you do it."

Her laughter made him smile. Despite all his concerns, she still had the power to brighten his mood.

"Dr Griffin," he said, using his serious voice, "I have no idea to what you are referring. Would you care to elucidate?"

"When did you ask Corky to add my name to the Queen Elizabeth Hospital's staff registry?"

"While Damian and I were waiting for the ambulance, why? Did Hamilton check your background?"

"Indeed he did. Nearly gave me a coronary when he practically chased me down the hall to apologise for double-guessing my treatment advice."

"Sorry about that. In all the kerfuffle, I forgot to mention it."

She sighed loud enough for him to hear down the phone line. "How did you know someone would check my credentials?"

"I didn't. Just like to try and cover all eventualities."

"At the time, I wondered why you claimed I worked in Birmingham."

"Corky's been helping DCI Jones for a while, remember. Although he has a gateway into most of the national data-bases, he's particularly familiar with the first responders' IT systems in the Midlands. Did you appreciate the job title he gave you?"

"Sorry. I haven't had a chance to visit the site. What did he make me?"

"Dr Elizabeth Griffin, Assistant Chief of Clinical Medi-cine. He wanted to make you the Chief, but I thought that role would go to a more mature consultant. Sorry for the demotion."

"You are forgiven. It amazes me how you think of such detail."

"Not much to do with me. Corky's the genius when it comes to building legends."

The earpiece clicked. *"Fanku, Mr K. Corky didn't know you cared."*

Corky's high-pitched chuckle mixed with Lara's gentle laughter.

"Damn it, Control. This is a private conversation!"

"If you wanted to keep it private, Mr K, you wouldn't be using this particular comms system—or the open phone line—yeah? You know Corky's built in an override facility. And 'sides, Corky had to cut into your call."

"Why? Over."

"Corky's got something to tell you, Mr K. Something operational."

Corky's reluctance to talk over an open line gave Kaine his cue.

"Understood, Control. Dr Griffin, I'll catch you later. Take care, and listen to Connor."

Kaine cancelled the call, powered down the mobile, and dropped it into his jacket pocket.

"Okay, Control," he said. "What do you have for me. Over."

"It's just that someone's closing on your location. Two hundred metres away. Approaching quickly along Rennie Row. He's about to turn the corner into your alley."

Damn it!

Kaine spun through one-eighty, pushed himself forwards, and lay prone in the sodden grass.

He pulled out his SIG, racked the slide, and waited.

Chapter Thirty-One

Monday 22nd February - Night

Rennie Row, Walthamstow, London, England

01:25.

Kaine's focus narrowed to a single point in time and space—the edge of the cone of brightness cast from the streetlight which backlit the turn into the narrow alley.

Background sound faded, his heart rate slowed, but his peripheral senses kept working. Protecting him against attack.

Using his well-practised breathing technique, he slowed his heart rate to a point where it wouldn't affect his aim. His hand on the SIG remained steady, dry. The index finger extended, resting on the outside of the trigger guard, prepared. He wasn't going to risk shooting an old geezer walking his pooch.

Movement.

A shadow cut into the cone, moving slowly.

Kaine slipped his finger through the guard and rested it gently on the trigger, taking up the slack, but adding no actual pressure.

The shadow stopped, its owner keeping to the blind side of the alley, out of any line of fire. Slowly, its arms raised and then stopped moving.

Kaine's earpiece clicked.

"Control to Alpha One, are you still there? Over."

Corky had finally discovered true radio protocol. Would wonders never cease?

"Alpha One receiving," Kaine whispered. "Not a good time. Alpha One, out."

Kaine released his left-hand grip on the SIG to tear out the earpiece.

"No, Mr K. Hang on. Don't shoot nothing. That there is what you'd call a friendly. Repeat, a friendly. Over."

"Repeat that, Control. Over."

"Alpha One, this is Control, Corky. Right? The geezer you is aiming your gun at right now is a friend. Corky warned you about his arrival so you wouldn't shoot him. Please let him approach and introduce himself. Over."

Kaine gritted his teeth.

"One day, Control. One bloody day you and I are going to have a serious falling out. Are you in comms contact with the newcomer? Over."

"Corky sure is. Over."

Kaine relaxed his shoulders but kept the SIG levelled at where the centre mass of the shadow would appear when its owner finally turned the corner.

"Tell your friend to step out into the light and keep his arms raised and his hands empty. Over."

"*Will do, Mr K. Just a tick. Corky, out.*"

Five seconds later, the shadow stepped forwards and fully entered the light. The man—above-average height, slim hips, wide shoulders, hands raised as instructed—stood still.

With a gun trained on him at a range of less than thirty metres—point blank in Kaine's terms—the stranger smiled.

Who in the hell?

Without losing the shot, Kaine climbed slowly to his feet and signalled for the stranger to approach, but kept his hand raised, finger extended to indicate the man should do it slowly. When the gap closed enough for them to speak without the need for raised voices, Kaine opened his hand again and the man stopped.

"Turn around. Three-sixty and do it slowly."

"Don't worry, Alpha One. I'm unarmed," the man said, his accent Mid-Atlantic, his voice calm and steady.

"Forgive me if I fail to take you at your word. Spin."

Kaine inverted his finger and rotated it. The stranger's smile didn't falter, and he obeyed the command.

Dressed in black from head to toe, the man's clothes hugged his taut frame—no loose cloth to flap about and give him away during a covert entry. Like Kaine, he wore his hair long and sported a full beard. Unlike Kaine, his muddy blond hair showed no trace of grey. Apart from the small, dark backpack which covered his upper back, he was clean—no obvious sign of a weapon.

When the man's back was turned, Kaine looked about him, in case the stranger's appearance was nothing but an elaborate diversion. Although why Corky would allow him to fall into such a trap eluded him.

Face to face again, the man's smile faded a little.

"Mind if I lower my arms, Captain? This backpack's smaller than yours, but heavy nonetheless."

Kaine nodded. The man lowered his arms, stepped forwards, and offered his right hand to shake.

"We're not quite there yet," Kaine said, turning the nod into a quick shake of the head. "Explain yourself."

"Happy to, Captain, but that cannon's making me nervous. Never did like guns, me. Would you mind?"

Kaine lowered the SIG, pointing it at the stranger's groin. "That better?"

"Not a lot, but I suppose it'll have to do. Please don't twitch. Although I already have a child, I'm quite keen to have others. Corky didn't give you much warning I was coming, right?"

"No, the little … person wasn't exactly forthcoming."

"Annoying little ratbag at times, eh?"

"*Hey, Corky heard that!*"

The stranger sighed and shook his head slowly. He tapped his left ear. Kaine's earpiece clicked in response.

"Control," the man said, "butt out, will you, buddy? Let the captain and me get to know each other. Over."

"*Okay. But time's passing, you know? Over.*"

"Just a second, Control. Can you let the doc know what's happening? She'll be having kittens about now, I'd imagine. Over."

"*Will do, Mr K. Control, out.*"

"As you said," Kaine said, de-cocking the SIG and sliding it back into its holster, "your friend can be a touch annoying."

"Good at his job, though."

"Agreed."

"Thanks for that, by the way," he said, pointing to the

323

holstered **SIG**. "Never could get comfortable with a gun pointed at the old family jewels."

"It's happened before?"

"Only once or twice, Captain." The smile returned and humour edged into the voice.

Kaine could probably grow to like a man prepared to use humour under such trying circumstances—assuming he passed the upcoming interview.

He backed further into the undergrowth and beckoned the newcomer to do the same. Keeping a little over arm's length apart, they dropped to one knee, and crouched at ninety degrees to each other.

"Okay, who are you, and what do you want?"

"Don't ever lose focus, do you?"

"Helps keep me alive. Come on, I don't have all night. Out with it."

"Straight to the point, okay. Like you, I use a few names these days, depending on the situations I find myself in, but you can call me Sean … Sean Freeman."

At the use of his full name, his intonation rose as though he expected Kaine to recognise it.

Sean Freeman?

Kaine repeated the name in his head a couple of times. Something about it tweaked a memory, but hell if he could pull it from the darkness.

"Rings a bell, but … sorry. Are you famous? If you were on a celeb TV show, forget it. I rarely make time to watch the idiot box."

"No, Captain. Like you, the last thing I'd ever want to do is appear on telly. Let's just say my name appeared in the media a couple of years back. Libellous claptrap, of course. Or is it slanderous?" He frowned and shook his head in apparent confusion. "Never can remember."

"Libel if it's written, slander if spoken," Kaine explained, although he suspected Freeman knew the precise meaning of each word.

"Well, considering my name appeared in the papers *and* on the TV news, I'm covered both ways. By the way, a mutual friend of ours sends his regards."

"Corky?"

"No, no. Not our esteemed hacker." He wrung his black-gloved hands together and shivered dramatically. "Forgot how cold it could be in the UK this time of year. Still, that's another story. No, our mutual friend is a grizzled, senior policeman by the name of David."

"DCI Jones?"

Once again, the easy grin transformed into a full-blown smile.

"Yep, that's the one. As it happens, he speaks very highly of you. I chatted with him only yesterday evening. He wishes your veterinary friend good health, by the way."

"Does he?"

"Indeed, he does. He also told me to say, 'archaeopteryx'. That mean anything to you?"

Kaine relaxed at Freeman's use of his and Jones' password of the week, which even Corky didn't know, at least as far as Kaine could tell.

"It does but, at the risk of repeating myself, what are you doing here?"

"When Corky mentioned your situation, I wanted to offer my assistance. It appears you want to scope out that there building"—he pointed in the general direction of the school—"and I have, shall we say, certain skills in that arena."

Although they continued their discussion in a more-or-less conversational tone, Freeman never took his eyes from the school. He seemed to be studying the building's every detail in much the same way Kaine had been doing off and on for the previous day or so.

The man was a professional. That much had become self-evident.

"By the way, I've heard a great deal about you," Freeman said, thrusting out his hand again. "Nice to meet you at last."

This time, Kaine gave the offered paw a firm shake.

"So," Freeman added, "what's the plan?"

"Don't have one yet. Corky gave you a full briefing?"

"Yep. We're looking to identify someone called TM and beat a confession out of him. That about right?"

"Possibly. I don't usually operate that way, unless I have to, of course. However, in this particular instance, I'm not averse to using a modicum of physical persuasion. TM is lowlife scum, leading other lowlife scum. One or more of said pondlife might be responsible for the death of someone under my protection."

"Glenmore Davits?"

"You and Corky *have* been talking."

"Yes, and I'm more than happy to assist any way I can."

"Thanks, I appreciate your offer, but I'm not sure what you can do to help."

"Fancy popping inside the school and taking a quick shufti around the place?" He grinned and nodded towards the crumbling, four-storey building again.

"Are you kidding?"

"Nope. Remember that business at the Stafford Museum a couple of years back?"

A memory tickled the back of Kaine's mind. A museum in Birmingham, a bungled heist ... A light in his head switched on.

"The Rajmahl Collection?"

"Aha," Freeman said, his smile broadening, "you *do* remember!"

"Hang on, you're *that* Sean Freeman? The one responsible for setting up the Parrish Gang?"

"Yep, that's me."

"You're one of the UK's most successful jewel thieves, according to the media. Dangerous, too."

"See what I mean about libel and slander? I only robbed places that could afford the losses and never once hurt anyone during a job. What's more, the police recovered all the jewellery I stole when they arrested Parrish and turned his place over. It seems some helpful soul opened the nasty man's personal safe, so the police didn't have the hassle. Wonder who could have done such a thing?" He tutted and shook his head.

"Okay, point taken. You have the relevant skills, but I imagine you used to spend time planning all your … operations. If we wanted to break into the school tonight, would it suit your MO?"

Freeman laughed quietly. "Truth is, I've been studying that building for a little while now."

"Really?"

"Yep. When Corky first mentioned your current situation I was in … well, let's just say I wasn't in the UK. Corky sent me the building's schematics, and I studied them during my flight. Meanwhile, Corky hacked into a military satellite, which gave me rather decent aerial coverage of the vicinity. He's also been reading me in on the research he's been doing for you."

Bloody Corky.

At least Freeman's explanation eased Kaine's concern about Corky's possible hidden agenda.

"To be honest, Captain," Freeman continued, "this intel includes the access and egress points. I've already formulated a plan of my own. Fancy a little fun?" Again, he rubbed his hands together. "It's bloody perishing out here. I bet it's much warmer inside that schoolhouse. Especially since they had fancy, new central heating installed a few months ago."

Central heating? Something Damian had forgotten to tell him. Kaine wasn't sure why the new information tweaked his interest so much. He needed time to think on it, but didn't have any to spare right then.

"Will you answer one question?" Kaine asked.

"If I can."

"Why are you offering to help me?"

Freeman put on a pained expression, and then he shrugged. "It's largely down to my wife's mother."

"Come again?"

"She's visiting our home. Since our daughter arrived, she's been spending every spare hour with us. Now, don't get me wrong, the wife's mother is a really lovely woman, really lovely"—again, he sighed—"but if I have to suffer another afternoon shopping for baby clothes, I'll bloody explode. I mean, how many threads does one tiny tot need?" He shrugged. "Don't know about you, Captain, but I need a little more excitement to pass the time. Fair enough?"

It wasn't, not really, but Kaine didn't intend to pass up any support. Especially if it came with a password-confirmed recommendation from the formidable DCI David Jones.

"Okay, fair enough," Kaine said. "What about breaking through the rear door? It's likely to be less heavily fortified than the front."

Freeman made a face like he'd chomped into a rotten apple. "A little crude, Captain. That might work for you crash-bang-wallop military types, but I prefer something a little more subtle. Before we do anything radical, what's our end goal here? I mean, do you actually have a plan?"

Kaine tried not to look abashed. "To be honest, I was just thinking of breaking in to take a little look around. According to Damian—"

"Who?"

"Damian Baines, aka Rhino. I thought Corky read you in on this."

"Ah, right. Helpful chap with the unfortunate scar on his neck," Freeman said, taking his turn to look embarrassed. "Sorry, I'm more interested in architecture than people's names. Apologies for interrupting. You were saying?"

Kaine checked his watch and made sure Freeman saw him doing it. "According to Damian, unless they're expecting a product delivery, the building's normally empty overnight. However, after what happened earlier ..."

"Your crossing swords with the Heavies, you mean?"

"Yes, exactly. It wouldn't surprise me for TM to hunker down for a while. Corky's studied the faces of everyone who left the building since the ... er, ruckus, but didn't see a standout candidate for TM. Didn't see a fellow called Barcode, either."

"Ah, Barcode. Corky explained why you're rather interested in catching up with that particular piece of pondlife. Any idea where he might be?"

Kaine shook his head. "None. But I'm renowned for being a patient man. I'll catch up to him soon enough."

"Don't think he's running scared, do you?"

"Scared of me? Bloody well should be, but I doubt he has the brains to be scared. Fear needs the kind of emotional depth I doubt Byron Codell has. Vicious and cunning he might be, but scared? Doubt that very much."

"So, let me get this right," Freeman said, glancing again at the school building. "Your plan is to break in and rummage around in the hopes of stumbling across something of interest. Or, better still, find someone in the know and to, erm … interview them. That about right?"

"It is now. I often find the direct approach works as well as any."

Freeman sighed and shook his head. "As I said, crash-bang-wallop. So damned … military."

"That's me," Kaine said, shameless.

After a gentle headshake, Freeman said, "The school will likely be full of cameras, motion sensors, and microphones. If so, what's to stop you tripping every alarm in the place the moment you step inside?"

Kaine patted the shoulder strap of his baby-Bergen. "I have a nugget of plastic explosive in here. Was planning to blow the mains power to the building before entry."

"You know where the junction box is?"

Kaine pointed to an overhead power cable anchored to a metal strut sticking out of the school's gable wall. From there, the cable ran down the outside of the wall and entered the school through a junction box.

"You're simply going to stick a bomb in that box and hope it kills the power to the whole building? What makes you think they don't have a backup generator?"

Good question.

It hadn't taken Freeman long to spot an obvious flaw in Kaine's rudimentary plan.

"You have a better idea, Mr Jewel Thief?"

"One or two," Freeman said, his smile returning. "See that skylight? The one on the left?"

He pointed to one of three tiny openings in the roof. The one he identified was around fifteen metres from the nearest chimney stack, whose brickwork looked as though it hadn't been repointed since Queen Victoria ceased to be amused. It also looked in imminent danger of collapse, as did the roof, many of whose tiles were cracked or missing.

"Are you serious? The roof structure's a real mess. And there's no way a man of your size could make it through that skylight."

"Correct, Captain Kaine. I'd never squeeze through that window. You, on the other hand, are a shoo-in."

For the first time since they'd met, Freeman's keen smile had started to grate on Kaine's nerves.

"What's the matter, Captain? I know all about your escapades in Scotland. There's no way you're afraid of heights."

"I don't mind scaling solid, granite cliffs with good anchor points, but that," he said, staring at the disinte-grating roof, "is a disaster waiting to happen."

"Of course it is, and that's half the fun, right?"

"Hmm," Kaine said, unwilling to say what he really thought.

"Knew you'd see it my way, Captain. Want to get going? It'll be daylight soon."

"While I'm scaling the north face of the Eiger without any climbing gear, what are you going to be doing?"

"Me?" he said, exuding nonchalance. "I'll be killing all the power in that building, including the backup generator they had installed in the cellar last autumn."

"Aha. I see Corky *has* been holding out on me."

"Don't blame Corky. I asked him to hold off telling you until we had this chat. Didn't want you gate-crashing the party without me."

Freeman patted the straps of his backpack in much the same way Kaine had done earlier. "As it happens, I built a special gizmo that's suitable for this very situation."

"You're an electronics man, like Corky?"

Freeman shrugged the backpack off one shoulder and swung it around to his front. "Sort of. I also dabble in mechanical engineering. Basically, I design and build the hardware, Corky develops the software. Together, we make a pretty good team."

"And this gizmo of yours is going to work?"

"Expect so. Been dying to run a field test."

Kaine grimaced at the memory of what happened the last time he had anything to do with field testing a piece of equipment.

Not the time, Kaine. Focus.

"C'mon then," he said, "let's get moving."

"Before we go, I need to explain a few things," Freeman said, matching Kaine's earlier grimace.

"Do we have time?"

"We need to make time. It's important."

"Okay. Mr Freeman, you have my undivided attention."

"'Mr Freeman' makes me sound ancient. Please call me Sean," he said, offering a smile.

"Is that it?"

"Not really. There's one slight problem with the gizmo. Not a deal-breaker as such, more of a side-effect."

Kaine allowed his shoulders to slump.

"Which is?"

Freeman unclipped the top latch of his backpack and loosened the drawstring. He removed a bubble-wrapped package about the size of a family bible. With the covering removed, it looked more like something a radio ham would knock together in his garage, all knobs, switches, and dials. It had a small, digital display in the centre.

"Highly impressive," Kaine said, unable to generate a great deal of enthusiasm.

Freeman shrugged. "Okay, maybe it won't win many design awards, but this little baby's taken me nearly a month to build from the motherboard up."

"Okay, I'll bite. What does it do and how's it going to help us in there?"

"Won't blind you with the detail, although I can if you like."

"Just imagine I'm your technophobic uncle and use small words."

"Can't exactly see you as that, but as a military man, you'll be familiar with electro-magnetic pulses and their effects?"

"EMPs are the bane of the electronic age. They can knock out comms, right?"

Freeman smiled again and nodded. "Pretty much. Trouble with EMPs is they do fatal damage to the devices they attack. Bit like taking a sledgehammer to a nut, kind of thing. Overkill. No finesse. This little darling on the other hand"—his fingers lovingly traced the outline of the dials and switches—"is much more surgical. A scalpel rather than a butcher's cleaver. When I power this up, it will knock out all the electronics within a selected radius, but without doing permanent damage."

"Can it change TV channels, too?"

"Very amusing, Captain. You should take that on tour."

"My apologies, Sean. Please continue," Kaine said, again glancing at his watch.

"For this application, however," Freeman continued,

apparently warming to his role as Kaine's impromptu lecturer, "I've identified two major challenges."

There had to be a catch, or two.

"Which are?"

"When I power this thing up, we'll lose our own state-of-the-art earwigs."

Kaine nodded. "I already made that assumption. Couldn't expect anything else. And the second flaw?"

"That's more technical. You see, the disruptor uses a specific form of rotating frequency modulation. As you probably know, most modern, digital, comms systems use microwaves with an intelligent, phased, encryption algor—"

"Small words, Sean. Remember?" Kaine said, raising a hand to stop the lecture mid-flow.

"Sorry. I get carried away sometimes. Anyhow, the upshot is, I can't simply power up the disruptor and leave it running. I have to adjust the signal in response to the input the system receives. Otherwise, I'd be joining you on the inside."

"That sounds like a major flaw with the device to me."

Another shrug. "It's a timing thing. Corky and I were working on a processor to automate the system, but … well, here we are. Pressing needs, you know."

"Sorry about that, but I didn't exactly beg for your help. Not that I'm ungrateful, you understand, but I am trying to pull my head around the idea that in a few minutes, I'll be trying to scale a rotten roof and squeeze through a tiny, little skylight while you blast a million microwaves at my backside. Now, is that all?"

Freeman scrunched up his face and made a passable impression of someone suffering from toothache. "Pretty much, but … it's just that … well, I wanted to make sure you know you can trust me, okay?"

What's this?

"Of course. Anyone who has DCI Jones' endorsement is okay—"

"Whatever happens in there," Freeman interrupted, holding Kaine's eye and being disconcertingly resolute about it. "Just go with the flow and trust me, right?"

"Trust you? Yes, right. Okay. Whatever you say."

Kaine had no idea what Freeman was implying and put it down to pre-match nerves, which affected different people in different ways. Perhaps the otherwise affable and confident jewel thief suffered from gloomy premonitions. Either way, it made Kaine antsy and he tried his best to brush the matter aside.

"Okay, Sean. Are we good to go?"

"Ready when you are, Captain."

"So, what are we waiting for?"

Crouching low, Kaine took the lead and they headed for the rear of the school.

Chapter Thirty-Two

Monday 22nd February – Byron Codell

Deal Road, Tottenham, London, England

00:11.

Barcode leaned against the wall, hidden by a long row of knackered, three-storey townhouses. The continual traffic noise broke what woulda been a nasty silence. An underground train rumbled by, vibrating beneath his jet blacks.

He hated the quiet. Gave him too much time to think.

In one of her rare lucid periods shortly before she buggered off, his useless witch of a mother took him on holiday to the country. Stifling it were. Soundless, ominous. Fucking terrifying. Give him the throbbing hustle of the city any time. This was his territory. The noise kept dark thoughts away.

The smells wafting from the shops on the main street—kebabs, curries, and pizzas—made his mouth water. Slicing Benjie's throat open had done nothing to ruin his appetite. If anything, that hot blood smell mixed with the fucking cold air made him hungrier, ravenous.

Perhaps he were part-vampire.

Damn.

But he'd sure as hell make one fine, black-assed member of the Undead.

When were the last time he ate? A chicken wrap for lunch and a can of cola.

Tasty.

Again, his mouth watered and his stomach grumbled.

How long since he had that wrap? Ten hours? No wonder his stomach moaned at him like a ho begging for more.

No time to eat just yet. Food could wait.

Across the road, the single-storey building—the collection point according to TM—stood squat, dark, and ugly. Surrounded by a chain-link fence that wouldn't stop a kiddie getting in, the place weren't a patch on Palmerston School. On the other hand, the bunker blended in with its surroundings well enough. Place seemed to fit the part of a temporary distribution centre. Although how TM gathered his knowledge, fuck knew.

Worry started to edge into Barcode's head.

What if this were nothing but TM's ploy to lower Barcode's defences and get him alone? Put him in a place where the Heavies could murk him easy and quiet, like?

Nah, if TM wanted him gone, he'd have done it in the Hub in front of the Tribe. Another example set to keep the little ones in line.

Suspicion could be a terrible thing. TM had given

Barcode a task. A test, for definite. Barcode would get the job done, and TM would make good on his promise.

Honour. That were the way of the Tribe. Always had been, even with the first TM.

Barcode had been standing in the same spot for the best part of two fucking hours. His feet was just about frozen to the pavement, and his calves had started to cramp. And, despite the black scarf wrapped around his face—one he stole months ago from the Black Bear foot soldier along with the souvenir button—the cold ate into the back of his neck.

Still, Barcode suffered in silence.

Movement might of given his position away. He refused to shiver. Didn't rub his hands together for warmth, neither. Barely even breathed for fear of raising a cloud of mist. He stayed put. Unflinching. A man of stone. He were ready. Ready for anything the Parksider assholes or their suppliers could throw at him.

If TM were true to his word, Barcode would soon be boss of a bigger patch and take home more paper. The biggest patch in the Tribe it would be, and he'd earn more income than anyone outside of the Heavies. A half-decent promotion, and one step higher up the ladder.

Upwardly mobile, that's what he'd be.

A climber.

As the new crew boss, Barcode would be managing a fifteen-man operation. He'd be facilitator, security officer, personnel manager, and a fucking wet-nurse to the newbies. He'd mosh around the hood, in charge of seven pitches, making sure of the product's availability and that it moved smooth from Hub to pitch, and on to the customer. And all with the minimum of fuss. Only he and the team leaders, Spook and Big Robert, would distribute the product itself.

The juniors, each one big and useful with knives and sticks, handled protection. They was junior only in rank, not in age. The titches, kiddies like Lil' Aran, crept around at the bottom of the pecking order. Gofers desperate for a slice of the action, they survived on scraps and tips, standing in when illness or the bacon took out one of the crew.

Barcode read the time off his cheap, digital watch—he'd left the distinctive, gold Rolex knock-off in his crib. Didn't want nothing giving him away.

Not long now.

Assuming TM's info were legit and not bullshit, Barcode was about to take care of the second piece of business that night, and he was still riding high from doing Benjie. Even though the gnawing cold and the icy rain had chilled his bones and frozen the skin on his face, he managed a happy smile. Getting his own back on the rat-faced weasel kept him warm during his long wait.

Benjie Harrington, aka Weasel, RIP!

Gone and good fucking riddance.

Another seven minutes passed and the temperature dropped with the speed of a ho's drawers as the wind whistling through the gaps in the houses increased. Fucking hell, it couldn't have been much worse.

Still, Barcode didn't stir from his hiding place.

Wait. What the fuck's happenin'?

A single headlight raked the alley, and the high-pitched whine of a moped—an ancient Aprilia RS50, according to TM—squealed through the noise of traffic on the far end of Deal Road.

Yeah, here come the mutha. 'Bout fuckin' time.

Barcode let the smile widen.

He flexed some warmth into his fingers. To take the asshole down, he needed speed and strength. Wouldn't get

KERRY J DONOVAN

none of them with frozen digits. He pulled out the knife, snapped open the blade, and watched as the stainless steel reflected the light from one of the streetlights.

The sharpened edge of stainless steel turned him on.

Fuck yes.

Barcode pressed harder against the brickwork, flattening himself out, melting further into the shadows.

Timing were everything.

He pulled the black scarf up and the hood down, leaving only a thin sliver of a gap. Enough to see through, but not enough to be recognised. Two jackets and a big, black coat changed his shape and the pebble in the heel of his right sneaker would give him a limp and alter his move-ment—a trick he'd seen in an old spy movie. Ain't nobody was gonna recognise him in his black rig even if he managed to step into range of some hidden snooper's surveillance camera. Let alone the boy on the moped, who'd be shitting himself the second he spied the blade.

Moped Boy, with a backpack dangling from his shoul-ders, leaned the Aprilia against the rusted railings surrounding the warehouse. He left the motor running and jogged along the path leading to the distribution centre's front doors. He'd parked under the working streetlight, presumably for security, making it easy for Barcode to read the number plate.

Well, fuck's sake.

The number matched the one TM made him memorise. Boss Man weren't pulling a fast one, after all.

Barcode's heart beat faster and his blood started pumping harder, spreading warmth through his body.

The second Moped Boy slipped through the front door and disappeared inside, Barcode pushed out from his hiding spot. He darted across the street, limping on his right leg, and crouched behind a green dumpster, twenty metres from the fast-idling moped.

If anyone in the warehouse spotted his move, Barcode's chances of surviving the night wouldn't be worth shit, but the bitter wind and low temperatures kept the guards inside the building, heads down.

Assuming TM's information held up, and so far, it had been dead exact, Moped Boy would only be inside for a few seconds. Then he and the Aprilia would return the way they'd come, heading back to the Parksiders' new base. Only they wasn't gonna arrive. At least, not in one piece.

Barcode started counting.

The short sprint had done sweet fuck all to warm him, and only made his legs scream out in cramp. But the cramp wouldn't last long. The Parksiders' loss of face and loss of product would more than compensate for Barcode's minor discomfort. He'd be warm soon enough.

By the time he reached an internal count of thirty-three, the big, metal door creaked open and Moped Boy jogged out. His backpack were fatter and hung lower on its straps, looking plenty heavier than it did when he arrived.

The fucker jogged down the steps, fastening the chin-strap of his helmet as he moved. He kept his head lowered and his eyes down.

Too fuckin' easy.

The kid finished adjusting his skid lid, pulled the Aprilia upright, and threw his leg over the saddle. The engine screamed and he peeled away from the pavement with what Barcode imagined was an attempted wheelie, but the under-powered piece of shit didn't have the guts and all the kid managed was a front wheel wobble.

Time this right, Barcode.

Moped Boy raced the Aprilia towards the dumpster.

The moment he drew alongside, Barcode stepped out and clotheslined the little fucker right off the saddle. With his arm protected by the sleeves of the two heavy jackets and a rolled up newspaper, Barcode felt nothing but a gentle thump.

The Aprilia carried on going and Moped Boy landed on his butt, rolled, and slammed into the low wall on the other side of the road. Ten metres away, the moped toppled and hit the tarmac. Orange sparks flew.

With his switchblade raised and leading the way, Barcode reached Moped Boy before the fucker knew what was happening. The first two knife swipes cut through the webbing straps holding the backpack across the kid's shoulders. The third sweep sliced through the back of Moped Boy's leg just above his sneaker.

The kid screamed. Tried to scramble away. Screamed again when Barcode lunged forwards, aiming a slash at the fucker's inner thigh, but missed.

Shit.

He slashed again and nicked the leg, but only lightly.

"What the fuck?" Moped Boy squeaked, still trying to back away, but being slowed by his fucked-up leg. "You insane? You know who I work for? Asshole!"

Barcode's blade dug in again, struck bone. Again, Moped Boy screamed.

"Black Bear Clan don't like bein' shafted, fucker!"

"What?" Moped Boy yelled. "You fucker, you fuck—"

Lights snapped on in the surrounding buildings. The warehouse shutters screeched open. Figures poured through the opening.

Barcode gripped the backpack, turned, and race-limped for the Aprilia. With its engine still running, he righted it, jumped aboard, and twisted the throttle wide open. The screaming moped took off like a butt-kicked ho.

Less than fifteen seconds. In. Out.

Job done.

He'd gotten away clean.

Barcode crushed down the need to yell in delight. Couldn't risk the chance of his distinctive laugh giving him away.

With a shift of his weight and a twitch of the handlebars, he turned right onto Harbinger Row, scooted around a slow-as-fuck taxi, and headed for the canal.

Chapter Thirty-Three

Monday 22nd February - Byron Codell

Landale Road, Tottenham, London, England

00:58.

Twenty minutes after ripping off Moped Boy, and with the empty backpack, the moped, and his disguise still burning in a disused car park, Barcode turned for home, searching for his next ride—anything ancient would do. He always boosted cheap cars made before the turn of the millennium since they didn't have no trackers.

'Course, he coulda walked home. Weren't all that far. Five, six miles maybe. Could stroll it inside two hours. But a huge, black guy schlepping the back streets alone and in the middle of the night would draw attention. It didn't pay to ask for trouble with the bacon, not with the load he were carrying. A kilo of blow and a surprise find — a roll of cash —was not something he could easily explain away.

"Oh no, Officer. This gear ain't mine. Just looking after it fo' a friend, innit," he muttered into the dark.

Ha!

Armed with his knife, he could take care of the average plod, but TM were expecting him in a couple hours and Barcode didn't wanna cause upset, not with him being so close to "made man" status. No. Current situation called for extra caution.

Barcode coulda tried hailing a cab, but the same rules applied. There weren't many cabbies gonna stop for a big, black man in the middle of the night. No fucking way. Yeah, and he coulda called one of the Tribesmen with a car for a lift, but that would mean he'd have to share the glory.

Nah.

Taking the Parksiders' latest delivery was Barcode's way into the big time. He weren't gonna share it with no one.

A twenty-five-year-old Ford Fiesta, parked badly with two wheels up on the pavement, were begging to be jacked. In passing, he plonked a butt cheek heavily on the bonnet. The fucking thing started wailing like a dog with its bollocks caught on a barbwire fence.

Shit!

To his right, a man shouted something obscene.

Barcode raced away, ducked down a side street, and continued sprinting, with the breath rattling in his lungs, his legs aching, and the sweat pouring. He only slowed when the car horn stopped blaring and the man stopped yelling.

Why run?

Shoulda faced the asshole down, sliced him open, but …

Getting into a dust-up with a civilian weren't gonna do much to keep his profile on the downlow.

Half a mile later, with the cramp finally easing from his calves, he spotted another candidate. A shitty, little Renault 5, in two-tone grey and rust. Perfect. The Frogs knew shit-all about how to build a thief-proof car. He repeated the ass-on-the-bonnet trick. This time, the rust box stayed silent.

During his time jacking cars, he'd learned all the tricks and carried tools for the job—slim jims, levers, wedges, cables, bump locks, screwdrivers, whatever. Although each had its strength and weakness, and offered entry to most rides without damage, they all took time. For the present situation, walking in the middle of a winter's night in a gathering rainstorm, he preferred the rapid, low-tech approach. With a rock picked up from a nearby garden, he caved in the rear passenger's window—ain't no one wanna sit on a driver's seat covered in sharp nuggets of glass. He pulled open the passenger's door, leaned inside, and unlocked the driver's side.

Fuck-all to it.

Ten seconds—and a screwdriver rammed into the ignition lock—later, the engine spluttered into life, and Barcode was off. He tried leaving the kerb with a tyre-burning screech, but the underpowered shit-box shot forwards with all the rage of a kitten playing with a ball of wool.

So what if the smashed window let in the freezing air and the winter rain? A fuck's sight better than walking, and his new ride's heater soon started pumping hot air onto his face and hands.

Fuckin' aces.

After racing from the area, he slowed to the speed limit and headed towards Walthamstow with a smile so wide, his cheeks soon started to ache and, again, his belly rumbled. Thieving and knife-work always gave him an appetite.

Since TM didn't expect him much before three o'clock,

he had plenty of time to pick up some food. A pepperoni pizza would go down almost as good as his favourite weekday slut, Deshonda.

Barcode pulled the shit-box Renault around the corner from the takeaway, parked in the darkest part of the street, and pushed through a steamed-up glass door into the bright, warm, delicious-smelling pizzeria. He sidled up to the counter and beamed at Petey, who took turns helping out his old man whenever he couldn't get outta it.

Barcode acted all calm and friendly, like. Relaxed.

Nothin' a matter here. Nothin' goin' on at all. No, sir.

"Wh'appenin', blood?" he asked.

Looking tired and bored to death, Petey nodded. "Wh'appening?"

"Things good?"

"Yeah, bro. Business jumping," Petey answered in his slow—some might say dumb-assed—drawl. But none would say it to the fucker's face. Petey was meaner than he looked, and he looked real mean all the time. "Pizzas are flying out the door and my dad's gonna be here in an hour. Then I'm due to hit my crib." He glanced over his shoulder at the kitchen door before leaning across the counter. When he spoke again, his voice was low, almost a whisper. "You been gone awhile. Some secret mission for TM, right?"

Barcode sucked air between his teeth and brushed a finger to the side of his nose. "S'right."

"Go okay?"

Barcode leaned back and opened his arms wide before patting the stolen stash bulging in his jacket pocket. "Hey, Petey, my man. When TM need somethin' done, he call on the only Tribesman who matters, y'know?"

Petey smiled. "I know, Barcode. I know well enough. Want yo' usual?"

"Sure 'nough. Double up on the pepperoni and add a Coke, 'kay? This nigga starvin'."

"Being out this late is likely gonna do that to you, bro," Petey said, while working the fresh dough onto a platter, spreading the sauce, and throwing on a load of mozzarella and a handful of sliced sausage. "I saw that Renault you pull up in. Make sure you leave it right away from my dad's shop, y'hear? We don't want no comeback from the bacon like wh'appened last time."

Barcode scrunched up his face. He didn't take kindly to being told what to do by a junior, but he let it pass. Didn't want nothing killing his buzz.

"No probs, Petey. I's on my way to the Hub now. Needed some o' your homemade pie 'fore my meet with TM. I'll dump the wheels far away from this place. 'Kay?"

"Thanks, bro," Petey said, lowering his head as though finally remembering his place in the Tribe's pecking order. As he slid the uncooked pizza into the oven, Barcode enjoyed the blast of heat that toasted his face.

Petey set the timer for seven minutes and looked up at him.

"You hear 'bout Rhino?"

Barcode just about managed to stop himself nodding. Far as the world were concerned, he ain't seen no one from the Tribe that night, and definitely not Benjie. No, definitely not Benjie the Weasel.

He frowned and shook his head. "Nah. Been busy. Wazzup with the man? Ariel drop the sprog or somethin'?"

Petey repeated what the weasel were in the middle of saying before Barcode sliced him open, ending with, "Yeah, bro. Demarcus and Crabapple drag him outta the Hub and into the courtyard. Man, he were screaming his innocence and crying like a baby. Then TM tol' us all to fuck off."

"Did you see Rhino make the signal?"

Petey shook his head. "Nah, didn't see nothing, me. Too busy concentrating on TM's speechifying. Impressed with what he said 'bout you, bro."

He offered a fist to Barcode and they bumped.

"Yeah? What he say?"

Petey shrugged. "Just how you was his main man. Headed up the ladder. Y'know?"

Barcode turned his sneer into a smile.

Don't you just know it, bro.

"You got that right, Petey. But 'bout the Rhino thing. You sure it weren't TM makin' one o' his points? Keepin' the Tribesmen in line, like he done 'fore?"

Again, Petey shook his head. "Not this time, bro. TM show us the recording. Look like Rhino was doing something sly, fo' sure."

"Dragged him out the Hub, you say?"

"Yeah, bro. Kicking and screaming, he were. Doubt we'll see him again. Not alive."

"Fuck!"

"What's wrong, man?"

"Rhino's one o' my crew. If TM had him murked, it's gonna reflect bad on me. I might have to smooth things out with TM."

"Oh. Didn't think o' that." Petey didn't look too disappointed with the idea that Barcode might be standing in the middle of a big heap of dogshit.

"How that pie lookin'?"

"Not long now, blood. Two minutes. Couple slices o' garlic bread there. Want some?"

For some reason, Barcode's hunger had eased a few notches, but he weren't about to let on to Petey. "Sure, man. Pass one over. Don't wanna kill my appetite fo' the pie."

Petey dropped the bread onto a paper napkin and handed it over. Barcode wolfed it down in one go, although it tasted of cardboard. He smacked his lips, wiped them with the napkin, then dropped it into the bin.

"C'mon, man. That pie gotta be ready now. I got a meet with TM. Can't keep him waitin'."

Petey shrugged. "If you say so."

He grabbed the flat, wooden shovel, dug the pizza outta the oven, and slid it into a waiting box. Then he ran the wheeled cutter through it a few times and passed the box over the counter along with a couple napkins and the cola. He waved away Barcode's offer of money. Barcode never did pay at Petey's dad's place, but always made the offer. Least he pretended to.

He up-nodded and they bumped fists once more.

"Take care, bro."

"You too, blood."

Keeping the pizza box level and dodging the rain, Barcode raced around the corner, dived into the Renault, and used the screwdriver to kick the car back into life.

During the short drive to the school, the smell of pepperoni and mozzarella set Barcode's mouth to watering again.

Although one of his crew mighta been playing for another side, it didn't necessarily reflect badly on Barcode, did it? After all, he'd just dealt the Parksiders a body blow. He done it single-handed and on TM's orders. Had to count for something, right?

'Course it did.

Barcode were cool. On the up. Fuck Rhino and his treachery.

He pulled the Renault to a stop across the road, a

couple hundred metres from the school, and started eating. Pizza were delicious.

So far, his day had gone perfect. All he needed was to run into the white bitch in a dark alley and it would round it off nicely. He could really use a bit of tight-assed, stuck-up white-bait about now. Yeah. He'd give her a good time. He had plenty enough dark meat. Maybe too much for her to handle.

Barcode allowed himself a trademarked cackle. He had that little delight to come.

The dashboard clock flashed over to 01:37. He had a great view of the front and side of the school and plenty a time to enjoy his pie.

———

AS THE FINAL segment of cooled pizza slipped down, Barcode belched loudly and excused himself to no one. He drained the last of the fizzy cola and dropped the can into the passenger's footwell along with the empty pizza box.

"Time to move, blood. Get this over with."

He reached for the handle on the driver's door to brave the rain. In the distance, on the roof of the schoolhouse, something moved. Something dark and man-shaped.

What the fuck?

Another man-shaped shadow moved in the courtyard out back. It slid along the rear wall, heading towards the back doors. Damn it, the school were under attack.

Parksiders?

Barcode pushed on the door. It screeched open, letting in a huge blast of super-chilled, soaking wet air. He swung his right leg out into the dark and the rain, then paused.

Wait, blood.

He needed to think.

Barcode pulled his rain-soaked leg back inside the car and slammed the door shut. No need to rush. Time to deliberate. He lit a cigarette.

Think it through, blood. Think it through.

Rhino had been caught signalling someone. Maybe he'd turned on the Tribe and joined with the Parksiders.

Perhaps it weren't nothing more than a coincidence.

What about the asshole on the Aprilia, Moped Boy? Did the little fucker recognise him through his disguise? Were the Parksiders retaliating already?

It were common knowledge the schoolhouse was usually empty overnight, but no one with any brains would dare break into the place. Not normally. Maybe they'd do it in retribution for his act of war—for maybe for the way Barcode dealt with Beanie Boy and his crew?

More than likely, this weren't an all-out attack. Maybe they was planning to trash the place and search for some product. If so, the Parksiders would be getting more than they bargained for. They be walking into a shitstorm.

On the other hand, just because he'd only spotted two men so far, didn't mean the Parksiders weren't there in full force.

What was he supposed to do?

Barcode wiped a hand across his mouth.

Should he crash into the school and raise the alarm? No fucking way. If the Parksiders were launching a full-scale attack, he'd be exposing himself to risk.

Fuck that.

He were gonna sit back, wait for the dust to settle. If TM were in the Hub, the Heavies would be there, too. The Heavies got paid to protect TM and the Hub. That's why they earned the big bucks. Weren't Barcode's job.

If he'd really fucked up and set the Parksiders on the Tribe, he'd be safer outta the firing line. Outta town, even. Fuck's sake. He might not even be safe if he left the shitting country.

Barcode breathed deep. He needed a backup plan. Play the odds. Warn TM.

He sucked on his tab and blew the smoke through the gap in the window.

Yeah. Too fuckin' right.

Keep a safe distance, but warn the Heavies and the Geeks inside the school. Then, he'd wait.

He leaned back in his seat, stretched out his leg to allow access to the pocket of his wet jeans, and dug out his phone.

Each Tribesman was ordered to memorise an emergency number in case the bacon raided or someone needed help. Geeks manned the number around the clock. It were one of their main jobs. On the promise of some pretty grim consequences, the emergency number weren't to be used lightly or for social calls. Far as Barcode knew, no one had never dialled it before, but this seemed like the situation it were made for.

He powered up his phone and keyed in the number.

The shadow on the roof slid around for a bit then slipped through one of the skylights. Whoever it was were small, or he woulda never been able to squeeze through the tiny opening. Barcode sure as hell wouldn't have managed it.

He finished dialling and hit the green button.

Silence.

"C'mon, Geeks. Answer the damn phone."

Chapter Thirty-Four

Monday 20th February - Night

Palmerston Road School, Walthamstow, London, England

01:52.

The cold, gusting wind tugged at Kaine's clothes, trying to push or pluck him from the school roof, depending on its direction. The slippery tiles didn't help, and holding on to the chimney's crumbling brickwork offered very little sense of security. On the plus side, the rain had eased a little.

Small mercies.

In his ear, the comms unit clicked.

"Alpha Four to Alpha One. Receiving? Over."

Kaine smiled. It seemed that Corky's buddy hadn't learned radio discipline from the hacker.

"Alpha One to Alpha Four, reading you full strength. Over."

"Sitrep. Over."

"On the roof, prepping for entry. You? Over."

"Entry effected. Disruptor in place and warming up. Prepare for comms blackout in sixty seconds. Over."

"Thanks for the warning, Alpha Four. Over."

"Good luck, buddy. Alpha Four, out."

Buddy? When did we become buddies?

The earpiece clicked again, and Kaine was alone. Alone on a ramshackle roof, on a filthy, black night in the middle of winter.

Lovely.

The dilapidated, A-frame roof stretched into the gloom ahead of him. Up close, the structure looked to be in an even worse state of disrepair than it had from the wonderful safety of the ground. The intact tiles that remained in place were slick with rainwater and covered in large patches of moss, mould, and dead leaves. Others were broken and some were missing altogether. The gutters had disappeared long ago. If he lost his footing on the treacherous surface, nothing would interrupt his fall but the concrete courtyard four storeys below.

The situations he allowed himself to fall into.

"Fall"? Why use a word like "fall"?

The skylight, his initial target, was located halfway between the first two chimneys, fifteen metres distant, and it hung one and a half metres below the apex—just about within an arm's stretch. The semi-circular ridge tiles ran in a relatively unbroken line to the second of three chimneys. They *appeared* strong enough to take his weight. At least, he hoped so.

Only one way to find out.

With his back to the first chimney, Kaine lowered himself carefully to his hands and knees, and spider-crawled forwards.

He took it slow. Really slow.

The wind whipped around his head, laughing at him, taunting, playing with his mind, and the rain washed the sweat from his face. The crepe soles of his military boots and the pads of his leather gloves added some traction, but very little, and not enough to offer him anything in the way of confidence.

Carefully, he pushed forwards.

Five metres away from the relative safety of the chimney, another ten before he drew level with the skylight, Kaine slid his right hand forwards a few centimetres. Beneath his palm, parts of a ridge tile broke free.

His hand slipped, he wobbled, dropped down to his chest and hugged either side of the ridge with arms pressed wide and his legs gripping at the knees. The tile slipped and rattled down the rear roof slope.

With his balance regained, Kaine watched the largest shard fall. As the orange fragment reached the final row of tiles, it teetered on the edge of the roof for a second before dropping.

In the whistling wind, Kaine couldn't hear it land.

Anyone standing in the courtyard below who wasn't decapitated by the falling roof tile would look up, but Kaine would be hidden by the walls and the pitch of the roof. To see him, they'd have to step well away from the wall and out into the full force of the wind and rain. Unlikely, but possible.

Kaine swallowed hard and slithered forwards another two metres ... three ... four. Over half way. He had to hurry. The longer he took on the roof, the greater the danger of being spotted, and the more chance the roof would collapse under his added weight.

Another metre.

Another.

The creaking and groaning beneath his hands and knees didn't offer much in the way of relief. Kaine paused and looked around. Not a good idea. Another gust of wind whipped up from the roof, tugged at his clothing, threatened to lift him from his risky perch.

Lights and movement struck his peripheral vision—the interior light of a car parked on the street a couple of hundred metres distant.

Kaine stopped moving.

The car's door screeched open, the driver started to get out, then changed his mind. The door slammed shut again.

Kaine waited, hugging the tiles, but the driver stayed in the car. A cigarette lighter flamed into life, flickered, and died. The red ember of a lit cigarette glowed brightly and faded. A smoker enjoying a final, surreptitious cancer stick before settling in for the night? A husband trying to hide his secret passion from his partner?

Kaine breathed again.

One good thing—the cigarette's glowing ember would impact on the smoker's vision, keeping Kaine hidden. He couldn't hang around, though. The ciggie wouldn't last forever.

After scrambling forwards another three metres, the skylight lay directly beneath him.

Kaine spun through ninety degrees, until his midriff was balanced on the roof's apex, and stretched out his arms. Nope, too short. His fingers fell centimetres shy of the skylight's wooden frame. He squirmed forwards, snake-like, until his hips met and then cleared the ridge tile, flattening his gloved palms against the tiles to increase the traction.

In this position, he'd pushed the safety envelope so far that it no longer existed, but with no secure anchoring point he couldn't have used a safety rope anyway.

Ridiculous lack of preparation.

Back in his military days, if any of his subordinates had suggested this method of entry to Kaine, he'd have drummed them out of the troop.

How times change.

There he was, balanced precariously on the roof of a decrepit building, searching for the identity of a person who may or may not have something to do with the death of an old man Kaine had never even met.

Stupid, stupid, stupid.

It defied all logic. But who said he had to be logical?

His fingertips met the wood of the skylight frame. Rotten, sponge-soft to the touch. A good sign in terms of forced access, but in terms of his overall safety, not so much.

With one hand on the upper frame for balance, he punched the glass lightly with the side of his fist. The thin pane rattled and cracked, but held. Glazing putty, powdered with age, fell away. He hit it again, this time with a little more force. The glass shattered and fell inside. A fraction of a second later, glass rattled on bare floorboards.

Relief swept through him, and he took a steadying breath.

The time lapse between smashing the window and when the shards hit the bare boards was short, almost instantaneous, confirming that the internal floor was intact and no more than a couple of metres below the skylight.

The architect's blueprints had indicated a small room and a floor below the skylight but before that point, neither he nor Freeman could be certain the floor still existed in its original state. For all they knew, the boards could have disintegrated during the years since the building had been abandoned, resting, as it was, directly beneath such a rotten roof.

The rain increased in force again. Huge dollops hammered into cracked tiles, bouncing high. Spray flew into his face.

Okay, Kaine. In you go.

Working with his hands and hips, Kaine shimmied backwards until his waist lay on the ridge tiles once more. He shrugged off his baby-Bergen, lowered it through the opening, and let it fall. It landed with a satisfyingly solid thump. He waited for his breathing to recover before rotating through one-eighty degrees.

After checking his legs lined up with the broken skylight, he gripped the half-round ridge tiles, wriggled backwards, and lowered his feet into the empty blackness.

Chapter Thirty-Five

Monday 20th February – Pre-Dawn

Palmerston Road School, Walthamstow, London, England

02:03.

With his legs dangling inside the school, feet searching for purchase, Kaine angled his shoulders to line them up with the diagonal of the window frame and shimmied lower. A tight squeeze. Too bloody tight. His body wedged in the frame, pinned at the upper chest beneath his armpits. The rotten wood of the window creaked and splintered, but held firm.

He froze. Struggled. Kicked his legs against nothing.

Stuck.

Bugger!

Momentary panic drove into his head, but he forced it away. No value in it.

Relax. Slow down.

Kaine stretched his arms high over his head, took a deep breath, and released it slowly. He forced the air out, emptying his lungs, narrowing his chest.

All the while, he was being soaked and frozen by the latest heavy shower—sleet mixed in with the rain.

With a sharp crack, the wood pinning him crumbled, gave way. He slipped through the opening, gathering momentum the whole time.

He was free!

Kaine softened his knees and ankles, preparing to drop into a paratrooper's landing roll if necessary.

An instant later, the toes of his shoes hit bare boards. The woodwork screeched like an old rocking chair, but otherwise held firm.

Bent at the knees and waist, Kaine held stock still in the pitch black, his eyes and ears open, watching and listening for anything unexpected. His vision and hearing told him nothing, but the smell of dust and decay confirmed the room hadn't been used in an age.

He sucked in a deep breath as he stood slowly, hands held high to prevent his head hitting a roof truss. The old school building creaked and groaned under the weight of age and the power of the growing storm. Otherwise, the room remained silent.

By touch alone, he found the small rucksack at his feet and fished inside for his lightweight, high-resolution, night vision goggles. He pulled the single lens over his non-dominant eye and scanned the room in all its optically enhanced, green-tinted glory—and found nothing special.

As the architect's drawings indicated, he'd dropped into

one of a dozen attic storerooms. Save for cobwebs, a rust-encrusted bed, and an old wardrobe, this one stood empty.

Keeping to the edges of the room where the floorboards were anchored directly into the brickwork and likely more secure, Kaine worked his way to the room's only door. He twisted the old-fashioned, ball-shaped handle, expecting it to be locked, but it screeched as it turned. The lock disengaged and the door opened inwards.

The narrow corridor beyond was equally as dark as the storeroom, but the NV goggles worked their magic. Closed doors, the same design as the one he'd just opened, lined the internal walls. Eight in all.

According to the plans, the corridor ran the full length of the school, chimney stack to chimney stack, each end terminating in a landing at the head of a staircase. Kaine turned right, heading for his first target which lay one floor down, more or less directly below where he stood.

He reached the head of the stairs and stopped. Still no sign of life in the building. For a brief moment, he wondered where Freeman had ended up, but didn't waste time on the matter. Freeman had his task, and Kaine had his own search to conduct.

Tentatively, he lowered his foot to the top tread and added his weight slowly. Again, the woodwork creaked in protest under the loading, but the ancient timbers held. Stepping on the outsides of each tread, Kaine descended to the third floor and turned back on himself. He counted off three doors on the rear of the building and stopped. The faint but familiar, acrid tang of gunshot—nitroglycerin, sawdust, and graphite—hung in the still and musty air.

Kaine turned the handle. This time, the lock held firm and the door stayed shut. The old-fashioned lock mechanism wouldn't be difficult to pick but, standing exposed in an open hallway made the little hairs on the back of his neck prickle, and he didn't have the time for finesse.

Kicking the door in would have worked, but the noise…

He twisted the handle again to disengage the latch bolt, pressed his shoulder against the door, and added more weight. The vertical jamb—rotten and weak—cracked and the door squealed open.

Kaine paused for a moment. Breaking the lock had taken less force and created less noise than he'd expected, but only a hard-of-hearing optimist would have called it silent.

The building still creaked and groaned, breathing under the stress of the wind and rain, but otherwise, all remained quiet.

He stepped inside what might once have been a bedroom for the workhouse staff, but now contained cardboard boxes, stacked four high against the interior walls. A single small window looked out over the rear courtyard and the rail tracks beyond.

Inside, the scent of gunpowder was much stronger. Little air movement in the room meant the molecules holding the odour would take a good while to dissipate, and it had only been a few hours since the shooter, probably TM, had taken the wild pot-shots at him.

Kaine inspected the window and the sill. Both indicated recent activity. Clear areas in the dust that had built-up over the years showed where TM had rested his elbows to steady his aim. The window catch hadn't been fully re-engaged, and scratch marks on the frame revealed where the casement had been forced open to allow the shots without the need to break any glass.

The shots—downhill and in the dark, but close range and relatively easy—had been wildly inaccurate. Much less accurate than a shot he'd expect from a regular, weekend hunter. It indicated little skill or marksman training. By poking the muzzle through the window, the shooter had allowed his target to see the weapon which had given him time to escape. No properly trained soldier would have been so careless. An amateur. As such, the shooter might have made other rookie errors.

Kaine searched the bare floorboards below the window.

Yep, there it was, shining bright in his optics. A spent shell casing. He picked it up and examined the markings pressed into the base. A 7mm-08 Remington. US made and designed for small game hunting. Millions of rounds were sold annually in the States, but they were illegal in the UK.

Interesting.

Most illegal weapons in the UK originated from the former Eastern Bloc, like the AK-47, and the majority of which were chambered for 7.62 Soviet cartridges. Other illegal weapons on the UK streets tended to use the slightly more accessible 5.56 NATO ammo. The Remington casing was relatively rare and therefore significant.

Whether through carelessness, ignorance, or overconfidence, TM had ignored another basic rule of sniper training. The fool hadn't policed his brass. In all probability, he'd left some trace evidence on the casing, too. At some stage in the not-too-distant future, Kaine expected the Palmerston School to be the focus of a police forensic investigation. Kaine returned the casing to the floor, but tucked it under one of the cardboard crates, nicely out of sight of the casual viewer.

He stood back from the window and cast his eyes around the room. This time, he found nothing else of interest and, after making sure no sign of his presence remained, he left the room, pulling the door tight behind him. Despite his clumsy break-in, the door held closed and looked no more damaged than any other he'd seen in the building so far.

Outside in the hallway once more, Kaine reversed his steps and headed down to the next floor. On the half-landing, he paused. Below him, somewhere in the bowels of the school, a door creaked open and slammed shut.

Not Freeman. No skilled jewel thief would make such a racket.

Voices.

Male voices, muted by the distance, but growing louder, drawing closer.

Kaine padded down the rest of the stairs two at a time, fetching up on the first-floor landing. On tiptoes, he raced along the corridor, pausing only long enough to test each door in turn. On the fifth try, he struck lucky. The door opened and he ducked inside another empty, dust-filled room, moments before the light from a torch lit the stairwell.

He closed the door softly behind him and leaned against it, breathing deep and slow, listening hard.

Heavy footfalls climbed the staircase, moving slowly. The voices grew sharper, clearer. Kaine pressed his ear to the door panel.

"...see him? Spitting nails he were. Nearly wet m'self, didn't I? I mean, literally," the first man said. His voice was fairly high-pitched and youthful, the accent pure Essex.

"Who are you talking about?" the second man asked, the voice quieter, the accent almost scholarly in comparison to the first.

"Demarcus Williams, you pillock. Like, who else would I be talking about?"

"He's back?"

The footsteps stopped and, by the sound of it, close to the top of the stairs, but the conversation continued.

"Yeah, man. Apparently TM called him back in, before the blackout. Didn't you hear him, Demarcus Williams, I mean, cussing and swearing? Sounded like a scalded cat, man. Kept saying as how he were gonna take them Parksiders apart on account of making him look bad and ruining his fave jacket. Hilarious, y'know? Like, I nearly pissed my pants. Literally."

"I just arrived, man. What did TM have to say about it?" Scholar asked, and the footsteps started up again.

"He starts laying down the law, y'know? Saying as how nobody does nothing without him giving the orders. Fucking man's a megla… megala …"

"Megalomaniac?" Scholar offered.

Essex Boy laughed. "Yeah, man. That's what I meant. You and your big words is rubbing off on me. TM's a fucking nut job."

"You wouldn't be saying that if he could hear you. Right?"

The footsteps stopped again and a door handle rattled.

The Heavies were running a security check.

Kaine leaned harder into his door and jammed the heel of his boot against the kickplate and into the floor. He slipped the SIG from its holster, quietly racked a shell into the breech, and placed his finger along the trigger guard. He had no intention of shooting these idiots, but he understood the petrifying effects of having a loaded gun pointed at you by an unknown madman. Simply showing them the weapon would likely end all resistance.

"Too fucking right I wouldn't, mate," Essex Boy answered, lowering his voice to a stage whisper. "Like, I mean, what's up with this blackout, man? Nothing works. You got any idea?"

His voice grew even louder and another handle rattled.

"Search me, man. All the landlines are dead, and I can't get a signal on my phone. It's weird."

They stopped outside Kaine's room. He raised the SIG to eye level, pointed it at the panel, and braced himself. The handle twiddled and rattled, and the door shook against the jamb.

"This is a waste of fucking time, yeah?" Essex Boy said as the footsteps restarted and the Heavies carried on their way.

Kaine relaxed a little.

"Agreed," Scholar answered. "No one in the neighbourhood has the balls to attack this place, not even the Parksiders. On the other hand, Demarcus Williams is unlikely to rescind his order to search on your say so."

"Huh?"

"Forget it."

"Yeah, right."

Two doors further along the hallway, the lock disengaged and the Heavies entered. They searched loudly for a short while, moving what sounded like heavy boxes and metal furniture, before slamming the door closed and carrying on. More handles rattled.

"You hear what happened with Red?" Essex Boy asked.

"No. Tell me."

"Fucking scarpered, didn't he! Never knew the slimy fucker could run so fast, man. Like, I always knew he were a coward, but fancy taking off like that. Scalded cat, man. A scalded fucking cat."

"Doesn't surprise me. Anyway, good riddance, I say. Probably halfway back to Ireland by now. Him and his, 'I was in the IRA before the Good Friday Agreement fucked everything up'. Total bullshit, you ask me."

"Yeah, what you said," Essex Boy said, hesitantly.

Kaine doubted Essex Boy understood the reference to what, to the lad, would be a historical footnote to the ending of The Troubles.

"Yeah and anyhow, like, what about them rifle shots? You should of seen it," Essex Boy said, his voice fading into the distance. "Bullets weren't far off plugging Crabapple in the arse where he were laying."

"Really?" Scholar answered over the creak of another door opening.

"Yeah, man. Saw it with my own eyes, I did. Heard it, too."

"You know what that means?" Scholar asked after a slight pause.

"Nah. What's it mean?"

"TM's still in the building."

"Really? You reckon?"

"Well, think about it, mate. Who else around here would have a rifle?"

"Like, er … Demarcus Williams always carries a shooter. Keeps flashing it around like he's a fucking cowboy."

"Robbie, sometimes, you can be a real plonker."

"Whatcha mean by that?" Essex Boy Robbie, asked, his voice rising in pitch.

"Demarcus Williams has a handgun, not a rifle. And the way you tell it, the big, black fucker was flat on his face at the time, on account of being laid out cold."

"Oh, yeah, man. Like, I didn't think of that." A door slammed shut, cutting off another of Essex Boy Robbie's embarrassed cackles.

Kaine de-cocked and holstered the SIG and buttoned the retaining strap before stepping cautiously back out into the hall. Far from being empty, it seemed as though the school was crawling with Heavies. Another problem with attacking a building without a full, advanced recon—he had no idea how many troops he faced.

He read the digital numbers on his watch. 02:38. Time was flying.

According to his briefing, Freeman wouldn't be able to keep the blackout running all night. Kaine needed to take his leave of the school, discretion being the better part of valour and all that. He would return another day, preferably armed with more backup.

Retracing his steps to the roof was out of the question. Without a rope, a roof ladder, or a bunk-up, he'd never reach the ridge or the chimney. He had to find an alternative exit. And so added another highlight to the problems associated with a half-baked, half-cocked plan.

Kaine, you are a bloody idiot.

He reached the head of the staircase and stood still, listening to the increasing sounds of foot traffic and raucous conversations filtering up from below, some of it little more than expletive-filled ranting.

Demarcus Williams' high-pitched, testosterone-fuelled harangue sounded loud over the others, practically screaming his orders. Heavy boots pounded throughout the ground floor, lights flickered on and lit the previously darkened ground floor.

Lights!

Something had happened to Freeman's disruptor. The return of power had certainly excited the ants below.

Kaine ran the calculation. The standard mag on his SIG held fifteen rounds. He had a full mag in the weapon, and he carried one spare. With his marksmanship, thirty shots would be plenty to force an exit, assuming he didn't mind injuring a bunch of drug-pushing thugs, which, given the changed situation, he didn't. Not in the slightest.

According to the architect's plans, the gable end of the school led to the door to the rear courtyard, the layout of which he knew pretty well. Fieldcraft 101—if in trouble, withdraw to familiar terrain.

Kaine turned, intending to start back along the first-floor hallway. He didn't get far before a shout stopped him dead.

"Griffin!" Demarcus Williams yelled from somewhere in the depths of the school. "Oh Griffin! Come out, come out, wherever you are!"

Kaine grimaced. They not only knew he was in the building, but knew his identity, too. It could only mean one thing.

Kaine eased away from the staircase, treading soft, breathing shallow.

"Griffin? Oh Griffin," Williams howled from the ground floor, somewhere near the bottom of the main staircase, "I know you're up there somewhere, you asshole. If you don't show yourself in the next sixty seconds, your blond friend gets a bullet in the kneecap. Sixty seconds after that, he loses the second kneecap. Sixty seconds later, an elbow. A minute after that ... Get the message, asshole?"

My blond friend?

The Heavies had found Sean Freeman!

Chapter Thirty-Six

Monday 22nd February - Byron Codell

Palmerston Road, Walthamstow, London, England

02:31.

Barcode lit another Camel and blew the smoke through the small crack he'd left between the window and the door frame. With the back of his hand, he wiped the mist off the windscreen and flicked the wipers to clear it of rain and sleet. If things got much worse, he'd have to turn the car at an angle so he could see the school through his half-open window. Fuck that, though. Too pissing cold.

At the end of his smoke, he cranked the window a little lower and flicked the lit butt into the night. The embers died before joining its three mates on the pavement.

He stretched the cramp from his shoulders, cricked his

neck a couple times, and tapped the screen on his phone. Still plenty of charge left. He dialled the emergency number for the thousandth time and, again, the automated voice told him the line was busy and he should, *"Please try again later."*

What the fuck were going on inside the school?

Barcode shifted in his seat. The stuff from jacking the Parksiders was starting to weigh more heavy, burning a hole in his pocket. If nothing happened soon, he'd have to make a decision, and there were only one he could make. If he took off with the stash and the money roll, his plans would be fucked, and he didn't give much hope for his chances of survival in the longer term. TM would think he gotten greedy and would send Heavies after him.

Nah, he'd have to grow a pair and head into the school. Maybe he'd make the difference between the Heavies winning or losing the battle, if there were a battle going on. Pretty damned quiet in the school, though. No gunshots meant Demarcus Williams hadn't been let loose. At least not yet.

Whatever those fuckers who broke in was up to, they was doing it all quiet, like.

He'd give it another half hour before calling again. Three o'clock would be a good time to start the rest of his life—or end it.

———

THE DASHBOARD CLOCK TICKED ON. Barcode finished another smoke. All the while, the sleet and rain landed on the car with the force and volume of a hammer drill. Started to give him a headache. Or maybe it were down to the ciggies.

Should think about givin' up again.

Would do, too, but the buzz it gave him helped even out the stresses of the executive lifestyle.

He sniggered at the idea of him, Barcode, being an executive, wearing a business suit.

Ha!

Wouldn't be a bad idea, though. Wearing a suit would improve his cred. And the contract killer in that movie, the one he got the idea of the barcode tattoo off of in the first place, always wore smart threads. Somehow, the suit made him look more scary. Yeah. He'd buy himself a nice suit.

Barcode grabbed the phone from the passenger's seat, swiped life into the screen, and …

The ground floor of the school lit up like a playing field on bonfire night. The floodlights out back lit up, too.

Barcode blinked against the dazzling brightness compared with the surrounding gloom.

What the fuck? 'Bout time.

He thumbed the numbers and hit the call button.

"Yeah? Who's that?"

He recognised the voice as one of the Geeks who manned the computers in the Hub, but never did catch the runt's name. No point filling his head with worthless shit.

"It's me, Barcode. What the fuck's goin' on, man? Been tryin' to call for a fuckin' hour."

"Hold for TM," the runty Geek said, and the call went silent.

Rude fucker, but it stood to reason TM would let the Geeks know to put him through right away. After all, Barcode were holding a load of product and readies.

Play it cool, Barcode. Be the iceman. You don't know nothin' 'bout what's goin' on at the school.

"*Barcode, where the fuck are you?*" TM's voice crackled in its usual electronic way, but he seemed more aggravated—speaking faster than normal.

"Sorry, TM. Had to take a roundabout route. Avoidin' the Po-Po, y'know. Been tryin' to call for the past hour, but—"

"*Yes, right. We've been experiencing some ... difficulties with the power supply ...*"

Barcode sneered.

Sure you have, asshole.

"*...but things are working now. How did your ... mission proceed?*"

"Went down just like you say it would, TM. Smooth as a young ho's butt cheeks. I got the goods and even found a roll of foldin' money."

"*You have such an interesting way with words. How far away are you?*"

"Couple miles. Had to ditch my wheels and use my heels, man. Didn't wanna risk takin' a cab. Be there inside thirty."

"*No. I have some business to take care of right now. Hold off until five o'clock on the dot. One minute later, and I'll send someone to escort you here. Understood?*"

Barcode ground his teeth. What were with the hidden message? Why not deliver the threat out front and in the open. Stupid cloak-and-dagger bullshit.

"Five o'clock? Yes, TM. I won't let you down, boss."

At least not yet, fucker.

The connection ended.

Two hours to kill. So fucking boring.

He dropped his phone onto the passenger's seat and chilled. Maybe he'd take a nice, little nap. Been awake for nearly two days straight. What with servicing the ho overnight, the earlier excitement, and his cracked head, he needed sleep, big time.

He settled back, rolled his shoulders into the soft upholstery, and closed his eyes, but snapped them open again a moment later.

Fuck's sake, blood.

What was he doing? Couldn't sleep. What if he missed the new deadline? He could always set the alarm on his phone, but what if it didn't wake him?

Shit.

He lowered the window fully, stuck his head out, and turned his face to the sky. The bitter sleet-rain shocked him awake. He blinked wide, pulled back inside, and shook the water from his eyes.

Man, what a blast. Mother Nature's version of speed. He took a deep breath, coughed, and spat into the street before winding up the window and sparking another tab, the last in the packet.

Fuck.

Did he have time to find an open petrol station with a ciggie machine? Damn it. Fancy running outta smokes in the middle of the night. Schoolboy error.

Nah, he'd better stay put for now. One of the Heavies would sell him a smoke at five o'clock. Might even give him one for free. After all, he'd be the hero, returning from his first, official, solo mission.

Again, the minutes ticked by in a dull, exhausting blur.

Chapter Thirty-Seven

Monday 22nd February - Pre-Dawn

**Palmerston Road School, Walthamstow, London,
England**

02:39.

Below Kaine, the lights shone bright. He removed the
NV goggles and stowed them in the side pocket of the
baby-Bergen.

The staircase dropped away into the bright lights of
danger.

"I'm going to start counting, Griffin," Williams
screamed, his excitement bordering on hysteria. "Sixty …
fifty-nine … fifty-eight …"

A manic giggle interrupted the countdown.

It resumed at fifty-three, by which time Kaine had

reached the intermediate landing and dropped into a squat, part-hidden behind a solid-oak newel post.

The final flight of twelve steps ended in another corridor, with oak blocks set in a herringbone pattern. Built for looks and to stand the wear and tear of time. Like the hallways he'd already traversed on the upper floors, the one on the ground floor would run east-west, most of the length of the building, ending at the Hub.

The solid treads and panelled balusters blocked Kaine's view to the end of the hallway. He was going in blind, with no idea of the strength or positioning of the enemy and couldn't use his gun, not with Freeman in the firing line. The only things going for him were his skills, experience, and the fact that none of his enemies knew exactly who they faced.

"...thirty-eight ... thirty-seven. This is getting real boring, Griffin. Don't you care about your friend? Such a shame. Thirty-one ... thirty ..."

Shadows moved at the far end of Kaine's range of vision. He slipped off the backpack, then unclipped the SIG and its holster from his belt and slid it into the front pocket. He tucked the whole kit into the darkest corner of the poorly lit landing. The most cursory of searches would find it easily enough, but it was the best he could do under the circumstances. He was gambling that the unprofessional rabble he'd witnessed so far wouldn't even bother to search the building once he'd given himself up. A longshot perhaps, but his only option.

"...twenty-five ..."

He stood, raised his hands, and descended the final set of stairs.

"Okay, okay. Enough with the counting already."

By the time he reached the parquet, four delighted-looking men of different sizes and ethnicities moved in to surround him. He recognised the baby-faced Delinquent from the courtyard, but none of the other three. They must have been the second shift.

Since Kaine had last seen the kid, Delinquent had grown a vicious bruise below his left eye and a fat lip, and he looked none too happy about it.

The Heavies wore a mishmash of quasi-military clothing—dark green sweaters, camo trousers, and black boots. One—a tall, squinty-eyed man—stood back, tapping the heavy end of a baseball bat into the cupped palm of his left hand, trying to look threatening. And failing miserably.

The other three carried nothing more deadly than one combat knife between them, and Delinquent held it in an overhand grip with the blade pointing up. The kid had never been taught knife combat and would be more likely to slice his finger off than injure a skilled opponent.

While Baseball stood his ground, Delinquent and his partner flanked Kaine, and the fourth, a heavily muscled black man in his mid-twenties, circled around behind him and grabbed his wrists. Kaine relaxed his arms and allowed the man to press his hands together and hold them into the small of his back.

The one with the muscles leaned closer to Kaine.

"Hold still, fuckwit, or I'll break your wrists, like what you done to Gerard." Kaine recognised the voice and the accent. He'd put a face to Essex Boy Robbie.

"...nineteen ... eighteen ..."

"Okay, okay," Kaine called out. "You've got me. Stop the bloody count."

Delinquent snapped out his free hand and tried to cuff the back of Kaine's head. Kaine ducked. Delinquent missed.

"Careful, lad. You'll make me angry and you won't like me when I'm angry," Kaine said, staring at the Heavy, who broke eye contact in a heartbeat.

Baseball laughed. "Why? You gonna turn green an' explode outta your vest?"

Kaine fixed the man with a cool smile. "Something like that, sonny."

The derisive laughter died in the tall man's throat. He glowered and took one pace forwards, the bat raised. Essex Boy Robbie tightened his grip on Kaine's wrists.

"...ten ... nine ..."

Kaine slumped, snapped up straight, and back-butted Essex Boy Robbie in the nose. The Heavy squealed and released his grip. Baseball hesitated long enough for Kaine to boot him in the groin. He grunted and fell faster and harder than a sack of coal dropped from the back of a truck. Unlike in the movies, in real life, fully operational men didn't recover instantly from crushed testicles. Baseball's face turned dark red, the bat fell from his hands and wobbled on the parquet. He puked. Vomit spewed over the floor.

Delinquent didn't move a muscle, but the colour drained from his damaged face.

"...five ... four ..."

Kaine ignored Delinquent and his mate, and took off at a sprint.

"...three ..."

"No, stop! Damn it."

The hallway seemed to stretch on forever. At the far end, a door stood wide open, bright lights flooded out, dazzling in the half-gloom of the corridor.

Kaine burst through into a huge, open room.

The Hub.

"…two … one. Bang!"

Raucous laughter followed from at least three different directions.

Kaine skidded to a halt, and half-turned fractions before a heavy load landed on him from behind, crashing him into the floor. The pointed weight of a knee dug into his lower back, pinning him down. Pain shot through his left kidney.

A man grunted and the weight shifted.

Hot breath tickled the back of Kaine's neck.

"You think you can hurt Gerard Coulthard and get away without extreme pain, *connard?*" the Frenchman whispered, seething venom.

The knee grinding into Kaine's kidney shifted again. Kaine tensed. Every muscle in his back turned into forged steel. He twisted. The Frenchman's knee slipped sideways, bounced off the tensed muscle, and slid down the side of Kaine's back. Kneecap connected with hard flooring.

Another grunt of pain, but this time, it wasn't Kaine who made it.

A hand on the back of Kaine's head pressed his face into the dirty flooring. Kaine twisted away, struggling to breathe, his ribcage restricted by the Frenchman's dead weight.

"*Hold it right there, Mr Coulthard.*" TM's electronically modulated voice crackled out of the speakers lining the walls and echoed through the room. "*You'll have plenty of time to hurt him later. Let the man up so I can see who's been wreaking havoc on my best people.*"

"Best people?" Kaine said into the floorboards. "If these clowns are your best people, I suggest you find a different employment agency, buddy boy."

Coulthard yelled and the hand driving Kaine's face into

the wood gripped his hair tighter, as its owner apparently tried to pull it out from the roots.

Shut up, Kaine. Can't bloody help yourself, can you?

As a kid, Kaine's mother used to accuse him of being his own worst enemy. Even in his forties, why did he still have to prove her right?

"Why not let Gerard have his play?" Williams asked, more controlled than he'd been during the countdown. "So long as I can have what's left over."

"*All in good time, Mr Williams,*" TM answered. "*You can all have your fun later, but I want to take a look at this gentleman. The gentleman who's caused me so many problems.*"

Coulthard released his hold on Kaine's hair and rolled away, grunting as he moved. As the weight lifted fully off Kaine, Delinquent and a bloody-nosed Essex Boy Robbie took hold of his arms and jerked him unceremoniously to his feet. This time they pinned his hands against his sides and stood at arm's length. A recently arrived, red-faced Baseball stood at a safe distance and watched.

Whatever anybody said about the skill levels of the average Walthamstow Heavy, these ones seemed to learn their lessons well. Kaine wouldn't be back-butting anyone in the nose any time soon, but there were plenty of other ways to break a man's grip.

As best he could, Kaine relaxed his arms, loosened his fingers, and slowed his breathing.

Coulthard stood in front and slightly to one side of Kaine and his guards. He had one wrist wrapped in a clean white cast, the arm cradled in a sling. It explained why he'd had to release Kaine's hair before rolling himself to his feet. The man stood still, glowering. His expression, comical in its intensity, almost made Kaine laugh out loud. If looks could kill, Kaine would already be a smouldering pile of ash. Thankfully, life didn't work that way.

It hadn't taken the Frenchman long to find medical treatment, but the bones in the wrist, the carpals, would take quite some time to heal. The injury would be painful and restrictive for months.

Such a dreadful shame.

Kaine smiled at Coulthard and threw him a sly wink. The Frenchman snarled and took one pace forwards before firing a glance at the wall monitor and holding himself in check.

In the momentary silence that followed, Kaine carried out a lightning sweep of his surroundings.

The Hub was pretty much as Damian had described it in the café—large, open, a former school assembly hall. Floor-to-ceiling windows, dark and covered with filthy curtains, broke into the west and south walls, designed to let in the maximum daylight in the years before electric lighting. The other walls—originally whitewashed, now a mottled patchwork of damp and mould—were interrupted by smaller windows and doorways, all but two of which no longer contained doors.

In one corner, a quartet of tables, two of them holding expensive-looking computer systems, formed Geek Junction. TM's huge, flat-screen monitor hung from the north wall, front and centre, imposing itself on anyone in the Hub. The blurred outline of the gang leader filled the picture. The outline shimmered as though TM were shaking with anger, but it may have been an artefact of the pixilation process.

Somewhere inside the building, the owner of the shimmering outline cowered in his protective nest.

Kaine kept each Heavy in his peripheral vision as best he could, ready for unexpected movement, but he reserved his full attention for the two men directly ahead, the ones between him and the big screen—Sean Freeman and Demarcus Williams.

Freeman sat on a hard, metal school chair, staring up at Kaine, shamefaced. A red welt bloomed on his right cheek. An open-handed palmprint with each finger and the thumb clear and isolated, it stood out angrily above his beard, showing clearly through the healthy tan.

Williams stood over Freeman, bent slightly at the waist, looking a little discomfited, no doubt still feeling the effects of Kaine's boot to his ribcage. In his right hand, he held a loaded and primed Glock 17, its muzzle pressed into Freeman's left knee so hard it puckered the trouser leg. Williams' finger curled around the trigger.

Freeman's chin trembled.

"So sorry, Mr G-Griffin," Freeman said, tears flowing from his dark blue eyes. "I-I was lost in concentration. Let the buggers creep up on me. I really am so … sorry. I had to tell them you were upstairs. Had to."

Kaine sneered and shook his head, not accepting the apology. Trust him, he'd said outside.

Yeah, trust him.

Williams grunted a little as he straightened and backhanded Freeman across his uninjured cheek, landing the blow with the butt of the Glock. Under such conditions, some might consider it a minor miracle for the weapon not to discharge.

Freeman squealed and curled into a ball, raising his hands and knees to protect his face.

"Please, please, don't hurt me," he wailed.

Kaine ground his teeth. He expected more from a cat burglar, more grit, but he hated the idea of standing by and watching a relatively innocent man being beaten.

Williams raised the gun again in preparation for another blow.

"Pack that in, you moron!" Kaine shouted.

He struggled against his captors, but made sure not to work hard enough or fast enough to break free. Not yet.

Williams stopped mid-swing and levelled the gun at Kaine.

"What'd you say, asshole?"

"Stop hitting him with the gun, you fool. It's likely to go off."

"Nah, safety's on. Only shoots when I pull the trigger. Says so in the manual."

"You really are a complete moron," Kaine said. "There is no external safety on a Glock." He twisted to look at the men holding his arms. "Don't know about you clowns, but if I'm going to be shot tonight, I don't want it to be by accident."

The man on Kaine's left, Essex Boy Robbie, looked uncertain. He eased his grip on Kaine's left wrist but didn't release it completely. Delinquent held firm, but kept flicking his gaze towards Williams and, no doubt, the Glock.

TM's voice cut through the room. *"Mr Griffin is quite correct, Mr Williams. Stop using the gun and start using what little brains God gave you. Use your fists, feet, anything, but not the gun."*

"Finally," Kaine said, addressing the outline on the screen, "someone with a modicum of sense. Now, TM, how about you and me having a quiet chat, face to face. Let's see if we can't straighten this whole thing out to our mutual benefit."

"Shut your mouth, you condescending prick!"

Kaine opened his mouth feigned shock.

"Condescending? *Moi?*"

"*The only way either of you is walking out of here alive, is if I let you.*"

"Don't be stupid, we all know you have no real intention of letting us go, but that's not the way it's going down," Kaine mocked.

"*And how is it going down, pray tell?*"

Now who's being condescending?

"You're going to let me and my friend leave here unharmed."

"Why the fuck would we do that?" Williams demanded, stepping closer to Kaine and away from Freeman.

"*Mr Williams. Shut your fucking mouth!*" TM screamed. A squeal of feedback echoed off the bare walls and bounced around the room, slicing into Kaine's eardrums. "*I'm the one conducting this interrogation,*" TM said, more controlled once the electronics had settled.

"Good to know someone's in command here besides me," Kaine said, smiling brightly.

"*Explain yourself, Griffin. Why would I let you go?*"

In a fluid, lightning-fast movement, Kaine rotated his left forearm, bent the elbow, and straightened again, breaking the already weakened grip. He dug his freed hand into his trouser pocket and pulled it out again, this time holding up his mobile.

To add shock and awe to the move, he yelled, "Bomb! Bomb!" and threw his hand up high. He pressed a key at random and held it down. Then he shrugged free of Delinquent's grip and stepped away.

"What the fuck?" Williams shouted.

"Williams," Kaine said, cool and calm, "lower the gun slowly and carefully to the floor."

"Fuck off. That's a phone, not a fucking grenade."

"Moron," Kaine said, twisting his lips and widening his

eyes into a manic stare. "This is a detonator. If I lift my thumb, we're all going to hell."

Staring at Kaine's mobile, and with his outstretched arm shaking, the big Heavy pointed the Glock towards an empty part of the Hub, and started to release his grip.

"No," Kaine said, softly. "Drop the gun and I might drop the mobile. Believe me, no one wants that."

"*Shoot him, Williams. Shoot him!*"

Williams flicked a disbelieving look at the monitor and shook his head. "But he's got a bomb!"

Kaine nodded and held his arm higher.

"That's right, Williams. All of you." He spun slowly to stare down everyone in the room in turn before facing Williams and the wall monitor again. "I planted a quarter kilo of Semtex upstairs. I let go of this button and we all die!"

The Heavies shuffled further away.

He couldn't believe they were falling for it.

"That's right, back off, all of you. My friend and I are leaving and no one's going to stop us. Williams, the gun!"

Williams hesitated for a moment, then bent slowly at the waist and knees, and lowered the Glock to the floor. He straightened again and made to kick the gun away.

"No. Just step away from it. You know nothing about guns, cretin."

Williams did as he was told.

Kaine looked at Freeman. "You ready, mate?"

Still cowering on his chair, Freeman shook his head, as though too terrified to move, but something in his eyes suggested otherwise. What was it, annoyance? Anger?

In a blinding flash, Kaine finally twigged.

"*He's right, you are all cretins,*" TM crowed, his electronically modulated voice rising to a scream. *"Look at his phone. Look at his fucking phone!"*

Kaine dropped the dead phone and dived forwards, grabbed the muzzle of the Glock, and fumbled with it, trying to reach the handle. Williams reacted faster than anyone could have expected. He snatched the Glock from Kaine's hands and swung a boot into his belly.

Kaine grunted, doubled up, coughed, and kept coughing.

Williams stood tall, aimed a kick at Kaine's head, missed. Aimed another. This time, he landed a blow to the temple. A blow that might have proved fatal had Kaine not pulled his head away at the last moment, but the glancing heel-strike still made him see stars and split the skin open. Blood dripped from the wound and flowed into his eye.

"No, don't hurt him," Freeman wailed from his chair. "Please don't hurt him."

The blond man, the self-acclaimed world's best jewel thief, still hadn't moved. Hadn't lifted a finger to help. From his position on the floor, Kaine twisted and skewered Freeman with a look of pure venom.

"You Goddamned coward," he mumbled, blinking hard and fast, trying to clear the blood from his eye.

Coulthard shuffled towards Kaine's mobile phone. He tilted his head to study it carefully.

"Merde," he said, stamping his foot and destroying Kaine's burner, "it is not even powered up. A bluff, nothing more."

Delinquent and Essex Boy Robbie looked at each other before bursting into relieved and embarrassed laughter. The Heavies started forwards, closing in on Kaine.

"What did you call me?" Freeman demanded, finding his anger at last, but aiming it at the wrong target.

Kaine, still bent at the waist, propped himself up on one elbow. "I called you a Goddamned, pandy-arsed coward."

The blond man jumped out of his chair. "Don't you dare call me that."

"Look at you. Sitting there, crying your eyes out like a little girl who's lost her dolly. Pitiful. You should be ashamed of yourself."

Freeman shot forwards and kicked Kaine in the stomach, the side of his soft-soled shoe landing in the same general area as Williams' heavy boot. Unsurprisingly, it didn't hurt.

"Arsehole." Kaine coughed and spat out the blood that had dripped from his head wound into his mouth. "Typical. Only a coward kicks a man when he's down."

"Fuck off, you prick!" Freeman screamed, spittle flying. "We can't all be former-military heroes. Remember, I know all about you … you traitor. And I know all about the reward on your—"

His eyes narrowed, swivelled in his head, and turned to the screen. He slapped a hand across his mouth.

"*What was that?*" TM shouted.

Freeman shook his head. "Nothing. Nothing. I didn't say anything."

Williams turned away from Kaine and pointed the Glock at Freeman's face. "What'd you say about a reward?"

The professional thief raised his trembling hands in surrender, turning his face away, cowering. "No, no. Don't shoot. Please, don't shoot."

"*You called Griffin a traitor,*" TM said, the image on the screen becoming animated, "*and said something about a reward. What did you mean?*"

Freeman covered his face with his hands. "No, I can't tell you. He'll kill me. He's a killer. A murderer."

The image on TM's screen stilled.

"*Let's make this faster,*" he said, his voice calmer. "*Mr Williams, if you would be so kind, restart the countdown from five. This time, don't shout 'Bang'. Just blow off this coward's kneecap.*"

"No!" Freeman squealed. "I'll talk. Don't shoot. Please. I'll talk."

"You little ratbag," Kaine shouted, scrambling to his knees and ending up in a sprinter's starting position. "Don't you dare. I'll kill you, understand? I'll kill you slowly. It'll take so long you'll beg to die!"

"*Shut up, Griffin!*" TM's outline moved. A hand waved at the side of the head. "*Everyone, watch him closely. If he moves, do some damage but make sure it's not terminal. He might actually be more valuable alive.*"

The Heavies closed further, surrounding Kaine, who stayed down on one knee, glaring at Freeman.

The memory returned.

"Trust me," the blond thief had said when they were outside in the dark. "Whatever happens in there. Just go with the flow and trust me, right?"

Surely this wasn't his plan all along?

"*Now, Mr Williams. Start counting, if you wouldn't mind.*"

A grinning Williams lowered the Glock, aiming it at Freeman's right knee. At such a close range, even he couldn't miss.

"Five ... four ..."

"Okay, okay. I-I'll tell you. I will. I'll tell you. Ask me anything you want."

"*Who is Griffin?*"

Freeman swallowed, looked from the Glock to Kaine, and then to the screen. "That's just it. His name isn't Griffin, it's—"

Kaine screamed and leaped to his feet. "You bastard! I'm gonna kill you!"

The Heavies reacted fast. Arms and fists flying, legs swinging, they backed Kaine against a wall and pinned him in place, Delinquent taking his preferred position on Kaine's right. Essex Boy Robbie grasped Kaine's left wrist tight and again used both hands.

"Who is that man?"

Freeman turned to face the screen, his back to Kaine. "Look closely. Don't you recognise him?" He half-turned and pointed a trembling finger at Kaine. "Last year, that animal killed dozens of people. He's the terrorist. He's Ryan Kaine!"

Chapter Thirty-Eight

Monday 22nd February – Sean Freeman

Palmerston Road School, Walthamstow, London, England

02:58.

Sean Freeman made the big reveal to a hushed audience and waited for a response. It didn't take long.

"*What?*" TM said, and the question was repeated in relay by at least three others in the room.

"You know," Sean continued. "Captain Ryan Kaine. The terrorist who shot down that plane over the North Sea and killed eighty-three people."

"Him?" Williams asked, incredulity in his question and written all over his face. "That wimpy, short-ass fool is Ryan Kaine? Fuck off. Kaine's a mass killer. A monster!"

"He took you and Mr Cox apart earlier tonight, Mr Williams. And look what he did to the others. Bring him closer to the camera. Let me get a better view."

The baby-faced thug and the other man dragged a struggling Ryan closer to the screen. TM's image dissolved, replaced by the infamous mugshot that had overwhelmed the TV screens and newspapers for weeks after the disaster. It revealed a wiry, clean-shaven man with a military haircut, piercing, light brown eyes and a small scar on his chin, a scar now covered by the bushy beard. Alongside the portrait, a rolling script scrolled through a list of physical characteristics, distinguishing features, and a short biography.

"Looks a little like him," Williams said. "The beard's new, and the eyes are the wrong colour, but … It say he's five-ten and about thirteen stone. Griffin looks about right. Could be him. And … fuck, would you look at that?" The villain with the gun used it to point to a line at the bottom of the bio which had stopped scrolling before reaching the most important part.

Clever, TM. Very clever.

Sean kept up his cowering and allowed his tears to flow.

And now, to reel him in.

Williams continued. "It say there's a reward on his head. Half a million notes."

One of the Heavies whistled.

Ryan's shoulders slumped and his head fell.

Sean snorted. "Chicken feed."

TM's outline reappeared above the mugshot and lines of bio.

"Five hundred thousand pounds is chicken feed?" TM asked.

Despite the bruises and the cuts on his face, Sean

managed to produce what felt like a crooked smile. "Y-Yes, TM, and you know why, don't you?"

The figure on the screen moved in what looked like a nod. "*I think I might. I really do.*"

"Y-Yes, and you … you know the implications. I'd really"—he glanced over his shoulder at Ryan and the Heavies—"like to keep the next part private. Can we take the rest of this discussion outside and talk face to face? Please?"

"*Not really. I value my anonymity.*"

"I-I don't blame you," Sean said, nodding in sympathy. "The captain feels the same way. Look what happens when people find out who he is."

"*We seem to be at something of an impasse. Why don't I simply get Mr Williams to beat the information out of you?*"

Sean winced, laying it on thick.

"Please don't. I-I … Listen, you could hurt me, and I'll probably talk, but … it might take a while and get a little messy. And you'd never be certain I've told you the entire truth."

Ryan struggled against the men holding him. "You bastard! I'll kill you for this."

Such forced bluster suited the world's image of a vicious, SBS hard man. It set the scene well enough, and the Heavies seemed to be lapping it up. Sean smiled internally, letting nothing show on his face. Things couldn't be working out any better.

"Yes, Captain," Sean threw back at him. "As you already said. But, given the circumstances, I don't see how that's possible, do you?"

"Bastard!"

"Yes, I am, but I've never blamed my mother. She was young and impetuous and so very much in love." He turned to face the big screen once more. "TM, I've known where Ryan Kaine's been hiding for months. A little internet friend told me. Why do you think I haven't turned him in for the reward yet?"

"*You know where the … merchandise is?*"

"Every part of it. It took a while, but … we've just been waiting for the right time to collect it. You see, the good captain is a very dangerous man. I didn't relish the idea of relieving him of the … merchandise only to have him hunt me down like a dog. And he would. He's extremely resourceful."

All around Ryan, the Heavies traded confused glances. They had no idea he and TM were talking about the millions of euros Ryan stole from Sir Malcolm Sampson. Information Corky had seeded into TM's personal internet search results.

"Sean," Ryan shouted. "No!"

Sean raised a hand and flicked him a dismissive wave. "Do you mind, Captain? TM and I are negotiating, here. What do you say, TM? There's plenty to go around. I'll share it with you and the Tribe. Fifty-fifty. All you need to do is guarantee my ongoing safety."

"*How can I be certain you have access to said merchandise?*"

"I have a friend inside Kaine's organisation."

"*Kaine has an organisation?*"

"Of course he does," Sean said, adding a heavy sigh. "How else could he have stayed hidden for so long with the combined ranks of the UK Police and Europol on his tail? He has a bunch of sycophants working for him. They all think he's a good guy who was conned into shooting down that plane, but he did it for the … merchandise. He's nothing but a mercenary. A gun for hire."

"*Your inside man, who is he?*"

"Ah … dear, old Corky. He's a whiz when it comes to the internet and technology. An absolute genius. The fellow's been wheedling his way into Kaine's good graces for months. He actually pointed Kaine towards Walthamstow when Glenmore Davits died. The nosey neighbour's intervention was pure gravy, and Corky manipulated the intel to suggest the poor, old fellow's death might not have been an accident. As luck would have it, the death occurred when most of Kaine's people were otherwise engaged. Couldn't have planned it better if we'd tried. Corky and I have been waiting for the right opportunity for months, and this timing is perfect."

As Ryan struggled impotently against the men pinning his arms, he aimed his expression—a powerful mix of fury and disgust … and understanding—directly at Sean.

He almost felt sorry for the "fallen hero", but it couldn't be helped. Not for the first time in his life, Sean had plans of his own.

"So, what do you say?" Sean asked the shadow on the monitor. "Have I convinced you of my bona fides yet?"

Again the image on the screen moved in the approximation of a nod.

"*Mr Williams, bring this man to the parlour. We need to discuss this somewhere quiet.*"

"Freeman!" Ryan bellowed. "You're a dead man. Hear me? A dead man walking!"

"*Freeman?*" TM squawked. "*Sean Freeman, the jewel thief?*"

Sean hesitated a moment before nodding.

"Yes, I … am. Why?"

"*God, man. Why didn't you say so earlier? I'm a great admirer of your work. Been following your exploits in the media.*"

Sean straightened, pulled back his shoulders, and allowed a smile to stretch his bruised lips. "You have?"

"*I have indeed. Is there any reason to keep Kaine alive? Will we need him for anything?*"

Sean turned to face the centre of the room. He gave the man wearing the sling, Coulthard, a sly smile and shook his head quickly.

"I … I don't think so. … No. None whatsoever. Your men can do whatever they like."

"*Well, Mr Coulthard? What are you waiting for?*" TM said through his laughter. "*Have your fun and make as much mess as you like. After the night we've had, everyone deserves to let their hair down.*"

Sean slid an apologetic smile to Ryan, who glared back, a menacing glint in his dark green eyes.

"I'm sorry, Ryan, but it's every man for himself, you understand?"

"You're going to rot in hell, Freeman!"

"I expect so," Sean admitted, "but not as soon as you, old friend."

The large screen faded to black.

Williams took a firm grip of Sean's upper arm, pinching the sensitive skin inside his biceps.

"Ow!" he squealed, wincing at the pain and trying, ineffectually, to tear his arm away.

As the thugs started hollering and whooping, and the blood started flying, the big man with the big gun pushed Sean through one of the two closed doors in the rear wall.

Despite the desperate cries of at least one man in real pain, Sean didn't look back. Neither did Demarcus Williams.

Chapter Thirty-Nine

Palmerston Road School, Walthamstow, London, England

03:08.

Demarcus Williams shoved Sean through a small corridor and into a large and windowless room that might once have been a kitchen. Cracked and filthy tiles clung to the walls and floor. The place reeked of mould and damp, as though it hadn't been aired since the school shut up shop decades earlier.

At the far end of the room, a narrow gap between the stainless-steel units forced Williams to release Sean's arm and let him take point. The opening led to another door, this one solid and shiny. An external lock, steel with a lever handle, held the door firmly closed. The upper part of the handle included a six-digit keypad.

Looks promising.

Sean stopped and waited.

With one of the pieces of kit he'd built in his teens and left alone, he could have opened the lock inside two minutes, but that would have defeated the object. He needed TM to come to him and there was no telling what lay beyond the security door. Maybe another five doors.

Williams jabbed his weapon into Sean's spine and leaned past to reach for the keypad.

"Ow. That hurts. Go easy with the gun. I thought we were partners now."

"We ain't partners, asswipe. The way you turned on your buddy back there, no way anyone's trusting you no more. No way, no how."

Sean sighed. The big man had a point. In Williams' position he wouldn't trust Sean, either. As for Ryan Kaine … that was another matter entirely. Sean hoped he'd understand.

Williams pressed the buttons 1-5-3-6 and worked the handle. The steel door released a loud vacuum pop as it opened inwards.

"Blimey," Sean said, "didn't expect that."

"Yeah, well don't get too comfy, fucker."

"You should try expanding your vocabulary. Wasn't it Spencer Kimball who once said, 'Swearing is the attempt of a dull mind to express itself forcibly.'? I paraphrase, of course."

"Fuck off," Williams grunted, adding emphasis by digging the gun harder into the small of Sean's back.

"Sorry." Sean smiled. "I talk a lot when I'm nervous. Say inappropriate things."

"You will be sorry, fucker."

My case rests.

Williams thumped Sean on the shoulder, driving him deeper into a room TM had called the parlour, although it looked more like the drawing room of a minor stately home.

The "drawing room" stretched away from them, with a deep-piled and highly patterned carpet, and walls lined with bookshelves and hung with landscape paintings from minor masters which almost looked original. At least fifteen metres wide and about half that deep, the place smelled of wax polish, leather, and cigar smoke.

Sean scrubbed the drawing room moniker and changed it to "smoking room".

A faux-antique, mahogany desk occupied the centre of the room, facing a huge, fake, stone fireplace, which contained a large TV. On its screen, a wood fire burned fiercely. Sean could almost feel its warmth radiating through the place, but the heat came up through the floor, not out from the walls. Underfloor heating. Expensive, modern, and nice.

"Good effect, but that's all it is, effect. Artifice," Sean mumbled to himself.

"Huh?"

"Sorry, those nerves talking again. Where's TM?"

Williams shrugged. "Dunno. Never seen him."

"Really?"

"Nah."

"You don't know who TM is?"

So much for disarming the big thug and pounding the information out of him. A shame, but that was always going to be the secondary option.

"Nope. Don't know who he is and don't give a fuck. All

I know is he pays well and likes his privacy. Only time I come in here is to let the cleaners in and watch over them while they work. TM don't come in unless no one's around."

"Hmm. I see," Sean said, again, mostly to himself.

"Yeah. Hmm. It's just you and me in here, fuckwit. TM ain't falling for none of your bullshit. No fucking way."

"So, what … what are we doing here?" Sean asked, swallowing hard and allowing a false tremble to return to his voice. "You're … not going to try and force the information out of me with that gun, are you?"

Williams leaned closer. Close enough for Sean to smell his breath. Halitosis didn't work too well with a spicy aftershave—or the ripe body odour.

"I hope so, fucker," he growled. "I really do hope so."

Something clicked, an electric motor whirred, and the middle three shelves of the full-length bookcase behind the desk slid apart to reveal a monitor the exact duplicate of the one in the Hub. On it, TM's blurry outline appeared, almost as large as life.

"Oh no," Sean said, trembling again. "Am I still in trouble? Aren't we ever going to meet?"

"*No, Mr Freeman. I'll be with you in a moment. In fact, I'm really looking forward to meeting you in person. I just need Mr Williams to run a magic wand over you. To make sure you're unarmed and not carrying any nasty surprises, like recording equipment.*"

"I don't have anything you need to worry about, TM. Honest I don't."

Without lowering the gun or taking his eyes from Sean, Williams slid open the drawer in a small occasional table, reached in, and pulled out a handheld scanner. Grey and gleaming. State-of-the-art. Sean had used something similar in the past. Williams' scanner detected both ferrous metals and electronic signals. It couldn't pick up ceramics, though. It wouldn't identify the knife hidden inside his leather belt, cunningly disguised as part of the buckle.

Sean never went anywhere without at least some defensive capability.

"Legs apart, arms out to the sides," Williams ordered.

"Why, are we going to dance? If so, can I lead?"

"Fuck off, funny man."

"Sorry. Sorry. Can't seem to help myself."

Sean stood still but trembled while the semi-literate buffoon swept over him with the scanner. Its ticking remained constant and even. No spikes or squeals seemed to confirm his claims. As far as the scanner was concerned, he was unarmed and had no recording devices.

"Satisfied?"

"More than satisfied, thank you, Mr Freeman. You'll forgive me for being hyper-cautious, but security is everything in our game."

Halfway through the speech, the electronic voice modulation deactivated and TM became less of a machine and more of a human being.

Williams' expression was a picture. Surprise etched itself into every line and crease of his chiselled face.

"Close your mouth, Mr Williams. There are no flies in this room for you to catch," TM said smoothly.

Williams snapped his mouth shut and swallowed. Slowly, the expression changed from surprise to confusion and then to recognition as a slim man of medium height and in his early twenties stepped through a door that had been hidden by one of the bookcases in the far corner of the room.

The man, dressed impeccably in a handmade suit and polished loafers, smiled broadly.

"You!" Williams said.

The scanner tumbled from his fingers, landed on the thick, pile carpet, bounced, and settled.

For a moment, the only sound in the room was the crackling of the false fire coming from the TV screen in the fireplace.

"Yes, Mr Williams. Me," the newcomer said, his accent educated and the voice gentle.

"Care to enlighten me?" Sean asked, although he knew the man's name the moment he'd stepped from the shadows.

Sean was playing a role and would play it through to the end.

Corky had identified all the players in the game, and had sent Sean all their dossiers, including a fairly thin one on the man who stood before him, wearing the expensive suit and the welcoming grin.

Chapter Forty

Monday 20th February - Pre-Dawn

Palmerston Road School, Walthamstow, London, England

03:07.

"You're going to rot in hell, Freeman!" Kaine screamed, struggling to free himself from the restraining hands.

"I expect so," Freeman answered, smiling with evident glee, "but not as soon as you, old friend."

They started in on him the moment the monitor on the wall powered off, and before Williams had finished pushing Freeman through one of the doors.

Delinquent landed the first blow, a rabbit punch to Kaine's right kidney. It did little damage. Kaine was ready for it, and the kid's punch lacked any real power, restricted as he was by the reduced wind up, and the fact he was still holding tight to Kaine's right wrist.

Essex Boy Robbie reacted slowly. Far too slowly.

Using their grip on his wrists as support, Kaine flipped his legs up and over his head. His wrists suffered friction burns, but the holds broke and he landed on his feet with both arms free.

Coulthard screamed something unintelligible. Baseball didn't move.

Kaine's instant, short-armed, left jab smashed Delinquent's nose. Blood flowed, quickly spreading into a red mask. Delinquent staggered backwards, screaming, hands covering the damage to his face.

Essex Boy Robbie turned, mouth wide open. Kaine's close-combat elbow strike broke his jaw, and the follow-up heel attack shattered the muscular man's right kneecap.

Two down, three to go.

A screaming, ranting Coulthard backed away, his good hand digging awkwardly into a trouser pocket, searching desperately for a weapon.

Kaine turned to the remaining two. Both big, both tough-looking. The one on the left, Baseball, had wide shoulders and stood over six feet tall. The Heavy had retrieved his bat from the outer hallway, but no longer tapped the fat end into his cupped hand. This time, he held the bat in both hands—right over left—and held it high, a batter at the plate.

The fifth man, as tall as his dark-skinned mate but slimmer and white, carried a flick knife in his left hand.

A southpaw.

Southpaws could be awkward in close combat and often

needed special consideration, but this one stood on Base-ball's right, which restricted his natural movement. The two would be getting in each other's way. The most basic of errors.

Time to finish this and get to Freeman.

Kaine rolled his shoulders and eased the stiffness from his neck. He took up the first defensive position, standing sideways to the two Heavies, leading with the left, right fist cocked and ready, the left foot slightly ahead of the right. Maintaining good balance, he stood still, calculating.

The two Heavies paused, swapped hesitant glances.

Apart from when he'd allowed it to happen, none of the Heavies had landed a decent shot on him, and their expressions showed him they knew it. Their indecision told the story.

A bit of bravado might end things quickly and safely. He clapped his hands. Both men blinked.

Coulthard, still backing away, had found his weapon, another butterfly knife, its eight-centimetre blade glinting as brightly as his first one. The Frenchman certainly loved his fancy knives, but he hadn't been as slick opening it with his left hand. He didn't look as comfortable holding it, or as confident.

"Okay, boys. Let's have some fun," Kaine said, adding a crazed laugh.

After all, as far as these plonkers were concerned, they faced a raving lunatic who'd intentionally blown up a passenger plane and cold-bloodedly assassinated all those innocent people.

Time to make the lie work for him for a change.

Smiling madly, Kaine relaxed his fists, flexed his fingers, and shook out his wrists. He rose onto the balls of his feet and shuffled forwards and back, swaying from side to side as though he were in a boxing ring, warming up before a bout.

"I've been looking forward to this. Come get me."

He danced forwards and threw a lightning left jab into Southpaw's ribs. The air rushed out of him in a whoosh. The knife fell from his hand.

Kaine sashayed backwards and performed a perfect Ali shuffle, ending with a feint to the left and delivering a solid gut-punch to Baseball's six-pack.

Baseball swung his bat wildly. It whistled through empty air, sailing high over Kaine's ducked head.

Kaine danced away again, untouched.

"Come on, boys. I'm getting bored with this," he said, still bouncing on the balls of his feet. "You know I'm a stone-cold killer. Famed for it, I am. Which one of you wants to die first?"

With Essex Boy Robbie and Delinquent still rolling about on the floor and groaning behind them, Baseball and Southpaw hesitated again.

"You with the bat," Kaine said, beckoning with his fingers, "come and have a go if you think you're hard enough. I'm gonna make you wear that thing like a rectal probe."

Kaine almost winced at his words and doubted either Heavy knew what a rectal probe might be. He should have told the man exactly where he was going to stick his bat, but he'd used enough unsavoury language for one night.

Baseball and Southpaw exchanged another rapid glance. Baseball nodded and dropped the bat. As it rattled on the floor, they turned tail and raced from the Hub as though the place had caught fire, or as though Kaine's bluff with the burner phone had been real. In his haste, Southpaw bowled into Coulthard, knocking him to the floor. He landed on the point of his elbow, knocking the butterfly knife from his hand. The knife, like its earlier partner, skittered away from its French owner, out of reach and useless.

Kaine dropped his guard, lowering his hands, flicking them out again. That had been almost too easy.

He strode purposefully towards the Frenchman, who scrambled away, one elbow and two feet scraping the parquet and polishing nice track marks in the dust and the grime.

When Kaine reached the grovelling Coulthard, he stopped and stood menacingly over him. The Frenchman snarled, raised his good arm in a pitiful attempt to protect his face, which was no longer as handsome as it had been earlier. Fear and swollen bruises would do that to a man's face.

"Not to worry, Gerard, old chap," Kaine said, turning on the charm, "you're safe enough. Don't believe everything you read in the papers."

"You're not going to kill me, *monsieur*?"

Kaine shook his head. "Not this time, Gerard. I've had my fill of killing for a while. And it's Captain, not *mister*. Captain Kaine, okay?"

Coulthard nodded.

"Now," Kaine said, sinking to his haunches beside the defeated man, but making sure he could still see the two flailing Heavies on his left, "since I've been so nice by letting you live, would you do me a little favour?"

Coulthard dipped his chin into his chest and looked up at Kaine through bushy, dark eyebrows.

"What?"

"Nothing too onerous, old chap. Just help your two colleagues out of here. If I see anyone on my return, I won't be so generous. *Am I making myself perfectly clear?*" Kaine added venom and a snarl to his question, and doing it so well he almost scared himself.

"*Oiu, monsi*—er, I mean, yes, *Capitaine* Kaine."

"Excellent, excellent. Hoped I could rely on you, old chap."

Kaine stood.

Essex Boy Robbie had turned onto his front and was struggling to push himself onto his hands and one knee. Delinquent sat in a heap, knees up to his chest, leaning against a wall, trying to stop the blood pouring from his nose with the sleeve of his jacket.

"One more thing. Will you answer a couple of questions?" he asked.

"*B-Bien sûr, Capitaine. Si possible.*"

Kaine pointed to the door through which Demarcus Williams and Sean Freeman had recently disappeared.

"Where does that lead?"

"To the kitchen and the back rooms, *Capitaine.*"

"Is that where TM is right now?"

Coulthard raised one shoulder in one half of a Gallic shrug, the other being hampered by the sling. "*Je ne sais pas.* I do not know. Why?"

Kaine rubbed his hands together. "Thought I'd have a word with him and catch up with my old mate, Sean Freeman."

He turned and headed for the kitchen.

Behind him, Coulthard grunted and used his good hand to push himself to a seated position.

"*Monsieur le Capitaine?*"

Without stopping, Kaine said, "Yes?"

"You are honourable, I think."

"And?"

"I, too, have honour. Demarcus Williams has a gun. I …
wanted to remind you."

Kaine reached the door. He stopped and turned to the
Frenchman.

"Thanks," he said, adding a sideways smile. "I hadn't
forgotten."

Chapter Forty-One

Monday 22nd February - Lara Orchard

Cambourne Cross Hospital, Leytonstone, London, England

03:08.

A shadow fell across Lara. She glanced up to find Connor Blake standing over her, but at a respectful distance. He held a plastic cup in each hand and smiled.

"Looks like you need a pick-me-up, Doc," he said, offering her one of the steaming drinks.

She sniffed the dark brown liquid before taking a tentative sip. Coffee, served in the military way—hot, black, and with something like three heaped teaspoons of artery blocker. She managed not to grimace as the scalding, over-sweetened drink burned her tongue.

"Thanks, Connor."

"Reckon you could do with some rest, too," he added, taking the chair alongside her.

He sat to attention, his eyes scanning the waiting area, never at ease. They were in a small bay, directly across from the pre-op suite, where Damian lay awaiting his turn in theatre. The last time Lara had entered the windowless room, Ariel had been seated at Damian's side, holding his hand with both of hers, crying silent tears.

For his part, Damian had fallen in and out of consciousness, fighting the debilitating effects of a punctured lung, broken ribs, and a significant blow to the side of the head.

A nurse marched along the hallway outside, glancing at notes on a clipboard. She stopped, smiled at Connor, and retraced her steps back along the halls, reappearing moments later carrying a clipboard of a different colour.

"Nurse Gorringe?" Lara said, standing.

The nurse's shoulders dropped slightly, but she barely slowed. "No news yet, Dr Griffin," she said. "Mr Shah is on his way in. He'll arrive shortly. Theatre is prepped and ready." Her voice faded out as she pushed through the doors at the end of the corridor—the doors marked "Operating Suite Three".

Lara returned to her stiff, plastic chair, the ones cunningly designed to be as uncomfortable as possible. Undoubtedly intended to stop visitors sleeping and encourage them to be on their way.

Beside her, Connor growled. Showing frustration for the first time that night.

"This is ridiculous. Poor bloke could be dying in there. I've seen more efficient medical cover on the battlefield."

"Can't be helped, Connor. It's the middle of the night

and you can't magic up a thoracic surgeon at the drop of a hat. I'm sure Mr Shah will be here soon."

"Sorry, Doc." Connor raised his hands in apology. "Not a big fan of 'anging around in 'ospitals, is all. Don't suppose you fancy doing the op yourself?"

She paused and slid Connor a questioning look before hiding it with a wince. It suddenly dawned on her that Connor might not know her actual qualifications. She and Ryan hadn't had a moment alone together since the reservoir, and he'd had no time to brief her fully on Connor's position in the group.

"I mean, after all," Connor said, leaning close, a serious expression on his angular and darkly handsome face, "cutting open a gang member called Rhino ain't all that different from operating on an 'orse or a cow, is it?"

He took a deliberately loud slurp of his coffee, smiled, and added a wink.

"So, you know," she said. A statement rather than a question.

"Yes, Doc. The moment the news broke about the captain and the trumped-up charges against 'im, I made a point of watching every news article and reading every bullshit word the idiot hacks printed on the plane crash."

He took another sip, this one silent, before continuing.

"You know there's a whole load of social media groups and hashtags dedicated to Flight BE1555 and the captain. Some say 'e's a wronged hero, others reckon 'e's the devil himself. Mind you, anyone who's ever met the captain will be on the first side of the argument. No way 'e's a terrorist. I ain't never met a more 'onest or 'onourable geezer."

Keeping her voice low, Lara said, "Ryan *is* innocent and we have the evidence to prove it."

Connor turned fully towards her, excitement etched into his face. "Yeah?"

She nodded. "Video evidence of a confession by Sir Malcolm Sampson—"

"The arms manufacturer?"

He spoke louder than she'd have liked and she patted the air between them to silence him.

"Yes," she said, checking both ends of the corridor to confirm no one was close enough to eavesdrop.

"Way I 'eard it, Sampson were banged up for tax fraud, yeah?"

"That's what the authorities wanted the public to think, but Sampson tricked Ryan into shooting down that plane. Or rather, paid a man called Gravel to trick him."

"Gravel? You mean Major Valence?"

Again, she nodded.

"The captain's boss and one of 'is oldest friends?" Connor added.

"Yes. I doubt anyone else could have pulled the wool over Ryan's eyes. … Still, Gravel did pay for his treachery."

"When 'is farmhouse exploded?"

"Yes."

Connor raised a little fist pump. "I knew that weren't no gas mains failure," Connor said and nodded to himself. "Poetic justice, you ask me. The captain's doing?"

"No," she answered, taking another sip from her cup. This time, she couldn't hide the wince.

"Not enough sugar?" Connor asked, not missing a thing.

"Too much. Sorry, but I normally take mine without sugar, and with milk."

"Sorry, Doc. My mistake."

413

"No problem." She lowered the cup to the table between them and slid it away.

"Not poetic justice or not the captain's doing?" he asked, returning to the subject.

"Not the captain. One of Sir Malcolm's minions ordered the hit, hoping to kill both Ryan and Gravel at the same time. They wanted to silence any witnesses. Which, by the way, would have included me. I was in that farmhouse along with Rollo and Danny Pinkerton. You know Danny?"

Connor smiled. "We've met. Nice bloke, but I wouldn't wanna take 'im on in a fist fight. Either 'im or Q, come to think of it. And as for the captain ..." He grimaced and shook his head slowly. "Never seen anyone with 'is skills. 'Ang about, Gravel's wife died in that explosion, didn't she? Collateral damage?"

"No, she was involved in the conspiracy all the way up to her botoxed forehead. No need to waste your sympathy on her. Ryan was actually trying to save her at the time." She looked away, focusing her eyes on nothing. "He's a good man. Kind. Honest. What happened to those poor people on that plane will haunt him forever. That's why we're here in London, trying to help the families of the victims."

"Understood, Doc. Wouldn't be 'ere myself if I didn't wanna 'elp."

"I thought you were here for the money," she said, smiling to soften any perceived insult.

He leaned away and threw a hand on his chest, covering his heart. "Ouch, Doc. That smarts."

"Sorry, didn't mean—"

"Not that the pay ain't important. After all, I do need to eat now and again. That said, I'm also choosy about who I work for."

"Speaking of work, back to my actual profession. You'd

have no problem with my treating you, should the need arise?"

"Not me, Doc. Especially since when the story first broke, there were a whole section on this *mysterious veterinary surgeon*"—he mouthed the words—"what saved the captain's life and ran off with 'im in the end. Some painted it as a love story worthy of a romance novel."

She sighed and managed not to roll her eyes, but her cheeks warmed.

He leaned closer, but not too close. "The way you two are together ... I mean, the way the captain looks at you. Seems them stories weren't total BS after all, yeah?"

Lara coughed. "Moving on ..."

"Yeah, okay. Got the picture, Doc." He finished his drink and placed the empty cup beside hers.

They fell silent for a few moments, allowing the noises of a busy hospital to swirl around them.

"Adding to the online conspiracy theories," Connor said, "within a month of the plane crash, all mention of this mysterious vet disappeared from the internet. No pictures, no bio, nothing. It's as though the animal doctor never existed. Funny that, eh?"

She nodded. "Yes. Funny."

"Wonder 'ow it's possible to completely 'disappear' someone from the internet. I bet there's a load of bad boys out there who'd love to know 'ow to make that 'appen."

She nodded again. "I imagine so."

"Anyhow, when Q invited me to join this particular shindig, the captain ordered 'im to answer any questions I 'ad. Seems 'e don't like to 'old nothing back from 'is men. Even if I 'adn't already known your background, Q would've told me about your ... unofficial status as medic of the team."

"And what *did* Rollo say about me," Lara asked, although she had a pretty good idea of what the huge, gruff marine might have said.

"Nothing much. Only that I could 'appily put my life in your 'ands should the medical need arise. Pretty 'igh praise from an old dog like Q, I reckon."

Lara smiled. "Rollo is too kind."

"Q, kind?" Connor scoffed. "Maybe to you, Doc, but you ain't ever seen 'im take charge of an exercise session."

She matched his scoff and added an emphatic nod. "As a matter of fact, I have. Rollo puts me through the wringer whenever the captain's away on … let's call them 'manoeuvres'. And before you give me that look, neither one takes it easy on this particular recruit." She dug a thumb into her sternum to emphasise the point.

Connor looked her up and down, and seemed to appreciate what he saw, at least in terms of her physical preparedness.

He jumped up, said, "'Ear that?" and headed towards the door to the prep room.

"What?"

"Damian. 'E called for Mr Griffin."

Lara hadn't heard a thing. She sprang to her feet and followed Connor across the corridor as the prep room door opened, and Ariel appeared in the opening.

"Dr Griffin," she said, her eyes puffy and her round face streaked with tears, "Damian's awake. He's asking for your husband."

"Bill had to leave. Can I speak with him?"

Ariel backed into the room and Lara entered quickly. Connor followed and moved to one side of the door, standing guard.

The patient lay in pretty much the same position Lara had left him, propped up on his good side, an oxygen mask covering his nose and mouth. His blood pressure and heart rate were slightly depressed but, encouragingly, the oxygen saturation had climbed a few points and had reached the low nineties. The oxygen mask was doing its job. Damian's eyes were open and they focused on her as she approached the bed.

She stood close beside him. He reached up to remove the mask.

"Mr G-Griffin," he said, his voice weak and rasping. "Where ..."

"Don't worry about my husband, Damian. Just rest. They'll be taking you into theatre soon."

She tried to replace the mask, but he brushed her hand away.

"He ... In the ambulance, he said somethin' ... somethin' about searchin' the school."

Lara glanced at Ariel, who nodded encouragingly. She must have known what Damian was mixed up in and how he'd received his injuries.

"No, Damian," she answered. "He just wanted to scout the area while the place was empty overnight."

"N-No ... He ... he gonna search inside the school."

Damian tried to sit up, but the movement brought on a spluttering fit. Wet, rasping coughs dragged up from deep within. Blood speckled his lips. The ECG machine on the shelf attached to the operating table flashed red and an alarm sounded.

Ariel cried out and tried to brush past Lara, but Connor held her back.

"She's a doctor," he said, firmly. "Let 'er 'elp."

Lara stepped in, forced the mask back in place, and held

Damian around the shoulders. As the spasm eased, she leaned him back into the bed's raised pad.

The door crashed open and a nurse in orange scrubs entered. Connor barred her approach.

Lara leaned closer to the patient.

"Damian what's wrong?" she whispered.

"TM and the ... the Heavies," he rasped.

Her heart lurched.

"What about them?"

"Waitin' for ... Barcode. School won't ... won't be empty."

Oh God.

Ryan was walking into a trap!

Lara stepped away and the nurse, muttering words Lara chose not to hear, brushed past her.

"Connor," Lara said, "with me."

Outside in the corridor, Lara turned right, heading for the emergency exit. Followed by her bodyguard, she crashed through the unsecured doors, pulled out her mobile, dialled, and waited.

After thirty seconds of her pacing, Ryan still hadn't picked up. She let the call ring.

"Bloody hell!"

"No answer?" Connor asked.

She shook her head. "Anything on the comms unit?"

"I've been on radio silence since we got 'ere." Connor tapped his earpiece. "Alpha Three to Control, are you reading me? Over."

She could only hear Connor's side of the conversation, but it soon became evident that Corky had lost contact with Ryan. Panic rose in her throat, restricting her breathing. Her stomach churned and her heart rate jumped.

Oh God. Ryan.

"Understood, Control. Keep trying. Alpha Three, out."

Connor tapped the earpiece and turned towards her. "It seems the comms are down intentionally." He paused a moment before continuing. "This guy, Control. What do you know about 'im? Is 'e any good? I mean, can we really trust 'im?"

"Corky?" Lara frowned. "We can trust him totally. He's an absolute genius. He's one of the two people responsible for my removal from the internet."

"Is 'e, by fu—'eck? Impressive. And strange."

"Why?"

Connor wiped his mouth with a hand and scratched at his stubble. "Turns out one of Corky's mates is 'elping the captain."

"A friend? Who?"

"Dunno. This Corky geezer would only give me 'is first name—Sean. Any idea?"

"Sean?" Lara resumed her pacing. The short landing which led to the emergency staircase only allowed six paces before she had to reverse direction. "Sean? I don't recognise the name. What about the comms?"

Connor scrunched up his face. "Seems like this Sean bloke built an anti-surveillance gizmo. Knocks out all the comms within a couple of 'undred metres. Power, internet, satellite, phones, the lot. Everything goes down."

"Oh God."

Lara clapped a hand to her mouth to stop herself shouting.

"Doc?"

She spun and reached for the staircase handrail. Connor's hand grabbed her wrist. She winced under his grip.

"Where d'you think you're going?"

Lara wrenched herself free and started down the stairs.

"I've got to warn him!"

"Doc, no. Wait!"

She reached the next half-landing before stopping and turning. Connor was halfway down the run. She held up her hand.

"Hold it right there, soldier!" she barked the order.

Connor stopped dead, years of training taking over. He held the handrail, his leading foot one tread down from the other.

"You are staying here!" she said, calm but firm.

"Let me go with you, Doc. You've no idea what's 'appening at the school."

"No. Your job is to protect Damian and Ariel. I'm armed," she said and tapped the side of her handbag which contained nothing more defensive than an illegal can of pepper spray that Ryan insisted she carry everywhere, but Connor didn't know that. "And I know what I'm doing."

"But—"

"You have your orders, Sergeant. Stay here. I'll be safe. Ryan has trained me for this. I know what I'm doing!"

Before he could argue any further, she threw him an encouraging smile and raced downstairs, taking them two at a time, glad she'd chosen a pair of flat shoes that morning.

She had absolutely no idea what she was heading into, but Ryan was in trouble and needed her help, and that was enough for her.

Lara loved him and owed him her life many times over. No way was she going to let him down.

Not ever.

Chapter Forty-Two

Monday 22nd February – Pre-Dawn

Palmerston Road School, Walthamstow, London, England

03:14.

Kaine pushed through the doorway and found himself in a dimly lit corridor. It stretched out straight ahead for about fifteen metres, running at right angles to the other corridors he'd walked that night.

The first door he reached led into the kitchen. At the far end, between two metal units, a solid-looking door stood ajar. Beyond the door, bright lights illuminated a plush room with carpets, wooden furniture, and a library of books.

"Ryan," Freeman called from inside the room, "that

didn't take you long. Come in, come in. Someone here is almost dying to meet you."

Kaine hurried through the disused kitchen, passed through the open door, and stumbled straight into a scene from a Victorian melodrama.

A broken, bloody mess that used to be Demarcus Williams lay on the hearth in front of a TV screen that displayed a blazing log fire. He didn't move.

Freeman sat in a wingback chair in front of a coffee table, sipping something that might have been whisky from a lead crystal tumbler, whose etched facets caught the light of a nearby desk lamp, adding multi-coloured sparkles to the amber liquid.

On the far side of a large, mahogany desk, a slim man in a business suit sat tied to a chair. Thin, nylon climbing ropes looped around his chest and neck, trussing him firmly to its back. The man's forearms were likewise bound to the chair's arms. The man screamed something, but the hood over his head and the gag tied around his mouth muffled his words, making them impossible to decipher. He struggled to free himself, but the knots didn't look as though they were going to loosen anytime soon.

A small part of Kaine's mind wondered where Freeman had found rope in such a fairy-tale library, but he couldn't summon the energy to ask.

Freeman pointed his glass towards one sitting on a silver coaster on an occasional table beside another upholstered wingback.

"I poured you a snifter. Please help yourself. TM won't mind. Will you, TM?" The man tied to the chair didn't respond. "Oops, there I go again, forgetting he can't hear us. Shame on me, but I've had a difficult evening."

"*Your* evening's been difficult?" Kaine wiped the blood

from his face with his sleeve to the background music of his new friend's increasingly irksome chuckle.

Freeman picked up a spare coaster from the table and threw it at the bound man's head. TM started rocking and screaming, the sound still muffled by the gag. Neither the ropes nor the solid chair moved.

Kaine crossed the room, trudging through a carpet with a pile so deep and plush, if it'd been in his house, he'd have considered running a lawnmower over the damned thing.

"Thanks, Sean. Been a long day."

Kaine lowered himself gratefully into the empty chair, sank into the well-sprung seat, and leaned back against the soft cushions, sighing loudly. He reached for the glass, inhaled the warm, smoky aroma of oak and distilled malt, and wet his lips.

"Nice," he said. "Very nice."

"Thought you'd appreciate it. When did you twig I was playing a game?"

"Took me a while," Kaine said after taking another tiny sip. "Thought I was going to have to teach you a lesson after I'd finished dealing with the Heavies."

"What gave me away?"

"The way you acted throughout, but mainly when you started talking about how Corky was setting me up. It didn't ring true. That's when I decided to play along."

Kaine used his glass to point, first at the deceased Demarcus Williams, and then at the hooded, still-struggling man in the chair.

"I thought you might need my help, but it seems I needn't have worried," Kaine said, knowingly stating the blindingly obvious.

"Nope," Freeman answered. He reached for a TV remote and hit a button. The big screen in the middle of the bookcase flicked on to reveal a widescreen shot of an empty Hub. Gerard Coulthard had made good on his word. Even Delinquent had manage to make it out in one piece—more or less.

"You did all right yourself. I watched you take care of the riffraff. Five against one. Impressive."

Kaine curled his upper lip and shook his head. "Amateurs. I've faced tougher opponents in the January sales."

Freeman narrowed his eyes in thought, and he drained his glass before nodding. "Yes, agreed. Those bargain hunters don't take any prisoners."

Kaine waited while Freeman poured himself another drink from a cut glass decanter that stood in a cruet set on the desk. Freeman offered him a top up.

"No, thanks, I'm good. Need to wrap up here before heading back to the hospital. I don't like leaving the doc on her own for too long." He lowered his voice when talking about Lara.

Although, the way the former gang boss was fighting his bonds, it didn't look as though he had the spare capacity for eavesdropping. But Kaine wasn't one to take chances.

"Don't worry about him, Ryan," Freeman said, nodding at the trussed man. "He can't hear us. Trust me. And if you were wondering about the ropes, I never set out on a job without bringing a few trusted tools of my trade." He pointed to his backpack, which sat on the floor next to the library door. "Ultra-thin climbing rope. You'll be surprised how many times rope comes in handy in my line of work."

"No, I wouldn't," Kaine said after another micro-sip. "By the way, all that, 'Please don't hurt me! Please don't hurt me!' Oh dear, oh dear." He shook his head slowly.

"What about it?"

"Hamming it up a little, weren't you?"

"What do you mean? That was award winning, my friend. Nowhere near your overacting. I mean, bloody hell. Cliché or what?"

Kaine frowned. "I've absolutely no idea what you mean."

"What was it? 'You're a dead man. Hear me? A dead man walking!' I mean, really. What were you thinking?"

Kaine wasn't a man to blush, but his cheeks warmed a little. "Yes, well, perhaps it might have been a little OTT. But, what about you and all that stuff with Corky and the money …"

"What about it?"

"A little close to home, I thought."

Freeman grimaced. "Yes. Sorry about all that, but I had to be convincing enough to reel this arsehole in." He turned and fixed his angry gaze on TM. "I had to out the murdering bastard."

"That leads me to an obvious question. What's your real role in all this? No way you're just here to help me. You're too involved and too well prepped. Come on. Out with it."

Freeman stood. "Before all that, would you like to know who this creature is?"

"Only if he can tell me what happened to Glenmore Davits. Can he?"

"There's a pretty good chance, I imagine."

Freeman strolled around the desk until he stood behind the chair and, with the flourish of a sommelier revealing a rare bottle of wine, released the knot holding the gag in place and hauled off the hood. He also ripped off the stereo headphones strapped to TM's ears with another length of climbing rope.

The former gang boss blinked hard, started hurling a high-pitched string of invective into the room, and redoubled his efforts to break free of the ropes. TM ranted and raved so much it took Kaine a moment or two to put a name to the enraged, blood-engorged face.

Tied to a chair in a room behind the Hub, in an abandoned school less than twenty minutes' march from where a disabled, old man had died, raged Darwin Moore—Glenmore Davits' grandson and the current heir to absolutely nothing.

Chapter Forty-Three

Monday 22nd February – Byron Codell

Palmerston Road, Walthamstow, London, England

03:17.

Near silence.

Echoing, aching silence. No, not quite silence.

Dripping water, running through drains, along gullies, down drainpipes.

Shit, something were wrong. Something were missing.

What?

Calm. Still. No wind, no rain.

Fuck.

Barcode tore open his eyes and rubbed some life into the dead thing that were his face where he'd pressed it against the ice-cold glass of the car's window. Something had woken him. What?

Shit, it had stopped raining!

When?

Time. Fuck's sake, what's the time?

The digital green numbers on the dashboard stood out bright but blurred. He blinked hard and rubbed his eyes. The digits sharpened into focus.

Jesus. Thank fuck for that!

Early. Still early.

He'd only been asleep a few minutes.

Barcode raked his fingers over his head, scratching some blood flow into his scalp.

Wake up, asshole. Wake the fuck up.

He hit the buttons to wind down the front windows, sucked in the cold air, coughed, breathed deep again. Fuck. Now he needed a piss. Couldn't wait no more or he'd wet himself.

Handle. Where's the fuckin' handle?

His scrabbling fingers found the plastic lever and pulled. The door opened, screeching loud in the quiet darkness. He shivered.

Bloody freezin'.

He took five steps into the deep shadow of a brick wall, lowered his fly, and shot a jet of steaming piss through a set of railings into a weed-covered front yard.

The relief of emptying an overfull bladder were fucking great, close to orgasmic. Still spraying like a horse, he craned his neck to take in the view of the school, making sure not to turn so much as to dribble over his nice, new trainers.

Every window on the ground floor of the school were lit up bright as though the building were ready to welcome him as the all-conquering hero. Whoever broke in overnight had fucked up. At a guess, they'd be feeding the fishes in the river before daylight.

Finally drained, he shook off the residue, tucked his monster back into its den, and worked the zip. How embarrassing would it be for the returning hero to arrive in the Hub with his flies open?

The school's front door creaked open, and the motion-sensitive, overhead light powered on.

Two men stumbled out, bundled up against the cold. The first one, Delinquent, stepped under the light and spied up and down the road. Look like someone had taken a blade to the poor fucker's face. A total blood-soaked mess.

Delinquent turned and nodded to the second one, Frenchie, who stood with his right arm in a sling.

What the fuck?

Together, they returned to the doorway and came back out with the idiot, Robbie, suspended between them, only using one leg. The fucker's jaw looked all wrong, swollen and screwed off to one side. Broken. Blood all over his face too. Robbie were even more of a mess than Delinquent.

What the fuck happened?

The Parksiders, or whoever had broke in, musta put up a hell of a fight to have fucked up them three so bad.

Barcode grinned. He'd missed a big rumble. Good job, too. He didn't mind a ruckus or two, but he preferred choosing the time, the place, and the opposition.

Barcode considered crossing the street and offering the injured Heavies a hand, but fuck that. TM told him to stay away until five o'clock, and that's exactly what he were gonna do.

Barcode were a good soldier. A good soldier who only fought when it suited him. He settled back into the deep shadows and watched the fucked-up threesome dance, shuffle, and groan along the street until they reached Gerard's shiny, black Beemer. He pointed the key fob, the locks clunked open, and they poured a screaming Robbie into the back.

Barcode chuckled the whole time.

Better'n the telly.

Frenchie, the least mangled of the three, slid behind the wheel, and struggled to stick the key into the ignition with his wrong hand. Took him three goes before he could fire up the engine. On the far side of the car, Delinquent only just managed to heave himself into the front passenger's seat and slam the door before the French fucker raced off in a squeal of burning rubber. It showed the advantage of automatic transmission for a one-armed driver.

The Beemer turned sharp left, rode the kerb, bounced back onto the tarmac, and disappeared behind a row of houses.

Frenchie normally treated that car better than his latest squeeze. Riding the kerb like that woulda fucked up his rims and hurt him worse than whatever he done to his arm.

Hope it's broke, you arrogant, French fuck.

Still smiling, Barcode rubbed his hands together for warmth, pulled the zip on his jacket right up to his throat, and checked the dash. A little after three twenty.

Still got plenty of time.

He slid behind the Renault's steering wheel and waited.

Waiting weren't no problem. Barcode were good at waiting. Could do with another tab, though. He were gasping.

Chapter Forty-Four

Monday 22nd February – Lara Orchard

Cambourne Cross Hospital, Leytonstone, London, England

03:22.

With the mobile phone clamped to her ear and the call still going straight to messenger, Lara skipped down the stairs, using the handrail for support. The absolute last thing she needed was to trip and fall. What would happen to Ryan then?

On the ground floor at last, she burst through the doors and rushed into the main admissions area, where she slowed to avoid raising suspicion.

"Dr Griffin!" Dr Hamilton called from behind her.

Damn!

Lara ignored him and continued past the reception area, heading for the main exit doors and the taxi rank.

"Oh, Dr Griffin? Might I have a quick—"

She hesitated before turning, balancing the worry for Ryan with the need to maintain their cover.

"Dr Hamilton, sorry. Didn't hear you. It's been a rather tiring day."

The young medic offered her a tired smile. "Tell me about it, Doctor."

"Is there a problem?"

"Not as such, but I … wondered if you were available for a quick consult. I have a rather diff—interesting case you might be able to assist with." He leaned slightly towards her, eyebrows lifted as though waiting for a response.

Lara glanced at her watch. If she dismissed the request out of hand alarm bells would ring. "I'm terribly sorry, Dr Hamilton, but my husband suffers from the occasional bout of vasovagal syncope. I'm afraid he's taken a bit of a tumble. Hit his head again. An emergency. You understand?"

The young doctor's expression turned serious. He nodded. "I understand, Dr Griffin. Perhaps we can discuss my patient when you get back?"

Lara gave him the most maternal smile she could muster. "Of course, Doctor. Of course. But, if you'll excuse me?"

Without waiting for his reply, Lara turned and headed for the exit, forcing herself not to break into an unprofessional trot. The young medic had cost her valuable time over a case probably no more tricky than an ulcerating sore.

Outside, the weather had closed in again and sleet mixed with heavy rain pulsed down from a black sky, smashing into the pavement and bouncing high.

Damn it.

Her coat. She'd left it in the upstairs waiting room. No time to go back for it. She'd have to put up with a soaking.

Keeping as close to the protection of the hospital walls as possible, she hurried to the taxi rank, dodging the incoming patients and jumping the deepening puddles.

By the time she reached the first of three cabs in the rank, Lara was already soaked to the skin and shivering. The cab driver took one look at her impersonation of a drowning rat and shook his head. He hit a button on his dash, and the clunk of locking doors sounded over the noise of the rain drumming on his car roof.

She slapped his window with her open hand. He jumped and turned to face her, anger burning in his piggy eyes. She made a "wind down your window" gesture. He yawned, shook his head again, and flicked a hand at her in dismissal.

"Lunch break," he shouted.

Selfish idiot.

Lara moved along the line. The second cabbie, a man with a full grey beard but no moustache, lowered his window.

"Where to?"

"Palmerston Road, Walthamstow."

He shook his head. "I not take young lady there this time of night. It dangerous place."

Oh for pity's sake.

"It's urgent. I need to get there right now."

"No. Bad place. I no take you."

"This is ridiculous!"

The rain beat into her shoulders and her hair hung in straggles around her ears. She hunched over to shield her handbag from the weather, tugged out her purse, and selected a note from the side pocket.

"Will you take me for fifty pounds?"

The full lip above the ugly beard twitched. The cabbie's eyes flicked from Lara to the note and back again. Greed won out over reluctance. He nodded and flicked a switch to unlock the rear door. Lara dived into the back, delighted to be out of the weather, if only for the few minutes it would take the driver to reach Walthamstow.

She leaned forwards and handed the note to the driver. "Here's twenty. You'll get the other thirty when we reach Palmerston Road. Ten more if we're there inside ten minutes."

The cabbie palmed the twenty into the inner pocket of his jacket, gunned his engine, and pulled out of his spot like a racing driver who didn't want to be booked for speeding —excruciatingly slowly.

Lara shrugged out of her light, soaked jacket, draped it across the spare seat, and pulled a packet of tissues from her bag. She dabbed ineffectually at her face and neck, but the tissues soon became a sopping mass of pulp in her hand. She lowered the steamed-up window a couple of centimetres and dropped the wedge of sodden paper into the night. The cabbie looked at her in the rear-view mirror.

"Biodegradable. It won't pollute the environment," she said in her defence.

Unlike this gas-guzzling Mercedes. What's wrong with electric?

"No, miss. I understand. You want proper cloth? Look behind."

On the parcel shelf, Lara found a green box marked "Biodegradable Cloths", which upgraded the cabbie's environmental credentials, at least in part.

She took out a couple, dried her face, neck, and hands,

and pulled a fresh cloth through her hair. Apart from the damp blouse that clung to her skin in all the wrong places, she felt better.

The driver's gaze flicked rapidly between the road ahead and the image in his rear-view which, to him, must have been the preferred option. Her disguise had mutated from "drowned rat" to "entrant in a wet t-shirt contest".

Men. One-track minds.

"In boot I have umbrella-brolly," he said, eyes back on the road since she'd crossed her arms.

"Yes?"

"You buy? Twenty pounds?"

Lara counted the dwindling number of notes in her purse—one twenty and four tens. Assuming they reached Palmerston Road inside the allotted time, she had enough cash. It would leave her flat broke, but what did that matter?

"Agreed."

"We have deal. I love London better than Mumbai."

The driver added some pressure to the throttle and turned left at a green light. He filtered into the empty bus and taxi lane and their speed increased to well above marching pace.

"Can you hurry, please?"

"I keep to speed limit, miss. Driving is my profession. We reach destination soon. Which end you want? North or south."

She had no idea.

"I'm heading for Palmerston School."

He pulled his foot off the throttle and the cab slowed. "No, no. Not good. Bad place. Tribe hang out there. Very dangerous. Really, miss. I tell you."

They'd slowed to a near-stop. Behind them a horn

blared illegally, and a white van sped past them, flashing his headlights.

"My husband is in …"

Bloody hell. How could she explain anything to a bargain-hungry hack who had such poor English?

"Okay, never mind. Drop me off at the end of"—she wracked her brain to remember the street names—"Brooke Street. I'll walk from there."

"You buy umbrella-brolly?"

Lara sighed heavily. "Yes. I'll buy the damn brolly, but please hurry."

The driver picked up speed again and made a turn into Walthamstow, eventually passing a darkened Denny's Grill —the first time she'd actually seen the café closed. A few turns later, the cab rolled to a stop two hundred metres beyond Glenmore Davits' house.

The ride had taken less than nine minutes although, to Lara, it had seemed closer to an hour.

The cabbie twisted in his seat, showed her the wide gap between his two front teeth in a smile, and held out his hand.

"Here in plenty time, as agreed. You pay forty pounds now, please. And twenty for umbrella-brolly?"

She pressed the money into his calloused hand and it retracted between the gap in the front seats faster than the hand in a novelty moneybox.

"The brolly?" she asked, one leg already out into the weather.

"I unlock boot from here. You be careful, yes?"

Lara slid out into the rain and raced around to the back. She levered the boot lid fully open and found a furled-up, black umbrella, just as the driver promised. She also found a light grey raincoat and something else she couldn't resist helping herself to—an L-shaped wheel brace.

The brace was heavy and cumbersome, but she had no idea what she'd face at the school and, as a weapon, it was better than nothing.

Apart from everything else, she'd paid well over the going rate for an excruciatingly slow, nine-minute taxi ride, and the odds on the cabbie having a puncture and needing to remove his wheel nuts were pretty low. She slipped one end of the brace between her belt and trouser leg, and allowed the right angle to act like a catch, hiding it and the raincoat as best she could with the "umbrella-brolly". She slammed the boot and rushed towards Palmerston Road, struggling to open the brolly on the move.

Behind her, the cabbie flashed his headlights, executed a U-turn, and trundled away.

Finally alone, Lara broke into a jog. She discarded the useless brolly, which turned out to be more of a hindrance than a help, and pulled on the raincoat. The colour didn't offer much in the way of camouflage, but at least it would keep the worst of the rain off for a while, and she could remove it if and when necessary.

She hurried along the empty street, gently steaming inside her oversized, waterproof covering.

How long had it been since Damian had given her the information? Thirty minutes?

Lara increased speed, her flat shoes pounding the pavement, splashing through puddles regardless. The wind grew in force, howling around her exposed head. The chill, wet air burned her lungs and tugged at her clothes. She shot past the alley where she'd dropped Barcode onto his backside.

How long ago that seemed.

All the long months Ryan had spent drilling military fieldcraft into her reluctant brain remained, but she ignored it in her frenzy to warn him. The need to spend time on reconnaissance and planning could go to hell. Ryan needed her help and she wouldn't let him down.

Lara raced on, turning right into Green Lane. She darted across the road, closing on Boothe Avenue.

Close now, she was close.

Two more turns and she'd be there.

Still at a full gallop, but breathing hard, she approached the end of the avenue, and slowed when she neared the junction with Palmerston Road.

Dear God. What the hell was she going to find at the school?

Chapter Forty-Five

Monday 22nd February – Pre-Dawn

Palmerston Road School, Walthamstow, London, England

03:25.

"You!" Kaine said.

After the life he'd led, he didn't think much would be able to surprise him anymore, but this?

"Yeah, me, you fucking—"

Freeman smacked Darwin's ear with a cupped hand. It rang loud in the quiet room. "Language, Darwin. I've had my fill of swearing this evening, thank you very much."

"Fuck you, arsehole!" Darwin screamed and received another cuffed ear for his troubles. "Let me loose and I'll kill you both with my bare hands."

"Hear that, Sean?" Kaine asked, unable to suppress a chuckle.

"Yes, I heard it. What do you reckon, bluster or a real threat?"

Kaine lifted a shoulder and dropped it again. "No idea. Untie him, let's find out."

"You sure?"

Kaine set his glass on the coaster, used the arms of the chair to help lever himself up, and stood in front of the desk. Fatigue had set in as the aftermath of the fight began to take its toll and the cut over his eye started to sting.

"Certain. Let him go and let's see what he's made of."

"I frisked him earlier. He doesn't have a weapon."

"Oh dear. That's hardly fair. Here, give him this."

Kaine pulled the butterfly knife he'd taken from Coulthard, and rotated and flicked it open in much the same, flashy way the Frenchman had done before hurting his hand, only faster and even slicker. With a rapid flick of the fingers, he reversed the grip, leaned forwards, and stabbed the blade deep into the desk's faux-leather insert. He released the knife and the handle halves flopped down, thumping into the desk.

"That's a little dramatic," Freeman said, shaking his head in rebuke. "Good job this table's a reproduction, not a genuine antique."

"And a cheap one, too," Kaine agreed.

"This whole room's like a film set. Nothing's real. All for show."

Darwin looked from Kaine to the knife and back again. The fear in his eyes was reinforced by his trembling chin.

"Don't want to play, Darwin?"

He shook his head.

"You're a soldier, a ... a killer. I wouldn't stand a chance."

"Neither did your grandfather. And by the way, I'm a marine, doofus."

Darwin frowned. "Same difference."

"Not quite, idiot, but I'll let it go for now. What happened? Did your grandfather find out about your little side-line? Did you kill him to shut him up?"

"I'm saying nothing. You don't have proof of anything. Pops fell down the stairs. It was an accident. An accident, you hear!"

"How did he manage to climb the stairs in the first place? I thought he couldn't leave his wheelchair."

"Yeah, me too. I didn't know it at the time, but his doctor gave him some new meds. Made him feel better, but he probably took too many. Way I see it, he was delirious, took it into his head to go upstairs and sleep in a proper bed, or something."

"Is that how he found out?" Kaine pressed. "Did you store some merchandise in your room? A good place to hide stuff. After all, who'd suspect an old man in a wheelchair and his college student grandson?"

Freeman moved far enough to his left for Darwin to see him without having to crane his neck.

"Listen, TM. We aren't the police and this isn't a courtroom. We want answers and we have all night. Hell, with that security door and all those surveillance monitors, we have all bloody week. No one's coming to save your sorry arse. Might as well answer our questions. Save yourself a great deal of pain. What do you say?" He smiled and waited.

"Fuck o—"

Freeman jabbed him in the left eye with a finger so fast,

Kaine almost missed it as a blur. Darwin didn't. He screamed, pulled his head as far away as he could, given his neck restraint, and kept screaming.

"I didn't see that coming," Kaine said.

"Neither did he," Freeman said, smiling. "The arsehole deserved it. I've seen the misery this creature is responsible for." He nodded to the corpse on the floor. "And that one."

"Care to elaborate? You still owe me a full explanation. No way you're just here to help me. You're too well-prepped and too highly motivated."

Freeman waggled his head a little before nodding. "In a sec. Let me just finish with this gentle interrogation."

Darwin stopped screaming and started crying, begging. His left eye streamed more than the right.

"I can't see … I can't see. Please don't."

Freeman leaned close again and placed a hand on Darwin's forehead. He forced the man's head into the back of the chair, and held it still.

"Darwin, open your eyes."

"No, I can't," he said as best he could through clenched teeth. "Can't see. I can't see!"

Still holding Darwin's head in place, Freeman reached into the desk tidy, rattled the pens loudly, and selected a fat, old-fashioned fountain pen. A Montblanc. A real one. Expensive. With finger and thumb, Freeman unscrewed the top and let it fall. The heavy top hit the desk, bounced twice, rolled off, and was lost in the deep undergrowth masquerading as carpet.

The noise it made when hitting the desk made Darwin open his remaining good eye. As he found focus on the pen's sharp nib, less than three centimetres away, the former gang leader whimpered. He squeezed the eye closed and tried pulling his head away.

Freeman held the head steady and used his thumb to pry and hold the eyelid open.

"Good, good. Now I have your full attention we can begin."

"W-What are you g-going to do?" Spittle flew as Darwin spoke.

"Ask a few questions. If I don't like an answer, I find out how well your eyeball stands in for a piece of paper."

Freeman spoke slowly and quietly. As he did so, he moved the Montblanc's gold nib closer to Darwin's eyeball.

It was masterful. Kaine couldn't have done it better himself.

"No, no. Please. Ask your questions, but don't hurt me."

Freeman twisted his lips. "Nah, sorry. Don't believe you."

The pen moved closer and the nib touched an eyelash on the lower lid. The captive squealed again.

"*Please. Please don't,*" he screeched, sounding remarkably similar to his electronically modulated alter ego.

Kaine hid a smile behind his hand.

Freeman pulled the pen away, but not far. Keeping the gang leader pinned and his good eye open, he turned to look at Kaine.

"What do you reckon, Ryan? Can we trust him to tell the truth?"

"Nah, start writing," Kaine answered. "After the evening we've had, I really don't mind watching him suffer."

"Okay, will do. Doesn't matter if he's blind. He has a pair of testicles, a todger, and all those fingers and toes we can work on. Think you can find something to slice things open with?"

Kaine didn't have to search hard. He pointed to the butterfly knife sticking into the desk.

"Will that do? Looks sturdy and sharp enough to me."

Darwin squealed again. "Oh God. No. Please, don't."

Freeman frowned. "Okay, okay. Stop your wailing. You're giving me a headache. First question. Did you kill your grandfather?"

"Yes, yes." He gagged. "W-Well, sort of. It happened pretty much the way Mr Kaine said. Pops found some papers in my bedroom, the one time I left the door unlocked."

"You use to lock your bedroom door?" Kaine asked.

"Y-Yeah. Fucking Primula Johnson. Nosey bitch had a key to the front door … didn't want her messing with my shit."

"Keep going," Freeman insisted, waggling the Montblanc once more.

"Yes, yes. Okay. So, Pops found some stuff I'd left out by mistake. P-Papers, not p-product. I'd never bring drugs into the house. N-Never touch the stuff. That poison's for morons. I … tried to bluff it out with Pops. Said it was part of my college studies. Research, you know. But he … he didn't believe me."

"So you pushed him down the stairs?" Kaine asked.

"No, no. It was an accident. He turned too fast, fell from the top step. I-I tried to catch him. Save him. Honest, I did but … but … I'm sorry. I couldn't save him."

"I've seen your grandfather's house," Kaine said. "Run-down, messy, broken central heating system, but you live most of the time like this." He swept an arm to encompass the room.

Darwin paused. He swallowed and took a moment to suck in a deep breath before continuing.

"Camouflage. The old house had to look the part. Anyhow, you didn't know the old man. If I'd tried to help him out, he'd have asked how I could afford it. Pops thought I was at university all week, studying hard, ramping up the student loans. How could I do anything for him?"

"That leads to a question," Freeman said. "If you were here all the time, playing TM, how come you're registered as attending every one of your classes and acing all your exams?"

Darwin looked at Kaine through his good eye and frowned.

"How d'you know that?"

Freeman touched the nib of the pen to Darwin's upper cheek and drew a small line. "We're asking the questions, idiot. Answer them."

"Sorry. Sorry. I-I hired a double. A kid who looks a bit like me and needed a free ride. In college, they almost never check IDs or take registration. It's not like at school."

Freeman turned to Kaine again. "That's something Corky should have known. I'll mention it next time I visit."

"You know where he lives?"

"Of course," Freeman said, grinning. "Look for the biggest toadstool in the forest, and you'll find Corky sitting cross-legged underneath it, playing a penny whistle."

Kaine smiled. Despite his annoying laugh, Kaine could easily grow to really like the amiable thief.

"You say it was an accident," Freeman said, lifting his thumb to release Darwin's eyelid, but still holding his head against the back of the chair, "but I'm sure the police could make a case for manslaughter. Now, moving on. Tell me about Southend."

"Huh?"

Freeman twiddled the Montblanc, dabbed the tip of his index finger to the point, and sucked air between his teeth.

Kaine had no idea where Freeman was headed with the

change of direction, but was happy to let him continue while he was on such a good a roll.

"Southend-on-Sea, Essex. More specifically, 124 St Helen's Park Road."

Darwin gasped. Renewed fear lit his good eye. The other was too bloodshot and tear-filled to read.

"Wh-What about it?" he asked, his voice hushed.

Freeman turned to Kaine. "You've heard of drug gangs running cuckoo's nests?"

Kaine nodded. "Yep. A coward's trick."

Freeman tested the sharpness of the Montblanc's nib with his fingertip again. He winced. Apparently, it hadn't grown any blunter since the first test.

Darwin, without doubt a fast learner, snapped his mouth shut, and kept it shut. He didn't lose sight of the pen, though.

"124 St Helen's Park Road was the Tribe's first attempt at running a cuckoo's nest. Darwin, here, sent in one of his prettiest girls to befriend the tenant. A young man with special needs. A gentle man with the IQ of a pre-teen. An easy mark. She moved in with him and brought a few friends along for the ride."

"And they set up shop, dealing drugs?"

"Yep, that's exactly what happened," Freeman said, turning his attention back to the captive. "Isn't that right, Darwin?"

The gang leader formerly known as Top Man, closed his eyes, squeezing out more tears in the process. It looked as though he finally understood the real reason for Freeman's presence, and the reason he'd played such a large part in the destruction of Darwin's business empire. Kaine still had no idea, but imagined he'd soon find out.

Freeman's hand slid up from Darwin's forehead and grabbed hold of his wiry mop, pulling hard.

"I asked you a question, arsehole!" he shouted, his voice spitting venom.

"Yes, yes. We did. But it wasn't supposed to go down like that. We had a good thing going. Barney wasn't being hurt. Alethia was keeping him sweet. The dummy never had it so good. Things were going great. Why would we want to mess that up?"

"Barney?" Kaine asked, although reluctant to interrupt the confession.

"Barney was the tenant with the special needs. Turns out he wasn't as slow as TM and Alethia originally thought. He worked out what was happening and threatened to call the police. Poor guy didn't stand a chance. TM sent that animal"—Freeman jerked his head towards the corpse on the floor—"to make sure Barney couldn't tell anyone anything."

"What happened?"

"A week after Williams' surprise visit, Barney's only living relative, his cousin, found his body in the bath with a belly full of sleeping tablets and his wrists slashed. The coroner concluded the poor lad committed suicide. Apparently, Barney became distraught when his new girlfriend left him unexpectedly. Case closed."

"But?"

"The cousin knew better. Barney could never swallow tablets and wouldn't have ended his life without talking to the cousin first."

"You were the cousin?" Kaine asked.

Freeman turned to face Kaine and shook his head. "No, Ryan. Not me. An old school friend. She contacted me through Corky, and the two of us decided to investigate.

"Corky and I put the bones of it together fairly quickly, but struggled to identify TM. I've been planning this little intervention for a few weeks now, which is why I built the disruptor. Then you received your the-83.com message from Primula Johnston, which caught the attention of one of Corky's clever, little bots. Couldn't have worked out better. The rest, as they say, is mystery."

"You mean 'history'?"

"Nope, not a fan of history. Prefer a good mystery thriller, me," Freeman said and double-hitched his eyebrows.

"Oh dear."

"Sorry, but it's been a long night and they can't all be gems. Jewel thief … 'gems' … get it?"

Kaine groaned and briefly closed his eyes. "Please stop doing that."

"Afraid I can't promise anything of the sort," Freeman said, still smiling brightly in spite of the bruises mottling his face.

"Changing the subject slightly," Kaine said, "I've just thought of something. Mind if I ask your prisoner a couple of questions?"

Freeman stepped away and rolled a hand in front of the captive. "Be my guest."

"You are so kind."

"I do try."

Kaine perched on the edge of the desk and faced Darwin full on. He narrowed his eyes and leaned closer to the hapless man, who simpered and jerked his head as far away as his restraints would allow.

"I asked you about this a couple of days ago, but I have a feeling you weren't being entirely truthful. Now that we've come to a better understanding, I'll ask the question again. Ready?"

"Yes. I-I'll answer anything, but please don't hurt me."

"What happened to that bank draft? Did you find it?"

"Y-Yes. Found it after Pops … passed."

"Did you cash it in?"

Darwin tucked his chin into his chest in an action Kaine read as a nod.

Kaine rested a hand on Darwin's shoulder. "That gives me a bit of a problem, Darwin, old chum. The money is meant for those who deserve it, not lying, thieving scumbags like you. Where is it?"

Darwin flicked a sly glance at a bookcase on the opposite wall to the fire before lowering his eyes to focus on the top of the desk.

Freeman clearly caught the look, too. He raised a finger. "Hold it right there a moment, will you, Ryan?"

Kaine shrugged, said, "Happy to," and squeezed Darwin's bony shoulder hard enough to make the young man squeal.

Freeman waded through the carpet and studied the bookcase for a moment before turning to Darwin.

"Oh dear," he said, "you've been holding out on us. Naughty fellow."

He pressed something on the side of the cabinet and a row of false books popped open like a door. Freeman swung the "door" fully ajar to reveal a brushed-steel safe with a digital keypad. He rubbed his hands together. "Lovely stuff. A 2015 Chumley Passive. Haven't opened one of these before. Let me get my bag."

Kaine sighed. "No need, Sean, my friend. We have the key right here." He squeezed Darwin's shoulder again, digging his thumb into one of a few pressure points he could have chosen.

Before he needed to ask, Darwin rattled off a five-digit number, which Freeman dialled into the keypad, looking a little disappointed. The safe clicked open. He peered inside and whistled, but his broad shoulders hid the contents from Kaine.

"Anything interesting?" Kaine asked.

"Not really. Unless you consider banknotes interesting." Freeman turned away to reveal a small safe neatly stuffed with bundles of cash.

Kaine nodded. "I do. How much?" He aimed the question at Darwin, to speed up the process.

"H-Half a million pounds," the prisoner mumbled without looking up.

The jewel thief stopped counting. "A quarter mil' each. Not bad for one night's work. It'll go a long way to help ease the pain from these bruises." He touched the side of his damaged face and winced.

Kaine shook his head. "Nope. All I need is the ten grand to cover the banker's draft. You can help yourself to the rest."

"You sure?"

"Well," Kaine said, after considering the issue a little further. "I did incur some costs during this mission, courtesy of the Tribe, but I'm sure you'll give the rest a good home."

"Oh yes," Freeman said, grinning. "I'll find something nice to spend it on. I am a thief, after all." He added a wink and threw Kaine four bundles of the crisp, unused notes.

Kaine caught the money and stuffed it into his jacket pocket while Freeman loaded the rest into his backpack. After he'd finished, he returned to the desk, dropped the backpack on top, and patted it lovingly. "I know a couple of drug rehab charities who will appreciate a sizeable donation."

"Really?" Kaine asked, allowing incredulity to seep into his tone.

"You thought I was going to keep it?"

"Well—"

"Shame on you."

Kaine tilted his head. "You did say you were a thief."

After delivering another wink, Sean said, "Don't believe everything you're told, Ryan. Especially if you hear it from a dishonest man."

"I'll take that on board for future reference, my friend," Kaine said. He pressed his hands against his thighs and used them to lever himself from the desk and into a standing position. "That only leaves us with one question."

"Only one?"

"One major question."

"Which is?"

"What do we do with this creature?" Kaine nodded at Darwin. "I'm not a big fan of killing a helpless—"

"Yes, I could tell that from the way you treated the Heavies."

Darwin's chin trembled and his shoulders slumped even further.

Kaine straightened his jacket and cleared his throat. "If you'll let me continue, I was going to say, I'm not a big fan of killing a helpless man, but in this case, I'm happy to make an exception."

"No, please. No!" Darwin cried, his shoulders jerking back up around his ears.

Freeman patted the man's cheek.

"Don't worry, old sport. You'll live past tonight. I know exactly what to do with you. You see, a good friend of mine has a buddy in the National Crime Agency. He's recently returned from extended sick leave after being shot in the line of duty. It appears that my friend's friend, Inspector Hook, hates drug dealers and murderers, and will appreciate a nice, easy case to work his way back into the job."

Freeman released Darwin's hair and stooped to retrieve the top of the Montblanc from the carpet. He twisted it into place and offered the complete pen to Kaine, who passed up the offer with a wave of his hand.

"No use to me, Sean. Can't remember the last time I needed a fountain pen. It's all keyboards and ballpoints these days."

"What about your good lady?"

Kaine tried to imagine how Lara might react to anyone having the temerity to call her a "good lady" and managed not to grimace. "No thanks, that's a man's pen. A little big for her, and it wouldn't feel right to give her stolen property."

"Good point. Highly laudable, in fact. However, I don't mind liberating this beautiful writing implement and giving it a good home." He slid the pen into his jacket's inside pocket. "Don't mind at all."

"So," Kaine said, standing and taking a deep breath. "Can I leave you to it? Don't really fancy being here when the boys from the NCA arrive to take this place apart. You don't really need me for anything, do you?"

"Nope, I'll be fine here on my own, thanks." He thrust out a hand and they shook firmly, both adding a forearm grip to the shake.

"Thanks for disabling the Glock," Freeman said. "Might have had a little more trouble from Demarcus if you hadn't locked the hammer."

Kaine frowned. "Sorry?"

Freeman tilted his head and pulled in his chin. "When you hit the floor and started fumbling with the gun. You engaged the safety catch, right?"

"Like I said in the Hub, Glocks don't have an external safety catch. They have three internal safeties. There is no lever, as such."

Freeman blanched and dropped his backside onto the desk.

"Blimey, I thought you disabled the damn thing. Why did you fiddle with it for so long?"

"Wanted to make it look good before Williams disarmed me. "

"You took a hell of a risk, though. What if Williams shot you?"

"A calculated risk. I didn't think TM would let him shoot me until after you'd spoken. Reckoned you'd be able to schmoose your way into a face-to-face meeting before that happened."

"You are a dangerous man, Ryan Kaine."

"So they tell me. Changing the subject, you don't know much about firearms, do you, Sean?"

"Not a whole lot. Clearly."

"Think about enrolling yourself in a weapons training course next time you're in the US. There's plenty about if you can pay the fees."

"Good idea. I'll think about doing just that," Freeman said, puffing out his cheeks.

"Begs the question, though," Kaine said. "How did you manage to take down Williams?"

"You're not going to believe it."

"Try me."

Some colour returned to Freeman's face. "When TM

arrived and I finally learned who he was, I punched the little ratbag in the face. Laid him out cold."

"Really?"

"Really."

Freeman started rubbing his face, probably trying to bring some feeling back, but winced when he touched the bruises and pulled his hands away.

"What did Williams do?"

"The bloke went apeshit. Started screaming and threatening me with the Glock. I just laughed at him. Must have sounded hysterical. Williams probably thought I'd lost it completely. He closed on me, pointed the gun in my face, and then I told him how you'd activated the safety. When he turned the gun to check it out, I jumped him. Started pounding and didn't let up until he stopped moving. Didn't even resort to this."

He dropped a hand to his belt and broke open the buckle to reveal a neat, little, ceramic blade.

"Nice gadget," Kaine said, "I've used something similar in the past."

Kaine turned his gaze from the knife to the bloody mess on the floor near the false fireplace and shook his head.

"You did all that damage with your bare hands?"

Freeman scratched the crown of his head.

"Well, he had been smacking me around most of the evening and threatening to shoot off my kneecaps. I'm embarrassed to say, I did rather lose my rag a little, and ..."

"And?"

"This helped."

He strolled over to the corpse and, with the toe of his shoe, lifted the dead man's shoulder. Beneath it lay the small, bronze statue of a horse.

"Grabbed that beauty from the side table after I thumped our little Napoleon here. I hadn't completely lost my mind."

The horse was missing its head and a foreleg.

Kaine didn't want to know the current location of either body part. No doubt the post mortem would turn them up, buried somewhere deep inside the corpse's pulverised head.

"Remind me never to make you angry, Sean."

"Normally," he said, "I'm a placid individual. I'm an artist. Abhor violence, me."

"You could have fooled me. Sure you don't want me to stay and help you clean up?"

"No, thanks, I'll be right. Actually, I'm used to tidying my own mess, and there's plenty of time."

"What about the Glock. Do I need to make it safe? Where is it, by the way?"

Freeman smiled again, this one was as sheepish as any Kaine had ever seen. Not even Danny could have matched it.

"Under the body. Williams is still holding it."

"Okay. Mind if I give you some advice for the future?"

"Don't attack a man who's pointing a gun at me?"

"Yep, that's part of it. The rest is, if you see a gun lying around the place, assume it's loaded, don't pick it up, don't pull the trigger, get the hell away from it. After that, everything's cool."

"Sounds reasonable. Thanks."

"You're welcome. Righto, then," he said, rubbing his gloved hands together, "I'd better be off. There's a hospital patient I need to visit, and a 'wife' I need to placate. Take care, Sean. Give my regards to Corky."

"Will do."

Kaine threw him a brief wave, spun away, and hurried through the security door without casting a backwards glance.

Chapter Forty-Six

Monday 22nd February - Byron Codell

Palmerston Road, Walthamstow, London, England

03:41.

Barcode's ears picked up the sounds quickly—the light splashes of someone running through deep puddles. Light, fast tread. A small runner. Travelling quick, making good ground, almost sprinting, but not breathing hard. Barcode couldn't hear no panting.

A jogger? Fucking moron. Couldn't they think of nothing better to do in the middle of the night. Like sleep, maybe?

The noise came from the junction where Boothe Avenue joined Palmerston Road. About a hundred metres away.

Holding his breath, Barcode waited.

The footsteps slowed, faltered, and stopped.

Movement. A shadow, lit by one of the few streetlights as still worked in that part of the hood, approached the junction.

Movement turned into a figure. It stopped at the junction, holding close to a set of rusty and broken railings. It crouched low, spying on the school.

What the fuck?

A raid?

Nah, no way.

The Po-Po wouldn't arrive on foot. They'd charge in, blue lights flashing, sirens screaming. TV news crews in tow, like as not.

Nah, this were something else. Musta had something to do with the crew that broke into the school and probably got their asses handed to them, stupid fucks. Maybe one of them Parksiders coming to check what happened to their buddies.

Too bad, fucker. Yo' peeps are toast.

The crouching man looked around him, head swivelling left and right like Delinquent had done. Fucker couldn't have seen nothing scary, because he stood up straighter, stepped out from behind the railings, and started across the road.

Fucker wore dark trousers and a grey, knee-length coat. Bare headed. No hat in this weather? Mutha must be desperate, or mad. Something familiar about the way he moved made Barcode's heart flip.

Fuck me!

Newcomer weren't no man, it were the fucking bitch who'd flipped him on his butt.

Griffin's woman!

Bloody hell, that meant one of them break-in merchants had to be Griffin.

Gold. Pure fuckin' gold.

Finally. He got the chance to get his own back on the bitch. Fucking hell, what a day. Revenge against Weasel, turning over the Parksiders—twice—and pulling vengeance on the bitch.

There is a God!

Barcode grabbed the steering wheel, grinning like it were his birthday.

Having loved the way he'd dealt with Beanie Boy, the crushed Parksider, cars were fast becoming one of Barcode's weapons of choice. Wouldn't replace a shiv for doing the deed up close and personal but cars would do. They'd do nicely.

Very nicely.

Barcode twisted the screwdriver in the ignition, and the engine fired. Caught first time. He slipped the stick into first gear, stamped on the throttle, and slipped the clutch.

The shitty, little Renault shot forwards like a cat booted in the butt.

Chapter Forty-Seven

Monday 22nd February – Pre-Dawn

Palmerston Road School, Walthamstow, London, England

03:39.

Kaine hurried through the empty Hub, avoiding the various pools of blood and stepping over the baseball bat and a knife—the debris of another battle he'd somehow managed to survive relatively unscathed.

To stop his hands shaking from the aftereffects of the adrenaline surge, he clenched them into tight fists. Then he opened his fingers, shook them out, and relaxed his hands, all the while taking deep, slow breaths to purge his system. Cooling down after battle was almost as important as the warmup before one.

In his head, he worked through the post-action debrief. Not that he needed to. It was simply one part of the end game process, his way to detox—to wind down. A way to cope with the aftermath of a life-threatening encounter.

What had he and Lara achieved from their few days in London?

They'd identified Glenmore Davits' killer. Kaine didn't believe Darwin's "accident" story. Not for a moment.

With the help of a techie freak and his strangely charismatic thief of a buddy, he and Lara had cleared up a death, destroyed a drug gang, and made some of the streets in Walthamstow a little safer. At least for a few days.

He grinned to himself.

The whole episode made them sound like a pair of comic-strip superheroes. So, why didn't he feel heroic?

One of the families he'd vowed to protect—one of The 83—no longer existed. Darwin Moore was the last in the family line, destined to spend most of the rest of his life in prison. Kaine had been, in part, responsible for the death of the mother, and he also bore at least some responsibility for Glenmore Davits' death. If he'd reacted sooner, visited the old man earlier, upgraded Glenmore's home, maybe even fitted a stairlift, maybe … maybe the old man would still be alive.

Pack it in, Kaine. That won't help.

Kaine shook his head and carried on at a fast march through the school.

No way should he think like that. What was done was done. If he could change the past, Flight BE1555 would never have crashed, the people wouldn't have died, and he wouldn't have to live with the nightmares. Wouldn't have to carry the guilt of so many deaths, either. On the plus side of the accounting ledger, if Kaine hadn't vowed to help The

83 and, as a result, investigate Glenmore Davits' death, Darwin would still be running the Tribe. At least he would, until Sean Freeman and Corky had worked out a way of stopping him.

Yes, all in all, they'd done a good thing. The only thing missing was to punish the bastard who'd laid his hands on Lara. Byron "Barcode" Codell.

Still, Kaine could live with that.

He wasn't about to go searching the streets of Walthamstow to find the thug and deliver vengeance. Such an act was beneath him. Besides, he needed to check in on Damian and Ariel, and he wanted to thank Connor for looking after them all.

As for Lara Orchard, the beautiful, wonderful, brave but vulnerable vet, he needed to find a way to return her to her old life, or at least a replica of it. Although it would kill him to let her go, he had to do what was best for her in the long run.

After a rapid detour to collect the baby-Bergen, Kaine reached the lobby leading to the once-grand school entrance.

In their hurry to escape, Gerard and the other two clowns hadn't even bothered to close the double doors fully. Kaine poked his head through the gap between the doors and peeked out into the dark night.

Off to his right, a car's starter motor chugged, the engine coughed, caught, and the high-pitched revving smashed the silence of the night.

Noisy bugger.

The car, a small, grey Renault, looked familiar. A memory surfaced. The image of a driver lighting a cigarette rose from Kaine's tired brain. The smoker, still there from what, two, three hours ago?

Why?

Headlights snapped on, illuminating wet tarmac, broken paving slabs, and a pedestrian in a light grey raincoat crossing the road stealthily. A woman, medium-length hair plastered to her head and face. Familiar gait. A recognisable sway to the hips.

Lara!

The Renault's engine whined, front wheels spun, found traction on the slick tarmac. The car lurched forwards, fish-tailed. Gathered speed.

"Lara! Look out!"

Kaine barged open the heavy, oak door, raced through the opening, and took the outside steps in one bound. He hit the pavement, shot forwards, angling his run to place himself between Lara and the fast-closing car.

Ten metres away, in the middle of the road, Lara looked up, her eyes wide, mouth open in shock.

Legs and arms pumping, feet pounding pavement, Kaine reached the road.

Five metres. Less.

Too far, too late.

The engine screamed louder and the lights grew brighter as the car approached.

Kaine dived, arms outstretched, caught her in the side, the hip.

Lara folded around him, flew away.

"Ryan!"

The impact.

Sudden and immense. Agonising.

The car struck, high. Shoulder, ribs, and hip. The sharp crack of breaking bones. Searing, excruciating pain in arms and legs. The world tumbled around him. A spinning, jumbled confusion.

Light grey clothing flew, landed, and rolled away. Safe? Buildings spun around his head, up, down, sideways. Something hard hit him.

It stopped his jagged flying-roll. Cracked his head. Bricks. A wall. A garden wall. Wet pavement, puddle … blood.

Chapter Forty-Eight

Monday 22nd February – Pre-Dawn

Palmerston Road School, Walthamstow, London, England

03:42.

Everything hurt. Mind fogged … Kaine closed his eyes to the pain … to the thumping, crushing headache. His arm throbbed. His side …

Someone needed him. Who?

Lara!

What happened?

The car. The Renault.

Sounds reverberated through the mists of his mind.

Metal crashed into metal. A booming crump. The racing engine died. A whoosh of air exploded from tyres.

Steam hissed from a cracked radiator. A car horn blared. Continuous blaring. Screaming.

Kaine opened his eyes, turned towards the noise, his vision blurred. The headlights still shone. The horn still blasted.

Lara. Oh God. Lara.

Where …

Stand. Help her.

Kaine pushed against the wall. Bone ground against damaged bone. His left arm gave way beneath him. He fell back, slumped against the brickwork of the garden wall.

He tried to sit up, roll himself onto his back, but something stopped him, held him pinned.

Kaine blinked hard. Cleared his vision a little, not much.

The Renault, fifteen, twenty metres away. It had climbed the pavement, hit the metal upright of a signpost. Its front end was up in the air, the wheels free of the ground, the one near Kaine still spinning.

Inside the car, behind the steering wheel, something moved. The driver. His head lifted and the horn cut out.

Eerie silence boomed through the air.

Pounding. The one in Kaine's head grew louder, deafening. His vision blurred again, faded.

In the Renault, more movement.

The head turned, and the driver's door screeched open. A foot wrapped in a black trainer pushed out from beneath the door, and with it, a leg clad in black.

Another screech and the door opened wider. A man stepped clear, a gash on his forehead poured blood down one side of his face, but he was smiling.

"Hey, honkey. How you doin'?"

Kaine shook his head, forced his vision to focus.

The man from the crashed Renault dug a hand into the pocket of his parka and pulled out a knife, its blade at least eight centimetres long.

Barcode!

Kaine tried moving again. Tried rolling upright. Nothing happened but blinding, grinding pain in his arm and his side.

Barcode swaggered away from the car, waving the blade in front of his bloodied face. His eyes shone in victory. He opened his mouth in a sneer. One of his front teeth was missing, but he didn't seem to notice, or if he did notice, didn't care.

"I's gonna gut you open like a fish, you fucker."

The big, black man took one slow, swaggering pace forwards, then another. The sneer grew.

"I gonna kill you slow, then I'm gonna have some fun with yo' ho of a wife."

Barcode laughed and turned to look at the place where Kaine had last seen the grey raincoat.

The drug dealer stopped dead. His head snapped to one side. Blood exploded in a bright, red mist.

Barcode's eyes rolled up into the back of his head.

His head snapped the other way. More crimson flew, and with it a piece of scalp.

Barcode's shoulders sagged. Slowly, his knees buckled, his skeleton seemed to turn to jelly, and he collapsed in on himself, flopping into a messy pile in the middle of Palmerston Road.

Behind him, Lara stood in her light grey raincoat, arms down in front of her, hands gripping a piece of bent iron—a wheel brace. Panting, and panting hard, she stared at the mess by her feet, surveying the damage, waiting for movement, guarding herself against reprisals that would never come. At least not from Barcode.

Never again from Barcode.

He'd taught her. In battle, she should never let her guard down, not ever. She'd listened. She'd learned.

Her training. The knowledge he'd drummed into her on the beach and the dunes of the Gironde had worked.

Lara was safe. He could relax.

Through his pain, Kaine smiled. So much for the "vulnerable" vet. She'd saved him. Yet again, she'd saved him.

God, how he loved her.

Lara lifted her eyes from the body, checked her surroundings, and dropped the wheel brace. It clattered onto the tarmac, ringing loud, a warning bell.

She turned to face him, pain and shock in her eyes.

"Ryan!" she shouted. "Oh God. Ryan, your arm!"

She hurdled Barcode's lifeless form and raced towards him.

Kaine looked down. His left hand and wrist turned in at the wrong angle. Not possible. The bones of his forearm didn't look right. Something else hurt. Another wound. The rusted end of an iron railing stuck through his side, between the lower rib and his hip.

Pinned, he was, like … like a butterfly on a display board.

No wonder he … couldn't bloody … move.

As Lara reached him, kneeled beside him, his vision faded again.

"Ryan, Ryan, stay with me, darling."

"Lara. I'm … okay, love … you. Lara … I …"

"Can you hear me, Ryan? Ryan can you …"

Eventually, his hearing faded, too. Kaine could no longer hear her worried, shouted words.

Chapter Forty-Nine

Monday 22nd March - Lara Orchard

The Villa, Gironde, Nouvelle-Aquitaine, France

With the villa at her back, Lara stood on the deck, staring out over the Bay of Biscay. She hadn't seen it quite as calm and inviting for months. Inviting, maybe, but she wouldn't dream of heading out there for a swim. Too bloody cold. Well, maybe not all that inviting after all. Although the sun still shone above the western horizon, having yet to hit the sea and extinguish its fiery glow for another day, the light wind chilled her to the core.

She pulled the collar of her woollen sweater tighter around her neck and hunched her shoulders. The wind huffed again, throwing a fine mist of dry sand into her face.

She blinked in reaction even though her sunglasses protected her eyes.

By God, it was so beautiful.

Rugged, magnificent. So wide and open, she could see the curvature of the horizon and imagine a whole world stretching out beyond it.

In different circumstances, the winter weather wouldn't have put Ryan off, oh no. If he'd been able, he'd be ploughing through the surf about now, and loving every moment of it. Loving the cold, the growing chop. In the water, Ryan would be in his element. But he couldn't, not now.

The fierce wind tugged at her hair, whipping it into her face, working some strands under and over the sunglasses, stinging her eyes. She tucked an errant lock behind her ear, but it worked its way free again almost immediately. Given a chance, she'd have shorn it off, made it more manageable for what she had planned, but Ryan liked it long, or so he'd said once, long ago. In a rare, poetic moment, he told her it framed her face in auburn glory. Silly man. Deep down, beneath the rugged exterior, he could be such a romantic.

No, her hair would stay long until she started the course. She'd do that for him. He deserved it.

The jittery, fractured images of Ryan bounding down the school steps, screaming her name, his whole body lit by the approaching headlights wouldn't leave her.

Not ever.

She'd been so scared. Terrified.

Once again, he'd risked everything to save her life. Her wonderful, honourable, heroic, but troubled man. Only the second man she'd ever truly loved.

The whole sequence seemed to happen both in slow motion and in stop-jerk triple-time.

Crossing the road, hell bent on warning Ryan, she'd tried to react to his warnings to her, but it felt as though she'd been swimming through mud. Before he screamed her name, she hadn't even noticed the car firing up until it crossed into her lane, aiming right at her.

Ryan dived forwards, knocked her aside, pushed her out of the car's path. She crumpled, the breath driven from her lungs, hit the road, and rolled away, the months of training kicking in, taking over. She survived with little more than bruises to her hip, elbow, and shoulder.

As she slid to a stop in a puddle, a puddle that had softened her collision with the tarmac, she saw it all.

The horror of the impact. Car versus human. No contest. The squelching crunch of breaking bones. Ryan, tumbling through the air, arms and legs flying, the car continuing in a squeal of rubber on road. The red spray of blood.

Ryan landed in a crumpled heap, arm bent and broken, bleeding from a head wound where he'd connected with something hard, either the wall, the pavement, or the car. The hideous, rusty end of the broken railing sticking out of his side, impaling him. Blood covering his face.

In that precise moment, Lara knew, she absolutely knew that Ryan—her beautiful Ryan—was dead.

She'd stopped moving, stopped breathing. All feeling had left her. Her man, her saviour, her love, was dead. Tears flowed, mixing with the driving, stinging rain.

The screaming crunch of tearing, rending metal impacting concrete, broke her from the stunned immobility.

She turned and there he stood, brandishing a huge knife.

Barcode.

The evil man, bleeding from somewhere, exposing a

gap-toothed smile, swaggered forwards. Laughing. Taunting. Taunting Ryan.

Lara stepped forwards to defend Ryan's dead body.
Something tugged at her waist, reminding her. She pulled
on the tyre lever. At first, it wouldn't move. Then it slipped
free of her belt.

Silently, she approached Barcode from behind.

So fixated on his immobile target, the vicious bastard
didn't hear her approach.

Lara swung the metal bar. Twice. Backhand, forehand.
As hard as she could. Each blow landed with sickening,
bone-crushing force.

Barcode stopped laughing. Fell and stopped moving.
Stopped breathing.

Lara spared him no pity. Allowed herself no guilt. She
stood over him, breathing hard, despite her world having
ended. She dropped the tyre lever, but she breathed.

Then, he moved.

Ryan moved.

The rest had turned into a heady, joyous blur. Ryan was
alive, but barely. She raced across the road. A man—blond,
tall, handsome, his face bruised—appeared at her side. He'd
seen it all from inside the Hub. He claimed to be a friend
and called himself Sean. She didn't care. Ryan was alive.
Alive!

Sean helped her drag Ryan from the metal spike and
staunch the blood loss. He carried Ryan to his car, and from
there to the safety of their hotel before the emergency
services could arrive and take him away, maybe forever. It
had been a miracle that no one had recognised him to that
point and she couldn't extend the risk.

Good as his word, Sean Freeman helped her bring Ryan
back to life. In the hotel, Sean had even acted as her

surgical nurse during the emergency operation to clean out his wound and sew him back together.

"Hey, lass. Are you going to stare into the sunset all night?" Ryan called from his reclining chair, wrapped in a heavy blanket. "An injured man can get awfully lonely, you know."

He peeled back the blanket and raised his left arm as far up as the sling would allow. The sling covered his whole arm, hiding the lightweight, waterproof cast, which Ryan insisted she fitted, claiming he'd be sea swimming soon and a standard plaster cast wouldn't last in the salt water.

Truly remarkable the way he healed so quickly. How his body managed it, Lara would never know. Already, he walked without a limp, standing straight and strong. The puncture wound in his side—miraculously, the rusted, iron rod had missed everything vital—was little more than a shocking memory. The scars, front and back, had almost completely healed with no sign of redness or infection.

The swift treatment, good wound care, and judicious use of medication helped. Of course it helped. But Ryan's incredible powers of recuperation fixed him faster than any patient she'd ever treated—animal or human.

In fact, the foolish man had been making noises about resuming full training in the morning, very much against his doctor's orders. Not that his personal medic, Lara Orchard, would ever issue them as orders. She offered cautious advice only. He rarely took notice however. Infuriating man.

She turned her back on the sea and made her way towards him.

"Okay, buster. Hold your horses, I'm coming."

She smiled as she spoke, but the horrific image of him flying through the air refused to leave her. She'd made her decision, and the discussion wouldn't, couldn't wait any longer.

Ryan lowered his almost-healed left wing and shuffled across, giving her room on the recliner to sit next to him in the lee of the wind. Lara obliged and they snuggled close. Warm and safe. At least for the moment.

What would she have done if he hadn't survived?

The thought sent a deep chill through her. She shivered.

"Come on, Lara," he whispered into the top of her head, his breath warm. "Out with it."

She pulled away, but only far enough to see his face. The cut over his left eye that let out all the blood and made her think he was dead, had closed nicely, barely noticeable amongst the light wrinkles.

"Out with what?" she asked, although she knew what he meant. He always seemed to know when she was troubled.

His right eyebrow twitched, the merest ghost of a movement. Yes, he knew.

Okay, here goes.

"That night at the school. It was terrifying."

She paused, stalling for time. Time to form her thoughts. He jumped in.

"You didn't have an option. Barcode had to be stopped. Don't waste your compassion on him. There's no need to feel guilty for ridding the world of that piece of human waste."

"No, no. That's not what I meant. It was you. At first, when I saw your injuries, I panicked. Froze. Although I'm supposed to be the team's medic, I had no real idea what I was doing. Sean … he helped, of course, but only with the lifting and the carrying. It was … Everything was down to me. I was terrified."

474

Ryan smiled and used his good arm to try to pull her close, but she resisted and he released her.

He frowned in question. He was confused, a rare event for her Ryan. "But you were brilliant, love. And here I am as living proof."

"No, no. Please listen," she said, leaning over to kiss him on his latest scar—one of so many. "If I'm to be an integral part of the team, if I'm to be its medic—"

"But you are. On both counts."

"If so, I need to be better prepared, better trained."

He sat up, leaning on the elbow of his injured arm. At least he tried to, but the sling didn't allow enough movement. He grunted and used his good hand to rip the bandage over his head. Then, he leaned back as he'd initially intended.

"That's better. Bloody hate slings, me. Okay, so what did you have in mind?"

She took a breath and dived in. "There's a company in Denmark. It runs specialist training courses. I've been visiting their website. One course in particular caught my eye."

Ryan lifted his chin. "Really? Which one?"

"Combat medic. Ten consecutive days, followed by an optional, one-week, clinical attachment to a hospital emergency department in South Africa."

He nodded, but said nothing.

"Ryan, this is important to me, to the whole team. If any of you suffers an injury, I need to know what I'm doing. Please, Ryan. You know this is the right thing for me. It's the right thing for us all."

He frowned again, scratched at his beard.

"There's a problem."

"Which is?"

"That title, 'Combat Medic', suggests you'll be close to the action. In danger. I don't want that for you. You need to be safe. Walthamstow was a disaster on every front. We could both have died."

"No, Ryan." She shook her head firmly. "That doesn't work for me. I can't sit here for the rest of my life, safe and secure and under armed guard, while you swan off saving the world. I need to be useful."

Ryan closed his warm brown eyes, admitting defeat. He opened them again, stared at her.

"There's no way I can change your mind, I suppose?"

"None."

He sighed and added a sharp nod. "No, I thought not. When's the next course?"

"It starts in two weeks, but I doubt there'll be any spaces left. The website says the course is usually booked up months in advance."

"No, they had a cancellation," he said, breaking out one of his wonderfully warm smiles. "I booked you in last night. At least, Corky did. Under the name Dr Grace Sloane. He's building your legend as we speak."

Her heart slammed against her ribcage.

"What? How … How did you know?"

"Oh, love, I mightn't be the world's greatest when it comes to IT, but I do know my way around a web browser. If you want to keep secrets, you really need to delete your search history during the day."

"You've been spying on me?"

She didn't know whether to be angry at the intrusion and lack of trust, or relieved that he supported her idea, but would probably end up defaulting to the latter.

He raised both hands, wincing only slightly.

"Sorry, couldn't help myself. Actually, it was an accident.

I was clearing my search history when I noticed where you'd visited. It didn't take a genius to work out your intention."

Lara relaxed. He'd put up a decent case for the defence.

"Okay, you are forgiven."

"Excellent," he said, leaning closer, angling his face for a kiss.

She obliged, long and loving and gentle, taking care not to damage her recovering hero.

"I guess we're heading to Denmark, then?" Ryan said, after coming up for air.

"What's this 'we' business? As your doctor, I'm in charge of your recovery, and—"

He kissed her to shut her up, and she gladly let him.

The END.

Next in the Ryan Kaine series

THE **RYAN KAINE** SERIES

KERRY J
DONOVAN

ON THE EDGE

For fans of
JACK
REACHER

vinci-books.com/ontheedge

**Danger's never far behind. For Kaine's team, the
mission never ends.**

Kaine and Lara's training in Denmark spirals into danger. Back in
Norwich, their associate Danny faces a deadly threat.

On The Edge: Chapter One

Saturday 3rd April – Evening

Blu Skandia Hotel, Valdemsgade, Aarhus, Denmark

Ryan Kaine slowed the hired BMW X4 and turned right onto *Valdemsgade*. The low, evening sun sparkled out of a powder-blue sky. It looked warm enough from the air-conditioned comfort of the car, but the dashboard's external temperature display showed four degrees Celsius, promising a chilly night and an almost inevitable ground frost. A bitter, Scandinavian evening in early April. No surprises there, but he'd made sure they packed accordingly. Kaine had visited Denmark on NATO missions a few times and knew the challenges the local weather could provide.

"Are we nearly there yet?" Lara asked from low in the

passenger seat, her voice deliberately wheedling and childlike.

Kaine shot her a sideways glance and smiled, still struggling to come to terms with her new look. She'd had her hair shortened and darkened specifically for the course. The new style looked good enough, but he missed the flowing, auburn tresses.

Still, needs must.

"Not long now. Couple of minutes."

She returned his smile, but it seemed forced.

A dark blue Volvo closed on his rear bumper. Kaine fed a little more petrol into the engine and nudged their speed up to the local limit, fifteen kph. After all the motorway and dual-carriageway driving they'd covered since the airport, it felt like little more than walking pace.

"Nervous?" he asked.

"A little." She nodded. "It's going to be tough. The things I put myself through."

"You'll walk it. I have every faith." He nodded his encouragement.

"Ten continuous days of intensive training with assessments at the end of each day. It'll be like being back at veterinary college. I struggled badly enough then, and I was a lot younger. Only a kid."

"I'll say it again. You'll walk it."

"I hope so."

She turned her head to stare at the low-level, commercial buildings flowing past the BMW's windows. Single-storey blocks, lights off, shutters lowered. Closed for the night and ready for the morning.

"You've been sweating over medical textbooks for months. You'll be the best-prepped medic on the course. And as for the strength and fitness side of things, you're as strong as any rookie I've ever worked on. You're ready, love. I promise."

She turned to face him again, eyes downcast.

"Thanks, but—"

"No 'buts'. You'll be fine." He winked. "Hopefully."

She sighed. "Thanks for the vote of confidence."

"If you're that worried about it, we could spend the night in the hotel, and head straight back to France in the morning. There's no need to put yourself under so much pressure."

Lara set her jaw.

"Not a chance, buster. I'm doing this course, and that's all there is to it."

"That's my girl," he said, allowing her another encouraging grin.

Following filter arrows painted on the road, Kaine indicated right and they turned into the forecourt of the Blu Skandia Hotel, Aarhus' most expensive and exclusive hotel. He parked in one of the bays marked in both Danish and English as, "Residents – Drop Off Only".

The concierge, a young, blond man wearing a top hat and a frock coat—both in a fetching shade of light blue—stepped through the revolving doors and approached their car. He opened the front passenger's door for Lara.

"Doctor Sloane?" he asked.

"Yes," she said, looking mystified.

The Blu Skandia's online booking process required them to provide photo ID and details of their vehicle. Kaine knew what to expect, but he hadn't forewarned Lara. Along with her ongoing, rigorous, exercise programme, she'd spent the previous fortnight cramming, adding to her already extensive knowledge of human anatomy, physiology, and pharmacology. He hadn't wanted to burden her with unnecessary information and imagined that the Blu Skandia's personal touch would go down rather well.

"I'm Robert. Welcome to the Blu Skandia Hotel," the concierge said in faultless English and stepped back to allow her out of the car. "I hope you have a pleasant stay."

"Thank you, Robert," she said, reaching for her matching, designer handbag and vanity case—both real, both ridiculously expensive, but essential to maintain their cover. Besides which, Lara deserved some pampering.

Kaine hit the button on the dashboard to unlock and raise the Beemer's tailgate. He had to open his own door, but just about managed the feat without assistance.

"Asger!" Robert called, signalling to the uniformed porter waiting near the entrance with a baggage trolly. The man hurried forwards to collect their luggage—three large, designer suitcases all matching Lara's hand baggage, two for her, one for Kaine.

Kaine retrieved his laptop case from the back seat, joined Lara and Robert on the pavement, and watched Asger load the suitcases onto the trolley. The porter treated the cases with a great deal of respect, not wanting to scratch such expensive pieces of overwrought nonsense. Kaine could have managed with a couple of Bergens.

"It's okay to park here?" Kaine asked.

Robert smiled and led them to the hotel's revolving doors.

"Frederik, one of our valets"—he pointed to another uniformed man—"will take your vehicle to our underground parking facility. There's no need to worry, Mr O'Keefe, Frederik is a first-rate driver, as are all of our valets. During your stay, we shall have your vehicle fully detailed. It is a complimentary service we offer to our premium guests."

Meaning, they included a car wash and valet as part of their exorbitant pricing structure.

Kaine smiled at the man and shrugged it off. He and Lara didn't often have the chance to luxuriate, and he intended to make the most of their extended stay in Aarhus —when she wasn't neck deep in simulated gore and medical textbooks.

Robert waved them through the doors and followed close behind. The three of them headed to the reception desk—a white, marbled affair that stood polished and gleaming under the subdued, mood lighting. Asger brought up the rear and rolled the loaded trolly towards the bank of polished, stainless-steel lift doors.

The receptionist, a dark-haired beauty with a dazzling smile, welcomed them with a well-rehearsed spiel, before handing Kaine and Lara a keycard, and ending with, "If there is anything we can do to improve your stay, please don't hesitate to ask. The reception desk is staffed at all times."

"Thank you," Kaine said, pocketing his card. "Dr Sloane and I will be leaving the hotel each morning at nine o'clock and will need breakfast served in our suite at six thirty sharp."

The woman's smile didn't falter.

"But of course, Mr O'Keefe," she said. "Simply make your choice from the breakfast menu overnight or one hour before service. Chef Marcel will be delighted to oblige."

Kaine nodded and turned away.

Robert walked them towards Asger at the lifts and held out his hand. Kaine took out his wallet, assuming the concierge expected a tip.

"No, no, Mr O'Keefe," he said, straight-faced. "I need your car keys ... for Frederik."

"Ah, I see." Kaine retrieved his key fob from his pocket and handed it across.

Robert dropped a little half-bow and slid away towards the revolving doors, leaving Kaine and Lara with the silently efficient Asger, who had already summoned the lift and rolled the trolly into the carriage.

Once inside, Asger pressed the button marked "PH", the doors slid together on silent bearings, and the lift raced upwards so quickly, it took Kaine's stomach a moment to catch up.

Within seconds, an electronic chime announced their arrival at the Penthouse Suite. The lift stopped, and the doors retracted to reveal a small lobby with a single wide door. Asger swiped an entry card over the reader and allowed them through to their exclusive accommodation for the duration of the course.

Asger rolled the trolley into the master bedroom and asked if they required room service to help them unpack. Kaine declined the offer. The last thing he needed was to try to explain away the surveillance gear they'd brought with them on the drive from France.

Before leaving, Asger gave them a quick tour of the suite, showing them the emergency exit and explaining how the fire door operated. On the way out, he pointed to the control panel on the wall.

"For privacy, you can press this button"—he pointed to a red switch on the panel—"and it will light up the 'Do Not Disturb' sign above the door outside. It will also prevent anyone entering the suite without your express permission."

"There's an emergency override, I imagine?"

The porter nodded. "The housekeeping staff have master keys, but will not use them when the sign is lit except, as you say, in an emergency. The sign can only be activated from the inside."

"Thank you, Asger."

Once the porter had left, with a healthy tip, Kaine marched straight to the picture window with its panoramic view overlooking the less-built-up, north-eastern quarter of Aarhus. It proved to be every bit as perfect as he'd hoped from his study of the hotel's website. With only one day before the course started, he wouldn't have wanted to relocate their base of operations at such short notice.

"That was generous," Lara said.

"What was?" Kaine asked.

"The tip."

"Probably, but we're high-rollers. We love splashing the cash. It gives us great pleasure to throw our money around to ensure that we receive great service from the 'help'." He shrugged and bent to unzip his case. "Besides that, it'll ensure our stay here is as comfortable as they can make it. The next ten days are going to be exhausting for you, and all I'm going to be doing is lazing around on my fat arse."

"Your backside isn't fat," she said, checking out his rear end in a full-length mirror in the walk-in wardrobe that was bigger than his safehouse in Camden. "Not in the slightest."

"Thank you, dear," he said, sighing.

"Some of my old girlfriends would have called them 'buns of steel'."

"Okay, that's enough. You'll make me blush."

Lara laughed.

Zip undone, Kaine opened his suitcase and started unpacking all the surveillance equipment he needed to maintain a watching brief on the most important member of his team—Lara Belinda Orchard.

IT TOOK an hour to lay out, set up, and connect the equipment to the hotel's Wi-Fi, and a further thirty minutes to receive Corky's assurance that the system was fully secure and cleared for use. Through it and the satellite coverage, Kaine would have a perfect, bird's-eye view of a specific area of the university's campus—some fifteen hundred metres distant as the crow flew. An area devoted to the practical components of the combat medic course that would occupy Lara's full attention for the following week and a half.

"Thanks, Corky," Kaine said to the smiling image on the laptop's screen.

"Happy to help, Mr K. If you need ol' Corky, he's only a comms call away. Cheerio, Doc. Knock 'em dead on Monday." His cheeks plumped as he cranked out a cheery smile. "But Corky don't mean that literally, mind."

His high-pitched chuckle cut off when Kaine ended the connection.

"Everyone's a comedian," Lara said through a yawn. "Okay, Ryan. After a day's travel, I need a shower."

"As do I. Which bathroom are you nabbing?" Kaine asked, trying his best to look innocent. The Penthouse Suite boasted three bedrooms, all with ensuites.

"I'll take the master," she said, smiling and moving closer. "And so will you."

Grab your copy…
vinci-books.com/ontheedge

About Kerry J Donovan

#1 International Best-seller with *Ryan Kaine: On the Run*, Kerry was born in Dublin. He currently lives with Margaret in a bungalow in Nottinghamshire. He has three children and four grandchildren.

Kerry earned a first-class honours degree in Human Biology and has a PhD in Sport and Exercise Sciences. A former scientific advisor to The Office of the Deputy Prime Minister, he helped UK emergency first-responders prepare for chemical attacks in the wake of 9/11. He is also a former furniture designer/maker.

kerryjdonovan.com